THE
LAWMAN

ADVENTURES OF U.S. MARSHAL RAND TRINITY

CONNIE SEIBERT

authorHOUSE®

AuthorHouse™
1663 Liberty Drive
Bloomington, IN 47403
www.authorhouse.com
Phone: 1 (800) 839-8640

Published by AuthorHouse 04/26/2016

ISBN: 978-1-5246-0561-2 (sc)
ISBN: 978-1-5246-0560-5 (e)

Print information available on the last page.

Any people depicted in stock imagery provided by Thinkstock are models, and such images are being used for illustrative purposes only. Certain stock imagery © Thinkstock.

This book is printed on acid-free paper.

Acknowledgments

M Y SON, WADE SEIBERT, has been such an encouragement to me that I wanted to mention him and tell everyone how much I appreciate his enthusiasm. He reads everything I write and loves my stories. He even carries copies to work in case he finds someone who wants one. Thank you, Wade, I love you, but of course I would love you even if you didn't read my books.

I'm sure there are some of you out there who are wondering about my sister Sandy. I'm happy to say we have not had a fight; we still love each other and she still helps me with whatever I need. To tell the truth I don't know what I would do without her. Thank you, Sandy, for being there for me.

Prologue

THE PIERCING SCREAM OF a young Red Tailed hawk drew the attention of a solitary figure who was standing on the edge of a meadow. The air was crisp and fragrant, smelling of damp earth from recently melted snow. Pine trees released their pungent perfume as the sun warmed their green needles.

The man pushed back the hood of his black wool cape and searched the skies. Shielding his eyes from the brightness of the day he smiled as he spotted the hawk riding the wind. The hawk circled and dropped then caught an updraft lifting him higher than before. He glided effortlessly a few more minutes then began a slow descent, spiraling in smaller and smaller circles until landing smoothly on the back of the man's leathered arm.

"Ah, Caesar, how I envy your flight." He fed the hawk a small piece of raw meat knowing the hawk cared for him only as a source of food. "I can only imagine the freedom you must feel to ride the wind and escape the cares of this earth. How I wish there was a way for me to escape my meaningless existence. No sense dwelling on it, though. Only a miracle from God can help me now and God seems fresh out of miracles when it comes to Peter O'Donnell."

Guilt washed over him as he remembered the few times he'd thought of taking his own life. "There must be some reason for me to be alive. It seems, Caesar, the only purpose I have now is to take care of you. That I will gladly do since you've been a comfort to me in my loneliness these last few months. That will come to an end someday soon because you are getting stronger by the day. You will take to the skies and never return. I will miss you but certainly not blame you."

Peter O'Donnell made his way up the hillside to the place he called home. The loss of everything he had ever wanted or loved threatened to overpower him again, but he refused to let himself fall into the pits of depression. He had visited there too many times during the last year. He knew that to give in one more time might be more than he could ever hope to pull out of again.

Chapter 1

"COME ON IN, THE door's open."

A tall, slender but muscular, young man opened the door and stepped into his commanding officer's presence. He immediately removed his cowboy hat, noticing the smile on Captain Sterling Cumberland's face. The older man was a U.S. Marshall in the Independence Missouri office. The captain's gaze swept over the red haired, younger man with bright blue eyes who offered his own smile and a handshake.

"Nice to see you, Rand," the captain said. "Thanks for coming in so early but this can't wait. You have a train to catch!"

"It's good to see you too, sir." Rand Trinity stood respectfully until his employer motioned for him to sit down. As he made himself comfortable, Rand thought of how proud his father would have been to see him in the U.S. Marshall's office. Rand was only fourteen when his father died but the horrible memory was burned into his brain. No matter what he was doing or what the topic of conversation might be, the memory was always there, right behind his waking consciousness. It was Rand who found his murdered father and then buried him. As far as he knew, the murderous gang had never been found and brought to justice. He often thought that his decision to go into law enforcement was a way to honor his father. Memories flooded his thoughts of when his father died and he ended up in a military prison in the North. His cousin, Aaron Trinity, miraculously found him and managed to get him released. His life with his cousin and uncle in the Dakota Territory had a lot to do with the life he had chosen as a lawman. Find the bad guys . . . bring them to justice! He was going to try, give it his best shot. "Where is this train headed that I have to catch?"

"I'll tell you in a minute. I want to tell you first that you did a fine job on your last assignment. That sheriff was mighty impressed and grateful you cracked the case and managed to catch the thief red-handed. You have a knack for this kind of work and I'm glad you're on our side."

"Well, thank you, sir. I appreciate that."

"How long you been with us now?"

"A little over two years, sir."

Captain Cumberland thought a moment before he continued. "Because you're so young I was hesitant to send you on this next assignment but after reviewing my options I decided you would be the best man for the job after all. You're going to have to stay sharp on this one. The Fitzpatrick's are involved. Do you know that name?"

Rand's eyes widened. "The *hardware* Fitzpatrick's?"

The captain nodded. "That's the one. After her husband died, Mrs. Fitzpatrick took over the business and built it to twice its size. She's an important lady and has asked for our help."

"What does she want us to do?"

"She's expanding their line of hardware stores to the west coast. Her son, Gerald Fitzpatrick, his wife and daughter, were traveling by train to be part of the joining of the railroads in Promontory Utah. Then they were going to travel on to California. The word I got was after leaving Cheyenne, the train wrecked on some torn up tracks. They said Indians were to blame, but something just doesn't feel right about the story. Anyway, they found the bodies of her son and daughter-in-law but not her granddaughter. There wasn't a sign of her anywhere.

"We're sending you down there to find the cause of that train wreck and find the granddaughter. A body doesn't just up and disappear into thin air. I guess it's possible the Indians took her, but I don't know, nothing about this sounds right. Since you lived in that area with your uncle, you know more about the Indians and the country around Cheyenne than anyone else we have. That's why I want to give you this assignment."

"What about Mason? Wasn't he down in that area?"

"Yes, but he got shot up pretty bad somewhere around Denver. They say he'll live but will be laid up for a good spell."

"Can you tell me more about the missing girl?"

"No, I can't, but you'll be able to find out whatever you need to know when you get on the train with Mrs. Fitzpatrick. Her two private cars will go as far as Cheyenne then they'll unhitch them on a side track. I don't know who's traveling with her but I'm sure you'll be well taken care of."

"Is there anything else I need to know?"

"Yes, you need to know there are a couple of Pinkerton agents who are already there. They're working the case undercover for the railroad. This agent runs the telegraph office at the train depot. Smart move on their part since you can hear a lot of things in a public office like that. His name is George Fisher. He has another agent working with him but I don't know anything about him. I think they said his name is *Joe*. Anyway, I want you to concentrate on the train wreck and find that girl."

"I'll do my best, sir."

"I'm sure you will. We've been asked to cooperate with the Pinkerton's so when you get there go to the telegraph office and ask if there are any messages for Rand Trinity. Then George will know you're on the job. People will eventually know you're investigating the train incident but be careful not to blow the cover of George and his partner. If for some reason you need to meet privately with George, go to the office and tell him you want to send a telegram to your Aunt Grace and he'll arrange a meet. That's about it. You only have an hour to get on that train so you better take off. Good luck, Rand, and watch yourself. Cheyenne has tamed down some but it's still a dangerous place."

Rand said goodbye to the captain, hurried to retrieve a few personal things, then made his way quickly to the train depot. The porter directed him to the last car of six cars where an older man was waiting and greeted him politely.

"Are you Mr. Trinity?"

Rand offered his hand. "Yes, I'm Rand Trinity."

The two shook hands. "I'm pleased to meet you, Mr. Trinity. I'm Nicholas Clench. Please bring your bag and come on in. You'll be riding in this car with me. Mrs. Fitzpatrick and her personal maid are in the one in front of ours." Rand stepped up onto the small platform at the back of the train and followed Mr. Clench into the car. "Our beds are back here. I've claimed the one on the right but if for some reason you want to switch, I would be happy to move."

"No, the left will be just fine, thank you," Rand said as he put his bag on the bed.

There was no other word than *luxurious* to describe the rest of the car. Plush chairs were anchored in deep carpets with designs in maroon. These matched the heavy curtains that were pulled back to let in sunlight.

Suddenly, a clatter and forward jerk caused both men to brace themselves as the train slowly began to move. "Looks like we are underway, Mr. Trinity. Make yourself comfortable and I'll find out if Mrs. Fitzpatrick is ready to meet with you."

Minutes later Mr. Clench was back. "Mrs. Fitzpatrick said she would see you in an hour, so we might as well relax. Did you have breakfast this morning, Mr. Trinity?"

"Yes, I've eaten, but I sure could use a cup of coffee if it's no trouble."

"No trouble at all. I just made some before you came. We can both have a cup and get to know each other."

Rand watched with interest as Nicholas Clench moved about the car. He appeared to be in his late fifties and was nice looking in spite of a slightly receding hair line, though his dark brown hair didn't have a bit of gray. Rand was puzzled about the man's relationship with Mrs. Fitzpatrick because Mr. Clench didn't fit Rand's idea of a butler. He was muscular, richly dressed and appeared to be in excellent physical condition. He handed Rand his coffee then sat down, Rand's curiosity caused him to broach the subject.

"If you don't mind, Mr. Clench, may I ask what your business is with Mrs. Fitzpatrick?"

Mr. Clench smiled in amusement. "Now, that is a good question. She usually refers to me as her friend or lawyer, but I'm more than that to her. I'm her body guard, killer of monstrous spiders and anything else she wants me to be. She's a remarkable woman, and . . . I love her."

His blunt confession surprised Rand. "I see."

"I hope you do, Mr. Trinity, because I want you to understand that I will do *anything* I can to protect her. I also want to be of any assistance necessary in finding Emily."

That was the first time Rand had heard the name. "Emily is her granddaughter?"

"Yes, Emily Fitzpatrick. She is one special young woman and I hate to see Cecilia so upset about her. She tries to hide it but I know her too well and can see through her brave front. Do you think there is any possibility Emily can still be alive, Mr. Trinity?"

"If we're going to be living in this car together for days, why don't you call me Rand. And as for your question, it's hard to say. There's always a chance, I suppose, if her body has not been found yet. I won't know until I get to the site of the train wreck and talk to the first ones on the scene. By now the area will be cold and trampled on so it'll be hard to tell much of anything. But not impossible."

Rand liked Mr. Clench and the two men sat and talked comfortably until there were three raps on the door leading to the next car where Mrs. Fitzpatrick was waiting. "That means we are being summoned," said Mr. Clench. "Are you ready to meet the ladies?"

"Sure," Rand said as he stood. "Lead the way, I'll be right behind you."

The car they stepped into was identical to the men's except the décor was in shades of blue. It was Mrs. Fitzpatrick that Rand noticed first. She was sitting in a plush chair and even though she wore a plain black mourning dress, she looked regal. Her black hair, with streaks of gray at the temples, was pulled back in a chignon. Her smile was warm and friendly. "Forgive me for not standing, but

I'm afraid I'm not used to the movement of the train yet." She gestured to a chair beside her. "Come sit over here and we can talk. Would you care for coffee or tea?"

"No, thank you. I've already had two cups with Mr. Clench."

"I'm not surprised. As you know, I'm Mrs. Fitzpatrick."

"Rand Trinity, ma'am. May I offer my condolences on your loss?"

"Thank you, Mr. Trinity." Her smile flashed again as she looked him in the eye and commented, "You are a lot younger than I thought you'd be. How long have you been a U. S. Marshall?"

"Its been a little over two years, ma'am."

"Well, you must have started quite young."

"I suppose I did, but I knew what I wanted to do with my life since I was fifteen, so why waste time?"

"Of course you're right. Now, what do you need to know?"

"First, I want you to tell me all you can about your granddaughter. You'd be surprised at the little things that might be important in finding her. Then I want you to tell me everything you've been told about the trip your son and his family were on and what you've been told about the train accident."

Mr. Clench sat close by and the three of them talked at length until a younger woman came into the room from the sleeping compartment. She was rather tall and slender and appeared to be in her early thirties. "Would you like for me to fix your lunch, Mrs. Fitzpatrick?"

"Oh, my, yes! The time has slipped by so quickly. Fix us all some sandwiches, Stella. And Stella, this is Mr. Rand Trinity. He's going to find our Emily!"

With a tight smile, Stella nodded but never made eye contact. "Pleased to meet you, Mr. Trinity." She then turned and went to the corner of the car that served as a kitchen area.

The atmosphere in the car changed, but Rand couldn't quite figure out what it was. *Almost like a frosty breeze blew through.*

Cecilia Fitzpatrick fought against the heaviness in her chest as the group ate their lunch. Talking about her only granddaughter brought up so many memories that emotions flooded her heart. Yes, she grieved for her son, but there was nothing she could do about Gerald now. Emily was the delight of her life. Not only was she beautiful but she had a sweet carefree spirit that Cecilia thought Emily had gotten from her. *My sweet Emily, where are you? Stay safe. I'm doing all I can to find you. How I long to hear you sing for me again.*

As if he could read her thoughts, Cecilia felt Nicholas Clench's eyes on her. She looked up at him. His reassuring smile warmed her heart. *Oh, Nicholas, thank you for being here for me. I hope you can see into my heart and know how much I've come to love you.*

Nicholas and his wife had been dear friends to her and her husband. Nicholas lost his wife and Cecilia's friend a year before her husband had died. He had been the Fitzpatrick's lawyer and advisor for years. Nicholas's friendship had slowly developed into something a lot more and Cecilia knew in her heart they would speak of it soon, perhaps after they found Emily. She would not let herself think of Emily as anything but well and alive, waiting to be reunited with her. *I'll find you, Emily, I'll find you.*

Chapter 2

PETER O'DONNELL SEARCHED THE skies one more time before he went into the cave he called home for the last year. Early that morning he'd spotted another hawk flying carefree in a clear blue sky. It was time for Peter to go for his supplies that he had arranged to be left at a designated place beside the railroad tracks twice a year. Cesar would have to be set free.

"This is it, Cesar. You must make it on your own now." The hawk cocked its head; black beady eyes stared at Peter a moment then turned away. Its wings began to stretch out and Peter pushed his arm up and away from his body as Cesar took to the air. "Goodbye, friend." He stood and watched a short time until he spotted two hawks in the distance floating on the breeze, dipping and diving in a game of their own.

Peter put on his black cape, pulling the hood over his head. He strapped a packing frame on his back and made sure his canteen was on his shoulder. Then he set out for his supplies. *When I get all my supplies up here to the cave I'll be set for the summer. They better be there. I'm about out of everything.*

It would take four trips down to the tracks and back to the cave to retrieve all the supplies. The pack frame Peter had made would carry only one crate at a time. At a steady pace he could make it down to the tracks and back to the cave in one long day. He knew the mountain well and chose his way carefully. Once on his way he made good time and hummed a song that was his favorite.

Much later, he glimpsed the designated spot where his supplies should be. He slowed and approached cautiously. The water tank where the train stopped before going into the mountains was where the supplies were supposed to be dropped off. They weren't there. *The train has probably been delayed. Guess I better find a place to stay the night. It's for sure I won't make it back to the cave tonight.*

Peter stayed in the trees and because the afternoon was warming up he pushed the hood off his head. *No one to stare at me out here.* This thought was punctuated by gun shots in the distance. Not wanting to get involved with people, but knowing someone might be in trouble Peter reluctantly made his way through the trees toward the sound.

He suddenly found the source of the gun shots.

"What in the world is going on?" He stood staring at a train wreck until his mind made sense of the scene before him. A large piece of track was missing on the downside of the hill. There was no way the engineer could have seen it in time to stop. The engine was leaning at a precarious angle threatening to tip over completely. Wood was scattered around two cars that were still upright on the tracks but the rest of the cars had to be on the other side of the hill. They had to have come loose from the rest of the train. More gun shots froze Peter's feet to the ground. He counted five men running

in and out of the cars. They were all shooting and shouting but he couldn't understand what they were saying. Realization finally struck him.

Realization finally struck him! They were robbing the train. Peter stayed hidden and watched with anger and frustration as the picture became clearer. *They're not wearing any masks and that's not good. They'll have to kill everyone so there won't be any witnesses.* Peter tried not to think about the fate of the passengers. *I've got to decide what to do next. It's for sure I can't fight all those men so I'll have to stay out of sight until they leave. At least maybe then I can get my supplies and help anyone who might be alive.*

The train robbers didn't give up until it was dark then they gathered a long way from the train at the tree line on the south side of the tracks. The north side was wide open prairie. Peter watched in curious fascination as they made a campfire then sat around talking. As quietly as possible, Peter crept closer to the gang until he could make out what they were saying.

"Maybe your girlfriend got it all wrong, Carl. There was only one girl on that train and she didn't have black hair or any locket around her neck."

"Maybe it came off when the train wrecked. Did you look around her body, Slim? Did you think to do that?"

"Well, sure, I looked around some. But that dog wouldn't even let me and Jack in that car. Jack had to shoot it! Shame too, it was a pretty dog."

"Forget about the dog, you idiot! We've got more important things to worry about than a dog!"

"Well, I like dogs, I'll have you know," Slim sulked. "I had me one that looked just like that one when I was a kid."

The gang member named Buck enjoyed taunting Slim. Slim was a loyal member of the gang but was a little slow to catch on to what was happening. "You like dogs, but you didn't mind killing those people on the train. You're one sick man, Slim," Buck taunted.

Slim was getting irritated. "I don't like killing people but it had to be done. Carl said it had to be done, so there won't be no witnesses. Isn't that right, Carl?"

"Yes, that's right, Slim. You all did good today except for *not* finding that black-headed girl with the locket around her neck."

The train robbers were quiet for a few minutes. Then the one called Ken spoke up. "She couldn't have walked away from the train. One of us would have seen her. I was the one who went in the last car she was supposed to be in with her ma and pa. I tore the place apart but she plumb wasn't there. The woman that was probably her ma had a broken neck from the car rolling down that hill. The man was knocked out so I put an arrow in him and scalped him like you told us to do. Don't like scalping people, but you said we had to make it look like Indians done it."

"You did everything right, Ken. Did you find any valuables in that car?"

"Just the cash and the jewelry I gave you."

"That's good," Carl said. "We got enough cash from the passengers to have us a time when we get back to Cheyenne."

Carl watched the one outlaw that hadn't said anything yet. "What're you thinking about over there, Jack?"

"I was just wondering what we're going to do now. If we don't have the girl we won't get any money out of the old rich lady."

"Oh, we'll get our money. Even if we found her we couldn't let her live. We'll just have to go back to that last train car and find something that belonged to her. We'll put it with the ransom note and no one will be any the wiser. But first, we're going back down there and tear those cars apart until we find her body. I have to *know* that she's dead. We can't have her showing up in Cheyenne. Her body just has to be down there somewhere. We just missed it, that's all. Course she could have found a hiding place we didn't see. First light we go find her, then we'll get away from this place before someone shows up. Get some sleep now. We've got us a long day tomorrow."

Peter didn't immediately dwell on what he had heard but quietly moved away from the robbers. In the dark he needed all his concentration to slip away without making any noise. When he was a good distance away he found a place to sit and think. As he looked out on the prairie there was enough moonlight that he could see the outline of the engine and the two cars that had remained upright on the tracks. When he realized he couldn't see the train robber's fire he knew what he would do first. *If I can't see their fire from here they won't be able to see the train engine and those two cars. I'll start there. Maybe I can find my supplies.*

A nagging voice began to echo in his head, *What about the girl? What about the girl?*

I don't know! If I find her, I'll help her. I guess she could have found a place to hide and they missed her. If I called to her she would be crazy to give up her hiding place. I wonder how old she is. Poor thing must be scared out of her wits. Yes, I'll try to find her. I'll have to be sure my hood stays in place or I'll scare her worse than the robbers would. Peter waited until the gang had time to settle down for the night then walked out to the engine. He moved along until he reached the two cars that were still upright. Their doors were wide open and faced away from the enemy.

Feeling relatively safe from the view of the robbers, Peter climbed into the first train car. He fumbled in his pocket where he always carried matches and struck one against the side of the car. The match flared to life. Before he took a step, he looked down at the debris around his feet and was surprised to find a lantern by the door. He quickly lit it and made his way around the car. All manner of boxes, crates, and sacks were strewn over the floor. He stepped carefully but was soon convinced his crates were not in that car nor was there any sign of a girl.

The night was eerily still and quiet as Peter blew out the lantern and dropped to the ground. The night air had a mixture of smells from green prairie grass, sage and cedars that confused his senses until he reached the door of the second car. It was only partially open and a foul smell emanated from inside. He stepped back a moment and steeled himself for the worst. *Death is in there, I know it! I'll find bodies . . . Heaven help me, I sure don't want to do this, but I have to look for my supplies.* Peter climbed inside and quickly lit the lantern again. *Oh, no. There's the girl with the dog.* He didn't need to touch the girl's body to know she had been dead for hours. It looked as if the dog had managed to drag himself to the girl and lay his head on her arm before he died. Peter clenched his teeth and swore under his breath. *What kind of animals would do such a thing? I have to find the other girl. I couldn't live with myself knowing I didn't try to save her from those monsters.*

Peter stood still a minute and spoke softly. "If you're hiding in here I want you to know I will not hurt you. The men who caused this train wreck are not very far away. They intend to find you in the morning, take your locket, and then kill you. They want money from your family. Please let me help you. I will take you away from here where they can't find you."

He stood very still, listening for the tiniest sound. There was no response so he lifted the lantern higher and searched the contents of the car.

Peter spotted the crates and knew they were his. As a joke the store owner wrote in big letters on the end of the crates, *deliver to Nowhere.* The man had laughed and said that's exactly where they would be delivered - nowhere. The four crates had been stacked at the front of the box car. The top one had fallen and landed on what appeared to be bolts of fabric. A box of blankets had fallen from somewhere above and were piled on another box that had broken open. It contained men's coats.

Peter lifted his fallen crate then stopped in mid-air, frozen on the spot. He heard a faint moan coming from under all the jumbled mess of fabric and coats. "I think I've found the other girl and it appears she's alive!" he mumbled to himself. Peter hefted the crate he was holding and set it by the door of the car, then quickly returned to dig through the mess that was on top of the girl. He saw her legs first. There was a nasty gash on the calf of her leg and a lot of blood. She made no other sound as he worked his way up to finally uncover her head. Dried blood was caked in her long black hair from a cut on the top of her head.

Peter stared at her for a moment then gently brushed a few strands of hair away from her face. "Can you hear me, Miss?" She offered no response so he carefully touched her shoulder and gently shook her. "Can you hear me?"

"Father, is that you . . ." she said in a voice so soft it could barely be heard. "I can't move my arm and it hurts so bad. I hurt all over, Father . . . help me."

Peter had not even thought of broken bones. His mind raced to find a way to help this young woman. For some reason, he thought he would be looking for a little girl. "Hush now, lass. I'll be helping you, but you must be brave. Tell me your name."

There was no response for she had slipped away from him. He lifted the lantern over her and watched her chest rise and fall in an even manner. *She's still breathing and thank goodness she didn't open her eyes.*

Just like with the crippled hawk, Peter now had a purpose. He would do everything in his power to keep this woman safe and protect her from what the evil robbers had intended. *I'll have to forget about the supplies. I'm going to need the rest of the night to get her to safety. Come daylight those men will be after me. It won't take them long to figure out what happened here. God help me!*

For a full five minutes Peter stood and looked at the pack frame then back to the still form of the young lady. *She's not very big. I'm sure some of the crates I've hauled up the mountain weigh more than she does.* An idea began to take shape in his mind and he immediately went to work. He padded the frame with blankets and a large man's coat.

The hard part was knowing what to do about moving the woman. He knew she probably had one broken arm so he decided to take a bolt of soft cloth that was in the pile of material and wrap her like a mummy to secure her arms to her body. Since her legs would be dangling, he wrapped them in the same fashion so they wouldn't flop around. It was laborious work to lift and wrap, lift and wrap, without hurting her anymore than she already was.

When he was satisfied with his work he placed the pack frame at the edge of the boxcar and gently lifted the young woman in his arms. He could feel her soft breath on his face and breathed a sigh of relief that she was still alive after his moving her so much. After placing her on the pack frame he buttoned up the coat then secured her tightly with the straps. Quickly, he jumped down, backed up to the door of the car then slipped his arms through the straps of the frame. Slowly, he moved away from the car until he felt the full weight of her body on his shoulders.

Peter blew out the lantern knowing he would need it in the dark places of the forest and quickly left behind the devastation the robbers had caused. It was a long hard night. He pushed himself more than he ever had before but his perseverance paid off. He breathed a sigh of relief when he entered a cave he was familiar with. He made his way down a tunnel and into a small room at the back of the cave. Carefully kneeling down he slipped the straps of the frame off his shoulders and lowered his bundle to the ground.

First thing I've got to do is clean her wounds and secure her arm . . . hope I can tell which one is broken. Then I've got to go try and erase any tracks up to the caves before those men wake up.

Chapter 3

WEARINESS WAS TAKING ITS toll on Peter by the time he finished cleaning the lady's head and leg wound. He smeared on some healing salve that he had doubted he would ever use but was now glad he had it. Her head wound didn't seem all that serious. But Peter was worried about the deep wound on the calf of her leg. It had bled during the night's walk back to the caves and started bleeding again when he cleaned and wrapped her leg. Leaving her in the cave was hard, but necessary. *I hope she stays unconscious while I'm gone. Poor thing wouldn't know where she is and total darkness can drive a person mad.*

The early light was enough to see any tracks he had made on the mountain, so he backtracked and wiped out any sign of his passing. When he came back to the cave he removed any traces that looked like people had been there and felt his way back into the deeper part of the cave where he'd left his patient. Peter got down on his knees and backed into a shallow cavity pulling the young women in with him. When he was sure they were both far enough into their hiding place that they couldn't be seen he wrapped the blankets around the girl and stretched out beside her. As his weary body relaxed, he drifted off to sleep, having strange dreams about running from an unseen enemy.

The sound of distant voices jolted Peter awake. He lay still for several moments while his befuddled mind remembered all that had happened. He wondered how the young woman was doing and cautiously reached over to her still form, only to receive another jolt. She was awake.

"Please don't hurt me anymore," she begged. "Who are you and what are you going to do with me?"

"Sh . . . Sh. I'll not hurt you, lass," he whispered. "It's the men out there trying to find you that will hurt you. But you must not talk now. Please, lay as still and quiet as you can. If they find us they will kill us both. I'll explain when it's safe to talk, but for now we must not talk or make any noise."

In total darkness it was hard for Peter to judge the passing of time and he didn't know how long he had actually slept. The voices came in and out of the cave, then all was quiet. He felt movement and knew the woman was probably getting ready to whisper to him. He firmly placed his hand on her arm and she stilled. Peter's instincts proved true, for then a voice called out, and right next to the hollow they were in, another voice answered.

"Jack, you in there?"

"Yeah, I'm still in here. Thought I heard something, but guess I was wrong."

"Carl said for me to find you. It's getting late and we're going down the hill where the horses are and make camp for the night."

"I'm coming out and I'll be glad to get off this mountain. We been crawling around this mound of dirt all afternoon and I'm sick of it. I don't think they're . . . ." The voices grew faint then all was quiet again.

"I think it's safe to talk now," Peter said. "But let's just whisper for a few more minutes. Are you feeling better, Miss? That's probably not a fair question considering all you've been through."

"I don't know how I feel. I hurt *everywhere*, and I'm . . . *scared*. Please tell me what happened and why those men want to kill me."

Peter told her what he had heard and seen, finishing his narrative with a quiet admission. "I'm so sorry. There was nothing I could do to help the other people on the train."

"Do you really think they killed all those people just to kidnap me?"

"That's what it sounded like and from the little bit I saw, that's what they did."

"That means my parents are gone," she started sobbing quietly. "And Susan, the girl in the car with me, and Taffy? Is the little dog gone?"

"Yes, a blond girl and her dog. I'm so sorry."

"Oh, poor *Susan*, poor *Taffy*. Taffy was my dog." She cried silently for a bit.

Peter listened to her sorrow, wondering how to comfort someone with such a heavy burden of bad news. "I can't tell you how sorry I am," he said again. "It's a lot of sad news to handle when you're so hurt yourself." He patted her shoulder." What's your name?"

"Emily," she sniffed. "Emily Fitzpatrick. What's *your* name?"

"Just call me Pete."

"Can I touch your face, Pete?"

The question startled him. "What . . . no! Why do you want to touch my face?"

"I've read that's how blind people learn what a person looks like."

"You're blind?"

"I must be now. I can't see a thing. When I hit my head I must have gone blind. I've heard of such things happening." She began to weep again.

"Emily, listen to me! Don't cry, just listen to me."

"What . . . ." She tried to stop her tears.

"Sh, listen. I don't think you're blind. We're deep in a cave and you're experiencing total darkness." With all his heart, Peter wanted to take this poor creature in his arms and comfort her, but he was afraid of hurting her arm and the rest of her battered body.

She sniffed and seemed to consider the possibility. "D-Do you really think so?"

"We'll find out in a minute. I'm going to strike a match, then you'll know. And *then*, I'm going to help you out of here."

Peter fumbled in his pocket and found his matches. He scraped one down the rock wall and the match flared to life, fumes of sulfur filling the air in their small hiding place.

"What are we going to do now, Carl?"

The gang sat around a campfire, sulking. They were all in a sour mood.

"I've been thinking on it and decided we're going to go back to Cheyenne with what we have. We could search in these mountains for days and never find that girl. If we move quickly maybe we can get the money from the grandmother and be out of the country before anyone figures out what happened. If we're gone it won't matter if she shows up. Just as long as we're out of this area, but we'll have to move fast."

"Sounds good to me," Buck said, agreeing with his boss's plan. "I'm looking forward to that good time you promised us."

Everyone mumbled their agreement while Jack threw out a challenge. "I've got half a bottle and a deck of cards in my saddle bag. How about a game of poker?"

Peter stepped out of the cave with Emily safe in his arms. He felt her turn her head and look toward the sky. "How wonderful to see the stars and breathe fresh air. I am ever so happy that I'm not blind."

"Yes, you can thank God above that you have your sight. I think He surely has his hand on you."

"You believe in God, then?"

"Of course. Can't say as we're on good speaking terms right now but I believe in God. Don't you?"

"I don't know, perhaps I do, but He seems so far away when I wonder about it. I'm not sure you can really *know* God."

Emily's answer bothered Peter a little, but he forgot about it when she asked him to set her down. "I would like to see if I can stand."

"All right, but be careful of your hurt leg. I don't want it to start bleeding again."

"I'll be careful. I have to know how badly I'm hurt."

He gingerly set her on her feet and instantly heard an intake of breath. "Does it hurt a lot?"

"Oh my, yes, it burns and hurts terribly! I won't be able to put any weight on it for now. Peter, I'm dreadfully thirsty. Can you help me over to that rock where I can sit? Is there someplace to get water? I feel a drink of water might help revive me a little."

"I asked you to call me *Pete*."

"I know, but I like the name Peter so much better. That *is* your real name, isn't it?"

"Yes," he said, grudgingly.

"Please let me call you Peter. What is your last name?"

Peter groaned inside but found he couldn't deny this young woman anything at the moment, *except* to tell her his last name. "Yes, you can call me Peter but my last name is of no consequence. I'll have to leave you for a while to get us water and I have plenty of dried venison in the cave where I live."

"Don't you live in this cave?"

"No, this one is the easiest to find. The one I live in is difficult to find."

"Peter, I don't want to be left alone. What if those men come back?"

Peter helped Emily sit at the entrance to the cave and lean back against the rock she had mentioned. "I'm sorry but it won't be long and I don't think they'll be back tonight. I'll have to go slow and be careful not to make any noise but I think I can make it back here in less than an hour. You must be brave and let me do this."

"What if a bear or some other awful creature finds me?"

"Can you shoot a pistol? I could leave mine for you if it'll make you feel safer."

"No, that would be silly, I guess. I don't know the first thing about firing a pistol. Just hurry, please."

"I'll go as fast as I can, you just rest while I'm gone." Peter looked up at the sky. "You could count all the beautiful stars."

Chapter 4

"WHAT DID THE CONDUCTOR tell you, Stella?"

"He said we would be in Cheyenne within the half hour."

Mrs. Fitzpatrick leaned back in her chair. "Do you have all of our luggage ready?"

"Yes, ma'am, we're ready. It'll be nice to be off the train and have a little room for a change."

"That's what I was thinking. What I'm looking forward to is a nice hot meal. We are so limited with what we can have on this train. Will you please knock on the door of the men's car? I would like to talk to Rand."

"Yes, of course, ma'am."

Moments later, Rand and Nicholas made their way into the women's car. "You want to talk to me, Mrs. Fitzpatrick?"

"Yes, I want to make sure you and Nicholas knew that we are all going to stay at the hotel instead of these train cars. I think we need a break from our small quarters. I'll rent enough rooms so we can all have our privacy. Maybe I'll rent a whole floor so we won't have strangers around us."

Rand nodded agreement. "If that's what you want to do, I'm fine with it."

"Will you join us for the evening meal, Rand?" asked Mrs. Fitzpatrick.

"If you don't mind, I'd rather be on my own. I want to interview a number of people and mingle with the locals. I'll probably spend most of tomorrow doing the same thing, then I want to get out to the site of the accident. More than likely that's where I'll find answers. I'll need to rent a horse and enough supplies to spend probably a week in the area of the wreck."

"And of course, you'll let me know what you find out before you leave?"

"Yes, I'll keep you informed every step of the way."

"Thank you, Rand. You go ahead and do what you need to do. Nicholas will watch over us while you tend to business. If you need anything, and I mean *anything,* let me or Nicholas know."

"Thank you. Where will we be staying, Mrs. Fitzpatrick?"

"At the Stanton House. I've been told it's the best there is except for the Cheyenne Club, but they also said the Stanton House is quiet and respectable."

"Sounds fine to me. Now, if you'll excuse me I'll go back and get my things ready. You all can go ahead and go to the hotel, I'll be along as soon as I can. I'd like to find the telegraph office and see if there are any messages for me."

"Very well," said Mrs. Fitzpatrick. "Here's a key to the train car in case you need to come back here. Will you check and see if there are any messages for me while you're there?"

"Be glad to. I'll see you later."

The train rattled, jerked, and wheezed into the station, stopping at the end of the platform. Rand watched the carriage that Mrs. Fitzpatrick, Nicholas, and Stella were in, drive away toward town, then he walked to the east end of the railroad station where there was a small building with a sign on the door that read, *Telegraph Office*. He entered and stood behind a man and woman who were writing a message.

"I'll be with you in a minute, young man," the clerk said.

Rand nodded his acknowledgement to a man he figured was at least fifty. The glasses perched on the end of his nose, and the balding pate made him look the perfect picture of a telegraph operator. As the clerk moved around the room, Rand noticed he took good care of himself and seemed to be in good physical shape.

After the couple left, Rand asked, "Do you have any messages for Rand Trinity? I just came in on the train. Also, any messages for Mrs. Cecilia Fitzpatrick?"

"No, nothing for Rand Trinity or Fitzpatrick. Where are you staying? If something comes in I'll have it delivered to you."

"I'll be staying at the Stanton House."

"Nice place."

"That's what I hear. I'll be leaving day after tomorrow for about a week. I'll check in with you before I go and when I get back."

The clerk nodded. "Be careful out there. Some bad things going on in these parts."

"I'll be careful and you do the same."

Rand then made his way off the train station platform and headed toward the sheriff's office. The walk felt good and he was amazed how Cheyenne had grown. The last time he had been here the town looked like many other western towns that had sprung up quickly. The store fronts were now painted, clean, and some had flowers growing in pots out front. There was respectability about the business area that surprised and pleased him.

Rand spent the good part of an hour going over a number of reports that the railroad had delivered from the crews who were the first to check on the train ambush.

"What do you think about all this?" Rand asked the sheriff, handing the reports back.

"Don't know what to think about it. There are several different opinions in those reports, but I figure it must have been Indians. They've been causing all kinds of trouble around these parts. Then, we've got a gang working this area, too. We've had a couple of businesses in town broken into and robbed. That's my problem, though, not this gang stuff out of the town limits."

Realizing he wasn't going to get much help from the sheriff Rand changed the subject. "Where can a man get a good meal?"

Rand didn't have much luck in finding any useful information as he went into different establishments and struck up conversations with the locals. Most people seemed to blame the train wreck on the Indians. One loudmouthed drunk repeated what the others had said, "It's got to be the Indians. They don't like the white man coming out here and taking the land, but they better get used to it cause we ain't leaving.

At the hotel, Rand was given a key to his room and ordered water for a hot bath. An hour later he stretched out on the most comfortable bed he had ever slept on and stared at the ceiling.

I'm going to try and leave tomorrow. I'll have a good breakfast, talk to Mrs. Fitzpatrick and Nicholas, go find a good horse and leave early afternoon. It'll be fun to be out on the prairie again. I've almost forgotten what it's like.

Rand pulled up the covers and soon was fast asleep.

A key rattling in the lock on his door brought him straight out of the bed. He pulled his pistol out of the holster that was on the table by his bed and was ready for whoever was coming through the door. Rand's face turned as red as his hair when he found himself pointing his pistol at the prettiest blond girl he'd ever seen, and even redder still when he realized he only had his long johns on.

A flicker of a smile was on her face as she turned away. "I'm so sorry, Mr. Trinity. I thought you had already gone down to breakfast with the rest of the Fitzpatrick party. I'll come back when you've had time to dress."

Rand just stood there with his mouth gaping open, not uttering a word as she walked out of the room and closed the door behind her. For moments he didn't move and couldn't think of anything but that sweet little mouth turned up in a grin. "Drat it! Why did I have to sleep so late this day? I better get dressed and downstairs in a hurry. He was embarrassed all over again when he opened the door to find the pretty girl . . . no, *woman*, getting ready to knock on his door.

"Is it safe to come in now?" Her voice dripped with sweetness.

"Sorry, guess I slept so hard I didn't know it was morning and you just startled me coming in *without knocking*." There. He felt justified for his actions.

"I did knock, Mr. Trinity. I always knock and when you didn't answer I let myself in so I can make up your room. I'm the maid on your floor this morning. Really, I'm glad I can talk to you alone for a few minutes. Are you the one who's going to look for Emily?"

"Yes, that's what I'm here to do. What do you know about Emily Fitzpatrick?"

"I don't suppose I know an awful lot but when she was here with her mother and father I was her maid, too. I liked her immediately and we were becoming friends by the time they had to leave Cheyenne. There was another young woman with the people who were on her train. Her name was Susan Draper. Her father was an important man with the railroad and they were headed to the joining of the rails from the west. Susan was a spoiled little rich girl and you would think Emily would be the same, but she wasn't. We had a grand time, though. Emily invited me and Susan to her performances here and at the Cheyenne Club. It was just marvelous. She sang like an angel."

After a deep thoughtful moment, the next thing that came out of the maid's mouth was, "I'm going with you to find Emily."

Rand heard the words but they didn't make sense to him. "You're what?"

"I'm going to go with you to find Emily Fitzpatrick." She said it like it was the most sensible thing in the world.

Rand blanched. "You most certainly are *not* going to go with me!"

She squared her shoulders. "Sure I am. You might need my help."

Rand's color changed back to red. "Are you out of your mind, lady? That is the most preposterous thing I've ever heard!"

Pretty, light-blue eyes glared back at him and Rand was sure he saw sparks in those eyes.

"Why is that preposterous?" she huffed. "Are you so proud you wouldn't accept help?"

"If I needed help I would *ask* for it, but it wouldn't be from some woman."

"And what do you have against women?"

"Nothing, as long as they stay in their place. Don't you have any idea how dangerous it is out there?"

"I can take care of myself. But never mind. I can see you are one of those men who can't be reasoned with."

Rand stormed off, muttering, "It's for *sure* I can't be reasoned with when it comes to you going *anywhere* with me."

The rest of the day didn't get any better. It didn't take long for Rand to realize his idea of leaving that afternoon was impossible. Later, on his way to rent a horse, he noticed a poster on the wall of an abandoned building and crossed the street to see if it was what he thought it was. Sure enough, it was a poster of Miss Emily Fitzpatrick, announcing her performances at the Cheyenne Club. *Wow, she's gorgeous!* Pitch black curls framed a perfect heart shaped face with dark eyes that seemed to dance with excitement. He stood looking and reading the poster until a voice interrupted his thoughts.

"What you starin'at, mister? You stare any longer an' all that red hair might burst into flame and burn up the pretty black cowboy hat on top of it."

Rand turned and glared at a scruffy, barefoot boy of about thirteen or fourteen, in baggy pants and a tacky shirt. His straight, dirty-looking, brown hair had grown long passed his ears. A big floppy hat hid his eyes but a dirty mouth with a black ring around it managed to stay visible. The black ring was obviously caused by the stick of black licorice he was chewing noisily on. Before Rand could think of a reply the boy gestured toward the picture. "Pretty ain't she?"

Rand turned and looked at the poster again. "I'm not sure *pretty* is the right word. I'd say she's *beautiful*."

"She's gone, you know." The boy smacked his licorice while talking.

Rand turned again to the boy. "Yes, I know. What are you doing here? Shouldn't you be in school?"

"It's summer, there ain't no school. Don't you know nothin'?"

"I know plenty. Like you should have a job or be helping your parents at home. First you need to take a bath and get cleaned up. No one would want to hire a boy who looks tacky and dirty. Doesn't your mother ever tell you to take a bath?"

"My mother is dead and it's none of your business when I take a bath."

"Oh, sorry about your mother." Rand dug down in his pocket. "Here, let me give you some money to buy some shoes and clothes. Might help if you'd get a haircut, too."

"You got a nerve, mister! I don't want your charity. I can take care of myself. Keep your stupid money. I only came to give you a telegram."

It didn't escape Rand that the dirty hand giving him the telegram purposefully left a big smudge of licorice in the middle of the paper. "Here, at least let me give you a tip. I didn't mean to offend you."

"Keep your tip, I don't need it." With that, the boy stalked off raising a cloud of dust around his bare feet.

"Didn't handle that any better than I handled that pretty woman this morning," Rand mumbled to himself. He turned to look at the poster again. He was looking at Emily Fitzpatrick but his mind was on the pretty blond maid. *When I get back I'll have to look her up and apologize. Probably won't do any good. She was a stubborn one. Pretty and stubborn.*

Chapter 5

THE TELEGRAM READ: *East end of telegraph office, 10:00 tonight*. It was signed by *Aunt Grace*. Rand folded the telegram and put it in his shirt pocket. Knowing the message was from George Fisher made him curious. *He must have some information for me. Ten o'clock is a long way off. I'll have time to go get a horse and supplies then maybe I'll go for a short ride*. The thought of taking a ride spurred him on to the stables.

Rand introduced himself to Jack, the stable owner, and was shown several horses. "The black gelding is the best of the lot. He's smart, fast, and gentle when handled right. Josie trained him so you know he's a good one."

"All right, I'll take your word for it. If you'll saddle him up I'll take him for a ride and see how we get along. What's his name?"

"Ducky."

Rand gave the man a puzzled look. "What kind of a name is *that* for a horse?"

"Josie named him. She says he's like a duck in the water."

"She? Josie is a *she* and you let *her* train your horses?"

"Yep, she's as good as any man when it comes to horses. She comes over when she can and works with mine. A lot of people are after her to train their horses. Right nice little lady, too. Maybe you'll get to meet her if you hang around Cheyenne for a while. I'll go saddle Ducky for you. Won't be long."

Rand watched Jack bring in the big black gelding and followed him into the barn. "What do I owe you?"

"Not a thing. A man came in this morning and told me to give you the best I had and send the bill to Mrs. Fitzpatrick at the Stanton House."

Rand nodded his thanks and headed out of the stables. The ride was nice. Rand enjoyed the feel of a well trained horse under him and decided Jack was right about the girl trainer even if she didn't know how to name a horse.

After a late evening meal with the Fitzpatrick party, Rand started to excuse himself when the pretty blond from that morning's episode came to their table. "How was your meal, Mrs. Fitzpatrick?"

"Absolutely wonderful, Josephine! They are truly lucky to have you as their pastry cook. The chocolate cream pie was the best I've ever eaten."

"I'm glad you enjoyed it. Is there anything you need for your room tonight?"

"No, no, we're just fine, thanks to you, dear."

"Good. I'm on my way home then. Have a good night, everyone."

Rand sat and struggled with his feelings. He'd had a number of women try to get his attention in the past few years but none had affected him like this pretty, blue-eyed blond who didn't seem to care one whit about him. *Irritating, that's all she is. Why am I even giving her a second thought? I can't get involved with any woman now anyway. There's no room for a woman in the kind of work I do.* He scooted his chair back and rose from the table. "If you'll excuse me I'll go on up to my room now."

"Of course, Rand. Will we be seeing you in the morning?" Mrs. Fitzpatrick asked.

"No, I plan on getting an early start. I don't know how long I'll be gone but I'll check in with you when I get back to town."

"Good luck, Rand, and find my Emily."

"I'll do everything I can to find out what's happened to her, Mrs. Fitzpatrick. Good night everyone."

Rand had an hour to wait when he got up to his room but after thirty minutes of pacing, decided to go ahead and make his way to the designated meeting spot. The town was slowly falling into the quiet hush of evening, at least on this end of town. By the time he reached the telegraph office it was quite dark and eerily still. He slipped around the east end of the building and stood motionless for some time, listening with every sense for danger or the presence of someone near. When he was satisfied that he was alone, he relaxed and leaned against the building.

"You're early."

So startled by the feminine voice just a few feet away, he jumped in spite of himself and had his gun in hand, not even realizing he'd drawn. "Tar-nation, woman! Who are you and what are you doing hiding in that barrel? I could have shot you!"

"I'm your *Aunt Grace.*"

Rand holstered his gun and tried to breathe evenly again. "Oh, then you have some information for me?"

"That I do," she said, climbing out of the barrel.

"Wait a minute," Rand demanded, coming closer. "I *know* that voice. What's your name?"

"I've been called a number of things but to *you,* I am Miss Fisher."

"The hotel maid?" He stared at the dark-clad figure trying to find a resemblance but it was too dark to even see her face.

"That's me. I need to hurry and tell you what I know because we have to hide where they're meeting before they get there."

This made no sense to Rand and he exploded in frustration. "What in *thunder* are you talking about, Miss Fisher! I'm not going to hide *anywhere* with you!"

"Oh, just hush and listen a minute." She began talking fast. "When I was in the kitchen late this morning making my pies there was a rather crude looking man who came to the back door of the hotel and asked me to deliver a message to Stella Harker. He handed me a piece of paper that was folded up several times, gave me a dime, and left."

"Did you deliver the message to her?" Rand asked.

"Of *course,* I delivered it to her," Miss Fisher huffed.

"I don't suppose you . . . no, I don't suppose you read what was in the note."

"Of *course,* I read it. How was I going to know what she was up to if I didn't read it? Anyway, it didn't make any sense that she would know any man here in town. Especially one like this rough looking character."

"Well, what did it say?"

"It was poorly written and a little hard to make out but someone wants her to meet them in the barn out back of Lilly's Hotel and Bar at midnight tonight."

"Hmmm, that *is* strange." Rand took his hat off and ran his fingers through his hair, was silent a moment, then put the hat back on. "Thank you for the information, Miss Fisher. Are you related to George Fisher?"

"Yes, he's my father."

"Oh, I hadn't heard anything about him having a daughter."

"I'm his one and only. Now, we need to go so we can get there before whoever is meeting with Stella gets there."

"*We?*" Rand turned to face the cloaked figure of Miss Fisher. "Do we have to go through this again? You are *not* going anywhere with me . . . it's too dangerous!"

"Really, Mr. Trinity," she said, drawing the words out with plenty of sarcasm. "Do *you* know where Lilly's Hotel and Bar is? Do *you* know the barn out back?'

"No, but I can find it."

"Well, I *do* know the hotel and the barn. I've been there any number of times and the women at the place know me. I can get you in that barn and hidden without anyone even knowing we're there. Now," she moved ahead of Rand, "follow me."

Miss Fisher didn't waste any time. She rounded the corner of the building and Rand had to hurry to catch her. *Confounded woman! Giving me orders and leading me around like I was her lap dog. I'd like to shake her good and . . . and . . . send her home to her father. Why is George letting her do something this dangerous? As stubborn as she is he probably can't control her either, poor man. Well, when this night is over she'll find out who's running this show!*

It was dark enough Rand couldn't see anything but the back of her form in a big coat and a funny hat on her head. When she stopped suddenly he ran into her.

"Oooff, sorry!"

Her elbow rammed into his stomach. "Sh, quiet."

Obediently, Rand stood still and listened. Miss Fisher then quietly moved on with Rand staying right with her. She slipped through the middle of a pole fence and led him through a door at the back of a barn where they both stood quietly right inside and listened.

"Good, we beat them," Miss Fisher said in a whisper. "Let's slip into this closest stall and wait. Lilly keeps guards at the front and back of her hotel to watch out for the working women. I don't know the guards very well." She didn't wait for a response but opened the gate to the stall and went in.

"I thought you knew *everything*, Miss Fisher," he whispered in irritation. A soft squishy feeling under his boot prompted a quiet groan. "Don't you dare say another word, *Missy*, or I will throw you over my shoulder and take you back to your father and see that he thrashes you good and proper for doing something dangerous like this."

Rand was surprised she didn't say anything but he heard a soft snicker that made his anger go up a notch. The two waited in silence, not saying a word to each other. Miss Fisher had found a box to sit on and Rand stood motionless in the dark corner of the stall. All his senses came alert when the barn door squeaked open. There was enough light from the hotel to see that a man entered the barn. Moments later, the door opened again and Rand recognized Stella Harker.

"Carl, are you here?"

"Right here, Stella. I see you got my note."

"How did you know I was here?"

"Me and the boys came into town yesterday and I saw them fancy train cars on the side track. Figured it had to be the lady with all the money and where she is I knew you would be around."

"You figured right, Carl. How did things go? Did you get her granddaughter?"

"Give me a kiss and I'll tell you all about it. I sure have missed you, darlin'."

"All right, just *one* kiss then you tell me everything."

It was quiet a few moments then Carl spoke again. "That's nice, Stella. I'll be glad when this is all over and you and me can go off someplace where we can live like the rich."

"That's not going to happen unless you've done everything I've told you to do. Did you kidnap Emily Fitzpatrick?"

"Well, it didn't work out like we thought it would, Stella."

"What do you mean?" Anger edged her voice.

"We couldn't find her. We killed everyone on that train like you told me to do and searched high and low for a black-headed gal with a locket around her neck. The only girl on that train was blond and there was a dog with her. We went back the next morning and found a place where blood was all over but no body, so I know someone was hurt at that spot, must have been her. Looked like she was taken off into the mountains. We followed the tracks and searched all day but just came to a dead end. Couldn't find any sign of anyone."

"That's bad, Carl. What are we going to do now?"

"I figured if we move fast and deliver the ransom note we can get the money and get out of town before she shows up. Or is found. I really think she's dead by now with all the blood we found."

"That might work but what can we put with the note to prove we have her? Without that locket I don't know if they'll believe she was kidnapped."

"Here's all the loot and jewelry from the car her ma and pa were in. Surely there's something that belonged to the girl that would work."

"All right, I'll look at what you collected when I get back to my room. I'll write the ransom note and put something that belonged to Emily with it. I'll figure all the details out when I get back to my room. But Carl . . .?"

"What, darlin'?"

"I want that girl *dead*. Send all the boys back to find her and get the job done. Tell them not to come back until they find her and make her *dead*! There's also a U.S. Marshall who's leaving in the morning to go find Emily. He needs to be killed, too. I've put up with a lot from those spoiled Fitzpatrick women. I've earned every penny I'll get. And, Carl . . .?"

"What, darlin'?"

"Would it upset you too much after we get the money if we left before the boys got back and go somewhere where they'll never find us?"

"That wouldn't hurt my feelings one little bit," he chuckled. "I know exactly where we'll go."

Stella's voice turned all sugary sweet. "I thought you might feel that way, Carl. I'll meet you back here tomorrow night and tell you how I decide to get this done quickly."

"I have a room in the hotel. Can you come in and stay with me for a little while?'

"No, I can't take a chance on being seen with you. I don't want to do anything to mess up this deal. We'll be together soon enough."

After one final kiss, Stella Harker made her way out of the barn.

Chapter 6

RAND AND JOSEPHINE WALKED back toward the telegraph office not talking until they were close to the train station. "Are you all right?" Rand asked.

"I guess. Yeah, sure . . . I'm fine. It makes me *so angry* those men killed Susan and all the other people! Poor Emily, we've just got to find her. Do you think there's a chance she can still be alive?"

For the first time, Rand felt something more than irritation for the bossy Josephine Fisher. He was sure he'd heard a tremor in her voice. He didn't want to give her false hope but he couldn't bring himself to dash what little hope she had that Emily might be alive. "I reckon as long as we don't have a body, there's always a chance that whoever found her can take care of her injuries and keep her safe. Why else would this person rescue her from those men?"

"What are we going to do?"

Rand huffed. There was that *we* again. "*We* are not going to do anything. *I* am going to do my job which is to find Emily Fitzpatrick. Do you know what your father does?"

"Do you mean that he's a Pinkerton agent? Of course I know."

"Then you're going to go home and tell George all that we learned tonight. He and his partner can go to the sheriff and take care of the situation in town. I would advise *you* to help by staying out of the way and doing your job at the hotel in a normal way. You can inform your father of whatever news you hear but don't get involved or do anything dangerous. Let your father handle things."

"Then there's no chance you'll change your mind and let me go with you to find Emily?"

"Absolutely no chance at all that I'll change my mind."

"Well, there's nothing more to be said then. Good night."

"Wait, I'll walk you to your house. Where do you and your father live?"

"Oh, it's just right over there and I don't need you to walk me home, I *know* the way," she said, unable to keep the smirk off her face which the darkness hid.

"Never-the-less, I'm walking you home."

Rand walked her clear up onto the porch of the small house. She opened the door and light from a lantern fell on a completely different looking Miss Fisher. Rand looked shocked. "What in the world have you done to yourself?"

She feigned innocence. "Whatever do you mean?"

"You heard me. What are you doing all done up like a . . . ."

"Oh, you mean the red wig?" She opened her coat. "And the way I'm dressed?"

"That's exactly what I mean. You look like one of the ladies at Lilly's."

"That's the *idea*, Mr. U.S. Marshall. I'm in disguise in case we got caught and I had to save your hide. I could tell whoever found us that I was a new girl at Lilly's and you were my . . . er . . . *lover*."

"Does your father know what you were doing tonight?" Rand felt his anger mounting.

"Of *course* he did. It was his idea."

Rand felt he was on the verge of losing his temper. He took a deep breath, glared at the woman in front of him and told her, "Go on in the house and get yourself cleaned up. When I get back to town I'm going to give your father a piece of my mind!"

She batted her eyes and made sure Rand saw it. "Now, why would you bother to do a thing like that, Mr. Trinity? I'm nothing to you."

"I don't know why, but by the time I get back I'll have it figured out and will give my opinion on what your father should do with you, whether he wants to hear it or not."

Rand stormed off the porch with the vision of a red headed Josephine Fisher made up like a floozy and wearing an outfit that showed more skin than any decent woman would think of showing.

As for Josephine Fisher, she closed the door and leaned back against it, a sly smile worked its way onto her ruby red lips.

"Peter, I can't stand it!" Emily was beside herself with frustration. "*Please*, put a piece of that fabric over my head again. The flies are driving me crazy!"

"It's the smell of blood on your clothes and in your hair. If you'll let me, I think I've figured out a way to help you." He gently draped a piece of fabric over her head.

"I would do about anything right now. I slept most of the day yesterday and I'm feeling better today. Maybe I could walk down to the creek . . . no . . . that wouldn't work. I can't wash my hair and bathe with my right arm all tied up. What did you use to hold my arm in place?"

"It's the top of an old boot. I wore the soles out last summer so I cut the top off and split it down lengthwise. Worked real well, don't you think?"

"Yes, it's very clever. The swelling must be going down since it's getting a little loose. I think so anyway."

"I'll tighten it up pretty quick but I have an idea. Since it's a nice warm day and if you'll let me, I'll carry you down to the creek and help you wash your hair. I'll take one of my shirts and a couple of blankets with us then you can take off your dress and I'll wash it in the creek. I don't know how clean I can get it, but it'll be better than it is now. I feel badly I had to cut the sleeve off such a pretty dress."

"Oh, this is dreadful! I can't possibly allow you to do that," Emily fussed.

Peter heard the distress in her voice. For the last two days she had cried and slept off and on all day, which was perfectly understandable. He was relieved to see her doing better this morning. "Don't think a thing about it, Emily. I had a sister and I know how important it was to her to have her hair washed. I suppose most women feel the same way."

"You said you *had* a sister? What happened to her?"

Peter groaned inwardly at the memories of a terrible night not so very long ago. He didn't like thinking about it, much less talking about it. But maybe it would take Emily's mind off her troubles for awhile. He decided to tell her some of his story.

"My mother and father had a fatal accident and left me with my younger brother and sister. My sister was a good girl and worked hard to be the lady of the house. One night after she had gone to bed, my brother and I had an argument that turned into a fight. He threw a book at me and accidentally hit the oil lantern which broke and spilled coal oil on me. My hair and clothes caught fire and by the time he managed to put out the fire on *me* and get me outside, the house was engulfed with smoke and flames."

Peter paused as the memory of that dreadful night crawled through his mind. He could almost feel the flames and smell the coal oil and his own burned flesh and hair. He choked on a sob but composed himself and continued. "My brother couldn't get to my sister, her bedroom was on the second story. He ran to retrieve a ladder but by the time he got it into place under her window, it was too late. They said the smoke killed her."

"How awful, I'm so sorry, Peter. Where is your brother now?"

"Well, after my sister's funeral . . . he hung himself. He left a note saying he couldn't live with the guilt."

Emily was touched by the grief she heard in Peter's voice, realizing it cost him a great deal to tell her about the loss of his family. "Why does there have to be so much sorrow in the world?"

"I don't know, Emily. I've wondered the same thing myself."

"Is that why you wear your cape with the hood up all the time, to hide your scars from the burns?"

"Yes, it's quite an ugly sight."

"I wouldn't mind if you take your cape off, Peter. It's such a warm day you must be hot under that hood."

"I don't want to talk about it anymore," he said abruptly. "I'll never take my cape off around people." He quickly changed the subject. "I'll go gather what we need to take down to the creek."

It turned out to be quite a chore but Peter managed to get Emily down to the creek to wash her hair. He built a fire beforehand to heat the chill off the water. "I'm afraid I'm getting more water on me and your dress than on your hair. Good thing I'm going to wash the dress." "It'll be worth it, Peter. I feel better already. Your soap stings the cut on my head; I hope it doesn't start bleeding again."

"I'll watch it carefully," he promised. He held a blanket up and turned his back as she took off her dress and wrapped in another blanket. He helped her as much as possible and still give her some privacy. "Are you all covered up now?"

"Yes, I'm covered. Here's my dress. I'm embarrassed that you have to do this."

"Please don't be. I'm going to go downstream a ways and wash a couple of my shirts along with your dress. There's some warm water left in the bucket to use however you want."

"Thank you, Peter. You won't go very far, will you?"

"No, I'll stay close, don't worry."

Emily watched Peter as he made his way downstream. *What a kind man he is. I wish I could see more of his face. With that scraggly beard I can't tell how old he is. Strange, but somehow he seems familiar to me.*

Startled by all the bruises on her body and exhausted from the effort of bathing herself, she used only her left hand and fumbled her way into Peter's shirt. A tear slipped down her cheek as she labored for a good fifteen minutes to button up three buttons. "That will just have to do," she mumbled to herself, then wrapped a blanket around her waist. She looked about, wondering what to do next. "Hair . . . I need to comb out my hair." She located Peter's comb lying by the soap a few feet away. Gingerly, she stood and tested her leg, putting a little weight on it. Carefully, she limped to the log, sat down, and began awkwardly trying to run the comb through her long, tangled hair.

Impossible! This is impossible! I know Peter would help me but I can't bring myself to ask him to do another thing for me. What am I going . . . what is . . . that? Emily listened intently for a few minutes. *That's Peter . . . he's singing!* Emily sat spellbound, listening. *What a wonderful voice. I can't believe it. He's singing Sweet Little Maid of the Mountain. That's one of Steven Foster's songs that I sang at my performance in Philadelphia.* A shiver of excitement and surprise skipped up her spine. *And . . . I know that voice! Can it really be him? It* has *to be him!*

Chapter 7

RAND DIDN'T WAIT UNTIL morning to leave Cheyenne. Knowing he wouldn't be able to sleep, he made his way back to his room, gathered up his things and went for his horse. Once in the saddle and out of town his mind began working on all that he had learned. "Well, Ducky, it's just possible she might still be alive. Let's go find her."

After a few hours of riding, Rand pulled to a halt. He took care of his horse then rolled up in his blankets without making a fire. Ducky's nickering woke him just as the sun was making its debut for the day.

"What is it, boy? Something making you nervous?" The horse bobbed its head and nickered again. Rand made his way to Ducky and stroked the horse's neck and side. "Thanks for the warning. I'll keep watch, it'll be all right." *For sure there's something out there. Probably a wild animal. I better ride careful today, Emily's life depends on me doing my job.*

By early afternoon, Rand spotted the place where the train had wrecked. A good number of men were milling around the area. Using ropes and horses, a crew was righting the engine on the tracks. Others had large fires going where they were tearing down and burning the train cars that had rolled and broken apart. Several wagons on the south side of the tracks had circled and made camp for the workers. Rand headed toward the camp.

A short distance from the cook wagon, Rand saw an old timer skinning an elk that was hanging from a tree limb. He went to offer his help. "Howdy! Could you use some help?"

The man glanced at Rand. "I've lived too long to turn down help, young man. Pull out your knife and let's get it done. I ain't had food since early this morning and I'm sure enough feeling weak in the knees. Cook says he'll feed me once I get this done." The old man chuckled. "What's your name?"

Rand had already started working when he answered, "Rand Trinity."

"I'm Valentine Matson," the man said with pride. "Most call me Val. Don't make no difference to me which one you use. I'll answer to both."

"Nice to meet you, Val. How long you been out here?"

"I was with the first bunch that came out. Never seen anything so ugly in all my life and I've seen some mighty ugly things in the past. This mess beats them all."

"Would you mind telling me what you saw and what you think happened?"

Val Matson stopped and gave Rand the once-over. "I *might* if I knew what business it is of yours."

Rand smiled at the old man and thought he could be trusted with the truth. "I'm a U.S. Marshall and I've been sent out here to find Emily Fitzpatrick. She was on the train."

"You don't say! I'm glad someone's looking for that young lady. I heard her sing at the Stanton House in Cheyenne. Sweet little thing. It's for sure God gave her the voice of an angel when she came into this world. Almost everyone thinks the Indians took her when they wrecked and robbed the train. Bunch of hog-wash, if you ask me."

"Why do you say that?"

"Anyone with any sense could tell it wasn't no Indian job. No one will go look for her cause they say it was Indians that done it. They think the military should track down the Indians and get her back."

"Tell me what *you* think happened."

"Sure. Looks like we're done here. Let's each take off a quarter and haul it over to the cook. I'll tell you what I think over a plate of food."

The two men found a place to eat and talk where no one was around. Rand got Val to talking again about the train wreck. "If you don't think it was Indians that robbed the train who do you think was responsible?"

"Idiots! That's who done it! Some idiot white men who don't know nothin' about Indians. There were three women on that train, not countin' your Emily. Not a one of them was scalped or taken. Even if they didn't want a captive they would have wanted that pretty blond hair hanging off their belts. There were a couple of arrows in two of the men's bodies and a few of the men were scalped. Messy jobs, too. Indians don't scalp like those jobs that was done. I saved one of the arrows and I promise you it wasn't made by no Indian. I'll show it to you if you want."

"Yes, I would like to see it. Maybe later, though. You think white men, maybe a *gang* did the job?"

"No doubt in my mind. Even the way the railroad tracks were tore up looked like a job done by white men. I've done some tracking in my time so I know how to read sign. And from the sign I read when we first got here I think that two of the girls were in the second car back from the engine. I don't know why they were in that car, but I suspect they went in to check on that dog. I was the first one in that car and it looked to me like the blond girl was knocked out when the train wrecked and Emily was thrown against the front of the car, then buried under all kinds of boxes and freight. That's why the gang missed her. They shot the blond girl and the dog." Val Matson stopped and reflected a moment. "I think the dog must have tried to protect the girls. Pretty collie. There's been times I wish I'd had a dog to keep me company. It gets mighty lonely roaming around out here."

"Who do you think took Emily? Do you have any ideas?"

"Well, now, that's a good question. I heard a man with the railroad say they deliver crates out here for a recluse who lives somewhere in these mountains. I figure he took her. The crates were still on the train, but one had been moved to the door. He must have found her under the freight and left the crates and took her. I think he carried her off cause the tracks leaving the train were deeper than the ones going in."

"Did you try and follow the tracks?"

"I did. They hired me to hunt game for meat for the crew that came out here, so I hunted in the direction the tracks went, but had to give up. Looked to me like that gang figured out what happened and went looking for her and the man that carried her off. There were too many tracks to figure out what they were doing. I did find where they camped at the base of a mountain, but I don't think they found Emily and the recluse. Anyway, I sure hope they didn't"

"Thanks for telling me about it, Mr. Matson. I'll be leaving in the morning and see if I can find them. Is there anything you can tell me about the country where the recluse might have taken Emily?"

"Not much. I knew a trapper who worked for gold in these mountains. He's been gone for a while, though. Had to go back east to see his sickly mother. He told me once he had a pretty spot on one of the mountains that had several caves. He lived in one that had a hidden entrance. Not sure where it is but sounded like a perfect place to be if you didn't want to be found."

"Would you point me in the right direction?"

"I'll do better than that. I'll take you part way in and then cut west. I saw a herd of deer over that way a couple days ago."

"I'd appreciate any help I can get," Rand admitted. "Can you leave early?"

"Sure, if you don't mind waitin' until after we get our morning's grub. They feed us about six."

"That'll work. Can't read the signs before then anyway."

Peter carried Emily up the mountain and laid her on the blankets she had been sleeping on. "I'll go back down in a while and get the things we left by the creek. I know you need to rest but we need to talk, Emily."

"I'm all right, Peter. What is it you want to talk about?"

Peter sat down on his bed that was across the cave from her. "I need to take you back down to the train. The railroad should know by now that something has gone wrong and they'll send men to check it out. You need to be with someone who can take care of you properly. That wound on your leg was deep and it would be awful if it gets infected. If we stay here any longer I'll have to leave you and go hunting for fresh meat. That's another thing. You need to be eating better so your body will heal suitably."

"I suppose you're right, Peter, but how are we going to get back to the train?"

Peter appeared to be deep in thought. "This is one time I wish I had a horse."

"I've wondered about that. Why don't you have a horse, or even a mule or donkey?"

"When I came out here I wanted to be alone. The man who told me about this place said the winters can be very harsh and taking care of an animal would be difficult, if not impossible. Also, a horse or other animal would need special care and would make trails that could lead people to me. So . . . I walk."

"I see," Emily said. "But the question remains; how are we going to get back to the train?"

"Well, I guess the same way I got you up here."

"I'm so grateful you saved me, Peter, but I *can't* let you carry me like that again. If you can find a walking stick and give me another day, I think I'll be able to walk on my own. I do love to walk and it's so beautiful here. I'll enjoy walking with you."

"I guess one more day wouldn't hurt unless your leg wound starts to look worse. I'll find you a good walking stick and see how you do tomorrow."

"Thank you, Peter. Thank you for *everything*. You've been so kind and taken such good care of me. I'll never be able to repay you."

"You're welcome and you don't need to repay me." He seemed embarrassed by her words of gratitude and suddenly stood up. "Now, let me check your leg wound before I go back down to the creek; it probably needs rewrapped. Maybe your dress will be dry by now. I got most of the blood washed out."

After her leg was bandaged, Emily lay down on her bed. She was aware of when Peter left the cave, knowing he had waited until he thought she was asleep. But sleep didn't come any time soon even though she was tired. Her emotions were in turmoil. *I can't believe I'm here in these mountains with Peter O'Donnell! I can't bear the thought of him living out here all alone. I've got to do something to get him to go back with me.*

Emily had gotten a glimpse of the scars Peter hid from the world when he carried her back to the cave from the creek. She'd laid her head against his shoulder when he had her in his arms and sneaked quick peeks. Only the left side of Peter's face showed the evidence of burns. Visible scars on his left temple pulled at his eye and gave it a squinty look. *Oh, Peter, how awful it must have been for you! You had the world at your feet and lost it in one awful accident. I've just got to think of something.*

Chapter 8

"WELL, TRINITY, I'M GOING to leave you here and go chase some deer," said Val Matson. "It won't be hard to follow their trail. Before too long you'll find where they camped."

"Thanks, Val. Will you still keep an eye out for any sign of that gang or Emily?"

"Sure thing, that's what I've been doing for the last week anyway. You be careful yourself, young man. That murderin' gang could still be in these parts."

"They should already be rounded up and in jail by now, but I'll be careful. You do the same."

Rand had enjoyed Valentine Matson's company but felt he could concentrate better on his tracking without the distraction of another person. He rode for a while then dismounted and walked, leading Ducky. By noon he found the cold campsite where the gang had spent the night at the base of a mountain. After a quick bite to eat, he hobbled his horse and spent the rest of the afternoon roaming the mountain. The only thing he found was a lot of tracks and a cave that certainly didn't have anyone living in it. And, a drop of dried blood on a leaf along the trail to that cave.

Rand felt perplexed as he made his way back to where Ducky was grazing. He was greeted with a nicker. "Glad to see you, too," he said as he stripped the horse. He made a fire and fried several thick slices of bacon, all the while contemplating his position. *Val said there is a cave up here with a hidden entrance. I'll go higher up in the morning and see if I can locate that hidden cave. I suppose it could be on another mountain, but I have a feeling, because of that drop of dried blood, this is where the recluse took Emily. I just need to find that hidden cave.*

Rand ate and surveyed the mountain one more time as twilight enveloped the area. A few stars had popped out and Rand made himself comfortable as the quiet and solitude of the night seeped into his soul. Eventually, he stretched out, wrapped himself in his blanket and drifted off to sleep, trusting Ducky to alert him of any danger.

He didn't know for sure how long he had slept but by the placement of the moon and stars he figured it wasn't very long. Morning was hours away but the strangest thing had just happened, bringing Rand straight up from his bed with all of his senses on high alert. He heard *singing*. A big smile crossed his face as he sat and listened. Rand remembered Miss Fisher saying Emily Fitzpatrick sang like an angel and that's one thing he couldn't argue with her about. If he hadn't been sitting on the hard ground he would have thought he had died and was on his way to heaven with an angel calling him there.

Reality struck when he remembered his job. This was the woman he was supposed to find. Slowly, he made his way toward the singing. It was tough going in the dark but he realized he had been wrong. The singing was not higher than the cave he had found, but lower and around the east side of the mountain. Emily Fitzpatrick stopped singing but Rand kept moving in the direction he thought the singing had come from. Soon he heard voices not too far away. He slowed and realized the voices were coming from behind an outcropping of rocks, brush and small trees. In the dark he couldn't see how to get through, so he just listened.

After Peter had retrieved all their belongings from the creek, he waited for Emily to wake from her nap. With his long bow in hand, he told her, "I'm going to hunt for a while and hopefully bring something back for supper. I'll walk up creek and if I'm lucky I'll get a rabbit or some grouse; that dried venison is getting tiresome. I won't be too long. Is there anything you need before I go?"

"I don't think so, Peter, unless you have something I could read."

"Sure do." Peter went to several boxes that were stacked behind his bed. "I have a box over here that has a few books in it." He placed the box beside Emily. "You have water and books, will you be all right for a short while?"

"I'll be fine. Please don't stay too long, though, or I'll worry. What if something should happen to you? I'd be lost out here."

"Emily, that is not true. If something should happen to me you need to turn left when you get out of the rocks and trees at the entrance of the cave and walk north. It will take you most of a day, but you will walk right to the train tracks. Someone will find you then."

"Oh, just don't let anything happen to you, Peter." She thought maybe she detected a smile behind his beard and wished she could see his eyes better to see if his smile reflected in them.

After he left, Emily let her mind drift back to the first time she had ever seen Peter. She was sixteen and had fallen hopelessly in love with the new young tenor who had a wonderful start to a career that would make him famous all over the world. After a time of reflection, Emily's eyes fell on the box with the books and she decided to see if there was anything inside that would interest her. She removed the blanket that was on top and began to look for a book. *I don't see any books in here. Peter must have gotten the wrong box. Oh, well, I doubt that I could keep my mind on reading, anyway.*

She lifted writing tablets out of the box and laid them and other papers on her lap. One by one she examined the writing. *He's been writing songs. That must be how he's passed the winter away. How wonderful!* She picked one up and studied the notes, then hummed the melody. *This is sweet, I love this one. It doesn't look like he's completely given up on singing.*

As she picked up the next writing tablet, a single piece of folded paper fell into her lap. She stared at the familiar paper for a full minute then cautiously picked it up and opened it. She was not prepared for what she saw or the emotions that swelled her throat. *He kept it . . . I can't believe he kept it!* A tear rolled down her cheek as she read his note at the bottom of the page. It said, 'I love this poem. I'll put it to music.'

Emily laid her head back against the wall of the cave and allowed herself to think once more of the dreams that were hers as a young women in love, knowing she could never have that special man who had captured her heart. *He would be surprised to know I've already put my poem to music and have sung it to him many times through the years. Would I dare sing it to him now and let him know that I know who he is? I wish he could have loved me instead of . . . .*

"Hi, I'm back," Peter greeted her. "Did you find something to read?"

"Yes, but not a book. I think you brought me the wrong box."

"I did? What was in the one I brought you?"

"Pages of music you've written."

Peter put his bow away and knelt at the box of music, peering in at the pages. "Just a lot of nonsense, but it helps me pass the time. I have a guitar that I play around with and make up little tunes. It's nothing of any importance."

"I think it's important. Some of them are very good."

He looked into Emily's face, his own half concealed. "And how would you know if they are good or not, Emily?"

"Well, I do have some experience with music. Would you mind if I play around with your guitar and maybe I'll sing to you after we eat."

"Are you sure you want to chance it? It might hurt your arm."

"Yes, please, I want to try at least."

"I'd like to hear you play, but not if it hurts your arm. Supper won't take long to cook. I only got one grouse; we'll have to split it. With the left over corncakes we'll have a good enough meal. Remember, we need to leave in the morning." He retrieved his guitar and laid it in Emily's lap.

"Yes, I know. I did pretty well walking today. Tomorrow I'll walk as much as I can. Who knows, maybe I can walk all the way."

"We'll see. Let's not worry about it tonight. We'll let tomorrow take care of itself. In some ways I hate to take you back to civilization. It will be lonely now without you."

"I guess you could always go back with me. I would like it if you would."

"I think by now you understand how I feel about that subject."

"Yes, I'm trying to understand."

"No one could completely understand how it is to have men cringe, children cry because they're afraid of the monster and women gasp and run away when they see you."

"Is that what she did, Peter, gasp and run away?" Emily asked, without thinking.

"Who are you talking about? They all run away."

Oh, how I wish I could see your face clearly. Emily looked right at him and made her decision. "I'm talking about Suzann Ramsey."

Peter stilled, his mouth tightened into a thin line, his voice hardened. "What do you know about Suzann Ramsey?"

"I know enough to know that she was not worthy of you."

Peter turned on her. "You don't know anything! It was *me* that was not worthy of *her*. She was so beautiful and full of life. I loved her dearly and don't blame her for running the opposite direction after my accident. I don't blame anyone who runs away from me."

"Well I do! When you love someone you don't run when things get difficult. You keep on working *together* through the difficulty and figure out what needs to be done to get through it."

"Some people are not as strong as you seem to be. Suzann was delicate, that's all."

"Delicate, ha! She didn't love you, Peter."

"You don't know what you're talking about!" Peter's voice rose in anger.

"I know a lot. Do you want to hear what I know?"

"Sure! Go ahead and tell me what you *think* you know!"

"All right." Emily closed her eyes and thought, *start from the beginning.* "When I turned sixteen I had heard of Peter O'Donnell. For my birthday I begged Mother and Father to take me to your concert at that new theatre in New York City. Mother refused to have any part of taking me to New York but when my grandmother heard about my wish, she convinced them to let that be her birthday present to me. A grand shopping trip and a visit to the new theater to hear you sing. Mother decided that since we were going to be shopping she would go along while my father stayed and took care of business. Mother never approved of me wanting to be a singer, saying it was not proper for a woman to display herself in front of hundreds of people. She cared more about being a part of proper society than she cared about my desires. Anyway, that's the first time I heard you sing."

After a deep calming breath, Emily continued, "A short time later, Grandmother helped me enroll in the Swanson School of Music in Philadelphia. That's where I heard you sing the second time. Also, I heard that you were to marry Suzann Ramsey. It broke my heart. I think I must have fallen in love with you the first time I heard you sing and after Philadelphia I didn't think I would ever love another man."

Peter stirred from his sitting position by the fire. "You were just a young woman, Emily. How could you know about love . . . and what does this have to do with Suzann?"

"After a while at Swanson, I was becoming quite popular and the school recommended me to sing at the Ramsey's Christmas gala at their wonderful mansion. I had been to fancy places before but never any place like that. If you were *anybody* in society you were invited to the ball at the Ramsey mansion."

"I remember that ball," Peter said. "Suzann was mad at me when I told her I couldn't go. Wendy, my sister, had become quite ill and I wouldn't leave her. Did you go and sing?"

"Yes, I went. Everything was so grand at first and I got a lot of attention from all the young men. A friend of mine told me that Suzann was jealous of all the attention I was getting and began intimating that I was mediocre at best and she was sorry she had let her mother talk her into letting me sing. I tried to ignore the innuendoes and enjoy myself but it really hurt and ruined the night for me. I didn't stay very long."

"That doesn't sound like Suzann," Peter said, shaking his head. "She was always so sweet and kind to everyone."

"Only when it benefited her, Peter. A couple of days later, I ran into that same friend of mine. She told me that after I left the ball, Suzann acted like a queen and carried on with all the young men who were now paying attention to her." Emily paused a moment. "Are you sure you want to hear the rest?"

"Yes, I'm sure. Suzann may have been a little spoiled but I loved her."

"I believe you, Peter. I'm sure you loved the person you thought she was."

"Go on, then. Tell me what you've got to say. I doubt it will make any difference to me but get it over with and say what you want."

"I don't know that it's what I *want* to say. I don't want to hurt you but I think you should know the truth. My friend happened to overhear Suzann's friend scolding her for being so brazen with all the men. She said to Suzann, 'How can you act like that and say you love Peter O'Donnell?'

"Her reply was, 'Have you ever heard me say I love Peter O'Donnell?' She laughed, then said, 'Peter O'Donnell is just a distraction for me. I'm hoping to make Gregory Abbot jealous. He's the one I plan to marry.' Her friends thought it was awful for her to lead you on, but she just laughed and flirted all the more.

"Peter, I had never felt hate like I did that day. I just decided it was not my place to do anything and I tried to forget you. Then I heard of your accident. I found out where you were and talked a friend into going with me to see you. They told me you were refusing to see anyone, so I left, and cried for days. Then there was no news, nothing. I couldn't find out anything about you or Suzann. So I concentrated on my singing."

Emily fell silent, picking at the strings on the guitar. Peter also was quiet as he went about the meal preparation. Finally, when they had eaten, he asked, "Are you sure about all the things you told me, Emily?"

"Yes, Peter, I'm sure. Please don't be hard on yourself and more than that, *please* don't hate me."

"It's hard to believe what you just told me. Maybe I was a fool in love and couldn't see the real Suzann. I don't know what to think, Emily, but I don't hate you."

Emily sighed with relief. "Thank you, Peter."

"I'm glad I know the truth. Maybe it will help me let go of the pain I've held for so long. I can still see the horror on her face when she walked into my room and saw me for the first time after the accident. She covered her face and ran from the room saying she couldn't bear it. Even then I loved her. I looked in a mirror only once after that and knew I couldn't blame her. I had almost died from the burns, but after that I almost died from not wanting to live."

Emily picked up the piece of paper she had laid carefully next to her. "When I was looking at your music I ran into this." She held up the paper. "Do you remember anything about this?"

Peter walked over and took the paper, studying it. "Not a lot. I remember it came in a card while I was in the hospital. I thought it was a beautiful poem of love and wanted to put music to it."

"Did you ever do that, put music to it?"

"No, I never could quite get a melody I liked."

"Would you like for me to sing it for you?"

Peter stared at Emily Fitzpatrick a long moment. He then sat down on his bedroll. "I'm not sure how you can pick up a poem and put a melody to it so quickly, but please, go ahead, sing."

"I can't play this guitar. You were right; it hurts my arm. Do you think you could play the chords while I sing? Start in the key of C."

Peter took the guitar from Emily and sat back down on his bed. After tuning it to his liking, he strummed a few chords. "All right, start singing, I'll follow you."

He wasn't sure what to expect but when Emily started singing, a jolt ran through him. She looked at him and sang the poem of love like she was singing it just for him. Her clear soprano voice was magnificent, he had never heard better.

My mind says it's folly, my heart says it's true,
When I look through the dream window, and I still see you.
Reality bids my heart to resist, dreams that will vanish sure as the mist.
Foolish dream window, won't go away, all is possible, it seems to say.

Dream window, dream window, don't tease me so cruel.
Dream window, dream window, am I your fool?

Suddenly his heart reacted when he realized she really was singing the song to him. The love in her eyes and voice told him that she had loved him and lost him, but would forever keep her love hidden in a secret place in her heart. Could it be that she had been the one to leave the card for him? Did she write the poem for him years ago? Entranced, he watched Emily as she continued to sing.

Like heaven's music, your voice lifted me,
To places of splendor, Oh, how can it be?
My young heart soared, with feelings all new,
A love song in springtime, so wonderfully true!

Soon it was there, my dream window came,
I'd sit by my window, and stare out the pane.
In time, as it should be, I was aware,
That I am in here, and you are out there!

Dream window, dream window, don't tease me so cruel!
Dream window, dream window . . . I'll be your fool.

They were quiet for a long time when she finished singing. Finally, Peter asked, "Did you write that poem for me, Emily? Did you leave the card and poem when I was in the hospital?"

Quietly, she answered, "Yes, I wrote it after I first heard you sing. I put the melody to it and sang it to you many times. I just never dreamed I would ever get to sing it to you in person."

"It's beautiful, Emily. Thank you so much. I wish . . . ."

Suddenly, a voice interrupted their quiet moment. "Hello, the cave! If you'll tell me how to get in, I'd like to talk to you."

Chapter 9

RAND DIDN'T THINK ANYONE was going to answer until a man's voice drifted out of the darkness. "Who are you and what do you want?"

"Name's Rand Trinity. I'm a U.S. Marshall looking for Emily Fitzpatrick. Is she there with you?" Silence followed for a few moments. Rand was just about to call out again when he heard the rustling of someone moving through the brush toward him.

"Where are you?" a man asked.

"I'm right here," Rand answered.

"Come this way," the man instructed.

Moments later, Rand felt a hand on his arm and was led through the trees and over a low boulder. A glow from a fire helped him see the entrance to the cave.

"Come on in," the man said. "Emily is inside."

Rand let his eyes adjust to the light in the cave and looked at his surroundings. He spotted Emily sitting on a blanket against one side of the cave. Even in her state of dishevelment she was beautiful, her tousled hair loose and flowing around her shoulders. He noticed her right arm was in a crude sling. Another bed lay across the cave. It was a pretty neat set-up, in a rough sort of way. A small fire was keeping the place warm, its smoke curling lazily up through a hole in the ceiling. Seeing there was no need for alarm, Rand smiled at the man in the black cape with the hood pulled up. "May I ask who you are?"

"My name is Peter O'Donnell, Mr. Trinity."

Emily quickly told him, "He saved my life. I would have been killed if it hadn't been for Peter."

"I knew someone must have been helping you," Rand said. "But didn't know who or what condition you were in."

"I'm doing fine, thanks to Peter."

"I have a lot of questions if you two are up to talking," Rand said.

The three talked until Rand realized how weary Emily looked. "You were planning on taking Emily back down in the morning, to where the train had wrecked?"

"Yes," Peter answered. "I figured the railroad would have men down there by now. She needs to be under a doctor's care."

"That's right and there is a crew working down there now," Rand said. "We'll all leave in the morning then."

"I won't be going with you, Mr. Trinity," said Peter. "I'm sure you understand why I don't want to be around people since you heard my story."

"I understand, but I'm going to have to take you back to Cheyenne so you can be a witness against that gang. I'll make it as comfortable for you as possible."

"Isn't there some way you can do it without me?" asked Peter.

"I suppose you could write out a statement and sign it in front of me. That might satisfy the judge."

Emily became upset. "Please, Peter, go with us! I want you to meet my grandmother and I know she would want to thank you for what you've done for me."

"Don't ask me to do that, Emily. You know I'm glad I could help you but I need to stay here."

"Will you at least go down to the train tracks with us?"

Peter thought about that. "Yes, I can do that. I need to get my supplies anyway."

"Well, now that *that's* settled, I'll go back down to where my horse is and get a few hours sleep. I want to leave as soon as we can in the morning, but first, you need to write out a statement for me to take back to Cheyenne, Mr. O'Donnell."

"I'll get it done in the morning," Peter promised.

Rand said goodnight and left the cave. Peter and Emily were quiet for awhile. But Emily couldn't stand the strain and began to cry. "I want to stay here with you, Peter," she managed between sniffles. "I can't bear to leave you here all alone on this mountain."

"Think of *me*, Emily. It's what I need to do. You have no idea what it's like to be so badly disfigured that people run from the sight of you. I tried to endure it for a while but finally decided I would be better off by myself. I didn't have any family left and desperately needed a place where I could have some peace in my life. That's when I met a man in the hospital who was visiting his mother. He told me about this place and drew a map for me so I could find it. It's lonely, yes, terribly lonely, but I have peace here. Please understand."

"I think I do, Peter, but that doesn't make it any easier for me to leave you here. Maybe God brought us together in this strange way for a purpose."

Peter watched Emily wipe the tears from her eyes. "So, you believe in God now?"

"Don't make fun of me. Yes, I believe in God. I've had time to think about it since that first night when you challenged me about my beliefs. But, I don't feel close to God. I don't even know how to begin to find Him."

"My sweet Emily. You don't have to find Him. He's already found you. All you have to do is open your heart to Christ, God's son, and acknowledge that you believe in what he did on the cross for you."

"You mean like when He died?"

"Yes, that's what I mean. He died on that cross in *our place*. If you believe that, you can be in heaven with Him when we leave this body in death."

"Do you really believe in Christ?"

"Yes, Emily, I believe. When you're ready you need to tell Christ you believe, too, and that you want to give yourself to Him so you can be in heaven when you die."

"That's all I have to do? I always thought a person had to grovel and confess everything they've ever done wrong and beg for forgiveness."

"Forgiveness is part of it, but not like that. You don't have to grovel and beg, but you do have to be sincere and admit that you've sinned. Do you understand *sin*?"

"I'm not completely ignorant about religious things," Emily said, indignantly. "I do know what sin is and I know I've done my share of things that God didn't like." She was thoughtful for a few moments. "I'll think about it."

"Good, now you need to try and get some sleep."

"Peter?"

"What?"

"Would you mind coming over here and sitting next to me? Hold me in your arms until I go to sleep."

"There's nothing I would love more than to hold you, but that wouldn't be a wise thing to do. You stay on your side of the cave and I'll stay on mine."

"Will you sing for me then?"

"I can do that. What would you like for me to sing?"

"It doesn't matter. Just let me go to sleep hearing your voice."

Peter hummed a lullaby that he remembered his mother singing to his baby sister. Then softly, he sang a few of his favorite hymns. Felling sure that Emily had finally gone to sleep, Peter slid down into his own bed of blankets. He fought feelings and emotions that threatened to destroy his resolve to stay on the mountain alone. The love that was developing between him and Emily was something he dared not let get out of hand. He must see her to the tracks and return to the cave, but he would treasure the memory of his time with her. *My sweet Emily, how can I possibly have come to love you so much in such a short time? God, please be close to her and keep her safe. Help her find your love and the love of a good man who will cherish her.*

He thought he would have a hard time falling asleep but it seemed only minutes when a faint light from the entrance of the cave roused him from slumber. His sleep muddled brain registered that his right arm felt numb. He started to stretch but realized something was on top of his arm. Blinking several times he cleared his vision and for a second was shocked. Emily was snuggled close to him, her head on his shoulder. She looked the picture of innocence.

Why did you do this, Emily? You test my resolve more than you know. Gently, he turned toward her and held her close, kissing her forehead and grieving the loss of her. It was not near long enough but in a few moments he released his hold. *I've got to get my mind on business. I'll go to the entrance and write down my story for the judge in Cheyenne.*

Sometime later, a sleepy voice asked, "How did you get away without waking me? Do you dislike being close to me so much that you jump up and run away?"

Peter turned to see Emily sitting up. "You're not a child, Emily, and I think you know why you shouldn't have done that."

"I knew I could trust you and besides, I was cold."

Peter ignored her last remark. "I have something I want you to do for me."

"What could I possibly do for you?"

"I'm going to bring you a piece of paper and I want you to write the notes to that song you sang to me. You know the poem you wrote. Can you do that for me?"

"If I'm careful and don't move too fast, I think I can."

"While you do that, I'll fix some corn cakes for breakfast."

"You've got to know it will break my heart."

"I'm sorry, Emily, but I would like to have your melody, if you don't mind."

"Very well, bring me the paper. I know the notes by heart."

Emily finished with the song and the two ate in silence until Emily asked, "Peter, do you think you could braid my hair before we go? Do you know how to braid? I can't stand the thoughts of anyone seeing me like this."

Peter groaned. "Yes, I can braid. I've helped my sister at times with braiding. I won't make any promises of how it will look, but I'll do the best I can."

"Thank you. I'll feel so much better with it pulled back out of my way. It's gotten so long I probably should have some of it cut off."

Peter got down on his knees behind Emily. "Sing your song for me while I braid your hair, then we need to go. I thought maybe Mr. Trinity would be up here by now but I guess we'll have to walk down to his camp."

Emily sang the song through. Peter was tying the braid off with a piece of fabric when Emily started to turn around. Peter stopped her. "No, don't turn around. Sing it one more time and I'll sing it with you."

"Why can't I turn around?"

"Please, Emily, just do as I asked."

Emily started singing and Peter beautifully blended his voice to hers. The cave fell into a strained silence when the song ended. Neither one spoke for a full minute as both were in a state of misery.

Peter made the first move. "Here is your walking stick. You can get started while I grab my pack frame then I'll be right behind you."

Almost at the bottom of the steepest part of the hill, Emily turned and started to plead again for Peter to come with her. "Peter, I . . . ."

"No more, Emily. I am going to come back here to this mountain when I get my supplies. Let's do what we know has to be done and get you back to your grandmother."

They finally came to the clearing where Rand had told them he was camping. Peter stopped in his tracks trying to make out the scene that lay before him. They stood staring at Rand Trinity . . . hanging from a tree!

Chapter 10

RAND'S WRISTS WERE TIED together with one end of a rope and the other end thrown over a tree limb, pulling him up into a stretch so that his feet could barely touch the ground. He had to stand on his tiptoes to take the pressure off his wrists. Peter realized too late that Rand was trying to warn him of danger. He and Emily were immediately surrounded by men with guns who Peter recognized as the gang that was after Emily.

"Well, now, this was a whole lot easier than I thought it would be," gloated one man, who was obviously the leader. "Thanks for bringing the little lady right to us. Jack, get that thing off his back and tie this feller up till we decide what we're going to do with him. And keep an eye on that girl!"

"Please don't hurt him," Emily pleaded. "He hasn't done anything to you. Just let him go. It's me you want."

Her pleas went unheeded and Peter was pushed to the ground. "Be quiet, lady, and sit down right there beside him."

Emily sat down beside Peter while another man came over and roughly tied Peter's hands behind his back then tied his feet together. "Hey, what's with the hood?"

Peter didn't answer. The man grabbed the back of the hood and jerked it down. He took a couple of steps back and stared.

Peter turned to Emily and quietly spoke. "I'm sorry you had to see me this way."

Emily smiled at him. "I told you it wouldn't matter to me. I love who you are."

One of the gang found his voice. "Lady, you got to be crazy! How could you love someone who looks like that! Wake up in the morning and look at that and it would scare a body plum to death!"

Another one made a face of disgust and added his opinion. "Ken's right, lady. He ain't nothing but a freak. I'd wear a hood over my head, too, if I looked like that. No wait, I think I'd jump off a cliff and save the world from having to look at one disgusting sight."

Rand felt anger rising up inside. He was gagged or he probably would have cursed at the men who had caught him off guard and put him in this predicament. His body ached, especially his head, from being beaten by the men who now had their attention on Peter O'Donnell. He felt sorry for Peter and Emily but at the moment there was nothing he could do."

When the men tired of verbally assaulting Peter, they turned to Carl. "What we going to do now, Carl?"

"Yeah, what we going to do?" Slim echoed.

"I'm thinking. Give me a minute and I'll figure it out. Slim, see if there's any coffee in that pot. We'll have us some coffee while I decide. That U.S. Marshall is the one that I want to disappear. We need to make sure no one will ever find him."

The man named Ken gave his opinion. "I think we should tie them up and get out of the country. They'd probably die before anyone found them."

"Shut up, Ken, we're not leaving until we get the money from that rich lady. Stella said she had more than she knew what to do with."

That caught Emily's attention. "Stella? Are you talking about Stella Harker?"

"Sure, she's the one who planned all this," Carl said with a sneer. "Now that she's dead, me and the boys is going to get all that money."

"Stella is dead?" Emily asked.

"That's what I was told. The sheriff and his deputy found her with the loot from the train and when they started to arrest her, she shot the sheriff with that little derringer she always carries, then the deputy plugged her right in the heart."

"Please, let these men go," Emily pleaded again. "I'll get the money for you. Just take me to my grandmother and I'll see that you get it."

"That's not what I been thinking," Carl said. "Boys, we're going to take this man . . . what's your name, freak?"

"It's *Peter* and leave him alone!" Emily screamed.

Carl laughed. "Don't worry, we're going to take you and your Peter with us." He turned to his men. "Remember that deserted shack out south of Cheyenne, the one we stayed in after we broke into the store in town? Well, we're going to take these two to the shack. Then we'll send the freak into town for the money. If he don't bring it to us, in a certain amount of time, we'll kill the girl and get as far away as we can. I'll have it all worked out by the time we get to the shack."

"What are we going to do with him?" Slim pointed at Rand.

"An evil gleam came into the leader's eyes. "Well, we're going to let you kill him any way you want, Slim. If I remember right, there's a shale slide not far on the side of that hill. We'll throw his body to the bottom and start a slide that will cover him real good. After he quits stinking, no one will ever know what happened to him."

Rand's mind was working frantically. His wrists were raw from struggling to free himself. *Maybe if the one who is going to kill me comes close enough I can . . . what?* Rand was feeling more helpless than he had ever felt in his life. He couldn't think of a thing to do, so he prayed. *Please, God, I need help! And I need it* fast!

Slim eyed Rand. "I don't want to cold-blooded kill him with him looking at me, Carl. Why don't we all aim and shoot at the same time? That way we can all say we done it."

"All right, Slim, we'll do it your way."

Emily tried pleading again and when they ignored her she started crying.

"Get your guns out, boys. We need to get this over with so we can get that money and go live it up."

All five men pulled their pistols and Carl gave the instructions. "When I say *three* we all shoot."

On the count of *one,* Rand shut his eyes. *Any time now, God, or I'll be seeing you soon."*

"*Two.*"

"Wait! Let *me* do it!" a voice interrupted.

Rand opened his eyes and couldn't believe what he was seeing. Standing inside the clearing, about twenty feet away, stood the testy kid from town who had delivered to Rand the telegraph message from George Fisher. The kid had on some nice looking cowboy boots but other than that everything about him was the same dirty, tattered clothes; same dirty, brown hair; and the same big, sloppy hat on his head. The kid didn't have licorice in his mouth but it looked like he had a wad of chew in his cheek.

The gang members were as startled as Rand was. "Who are *you?*" Carl demanded. "How did you get here?"

"I tracked you from town. It was easy," the kid said with a swagger.

"Why'd you track us?" Carl asked. "That was a stupid thing to do."

"I followed you to ask if I could join your gang."

"You must be touched in the head." Carl shook his own head. "Why would we want a snot-nosed kid with a smart mouth joining up with us?"

"Cause . . . you *need* me."

A couple of the men snickered. "And why would we need *you?*"

"Cause I've got *talent* that none of you have." The swagger was back.

"Keep going, I want to hear about your *talents,*" Carl scoffed.

Before the kid answered, he spit a steam of dark brown liquid right in front of Carl, then grinned. "I can crack open about any safe there is. The easier ones in five to ten minutes and the more complicated ones depends on how new they are. The new ones are a little harder. And, I can shoot better than most anyone I know."

Rand felt disgust when the kid spit another stream of tobacco. He didn't know why but he felt like he had failed the young man. *Wish I could have reached him before he came out here to be a killer and a thief.*

"What's your name, kid?" Carl asked.

"Call me Joe."

"Tell me, Joe, if we let you kill this U.S. Marshall, how would you do it? With your all-fired good shooting, or what?"

"*Knives!* I like knives." the kid answered.

"Whew! You're something else, Joe!"

Emily began crying again. "Please, *please,* don't do this. I beg you, *please,* don't do this!"

Carl became agitated. "Ken, put her on that black horse with the man behind her and get her out of here. I'm tired of her caterwauling. Slim and Buck can go with you. Keep the man's hands tied, though. Jack and the kid can help me finish this here job."

"Sure, boss, we'll go slow till you catch up."

Rand watched as Ken put Emily on Ducky and goaded Peter until he was mounted behind her. His hands were tied in front now, so he could put his arms around Emily and still guide the horse. "Just follow Slim and don't do anything stupid. I'll be right behind you just in case you get any idea about doing something dumb," Ken told Peter.

Peter did what he was told and the three men left with Emily and Peter. *Three down, three to go, God.* Rand felt foolish talking so calmly to God when he was about to die. *I don't know what I can do, God, it's up to you.*

"All right, kid, it's all your show now, get it done!" Carl demanded.

The kid who had asked to be called *Joe* produced two ugly looking knives. He sauntered over to Rand and laid the flat of the blade on Rand's upper cheek and slid it downward. "It's a sharp knife and won't hurt all that much, Mr. U.S. Marshall. You got anythin' to say to your maker before you leave this earth, to wherever you're going?"

Rand tried to talk around the gag in his mouth.

Joe reached up and pulled the gag down, then pushed his own floppy hat back far enough so Rand could see beautiful, light-blue eyes sparkling back at him. They looked suspiciously like Miss Fisher's eyes. "Now you can talk," Joe went on. "You better confess your sins in a hurry and make it good cause I'm affixing' to show these men what I can do with a knife."

Rand almost choked when Miss Fisher pulled her floppy hat back down and spit a stream of dark brown juice on one of his boots. Rand looked down at his boot and started to pray, "God, I've done things I'm not proud of. Please forgive me, Amen."

"Is that all you've got?" the kid challenged. "I think maybe there's more confessing you need to do."

Miss Fisher was taunting him and Rand knew it. He also knew what she was waiting to hear so he swallowed his pride. "Yes, there's more." He looked straight at the mouth that had a grin only he could see. "I want to ask forgiveness for being proud and arrogant. I need to ask to be forgiven for not listening to people who are trying to help me." Rand paused and tried to look contrite. "Do you think I'll be forgiven, Joe?"

"I reckon your prayers were heard. You ready to meet your maker now?'

"I'm ready."

Joe winked at Rand and sauntered back over to stand in front of Carl. "Should I make him suffer or get it over quickly?"

"Get it done, kid. I'm tired of waiting."

Rand knew Miss Fisher had a plan. He was just hoping it was a good plan and he was ready for whatever she was going to do. He cringed when she held one of the knives by the tip and prepared to throw. What happened next was a blur. She threw the knife; Rand felt the rope give and with his weight, pulled on the rope; he collapsed to the ground, immediately rolling toward the men. Miss Fisher also hit the ground and rolled into position to throw the other knife. It was a good throw and Jack jumped backwards with a look of utter shock on his face as he sat hard on the ground. In moments he slumped and fell the rest of the way down. Rand scrambled to his feet and dove for Carl, but was too late. Carl dashed into the trees firing a shot that grazed Rand's arm.

Miss Fisher had disappeared and Rand, without hesitation, did the same. Standing behind a tree he listened for movement. The sound of a horse galloping from the area gave him reason to believe it was Carl, but just to make sure, he stood quietly for a few moments longer.

Miss Fisher finally called out, "He's gone, Mr. Trinity!"

"Maybe, maybe not! Stay put, I'm coming to you!"

Chapter 11

SURPRISED THAT MISS FISHER didn't argue, Rand began making his way in the direction of her voice. He moved cautiously, stopping often to listen for Carl. He knew he was close to Miss Fisher but still jerked in surprise when she tapped him on his shoulder and stepped from behind a tree.

"I'm right here," she said. "We need to talk."

Rand's anger flared, but he quickly checked it. "Do you *have* to do that?" he managed to say in a relatively calm voice.

"Do what?"

Rand was amazed at the guiltless face before him. He knew better. "Scare the beegeebers out of me! I think you enjoy it way too much and *yes* we need to talk. The first thing I want to know is your real name. It's about time we started calling each other by our first names."

After spitting out a wad of something then wiping her mouth with her sleeve, she answered, "All right, Rand, you can call me Jo, Josie, or Josephine."

"It's for sure I'm not going to call you *Joe.*"

"Most of my friends call me Josie."

"Are you the Josie who trained Ducky?"

"That's me. Ducky is the smartest horse I've ever had the pleasure to meet."

"Well, you did a good job. He *is* well trained, for sure."

"Why, thank you, Rand. We need to make a plan now. What are we going to do? Do you think they'll still go to that shack they were talking about?"

There is that we *again. At least she's including me in the plan this time.* Rand thought a moment before he answered. "I figure they'll move quickly to the shack. They want to hurry and get the money from Mrs. Fitzpatrick."

"You could be right but I'm thinking about Emily. They would have to ride hard and fast to get to Cheyenne today. I don't think they'll be able to travel that fast with Emily and that man riding double. If they go back the way they came they'll stay in the trees and brush. And Emily probably isn't able to ride hard with her injuries. They'll probably stop for the night and I have an idea about where that might be. If we get out on the open prairie we can travel faster and get ahead of them at the lake where I think they'll stop for the night. That way, we can watch and make sure Emily is safe. Maybe we'll get a chance to get them away from the gang." Josie shrugged. "Of course, they could stop and try to ambush us."

"There's a chance of that but most gangs like this one will choose to do things the easiest way possible. Ambushing us would take some planning and patience on their part. I like your idea but how are we going to travel fast when they took my horse?"

"I'll go get my horse and see if by any chance they left the dead man's horse."

"All right, but be careful. I'll gather what things of mine they left and we can get going. Do you have an extra gun? They took my rifle and my hand guns."

"I have a number of knives, a small derringer and a rifle that's on my horse. You can use the rifle if you like."

"All right, I will. How did you learn to throw a knife like that?"

"Circus. I'll go get the horses."

Rand watched as Josephine Fisher dashed into the trees and disappeared out of sight. *I wonder if I'll ever get her to be still long enough to tell me what that means. Circus?*

It wasn't but a few minutes later when Josie came out of the trees with a brown mare in tow. She had washed her face and changed into clothes that were more suitable for a young woman. The wig was gone and her hair was down and tied back with something that Rand couldn't see because on her head was the big floppy hat.

Josie cleaned and wrapped Rand's arm with a cloth she had in her saddle bags. "You were lucky, it's not a very deep wound. Sure bled a lot but it shouldn't give you much trouble." She nodded toward the body on the ground not far away. "What are we going to do about him?"

"There's a lot of men by the railroad tracks. We'll have to go that way to get to open prairie, so I'll get someone to come back here and get his body." Rand noticed Josie was trying not to look at the body. "Is this the first time you've killed someone?"

"Yes, and I hope I never have to do it again. It's not a very pleasant feeling knowing you've taken someone's life."

"I know what you mean. I've had to shoot a few times, but only once did I kill a man. If any man deserved killing, it was him." Rand handed Josie her knives. "I retrieved your knives."

"Thanks, I'd hate to lose them. My knives are made especially for me."

"I want to hear all about your knives and what happened in town with the sheriff, but we need to go if we are going to get ahead of that gang."

"You're right. I'll fill you in when we stop later in the day."

"That'll work." Rand looked deep into blue eyes that still sparkled but had turned serious. "By the way, thanks for saving my life, Josie."

"Glad I could help, Rand."

Josephine quickly turned and mounted her horse. "You lead out, I'll follow."

After finding someone at the tracks to go back and get the dead outlaw, Rand and Josephine took off across the prairie. Rand was impressed with Josie's riding skills and especially the way she cared for her horse. Having time to think about all that had happened, Rand found himself thinking of Miss Josephine Fisher in a different light.

Later that afternoon Rand stopped for the third time to give the horses a breather. "Are we close to the lake?"

"Yes, we're just about right on. We need to go south into the trees now."

"Good, you take the lead now but keep your eyes open for trouble, especially when we get into the timber."

"All right. We'll need to go slow when we get in there anyway. I'll have to find the trail to get my bearings, but it looked like they had camped by that lake when I was tracking them to the mountain. I figure they'll stay there again. If we get up high we should be able to watch everything that goes on. I've got a spot in mind."

"I think I remember that lake from years ago and you're right, it would be a good place to camp for the night."

Josie's face registered surprise. "You've lived here before?"

"Yes, my cousin rescued me from a Union prison in the middle of the war back east. He brought me out here to live with him and his father. My father was killed in an attack on the train we were on. I was alone after that so my cousin brought me out here."

"Where's your mother?"

"I don't know," Rand answered, without feeling.

"I'm sorry, I don't mean to be rude but if you don't mind me asking, what happened to your mother?"

"Dad told me she had a wild, restless spirit and ran off when I was about six."

"That's awful. I don't understand how a mother could do that."

"There've been times I've wondered about it myself . . . but not anymore."

"Have you ever thought about trying to find her?"

"What good would that do? If she didn't want me when I was a kid I don't figure she'll want anything to do with me now."

Josie thought a minute. "Maybe she's changed."

"Maybe, maybe not. I'm not planning on finding out."

Josie smiled at Rand. "I bet you get your red hair from her."

"I don't know what that has to do with anything, but that's what my father told me." Rand changed the subject. "We better get going, you ready?"

"Hey, Buck, hold up a minute."

"What do you want, Ken?"

"I just want to talk a minute. Slim, keep an eye on these two while I have a chat with Buck."

"All right, Ken, find out if we can stop pretty soon."

Peter watched as Ken made his way around the horse he was on with Emily. He stopped close to Buck and the two outlaws talked quietly. Peter whispered in Emily's ear, "You doing all right, Emily? I noticed you've been holding your arm like it might be bothering you."

"It's hurting some, but I'm fine. I wish we could stop pretty soon. It seems like we've been riding for hours."

"We have been riding for a few hours. There's something else bothering you. Tell me what it is."

"I have been wondering, do you think they killed Mr. Trinity?"

"I don't see how he could still be alive the way he was tied up to that tree. Anyway, that's what I figured at first. Now I'm beginning to wonder, myself."

"What do you mean?"

"Well, where is Carl and Jack? They've had plenty of time to catch up with us and that gives me a little hope. But we better not count on Mr. Trinity being able to help us if by some miracle he is still alive. We just need to concentrate on keeping ourselves alive and watch for an opportunity to escape."

Peter stopped talking when Ken made his way back to Slim. "Cheer up, Slim, we're going to stop pretty soon and give Carl and Jack a chance to catch up. Think about going fishing. We'll have a mess of fish for supper tonight."

"Man that does sound good. I'm so hungry I could eat a whole pan of fish by myself."

As they started moving forward, Peter whispered in Emily's ear. "When we stop for the night don't do anything to draw attention to yourself. I don't like the way Buck has been looking at you. When we turn at an angle where the two behind us can't see, start working on the knots on the rope in front of you. Don't untie me, just loosen them up. Don't be afraid to let go of the saddle with your left hand. I won't let you fall."

Emily didn't say anything but Peter felt her nod.

Buck picked up the pace like he had a plan and was eager to arrive at some destination where they would stop and wait for their boss and Jack.

"Maybe I was wrong, Rand. Don't you think they should be down there by now?"

Josie had led Rand to the lookout spot she had told him about, where they could watch the lake and see anything that happened below. The trees and brush were thick enough to keep them in shadows. Trees were around most of the lake, but about a hundred yards around the water was rock, sand and scant vegetation. Sneaking up on the gang that held Peter and Emily, would be nearly impossible.

"I don't know, Josie. Let's give them a little longer."

"What should we do if they don't show up?"

"Do you know the shack they were talking about holding up in?"

"I'm pretty sure I know which one Carl meant. Dad and I ran into it last fall when we were hunting. It would be a good place to hide out, all right."

"Let's see what happens in the next hour and then decide. While we're waiting, tell me what happened in town. Did Stella Harker really shoot the sheriff?"

"I'm afraid she did. When I told Dad all that we'd learned, he went to the sheriff right away and told him all about it."

"Did you go with him to see the sheriff?"

"No, Dad had me go quietly to Mrs. Fitzpatrick and Mr. Clench and warn them. When the sheriff and Dad got to the hotel, they woke up Stella and searched her room. They found what they were looking for in one of her traveling bags. They brought her into the room where I was waiting with Mr. Clench and Mrs. Fitzpatrick to let us know what they had found. She was cold as ice, Rand! She pulled out that little derringer from her pocket and in a *blink* the sheriff was dead. She had two shots and aimed the other one at Mrs. Fitzpatrick but Mr. Clench threw himself in front of Mrs. Fitzpatrick, and Dad shot Stella. Stella's shot went wild. Dad took over and told Mr. Clench to stay and protect Mrs. Fitzpatrick while he rounded up a couple of men he trusted to arrest the gang at Lilly's."

"Evidently the gang got wind of what happened and took off," Rand guessed.

"We weren't sure where they went, but they were not at Lilly's place."

"Did your father send you out here to warn me?" Rand watched Josie's face carefully.

She didn't answer right away which made him curious. When she finally looked at him, he saw the look of a guilty child who just got caught with her hand in the cookie jar.

"No, I'll not lie to you," Josie admitted. "I left a note telling him what I was going to do. I knew he had to stay in town and make sure Mrs. Fitzpatrick was safe in case the gang hadn't left town. Besides, if I told him what I was going to do he would have locked me in the jail."

Rand frowned. "That's probably where you should . . . ."

Josie was saved for the moment from getting a scolding. "Shh, I think I hear them coming."

"Yes, I hear them, too. Looks like you were right, Josie. Don't move anymore than you have to."

Silently, the two watched as the riders made their way to the fire pit where they had camped before. The gang placed Peter, with feet tied together, and Emily close to the pit where they could be watched with little effort. As wide and open as the ground was around the lake there would be no slipping away without being seen. Rand was glad to see the two were in relatively good condition, but when he observed the outlaws setting up camp for the evening, his muscles clenched as he realized they had a problem.

A *big* problem!

Chapter 12

RAND MADE EYE CONTACT with Josie and her expression was proof she had realized the problem too. Carefully, the two inched their way back into the trees far enough that they couldn't be seen or heard.

"Where's Carl?" Josie had a scowl on her face.

Rand shook his head and thought a minute before he answered. "It's for sure he's not with his men. That could only mean one thing; he's followed *us* and is somewhere around here."

"Oh, fiddlesticks! That's not good."

"You're right. That's *not* good!"

"What should we do, Rand?"

"If I told you to stay here . . . would you do it?"

A smile touched Josie's lips. "If you tell me *why* and it makes good sense, I'll do what you say."

"Good. There's only about half an hour of daylight left. I want to walk back to the spot where the trail is narrow. I think from there I can see most of the way down the main trail. Maybe I can get a glimpse of him."

"What will you do if you see him?"

"I'm not sure. It'll depend on the situation."

"I'll stay here if you promise me you'll come back before you do anything."

"All right, it's a deal. You stay here and watch their camp. I'll come back when I figure out where he is. And, Josie?"

"What?"

"Please be careful and don't go anywhere else."

"I *told* you I'd stay right here."

"Yeah, I know, but you don't always do what you're supposed to, do you?"

"Ah, shucks! You figured me out." She motioned him away. "Go on, I'll stay put, but you better hurry or I might change my mind."

Rand picked up Josie's rifle and walked down the hill in the direction they had come. He was close to the narrow spot on the game trail where he was *sure* he could see if they were being followed. But only if there was enough light. When he stopped to search the hillside there were already deep shadows at the bottom of the hill where they had left the main trail. He watched for any movement. He was about to decide there was no one following, when he heard a faint whisper of movement behind him. Just as he started to turn, a blow to the side of his head knocked him off his feet.

Rand was barely conscious, with fireworks going off in his head, but it was instinct that kept him from receiving the blow that was meant to kill. He hit the ground and automatically rolled several times which sent him over the edge of the cliff he had been standing on. He couldn't see a thing but felt every obstacle his body encountered as he slid and rolled over rocks and brush, unable to grasp a hold or to stop or slow himself down. Suddenly, there was nothing but space. He was falling and had no idea how far it was to the bottom. There wasn't a thing he could do. *Dad, I failed! The bad guy wins again.* Deep inside, he rebelled at that thought. *God, help me,* was his last thought as his world went black.

Josie watched the activity around the campfire down below but her mind and ears were listening for Rand to return. *Where are you, Rand?* It was completely dark and she couldn't stop the worry that was starting to aggravate her mind. Inactivity was not one of her favorite pastimes. *You better hurry, Rand Trinity, or I'm going to break my word to stay put.*

About the time Josie decided she had waited long enough she heard someone approaching from the direction Rand had left. Relief swept over her as she felt her body relax. It was short lived, however, when she heard a horse close by. *Rand did not take his horse.* She listened a moment longer. *Whoever it is, they are very close. I better play it safe, than sorry. It's probably Carl.* Carefully stretching out along the log she had been leaning against, she forced her body to relax and mold into the log. With a great deal of effort she calmed her breathing and didn't move a muscle.

Cigarette. He's smoking a cigarette. Even though she now knew it wasn't Rand who was standing about twenty feet away, she almost gave herself away and nearly jumped when the man spoke.

"Well, kid, I know you're out here somewhere. You're a puzzle to me but that don't matter now. You tricked me, killed my friend and now I'm going to kill you. Your Marshall friend won't be around to help you, either. He met with an accident that takes him out of the picture. If I was *you* I'd high-tail it out of here as quick as I could cause if I ever lay eyes on you again you're a *dead* man! You better grow eyes in the back of your head, kid, cause you'll never know when I'll be behind you."

Carl took a couple more drags on his cigarette, then threw it to the ground and mashed it into the dirt. Even after she heard him leave, Josie didn't move until she heard the crunch of the horse's hooves from the rocks on the trail as horse and rider moved down the hill.

Slowly, Josie's muscles relaxed and she rolled onto her back staring at the beautiful night sky full of stars. Peace and beauty filled the little space she lay in but there was no peace or beauty any where inside Josephine Fisher. It was like every human emotion had gathered in her chest and was screaming to express themselves. She fought down fear, let her mind do battle with the raging anger that made her want to scream, but in her heart . . . she grieved for something she didn't understand.

A single star shot across the sky and disappeared in the blink of an eye. *God, he was so young. Just like that falling star his life goes out. God . . . .*

Suddenly, Josie had a thought that made her sit up and seriously consider the situation. *Maybe Carl was lying. I didn't hear a gunshot . . . of course, there are a lot of ways to kill someone. If he had shot Rand I would have heard it and he couldn't have snuck up on me. That's why he didn't shoot. Rand may be out there needing help, though. Maybe he's not dead. I need to find him. But how . . . .*

Josie watched the enemy's camp and saw Carl join his gang. They were happy to see their leader but when they gathered around the fire it was obvious he was telling them about her. They kept looking up in her direction, searching the mountain side. Peter and Emily were sitting close together and Emily was feeding Peter with her left hand. So far, they appeared to be all right. She quickly made her decision and moved back to their horses, left on a patch of grass. Relieved that Carl had not found the horses, she set out to find Rand.

Making her way to the narrow spot in the trail she kept that spark of hope alive. After more than an hour of walking, listening and quietly calling Rand's name, the spark died, and she realized the futility of what she was doing. *I'll never find him like this. Either he is badly hurt or he is . . . he is . . .* She couldn't think the word and she wasn't ready to give voice to her fear that Rand was dead.

After checking on the horses one more time, Josie found a different place to spy on the enemy. Knowing that lives now depended on her, she tried to formulate a plan as she kept watch.

When the camp below fell quiet, fatigue soon won her over and Josie fell asleep without any firm plan in mind.

Slim shook Peter and Emily to wake them, not that they had gotten any sleep. "Wake up, you two, but *be quiet*. I'll saddle your horse, then we should be ready to leave. The boss is in an all fired hurry to leave this morning."

"Why is he in such a rush, Slim?" Emily asked. Slim had been the kindest to them and had obviously been given the job of watching them.

"I figure he's thinking about all that money we're going to get," Slim replied. "And how we're going to leave this country as fast as we can."

Buck interrupted, "Slim, quit your gabbing and get those two on their horse. Boss says not to make any noise!"

"All right, but why do we have to be quiet?" Slim complained. "If he killed that Marshall we shouldn't have to worry about being quiet."

"Slim, you *heard* what the boss said. That kid who killed Jack is still out there somewhere, We want to get our money before he can make it back to town and warn the law."

"Oh, I didn't think about that. I'll hurry, Buck."

"You do that, Slim."

A short time later Peter and Emily were on Ducky waiting for the outlaws to mount up. "Peter," Emily whispered. "Do you think they really killed Mr. Trinity?"

"It sure sounds like it, Emily. Seems like our only hope is that kid. We can't depend on him, though. We need to watch for any opportunity to escape. Do you know who that kid was?"

"No, I don't think so. I've never seen him before."

Peter's tone of voice changed to concern. "Are you really all right, Emily? How are you feeling? I thought I heard you crying last night. I wanted to move closer to you but Ken tied me up so tight I could hardly move at all. Plus, they were watching me every minute."

"I'm fine, Peter, please don't worry. I'm stronger than I look. Guess I was just feeling sorry for myself last night. I got to thinking about my mother and father. I can't believe they're gone. Grandmother must be worried sick." Emotion tightened Emily's throat as she continued. "I feel so helpless with my arm broken and being barely able to walk. I want to fight back but how can I like this?"

"We'll fight back when the time is right, but we've got to be smart about it. Be ready when we get close to Cheyenne. We might be able to outrun them for a short distance but we sure can't outrun them this far away from help. Shh, they're coming this way."

Chapter 13

*T*HE NOISE OF A pesky bird caused Josie to jerk her head up. She scolded herself for falling asleep when she saw the outlaw's camp was deserted. She had been sitting at the base of a tree wrapped in the only blanket she had. The sun wouldn't reach the west side of the mountain for quite a while and she was cold. *Best thing to do is get up and move around.* Her mind immediately centered on Rand. There was an acute sense of loneliness as she made her way to get the horses. *I've got to know what happened to Rand. If he's not dead he might need help. I just have to know. God, please help me find him.*

Josie was greeted with nickers from the horses. She saddled them both and walked back down the hill. Moving slowly she searched for tracks but found none except for hers and Rand's. Then, coming close to the place that Rand had mentioned, she spotted something. *That's a different boot track, it has to be Carl's!* Josie searched around for any sign of Rand but didn't see anything until she mounted her horse and rode a few feet down the narrow trail. Being on her horse gave her the advantage of height and a glint of metal caught her eye. *My rifle . . . Rand must have gone down here.*

Her heart thudded with dread as she dismounted and carefully picked her way down the steep side of the hill to retrieve her rifle. It seemed to be in fair shape. She side-stepped down about ten feet then froze when she realized she was at the edge of a drop-off. *I'll have to go back up to my horse and get a rope to rappel down that.*

Josie scrambled up the hill and was shortly back in the place above the drop-off. She choose the strongest looking tree that was the closest to the edge and began tying her rope around the tree. She stopped a moment and sniffed the air, sure she smelled wood smoke and coffee. *I've got to be imagining things. Rand better not be sitting down there drinking coffee.* Then another thought made her stop and think about what she was about to do. *That might not be Rand down there, but who else could it be? I saw Carl join his men last night.* She gathered a bit of courage and took a chance by calling out. "Who's down there? Rand, is that you?"

A man's voice called back, "You tell me who you are first, then I'll give you my name."

"I'm Josephine Fisher and I'm looking for a friend."

"Hey, Josie, it's Valentine Matson down here!"

"Valentine! What are you doing down there?"

"Guess you'll just have to come down here and see. Where you at?"

Josie peered over the edge of the cliff. "I'm right up here."

"You come down that way and you'll end up in water. Move your rope over to your left. You be careful, now. Do you think you can make it?"

"Yes, I'll be fine."

Pretty quick Josie's feet hit solid ground. The drop-off was less than twenty feet but the ground was uneven where she landed. Valentine was there to steady her. "Whoa, there. Got your balance now?"

"Yes, thank you, Valentine. Did you see another man down here?"

"If you're talking about that U.S. Marshall fellow, Mr. Trinity, yeah, he's right over there."

Josie peered around Mr. Matson and gasped. "Is he . . . is he . . . ."

"Dead? No, he's not dead, but he's banged up pretty bad. Looks like someone clubbed him in the head and he rolled down the hillside you just came down. Good thing he landed on his back in that water. It took me a while to get to him and if he'd landed face down he would've drowned. That little old pool of water is ice cold snow melt and may have helped him, too. A lot of snow drifted in this draw and the sun don't hardly get in here. There's still a bit of snow around the edges if you look close. It stopped the bleeding and maybe kept his head from swelling too bad."

"I'm glad you were here to help but what are you doing here anyway?"

"I spotted you and Mr. Trinity when I was hunting this morning; noticed a man that looked like he was following you two so I followed *him*. Sure enough he was following you and doing it mighty sneaky. I was down on the road below and saw Mr. Trinity rolling down that hill and drop off that ledge."

"Where's your horse, Valentine?"

"Had to leave him and the pack horse down a ways. It's mighty rough going part of the way up this draw."

Josie looked in Rand's direction. "What do you think about Rand? How bad do you think he is?"

"It's hard to say, little lady. He hasn't moved a muscle since I been with him. Had to take his clothes off and dry them out around the fire. He's bruised all over but I don't think there's anything broke. Anyway, nothing broke that I can tell."

"I don't know what to do, Valentine."

"I think you better tell me the whole story then we'll decide what needs to be done."

Josie accepted a cup of coffee and sat at the fire close to Rand while she told Valentine what had happened the last few days. Rand moaned and moved his head from side to side a couple of times but didn't regain consciousness.

"I need to go warn my father, Valentine. Can you stay here and take care of Rand?"

"Well, Josie, I think it would be better if I go to warn your father. I can help him round up some dependable men. You stay here and take care of Mr. Trinity. I figure he's a tough one and will be coming around pretty soon. I'll go up the hill and bring your horses down where mine are and leave my pack horse with you. Use anything you need in my bags. It's not very far down. You'll see how I make it through."

"All right, Valentine, if you think that's best."

"I won't come all the way up here again. When I get your horses to where mine are, I'll skedaddle and get on to Cheyenne."

Mr. Matson didn't waste any more time. He left quickly and not much longer Josie heard him down in the narrow draw they were in. Then all was quiet. Ordinarily, she would have loved every minute of her time in the woods but worry over Rand kept her tense and frustrated. She used Rand's neckerchief and wet it in the cold pool of water he had fallen into. Kneeling beside him she began bathing his face. She couldn't keep from smiling as she brushed his wild red hair back and washed his scruffy, bearded face. *You are a handsome man, Rand Trinity. A very stubborn, independent, handsome man.* Josie was surprised and a bit confused when tears came to her eyes. She couldn't figure out her strong feelings for this red-headed Marshall. *You just have to be all right. Please, wake up, Rand!*

Josie saw that the wound on Rand's head was oozing a little, so she turned to the cold pool of snow water and drenched the neckerchief in then hurried back and placed it over the nasty looking goose egg that Carl had given him.

Her stomach rumbled. She realized suddenly how hungry she was. *If I'm going to take care of Rand I better keep up my strength. I haven't had much to eat yesterday and this morning.* After warming the bit of cold coffee left in her cup, she pulled out a small sack from her pocket and loosened the string at the top. Pulling out a big wad of the contents she shoved it in her mouth.

"Do you know that's the most disgusting thing I've ever seen?"

Josie's eyes lit up. "Rand, you're awake!" She moved to his side. "I've been so worried. How do you feel?"

"Spit that stuff out of your mouth and I'll tell you."

Josie grabbed her coffee cup and swallowed the wad in her mouth, washing it down with coffee. "Never mind that, it's only shredded dried beef. How do you feel?"

The only part of Rand that moved was his eye lids. "I don't know. It hurts just laying here. I can't imagine how it's going to feel when I try to move."

"Just move slowly."

Rand drew his right hand out from under the blanket then dropped it quickly, clutching the blanket to his hairy chest. "For crying-out-loud! What did you do with my clothes?! Oh, that hurts." Rand closed his eyes with a grimace.

"I told you to move slowly. What hurts?"

"It would be easier to tell you what *doesn't* hurt." Rand carefully turned his head toward Josie. "Did you undress me? Please tell me you didn't."

Josie had a hard time keeping a straight face. "Do you see anyone else here?" She realized how her teasing affected Rand, so quickly told him the truth. "I'm sorry, I shouldn't be teasing you. Valentine Matson found you. When you didn't come back last night I realized something was wrong. I tried to find you but it was impossible in the dark. Carl almost found me but I managed to stay hidden. Rand, I thought you were probably dead. Carl and his gang left early this morning and I came again to look for you."

Josie told him how Valentine had seen Carl following them and so he followed Carl. "He's the one who found you last night and pulled you out of the pool over there. Val took care of you until I came down the hill this morning. You probably would have died if he hadn't found you, dragged you out of that ice cold water, took off your wet clothes, and built a fire to warm you up."

"Guess I'll need to thank him. I sure thought I was a goner when I went over that cliff. Where is he anyway?"

"He went to Cheyenne to warn my father about the outlaws and what they're planning. He's only been gone about an hour."

"Good, we need to get going, too."

"You don't even know if you can ride."

"I'm not going to find out until you bring me my clothes and give me some privacy."

"All right, don't growl at me. I'll go down to the horses and see if I can find something for us to eat. Val left his pack horse and said for us to use anything we want. They're all down past a thick stand of trees and shrubs. I'll water them and give you time to get dressed."

"Thanks . . . you . . . wouldn't . . . ."

Josie turned her back and called over her shoulder, "Don't worry, I'm not interested in peeking around the bushes to see your skinny hide."

By the time Josie returned, Rand was up and slowly moving toward the coffee pot. She watched as he picked up her cup and poured the last of the coffee in it. "Well, you're walking so it doesn't appear you broke a leg. How's the rest of you doing?"

Rand turned slowly and smiled. "I don't think anything is broken. I feel a might weak but I'll be all right."

She smiled back. "Valentine said you were tough. I guess he was right."

"You find anything to eat?"

"I found enough to fix a good breakfast. I think Valentine really likes his food. Think you can manage to put a few more sticks on the fire?"

Josie waited for Rand's response but he just stood there and looked at her for a full minute.

"What?" she finally said.

"I was just wishing I had a piece of your chocolate cream pie to go with this coffee. I've never tasted anything as good as your chocolate pie."

"Thank you." Josie felt herself blushing. "Is that all you were wishing for."

Rand grinned impishly. "No, but that's all you're going to hear about."

Josie moved about fixing a simple breakfast of bacon and flapjacks. She moved with complete confidence and total femininity. Rand didn't doubt she was as comfortable around a campfire as she was in the hotel kitchen. *She's something else! Any man would be blessed to have such a pretty woman as a wife. Besides, she can cook, which is an added bonus.* Rand tried to put himself in the picture that his mind was conjuring: A beautiful ranch house, a big front porch, with two rocking chairs on it. But for the life of him, he couldn't put himself in one of those chairs. High in a tree a bird chirped noisily. Rand searched the branches trying to locate it until his mental picture shattered. *What am I doing day-dreaming about such things? My life isn't suited for marriage and a family. I better keep my mind on my job of getting Emily Fitzpatrick back to her family.*

"What're you thinking about?" Josie asked, intruding into his thoughts. "You're awfully quiet."

"Nothing much. Just trying to put myself in the mind of that murdering gang. Do you figure they'll still go to that cabin they talked about? I can't think of any reason why they wouldn't, can you?"

Josie handed Rand a plate of food. "There's molasses in this container. You go ahead and use it, I'm not real fond of the taste except in cookies."

"Thanks, sure smells good. Is there any more coffee?"

"No, I didn't find any in the packs but the canteen here has water. Sorry." Josie sat down and ate out of the skillet she had cooked with. "To answer your question, yes, I figure they'll still go to the cabin. They think you're dead and I don't think they'll be worried about me. Carl told me to leave the country and if he ever saw me again he would kill me. Of course, he thinks I'm a dirty, smart-mouth boy."

Rand jerked his head up, a scowl plastered on his face. "When did you talk to Carl?"

"I *didn't* talk to him. Last night after he clubbed you in the head he came looking for me. He knew I was somewhere around the trail but he couldn't see me. He just smoked his cigarette and talked out loud like I was standing right in front of him."

"Is that all he said?"

"That's about it except he told me I better grow eyes in the back of my head."

"I don't like the sounds of that," Rand said around a mouthful of flapjacks."

"Don't worry. He doesn't know who I really am."

"Let's hope he doesn't figure it out." Rand took the last bite of his food. "I want to get moving as soon as we can. I can't wait to get this gang locked up."

"I'm about ready. Grab what you can carry and head through the brush down there. I'll wash this skillet out and be right behind you."

Chapter 14

"H ey, Carl," Slim called out. "What you want me to do with these two?"

"Put the freak in the storage room, there's no windows or any way for him to get out of there. The girl goes over there in that corner so we can keep an eye on her."

"Should I tie her up, boss?"

"Just tie her feet."

Buck pushed his way over to Slim. "You take care of the freak, *I'll* tie the pretty lady up."

Emily was repulsed as Buck manhandled her to the corner and pushed her to the rough floor. Squatting in front of her, he pulled her feet out straight, pushed her dress up to her knees and crudely ran his hands down her legs to her ankles, not bothering to be careful of the wound on the back of her leg. Emily tried to jerk her feet back but Buck's callused hands held her tight. He slowly began tying her feet together, his eyes roaming over her. "Nice, really nice," he whispered just for her to hear. "You better be nice to me, you might need a friend before this night is over."

As soon as he finished tying her ankles, Emily quickly pulled the skirt of her dress down to cover her legs. No matter how hard she tried, she couldn't hide the trembling in her hands. This made her angry with herself. Buck noticed, laughing as he moved away. She closed her eyes and her mind raced with the implications of Buck's words. *What could he mean by that?* Her heart thumped and tears stung her eyes but she blinked them back. *They don't intend to let me go and I don't want to even think what they might do. I'm sure that's what he meant. When they get the money, they're going to kill me and Peter.*

Emily's attention was drawn to the conversation going on between the outlaws. Ken seemed irritated. "What are you going to do, boss? I don't like hanging around here any longer than we have to. Let's get it done and get out of here."

"Keep your britches on, Ken. We'll be out of here by morning."

"Why don't we send the freak to town right now?"

"Cause I don't *trust* him. As soon as it's dark I'm going to sneak him in to the back of the hotel where the old lady is staying. I'll wait outside for him and make sure he brings the money out with him. We'll ride hard and fast back here and then we'll divide the money and you all can go with me or go your own way. How does that sound?"

Ken wasn't satisfied. "What if she doesn't have very much money in the hotel?"

"Of course, she don't have it with her in the hotel! But, she's got enough clout to wake up the banker and get her hands on the twenty five thousand we're asking for."

"How long you going to give her to get the money?" Buck asked.

"Two hours from the time I send the freak into the hotel. If he's not out the back door with the money in two hours, I'll ride back here and we'll kill the girl and leave. You all need to be ready to leave as soon as I get back."

"I guess that'll work." Buck seemed to be satisfied with the plan.

Ken still wasn't so sure. "What if something goes wrong in town and they capture you? We won't know a thing until they bring a posse down on us."

"Quit trying to dream up trouble, Ken. They ain't going to catch me. Have any of my plans ever gone wrong?"

Ken stared long and hard at his boss. There was no conviction in his voice when he finally said, "No, I guess not."

"All right then. Let's fix us something to eat and rest up for our ride out of this country. It's stuffy in this here cabin; let's build a fire outside in the fresh air. I think it's a beautiful day for getting rich!" Carl chuckled on his way out the cabin door.

"We're getting real close, Rand. We better tie the horses here and walk the rest of the way. If I'm right, that cabin is over the hill. It's kind of hidden and we're coming at it from a different direction than I've ever been. I could have it all wrong."

"No, I don't think you're wrong. Look real close over there. I think that's smoke from a fire lifting out of the trees."

"Maybe, it's hard to tell."

Rand let his eyes roam the terrain. "If we walk south up to that ridge we'll be above them, or at least, come at them from a direction they won't be expecting."

"Makes sense. How are you feeling, Rand? Are you up to this?"

"I've had a headache for a while now, but I'm all right. My biggest headache will be taken care of when we get these outlaws in jail." Rand started walking after taking Josie's rifle and the only two canteens they had. "What I really wish is that I had my gun belt and pistols."

Again, Josie and Rand found themselves looking down on the enemy camp. All four of the gang members were gathered at a fire at the front of a rough-hewn cabin. They were lounging around, eating and laughing like they didn't have a care in the world.

"What do you suppose they're up to?" Josie asked.

"Looks like they've let their guard down and that's good. They must really think I'm dead and you're out of the picture. Maybe they'll get careless."

"Peter and Emily must be inside the cabin. Oh, I sure hope they're all right," Josie said.

"I'm sure they are or will be until those men down there get the money they want. Then you know what will happen."

"I don't want to think about it."

"Well, if I have anything to say about it they won't get a chance to harm Emily or Peter."

The two sat and watched the gang in silence for a while. They watched as Slim took food into the cabin then come back out to join his partners again.

"Josie, I have a hunch," Rand said, excitedly.

"What is it?"

"I think they're waiting for dark. Then one of them, maybe two, will take Peter to get the money. I want you to leave right now and ride into town and tell your father the new plans. He can get some men to watch the hotel and arrest the one who takes Peter into town. It will probably be Carl. I don't think he'll trust that to any of the others. I'm suspicious after hearing what Stella and Carl said in the barn. I figure Carl will go alone with Peter and when he gets his hands on the money he'll take off in the other direction, leaving his gang out here."

"You *know* I don't want to leave you."

"Yeah, I figured you wouldn't, but surely you can see that it's the smart thing to do."

"Yes, you're probably right, and I *will* go. What are you going to do here?"

"After dark, when Carl and Peter leave, I'll move closer to the cabin. If I can, I'll wait for you to bring three or four men back to help arrest those holding Emily. If they try to harm her, I'll just do what I have to do."

"I better get going then. I'll be back with help."

Before Josie moved away, she placed her hand on his scruffy cheek that had a few days growth of reddish beard. "Rand, please be careful."

He looked into her beautiful blue eyes and saw emotion there that made his heart race. Unable to help himself, he leaned down and tenderly kissed her lips. Josie didn't say a word, just smiled then turned and hurried toward her horse.

Rand's heart didn't slow down much as he watched her walk out of sight but he forced himself to turn his attention back to the cabin and the job he had to do. An hour went by with his only problems being flies, heat, and hunger. But those miseries were insignificant compared to the affect that one sweet kiss had on him. *Stupid, stupid, stupid! I shouldn't have kissed her. What was I thinking?* A smile touched the corners of his mouth. *I wasn't thinking and I know good and well if I could turn time back to that moment I'd do the same thing all over again, only I might have gone for a second kiss.*

Rand looked west and saw the sun was just touching the horizon. *I better start moving down to the back of the cabin. It's going to be dark soon and I want to be able to hear what's going on and take action if I get the chance.*

Moving from tree to tree, he unexpectedly came upon a deer carcass, probably shot earlier that day. His movements disturbed a couple of magpies feasting on the leftover carcass, causing the pesky birds to squawk and fly to nearby trees. Rand hunkered down behind a tree, waiting a few moments, then slowly checked the cabin area to see if they had been alerted to his presence.

The outlaws were milling around but seemed unaware of the commotion the birds had made. Ken added wood to the fire while Buck whittled on a piece of wood. Slim was tossing rocks at something Rand couldn't see, and Carl sat starring into the campfire. Suddenly, Carl stood and called to the men, "Get on over here, ya'll, we need to talk before I leave." He waited until they had joined him by the fire. "This is the night we've been waiting for and I don't want anything to go wrong."

Rand moved like a stealthy panther until he was at the back of the cabin. He inched his way close to a window cut in the side of the cabin with only a screen covering it, then sat still as a post listening to the men.

"It's almost full dark now and I'll be leaving with the freak in a few minutes," Carl said. "I'll hide out close to the back of the hotel and send him in. If he doesn't come out in a couple of hours with the money. I'll ride back here and we'll kill the girl and get out of the country."

"Do you think that's long enough for them to come up with that amount of money, boss?" Buck asked.

"I might give them a little longer but not much. I'll decide when I get there. Anyway, as soon as I get the money I'll bring the freak back here and we'll skedaddle out of the country. The only thing the three of you need to do is make sure you're ready to leave when I get back. You got that, Slim? I want you to do what Buck says. I'm leaving him in charge."

"Sure, I got it, boss. I'm not stupid."

Ken harrumphed, signaling his disagreement. "Why are you putting Buck in charge? I should be the one to be in charge when you're gone. I've been with you longer than Buck. Besides, he's a hot-head with a nasty temper."

"Watch your mouth, Ken!" Buck challenged. "Carl knows he can count on me to do what needs to be done."

"Knock it off, you two," Carl snapped. "Since that kid killed Jack I haven't even thought about who would take his place. You're probably right, Ken, but what I said goes for now. Buck is in charge this time."

Ken mumbled some reply that Rand couldn't hear but figured it wasn't good. *I'll have to remember that. Ken and Buck don't like each other. Maybe I can use that to my advantage. I wonder what part of the cabin Peter and Emily are in. I'd like to peek inside this window. . . .*

Carl began issuing orders and Rand slipped to the back of the cabin. "Slim, go saddle my horse and the black one the freak has been riding. Buck, get the freak out of that closet and make sure his hands are tied *tight*. Ken, come with me, for a minute."

Rand was well hidden in the shadows and watched as Carl took Ken a short distance away. He couldn't hear the conversation but when they turned back toward the cabin, Ken had a grin on his face. Carl slapped him on the back and asked, "Can you do that, Ken?"

Ken's response was, without a doubt, something he was going to enjoy doing.

It's definitely true that there is no honor among thieves. Carl is probably going to have Ken kill the others . . . then he'll kill Ken.

Buck shoved Peter out into the main room of the cabin, causing him to stumble but quickly regain his balance. Peter's eyes zoomed in on Emily sitting on the floor in the corner. She steeled her gaze with complete calmness in her features, not allowing her fear to show through. "I'm sorry, Emily," Peter managed to say.

"Don't worry, Peter, just go get the money and come back for me."

"I'll do my best."

"I know you will."

"All right, enough of that mush! Get going, *freak*." Buck shoved Peter forward.

He started through the door when Emily called to him, "Peter!" He turned to her. "I love you," she said.

"I know. I love you, too, Emily. God be with you."

With another shove, Peter stumbled out of the cabin.

Emily sat very still, listening to the horses ride away. A sense of loneliness hovered over her. It was loneliness like she had never known before. *Oh, Peter, will I ever see you again? Please, God, take care of Peter. He's had so much pain in his life. It hurts to see him suffer at the hands of these evil men. I've never asked for anything from you before but I beg you to hear me now!*

Chapter 15

"**J**osie! Girl, you're a sight for sore eyes! Come in here and tell us what you know. Are you all right?"

Josephine had ridden into town, first checking on her house then the telegraph office, but her father wasn't in either place. She rode to the sheriff's office, finding a good number of horses lined up at the hitching rail. She went through the office door and when her father laid eyes on her, he greeted her with a hug.

"Yes, Dad, I'm fine. Did Valentine make it to town?"

"Yeah, I'm right here, Josie," Valentine said. "Is Rand with you?"

"No, we followed the gang to a cabin they've probably used for a hide out before. Rand stayed there to keep an eye on things. He sent me to get a few men to come back to the cabin and arrest the ones there. Rand thinks Carl, the leader of the gang, is going to bring the man who helped Emily, into town to collect the ransom from Mrs. Fitzpatrick. We need to post some men around the hotel where Mrs. Fitzpatrick is staying and arrest him."

"Whoa, Josie, you're talking too fast." George led her to a chair. "Sit down and let me make sure I understand what's happening. The outlaws are at a cabin they use for a hide out, and Rand is there keeping an eye on them. He thinks that this leader, named Carl, is going to bring the man who helped Emily Fitzpatrick, to the hotel to collect the ransom, and we're supposed to be ready to capture him. Am I right, so far?"

"Yes, and Rand wants me to bring back a few men to help him get the three that are at the cabin with Emily."

"Do you have any idea when Carl will be coming into town?"

"Not for sure. Rand seems to think they will wait until it's dark. Do we have enough men, Dad?"

"Sure, we've got a lot of men. When Val came in we spread the word and there are plenty of men who are tired of this gang and have come to help."

"Good! If you can pick out some men for me, I'll leave right away."

"You look real tired," George said. "Are you sure you're up to going back? You could just draw us a map."

"I want to go, Dad. I'll be all right. Emily might need me and I want to be there for her."

"That's a good idea. But before you go anywhere, head on over to the hotel and get something to eat. Then talk to Mrs. Fitzpatrick and Nicholas Clench. Tell them what's going to happen and they should stay put. I'll have four men out front of the hotel when you're ready."

"Thanks, Dad. Please be careful. Carl is a bad one. He needs to be put away for a long, long time."

"Wish I was going with you, Josie, but Rand will take care of things at the cabin. Go on, now, and take care of yourself."

Josie hugged her father and rushed out the door. The hotel staff was happy to see her and went to work fixing her something to eat. "Honey, you go on up and talk to Mrs. Fitzpatrick. We'll have you something to eat in no time and we'll fix extra if you want to give some to your Marshall friend."

"Thanks, Dorothy, you're a sweetheart. I'm sure Rand is starved."

Dorothy beamed and shooed Josie off. "Off with you, girl, so I can get to work."

Mr. Clench opened the door at Josie's knock. "Yes, what can I do for you?" Recognition showed in his eyes and he grabbed her hand and pulled her in the room shutting the door behind her. "I almost didn't recognize you. You look like you've been on the trail for a week. Are you all right, do you have any news?"

"Who is it, Nicholas?" Cecilia Fitzpatrick came in from a side room.

"It's Josie, Cecilia."

"Oh, it sure is. Josie, come in and sit down. Do you have news? Is Emily with you?"

"No, she's not with me but I've seen her. She had her arm in a sling and limped a little, but she looked pretty good other than that. She's stronger than she looks, Mrs. Fitzpatrick. She'll make it just fine."

"Oh, Josie, is she still in danger?"

It went against Josie's beliefs to tell a lie. But, it broke her heart to tell them the truth. She told the two people hanging on her every word, the truth. "I won't lie to either of you, but, yes, Emily is still in danger. The outlaws took her and Peter to a hideout cabin. Rand and I followed them and have been waiting for a chance to rescue them. We never had a chance without endangering Emily and Peter."

"Wait, Josie," Mr. Clench stopped her. "Who is this Peter?"

"He's the one who rescued Emily from the train. He's been taking care of her."

"God bless him," Mrs. Fitzpatrick quietly spoke as a prayer. "Please, go ahead and tell us the rest."

"Don't give up hope because we have a plan in place. Rand is still at the cabin. He thinks the leader will bring Peter to the hotel to get ransom money from you. His name is Carl and he wouldn't dare show his face in town, so he will probably hide somewhere at the back of the hotel and send Peter in here to collect the money. I've told my father all of this and he will have men waiting and ready to arrest him."

A knock on the door interrupted their conversation. Nicholas let in a young woman carrying a tray of food for Josie and said she left a sack of food at the desk by the front door.

As soon as the kitchen lady left, Josephine apologized. "Please, forgive my manners but I'm starved and I'm going to go ahead and eat while I talk." She took a big bite, while gathering her thoughts. "Dad is sending four men over here for me to take back to the cabin where Rand is. They are going to arrest the three men that are keeping Emily there. I want to leave as soon as I can so I can be there for her."

"I'm so glad you're going to go to Emily. Do you think the three men will try to harm her while their leader is away?"

Josie swallowed the bite of food in her mouth, took a deep breath and slowly exhaled. "Those three men are capable of anything. But I trust Rand. That's why he's there. He will be close enough to defend her, even if he has to die. That's just the kind of man he is. Of course, I've never seen him in action like in a gun battle but everything in me says he's good at what he does and he won't let anything bad happen to Emily."

Talking about Rand dying caused Josie's heart to ache and made her stomach clench tight. "I don't think I can eat any more." She picked up a handful of cookies off the tray. "Maybe I can eat these on the way." When she reached the door, she turned to Cecilia and Nicholas. "I need to warn you about Peter."

"Warn us? Whatever do you mean?" Mrs. Fitzpatrick asked in alarm.

"I don't mean like you're in danger. Quite to the contrary. The little I've heard and seen is he's probably a wonderful man. But, you might become alarmed when he shows up in a long black cape with a hood. He wears the hood up all the time to hide some ugly scars from burns he suffered from in a fire. He will have to tell you his story, himself, because I don't know any more than that. I imagine he's been through an awful lot. Keep him here, if you can, at least until my father tells you they arrested Carl. You can let Peter know what we're doing. From what I witnessed, Emily cares a great deal for Peter and he seems to return those feelings."

Tears came to Mrs. Fitzpatrick's sad eyes. "Thank you, dear Josephine. Please take care of my granddaughter and keep yourself safe, also."

"I will. Please keep praying for us until we get back." Josie left and hurried down the stairs. Just as he promised, George Fisher had four men waiting in front of the hotel. Josie was glad to see Valentine Matson was one of them.

"Mind if I go along with you, Josie?"

"Not at all, Val. I'm glad to have you along."

"I took your horse down to the stables and brought you a fresh one," he told her.

"Thanks, I appreciate that." Josie mounted her horse. "I'm ready."

"Lead the way, little lady," one of the men said. "We'll be right behind you."

"Nicholas, come and sit with me," Cecilia said. "You're going to wear a hole in the floor."

"Cecelia, dear, you know that's hard for me to do. Being confined here in this room would be hard on anyone."

"You can go on outside and get some fresh air. Or, why don't you go ahead and take a walk?"

Nicholas stopped pacing. "Now you *know* I'm not going to leave you by yourself. Not now that it's dark and that man might be coming any time. Josie might trust him but I'll have to decide that for myself."

Cecilia looked longingly at Nicholas. "Thank you for being here for me. Do you know I love you, Nicholas Clench?"

Nicholas smiled at Cecilia. "You've never said the words to me, but I was sure I could see it in your eyes and hear it in your voice." He cleared his throat. "I was going to wait until we found Emily but I've wanted to talk to you about . . . about . . . . *us*."

"What about us?" A shy smile worked itself onto her lips.

But a light knock on the door interrupted Nicholas's marriage proposal. They both looked at the door. Nicholas shrugged. "Sorry, I'll have to ask you later."

Cecilia stood and looked lovingly at Nicholas. "Never mind asking me later. The answer is *yes*. Now, go answer the door." Since Valentine Matson had come with news that the outlaws were coming into town for ransom money, he wouldn't allow her to even answer the door to her rooms.

"Who's there?" Nicholas spoke through the closed door.

"Peter, a friend of Emily's."

Nicholas was glad Josephine had prepared them for this man. He opened the door to a tall figure draped in a black cape with only the lower part of his bearded face showing.

"Please, may I come in and talk to you?"

"Yes, of course. We've been expecting you."

The hooded man stepped into the room. He hesitated. "What do you mean, you've been expecting me? How could you possibly know I would come here?"

"It's a bit of a story, Peter. Let's sit down and I'll tell you about it. First, let me introduce Mrs. Cecilia Fitzpatrick to you. And my name is Nicholas Clench."

Cecilia offered her hand to Peter. "My dear man, I will be forever grateful to you for all the help you have given my granddaughter. I understand you saved her life. Come, let's all sit down. We need to tell you what is happening."

Peter tentatively took a seat and listened while Mr. Clench and Mrs. Fitzpatrick told him what they knew about the situation. They assured him that Carl would be arrested by men who had hidden at the back of the hotel. "What about Emily?" Peter said in alarm. "If I don't return with Carl and the money, they'll kill her!"

Again, another knock interrupted them. "Wait a minute," Nicholas said. He got up and went to the door. "Who is it?"

"It's George Fisher. I've got good news."

Nicholas opened the door and invited Mr. Fisher in. "We could use some good news."

"We got the gang member named Carl," said Mr. Fisher. "Didn't even have to fire a shot. I wish you could have seen his surprised face. We had him before he could put up a fight."

"That is good news!" Mr. Clench said. "I suppose it's too early to hear from the other group that went with Josie, isn't it?"

"I'm afraid so. You all might as well relax, since it'll probably be a while."

As Nicholas said goodbye to George, Peter got up and walked to the window, looking down into the darkened street below. Cecilia walked over and put her hand on his arm. "Are you all right, Peter?"

"I don't know," he responded. "I'm not sure what to do now. I should try to go back and rescue Emily but I'm not sure I can find it in the dark."

"I don't think you need to go back, Peter. Josie gathered some men and they went back to help Rand Trinity arrest the other gang members and bring Emily back here."

"I don't know who Josie is and where is Mr. Trinity?"

"Josie is a friend of Emily's. Rand and Josie tracked the outlaws to the cabin where they took you and Emily. Rand sent Josie back here to get help. That's about all I know. We'll just have to wait for Rand to bring Emily back."

Peter's shoulders slumped, his hands went to the window frame. Bracing himself, he put his head on the cold glass. "I don't think I could stand it if anything happened to her," he said, softly.

"I don't want to hear talk of something bad happening to my Emily. There is still hope."

"I'm sorry," Peter murmured. "The last few days have been rather difficult. I'm just so tired."

Cecilia tugged on Peter's arm. "I'm sure you are. Come and have some tea with me and Nicholas, then I'll show you to a room where you can rest."

Chapter 16

RAND STAYED IN THE shadows at the side of the cabin. One thing he had learned was to be patient and wait for the right moment to make his play. He wanted desperately to call through the screened window and talk to Emily but was afraid he would be heard by the outlaws. He glanced around the corner of the cabin and saw Ken and Buck talking quietly by the fire. Slim was looking for more wood when the two by the fire started laughing. Buck got up and walked to the cabin.

Slim was curious. "What's Buck up to? Y'all sure were having a good time laughing about something."

Ken just laughed again. "Oh, you know Buck. He's always laughing at something stupid."

Every muscle in Rand's body stiffened when he heard Emily's voice coming from inside the cabin. "Stay away from me!"

"Now why would I want to do that?" a husky voice answered.

Rand imagined a sneer on the outlaw's face. He desperately wanted to wipe it off with his loaded rifle. Well, Josie's rifle, anyway.

"Get your dirty hands off of me!" At the top of her lungs, Emily screamed, "Slim, help me! Please, don't let him hurt me!"

Like a knight in shining armor, Slim raced into the cabin.

It's time to move! Rand had to take Ken out, now that he was the only one outside. Just as he reached Ken, the outlaw turned to see who was coming at him. Rand smashed him in the head with the butt of his rifle. Ken fell to the ground like a sack of grain thrown from a wagon, and didn't move. Quickly, Rand rushed to the door of the cabin and stopped just out of sight. The two inside didn't seem to have noticed the commotion outside. They were in their own battle of wills.

"Leave her be, Buck."

"Get out of here, Slim. It's none of your business what I do with the little lady."

"I'm making it my business. Just leave her alone, she's a nice lady and we shouldn't hurt her."

Buck was getting madder by the minute. "Shut up, you *stupid* idiot! You've known all along we're going to kill her and the freak when we get the money."

"I know that's the plan, but I want to talk to Carl when he gets back. I think we should let them go."

Buck pulled his gun out of its holster and pointed it at Slim. You don't have a brain in your head, Slim. Carl left me in charge while he's gone so get yourself out of here or I'll shoot you where you stand."

Rand couldn't see exactly where everyone was but he could picture from the sound of voices approximately where the men and Emily were. *I can't let Buck get the upper hand. Emily is probably right behind Buck and might be in my line of fire. If I call out he'll grab her and shield himself. I need to surprise him and shoot quick and not miss. Maybe Slim will be too stunned to move fast. I gotta get it done, NOW!*

Rand dove through the door, hit the floor, and fired, hitting Buck in the chest. He rolled and saw Slim drawing his pistol so he fired again. Buck had dropped dead on the spot but Slim looked confused and crumpled to the floor.

Collecting the pistols from the outlaws, he hurried to Emily. "Are you all right?"

Stunned, Emily just stared at Rand for a moment. "Yes, yes . . . I'm all right. I thought Carl killed you."

"He tried but didn't quite make it. Let me get these ropes off you."

"Is he dead?" Emily nodded in the direction of the outlaws.

"I know Buck is dead. I'm not sure about Slim."

"Help me, Mr. Trinity. I want to go to Slim."

Rand helped Emily to her feet and led her over to where Slim lay. Emily went down on her knees beside him. "Slim, can you hear me?" With her left hand she stroked his face. "Can you hear me?"

Slim's eyes opened and he focused on Emily's face. Rand was standing above Emily looking down at the dying man. He heard the outlaw whisper, "Sing for me, pretty lady."

"Of course, I'll sing for you, Slim. Thank you for standing up for me. You were so brave."

"Only decent thing I ever did."

"What do you want me to sing?"

"*Rock of Ages*. Ma used to sing that all the time."

"I know some of it. I'll do my best."

Slim just smiled and Emily began to sing. "Rock of Ages . . . Cleft for me . . . Let me hide myself in thee . . . ."

She faltered and Rand quietly prompted her, "Let the water and the blood."

Hearing the words triggered her memory and Emily finished the first verse. Rand helped her with the words to the second verse. Even though he heard horses approaching the cabin he didn't move.

A subdued group stood just outside the door watching and listening to the scene unfolding in the cabin. Once Emily's memory was refreshed she sang the song through again. Slim still had the smile on his face as life left his body. All was quiet until Josie stepped up into the cabin and stood by Emily. "That was beautiful, Emily."

Tears were streaming down Emily's face as she looked up and saw Josephine Fisher standing above her. "He was good to me, Josie, and he tried to protect me."

Rand and Josie helped Emily stand then Josie led her out of the cabin.

Valentine Matson put his hand on Rand's shoulder when he came out of the cabin behind the girls. "Looks like we missed all the excitement."

"Oh, you didn't miss all of it. We've got to get that one over there to jail."

Everyone looked in the direction Rand had indicated. Ken was gone. Looking toward the small corral it was plain to see that Ken had managed to get on his horse and ride out. "Guess it's not over yet. One of them got away. I hit him in the head pretty hard but evidently not hard enough."

"What do you want us to do, Mr. Trinity?"

"First, tell me how things went in town."

"We don't know how it turned out, but they're ready to get the one who's coming in for the money. He won't get away this time."

"That's good news. I guess what we need to do here is get the bodies of the two in the cabin on their horses. And men, be careful, the outlaw that got away could still be around. If he has any sense he'll try to get out of the country. Let's hurry. I'd like to get Emily back to town as soon as we can."

"You've got it. Come on, men, let's get it done." Valentine took charge while Rand and Josie helped Emily to a stump-chair by the fire.

"Will you be all right, Emily? We'll be right back after we get those horses saddled."

"Sure, I'm fine, Josie. I'm not going anywhere so you go ahead and help."

When the group was ready to go, Rand suggested they go on without him. "I need to ride over that hill and get the horse I was riding and Val's pack horse. You all go on and I'll catch up."

The fire had been doused and there was very little light but Rand was close enough to see Josie open her mouth to protest. Their eyes met, and in the dim light, Rand had to turn his head to keep her from seeing his smile. She closed her mouth for a moment, but then said, "We'll go *real slow* till you catch up." Her tone was frustrated as she added, "Don't dilly-dally or we'll be right back to find you. You seem to have a knack for getting yourself into trouble."

They all heard Rand mumble, "I'll be so fast you won't even know I'm gone."

Josie *harrumphed* and mounted her horse behind Emily. "Valentine, will you lead out? Emily and I will be right behind you."

"Sure enough, Miss Josie. How *slow* do you want me to go?"

"Oh, Val, I didn't mean to sound so grouchy. We can't go fast through the trees anyway, and when we get out in the open Rand will be able to see us pretty easy with the moon almost full. I don't know what my problem is tonight. Guess I feel kind of *jumpy* knowing that one of those outlaws is still out there."

Val chuckled. "Maybe you're just in a dither over that nice looking Mr. Trinity gettin' out of your sight cause you're gettin' kinda attached to him. Hmmm?"

"Hush, Val, or you won't be getting anymore of my apple pie."

Val laughed. "Now that is a cruel threat but I'll keep my mouth shut if that's what will get me some of your apple pie."

In no time, Josie heard Rand ride up behind them and speak to the men who were leading the horses with the bodies of Buck and Slim. They asked about the horse he went to get. "Couldn't find him, huh?"

"No, he either got loose and wandered off or Ken took him." Riding up to Josie, he said, "Did you miss me?"

Val called back over his shoulder, "I missed you!"

A few chuckles came from the men as each one added their sentiments of missing Rand. Emily's female voice chimed in, "I missed you, too!"

All was silent until Josie huffed, and admitted, "All right, I missed you, too! And, I want to apologize."

"What for? For missing me?"

"No, for what I said about you having a knack for getting in trouble. I'm sorry."

"Well, it seems on this job you might have a point. If you hadn't been there to rescue me from Carl and Jack, I would be a dead man. And Val saved my bacon when I went down that hill. It's downright humiliating to have to be rescued by a woman and an old man."

Val laughed, but Emily was confused. "What are you talking about?" she asked. "How did Josie save you from Carl and Jack?"

"Remember that dirty, obnoxious kid named Joe? The one who wanted to join the gang so he could kill me?"

"Yes, I remember. He was about the crudest boy I've ever seen. What happened to him?"

"You're riding with Joe right now."

There was silence for a full minute as Emily processed the information. "No! I don't believe it! It couldn't be! That was *you*, Josephine Fisher? Tell me the truth, was that you?"

"Guess my secret is out now. Yes, it was me."

"Why, how . . . How . . .? Emily stammered.

"I'll tell you all about it later," Josie said.

The weary group rode into town in the wee hours of the morning. The men scattered to wherever they were going while Rand and Josie delivered Emily to her grandmother. After a period of tears and celebration, Emily asked her grandmother, "Where is Peter, grandmother?"

"He's resting in the room next to Rand's."

"I'll go get him," Rand offered. "I need to talk to him anyway."

Rand came back in a few minutes with a piece of paper in his hand. "He's gone. All he left was his statement for the court."

Chapter 17

BY THE TIME THE group that had gathered in Mrs. Fitzpatrick's rooms to answer her questions and tell their stories the sun was up and life in Cheyenne could be heard down on the streets. Mr. Fisher had joined them earlier and as he said his goodbyes, Rand joined him. "I'd like to walk with you, Mr. Fisher."

"Sure, come on with me to the sheriff's office. I need to check on the young deputy, Garth Jones. He's holding things down until the town can decide what to do about a new sheriff."

When they were away from the hotel, the two men talked about what would probably take place in the next few days. "I sent telegrams this morning and from past experiences I figure the judge should be here in about five days," Mr. Fisher said.

"That sounds good. Sometimes it takes a lot longer than that to get a judge out here. Our only loose end is Ken, the outlaw that got away."

"Yeah, I thought about going after him," George confessed.

"Well, don't think about it anymore. I'm going back to that cabin and see if I can find his trail."

"You've got to be tired, Rand. Why don't you get some rest today and start out fresh in the morning?"

"If I crawled into that bed in my room I might not wake up for a week. It's the best bed I've ever had the pleasure to sleep in. Besides, I'd rather go out today. If we get a rain or a wind storm later on, it might wipe out any sign he left. I plan on going back to my room, taking a nice hot bath, getting a good meal and riding on out to the cabin. I'll find a place later in the day to get some sleep. And, George?"

"Yeah, what is it?"

"Will you do something for me?"

"If I can, I'll sure try."

"Thanks. I know it'll be hard but would you please *not* tell your daughter what I'm going to do? Just don't mention me today and maybe everyone will think I'm sleeping. If she finds out, just keep her busy in town."

George laughed. "You do know that you're asking something very difficult of me."

"Well, I got a good taste of her independent spirit, if that's what you mean."

"Ever since she turned twenty she keeps reminding me that she's a full grown woman and can do what she wants. I've raised her to be able to take care of herself. Since I'm the only living relative she has, when I'm gone, she'll have no one. Actually, Rand, I couldn't ask for a better daughter even though she holds it over my head that I couldn't do without her cooking and cleaning for me. She makes the best peach cobbler you ever tasted. Makes me hungry just thinking about it." George rubbed his stomach in appreciation of the thought of peach cobbler. "As for your request, you've got my word that I'll do the best I can to keep Josie in town. I figure she'll be busy with Miss Emily most of the day."

"Yeah, I heard Josie offer to stay with Emily for a while. She's going to help her clean up before the doctor comes to check her out. Then I wouldn't be surprised if both girls sleep the day away."

"You sure don't know girls very well, Mr. Trinity. Those two will talk for hours, fuss with all those things girls do to look beautiful and go to sleep tonight just to sleep late in the morning."

George stopped at the door to the sheriff's office. "You going to come in?"

"No, if you can take care of business here, I'll be on my way."

"I can take care of things here. You go on. And, Rand . . . be careful."

"I will, sir."

In a couple of hours Rand was shaved, bathed and with clean clothes on, he went down and ate a big breakfast. A short time later with Ducky under him he felt like a new man. Rand was cautious but let his mind wander as he rode across the prairie toward the low lying hills to the south. *Where did Peter go? I know he didn't want to be around people but to just walk away seems strange to me. Well, I can't worry about that now. There's more pressing things to take care of. No sense going back to the cabin cause with the horse I was riding and Val's pack horse gone it's a pretty good guess that Ken took them. Nothing left to do but find his trail and follow the tracks.*

At first it was easy going. Ken didn't seem to be hiding which way he was going. Then suddenly, he changed directions and headed north. It didn't take long to see the outlaw's strategy when he hit the main roadway the wagons took going to Oregon or California. *I'll have to give it to this outlaw, it was a smart move to come here to the main trail west. There are so many tracks it will be pure luck to figure out which way he went.* After studying his options, Rand made his decision. *Might as well ride west for a while. Maybe I'll get lucky and find tracks of three horses leaving the main trail. I'm pretty sure after following their tracks I'd know if it was Ken's, cause that pack horse has a shoe on the right front that has a funny notch in it.*

By mid-afternoon, Rand had covered a lot of ground but found no signs that the outlaw had left the main trail. The hot sun and lack of sleep were taking their toll on him so when he spotted a small grove of trees and high willows he headed in that direction knowing it probably meant water and shade.

In a small shaded area by a creek that would be dry in another month, Rand ate and stretched out to rest. Sleep took him hard and fast.

It was the sound of wagons, men, women and children that brought Rand out of his sleep. He lay still for moments letting the sounds register in his brain. There was nothing that alerted his sense of danger so he slowly sat up and found himself looking in the face of a boy about fifteen with a rifle in his hands. He was a tall, skinny boy with brown hair that looked like it hadn't been combed in a month. "Hi," Rand greeted him. "You with the wagons?"

The boy's eyes roamed over Rand and the small area where he and Ducky were. "Yes, sir, I'm with the wagon train. Most of the folks on the wagon train are right nice folks, but if you're an outlaw you probably want to skedaddle out of here. These are law abiding folks and if my pa thought you were an outlaw he'd string you up in a minute."

Rand stood up and brushed himself off. "I'm not an outlaw, but I'm looking for one."

"You a sheriff or something like that?"

"Yeah, I'm something like that. Have you or anyone on the train seen a man with an extra mount and pack horse?"

"No, not that I've heard of. Pa picked up a man wanting a ride to the other side of Ft. Laramie. He gives me the creeps cause he wears a black cape and has the hood up all the time. The boy shivered. "Gotta be something wrong with a guy like that."

"Don't be so quick to judge a man before you know him. I happen to know him and he's a mighty fine man. Just had a bad accident and got burned real bad. He keeps the hood up to cover the scars."

The boy scowled, then looked thoughtful. "Oh, never thought of something like that. You want to talk to him?"

"Yes, I would."

"I'd take you but pa sent me to follow this stream up the hill and see if I can find some fresh meat for us. The man wearing the cape is in the wagon with the pinto pony tied to the back."

"Thanks," Rand nodded to him. "Good luck on your hunt."

The boy started up the creek. "Thanks, maybe I'll get lucky if I get going before some of the other men start hunting and scare everything out of the country."

Rand led Ducky to the creek and let him have his fill, saddled him, and made his way over to the wagons which were circling for the night. He found Peter looking around for firewood. "Hi, Peter! Glad I ran into you."

Peter heard Ducky approaching and looked up. "Hello, Rand. I left my statement at the hotel. Didn't you find it?"

"Yes, I found it, but I'd like to talk to you about some things if you don't mind."

"No, I don't mind. I'll talk with you but I'll tell you right now that if you're going to try and talk me into going back to Cheyenne . . . it won't work!"

"Thank you Josie for arranging this. I don't think I could bear to be around anyone yet. A nice quiet supper with a friend is just what I needed."

"It was nothing, Emily. Dr. Mayfield said you should take it easy for at least a few more days. To be honest, I didn't feel very enthusiastic about going out to eat either. We're both really tired and drained after the last few days. I can't believe you talked the doctor into letting you leave that old boot top on your broken arm."

"Well, the way the doctor wrapped it, no one will even know it's there, but I'll have a memento of Peter close to me. Besides, the doctor said it was quite ingenious how Peter thought to use the top of a dried up old boot."

"He is a strange man, Emily. I can't believe he just walked out and never said goodbye to anyone, especially you."

"It's not so strange, Josie. You saw his scars and heard what those horrible outlaws called him. He wouldn't shame anyone he loved by putting them in a position to be laughed at and ridiculed for being around him. He has a big heart and is very determined to live the rest of his life away from people."

Josie saw that Emily was getting emotional, tears were flooding her eyes. "I'm sorry, Emily, I didn't mean to make you cry. I guess in a way I can understand how he feels. I just hate to see you so depressed."

"It hurts terribly, but there is nothing I can do about it. I know grandmother is worried about me, so I need to act like I'm fine. With mother and father dead, I'm so glad she and Nicholas are finally going to be married. She will have someone to care for her when I'm gone."

"Do you know what you are going to do?"

"No, not really. I'll go back east with grandmother and stay with her until she is settled, then I think I'll go ahead and make the trip to San Francisco. I was really looking forward to singing there. What are you going to do, Josie? Will you stay here in Cheyenne?"

"Right now I don't know. I'll just follow my dad wherever his company sends him. The railroad is sending a replacement for the telegraph so it probably won't be too long before we get our next assignment."

"Will you come and see me if you ever get close to Philadelphia?"

"You know I will. I may even make a special trip to see you when dad finds out where he's going to be."

"Oh, that would be wonderful! Promise you'll come."

"I promise. Now, I'm going to leave so you can get some rest. I need to go to the sheriff's office and take the deputy and his prisoner some supper. Is there anything you need before I leave?"

"No, I'm fine. Thank you so much for being with me today. It has helped more than you know."

"You are welcome and I'm glad we had this time together. I'll see you tomorrow but not early. I plan on sleeping as long as I want in the morning. Good night and sweet dreams."

"Goodnight, Josie, see you tomorrow."

Josie let Mrs. Fitzpatrick know she was leaving, went down and picked up supper for the two men at the jail, and headed down the boardwalk. As she got close to the office, a young boy ran out and darted down the street. *I wonder what that's all about.*

She stepped into the office to find Deputy Jones pacing the floor. "Thank goodness someone came! I need to hurry and get home to my wife. That kid that just ran out of here came to tell me my wife fell and her labor started early. He's going to get the doctor then go tell your dad."

"You go ahead, I'll stay until my dad gets here."

"I don't know, he may not like me doing that."

"It's all right, you go on. What could happen in the next few minutes anyway? It won't take him very long to get here."

"If you're sure."

"I'm sure. You go on, your wife needs you."

"Thanks, Josie, I owe you."

Josie smiled as the deputy ran out of the office, jumped on his horse, and tore down the street like he was being chased by a herd of stampeding cattle. Her smile didn't last long.

A voice boomed from the back of the jail. "Hey! What's going on out there? When do I get my supper? A man could starve to death in here."

She almost waited for her father to come before going in to give the prisoner his supper, but he started yelling again so she took one of the plates of food and opened the door that led to the jail cells. A short hall with a window at the end separated the cells, two on each side of the hall. Carl was in the last cell on the right. She told him to step back from the bars. He obeyed and she pushed the plate under the bars with a tin cup of water. As she stood up to leave, Carl stopped her. "Wait a minute! Your voice sounds familiar. Do I know you?"

Josie quickly walked down the hall with her heart in her throat. She didn't look back or say anything. She closed the heavy wooden door and leaned her forehead against the rough boards. *I didn't see that coming. I hope he doesn't figure it out. I'm so stupid! I should have waited for Dad to get here.*

She turned from the door to find a sneering Ken standing just inside the room, a pistol pointed at her. "Well, now ain't this nice. Just turn right around, little lady, and walk on back in there where my friend is. And while you're at it, grab the keys right there on that peg."

Chapter 18

*I*T WAS DARK WHEN Rand rode up to the hotel. As he went through the lobby he spotted Mrs. Fitzpatrick and Nicholas Clench having their evening meal. *Might as well go report now. Wish I had some good news and could wrap this whole affair up. Never had so much trouble getting a job done before.*

"Hello, Rand. Come and have some supper with us," Mrs. Fitzpatrick invited.

"I'll sit for a minute but I'd like to clean up before I eat." Rand pulled a chair out and sat.

Nicholas leaned toward him. "Have any luck finding the trail of the one that got away?"

"Oh, I found his trail all right. He wasn't hiding it. He's a little smarter than most outlaws. He went south then doubled back to the main trail. Looks like he hit the main road in front of a wagon train. There was no way to tell which direction he went."

"Are you going to give up?" Nicholas wanted to know.

"No, not now anyway. I've got a few more things I'd like to check out before I give up. I'll put out wanted posters on him. Do you think Emily might be able to help someone draw a picture of his face?"

"I don't know," Mrs. Fitzpatrick answered. "I'll mention it to her, but I don't want anything to upset or worry her for a few days. Her body needs a chance to heal. I'm afraid her heart will take longer to heal than her body, though. Mr. O'Donnell leaving without saying goodbye, hurt her terribly. She tries to hide it but it's obvious to me how she feels. I'm afraid she has fallen in love with the man."

"I think you're probably right," Rand agreed.

A waitress came by with the coffee pot. "Anyone want more coffee?"

"I think we are all through, Susan," Mrs. Fitzpatrick answered. "Weren't you going home earlier?"

"Yes, but I have to wait until Josie gets back. She took meals to the deputy and the prisoner some time ago. Don't know what's keeping her. It's not like her to be gone so long."

A nagging uneasiness gripped Rand, but he dismissed it, excused himself and headed upstairs. He reached the top of the stairs and that uneasiness had built to where he couldn't ignore the feeling that something wasn't right. Taking a deep breath, he turned, went back down the stairs and out to his horse. Ducky nickered and nudged him as he ran his hand down the horse's neck. "I know you're tired, too. One more stop and I'll take you to the stables."

The sheriff's office was dark when Rand rode up. He stayed mounted as he watched the two windows in the front of the building. *I don't like this. There should be a light in the office.* Not seeing any movement from either window, he dismounted and walked to the front door. There was no sound coming from inside so he turned the door handle and cautiously pushed it open, staying out of the line of fire. *Quiet as a tomb in there.* Slowly, Rand stepped around the door frame and made his way into the office. There was enough light to see that no one was in the office. He spotted a tray with one empty plate and a cup on the desk. Rand's senses went on high alert. *Something is definitely wrong. Where is the deputy and where is Josie?*

The door to the back room where the jail cells were was slightly ajar. *I won't be able to see anything in there without a light. Where is a . . . .* Rand located a lantern, found some matches and lit the lantern. Crouching beside the door he pushed it open far enough to set the lantern in the room where Carl was supposed to be locked up. There was nothing, no movement, no sound, only silence. *Here goes!*

Rand pushed the door wide open and stepped into the room, his pistol ready for what might confront him. At first he didn't see anything but as his eyes swept the room he saw what looked like a body on the floor of the last cell on the right. He picked up the lantern and quickly went to the door of the cell. Sprawled on the floor was George Fisher, his head in a pool of blood. The cell wasn't locked so Rand knelt on the floor beside Mr. Fisher. There was so much blood on his head and the floor that Rand was quite surprised to find he was breathing. *I can't believe he's still alive! Must not be a gunshot wound. Probably just bashed in the head with the butt of a pistol.*

"Mr. Fisher, can you hear me?" Rand shook the man's shoulder, trying to get him to respond. "Mr. Fisher, this is Rand Trinity. Can you hear me? It will help a lot if you can tell me what happened." Again, there was no response. *I've got to get some help.* Rand hurried out on the boardwalk and looked up and down the street. A couple of men were walking toward the stable. A loud whistle from Rand stopped the men, who then turned to see what was happening. Rand motioned for them to come over. "I need some help!" he yelled, and was grateful when the two men hurried to reach him.

"What's going on?" one of the men asked.

Rand pulled them inside the office. "There's been a jail break and George Fisher has been hurt. Will one of you run and get the doctor? I'm afraid he's hurt pretty bad."

"I'll go," one of them offered, turning to the door.

"Wait!" Rand said. "I want your word that you won't tell another person what has happened here and tell the doctor not to say a word, either. There are probably two outlaws still in town and I don't want them to know I'm looking for them. Hurry, but act as normal as possible."

"You got my word and I hope you catch those two!"

The other man asked, "What can I do to help?"

"Will you find another lantern, water and a rag so I can wash some of the blood off his face. I'll see if he's hurt anywhere else."

"Sure thing. My name's Dick Rider and I'll do whatever you need me to do."

"Thanks, Dick, I appreciate your help."

Rand heard a moan from the back cell and hurried to see if George had regained consciousness. "George, can you hear me? It's Rand Trinity."

With surprising strength, George grasped the front of Rand's shirt. "They got Josie, Rand! They got Josie!"

"I was afraid of that. Can you tell me anything else? Do you have any idea where they took her?"

Mr. Fisher mumbled something Rand couldn't understand then blinked his eyes and looked straight at Rand swiping at his eyes to try and clear the blood away. "They took her to open the safe at the bank."

Dick handed Rand a wet rag. "Here, this will help wash the blood out of your eyes."

Rand started to help George but he grabbed Rand's wrist. "Don't waste time on me! They should still be there. Go get my girl!"

He understood George's fear but didn't like Mr. Fisher getting so agitated. And there was nothing Rand wanted more than to go get Josie. He stood and addressed Dick Rider. "Will you stay here with him until the doctor and your friend come back?"

"Of course, I will."

"Good, and all of you stay *here* unless it's life or death, until you hear from me."

"Don't you worry about anything here. That Miss Josie is a fine girl so you go make sure you get her away from those outlaws. You might save the town from a hanging if you take care of those two like they need to be taken care of . . . if you get my meaning."

Rand didn't answer, just walked away. He'd been mad before but never had he felt such anger as he was feeling now. It was boiling up so hot and fast he thought he might choke. Walking between two buildings across the street he stood a few moments in the shadows and cleared his mind of everything except what he now had to do.

If they're still at the bank, they'll probably have their horses in the back. I'll check there first to make sure. I wonder if Josie really knows how to open a safe. That's another thing I'm going to have to find out about that girl.

Rand started moving into the shadows until he reached the only bank in town. He had been right. Two horses were at the back of the bank building. Cautiously, he checked the building and found no windows except two large ones at the front. *That is going to be a problem. I'll have to get in through the back door.*

Carefully turning the knob, Rand realized the door had been busted up around the frame and was elated that it didn't squeak when he opened it enough to step through. His first few steps were completely quiet. He stopped and quietly pulled his gun when he heard a man threatening someone. Was that someone Josie?

"You better get it open *this* time! And if you're lying to me, you'll be sorry you were ever born."

That voice belonged to Carl, Rand was sure.

"I'm not lying to you. I can get it open but it would be easier and faster if I had some light. Every time I hear the tumblers fall, I can't see the number and I have to start all over. I only needed one more number this last time, but now, I've got to do it all over again."

Yep, it's Josie.

"Boss, I've got a piece of a candle in my saddle bags. If we stood in front of it, I don't think anyone could see it, and it should give her enough light to get the safe open."

And . . . there was Ken. The two outlaws in one room. How convenient.

"Go get the blasted thing and *hurry*! We need to get out of here."

Rand didn't have time to hide. Ken was right next to him before he had a chance to think what to do. In the dim light, Rand saw the startled outlaw go for his gun. Rand acted instinctively and fired. The man was so close, Rand didn't have to aim, just pointed and shot. The outlaw's gun went off harmlessly into the opposite wall then a loud thud sounded as Ken's body collapsed to the floor. Rand made his way quickly to the front and stood just behind a partition. He heard Josie gasping and realized Carl had her in a chokehold.

"All right, Carl," Rand called out. "It's all over! Those shots will bring the town here in no time. You might as well give it up."

"I've got the girl, remember! I'll kill her if you don't step out here and let me go out the back door."

"You harm her and you're a dead man for sure!"

"Maybe, maybe not. Either way I'll have the satisfaction of knowing she's *dead*. She killed Jack and played me for a fool, so she's dead no matter what!"

"Quit hiding behind the skirts of a woman! Let's fight it out man to man. I've heard you consider yourself a fast draw." Rand knew most outlaws thought they were always faster than the other man and figured Carl would be no exception.

"You mean *guns?*"

"Sure, why not? We'll both holster our pistols and see who's the fastest. If you win, you can do whatever you want. That is, if you hurry. I see some men coming across the street right now. You shoot me and you'll still have a chance to get away."

"How do I know you'll holster your gun and make it a fair fight?"

"You've got the girl. I'll step out and we'll holster our pistols together. When you push the girl to the side, we'll draw and fire."

Carl's voice was tinged with panic. "All right, step out!"

Rand stepped out from behind the partition and into the dim light of the main room. Both of the men had their pistols pointed at each other. Rand slowly started lowering his gun, as Carl did the same, sliding them into their holsters. Tension hung thickly in the room as the men kept their eyes on each other. A voice called through one of the windows, "What's going on in there? Is that you, Rand?"

Rand recognized Valentine's voice. "It's all right, Val, stay out there. I've got it under control in here."

"You just *think* you have it under control," Carl sneered as he went for his gun. He didn't push Josie aside but what he didn't expect was for Josie to drop out from under him. She just fell straight down like a wet noodle, giving Rand a clear shot. Her timing was perfect and her actions threw Carl's shot off, barely missing Rand's head. Rand's shot did not miss and the outlaw named *Carl* was dead in moments.

"Rand, did he hit you?" Josie cried out.

"He *missed*, thanks to you. Are you all right?" Rand was at Josie's side in a flash, trying to help her to her feet.

"No, I'm *not* all right and leave me be for a minute," she ordered, her voice quaking.

"Tell me what's wrong with you. Are you hurt?"

"I'm shaking so badly and my knees are so weak, I don't think I can stand."

"I'll help you," Rand said, taking hold of her arm.

"No! I want to sit here a minute."

"Can I do anything to help? Tell me what to do!"

Josie said softly, "Come down here and hold me a minute."

Rand could see a group of men peeking in the windows trying to see what was going on, but at that moment, he didn't care. He got down on the floor, put his hands on Josie's shoulders and pulled her into an embrace. There was no resistance from Josie. She just melted into Rand's arms and started to cry.

He smiled when he heard Val tell everyone, "Rand's got it all under control. Let's go over to the jail and see what's going on over there."

"I was so afraid he would kill you," Josie sobbed. "That was such a crazy thing to do."

"It wasn't such a smart thing for you to tell them you could open that safe either."

"I had to do *something,* they were beating my father to death! It was the only thing I could think of that would get them to leave him alone. Carl had been suspicious anyway because he thought he recognized my voice earlier. But when I told him I would open the safe if they would leave my dad alone, that's when Carl realized who I was. I thought he was going to kill me on the spot but his *greed* got the best of him." Josie's tears were slowly drying up and she moved away just enough to reach into her pocket and pull out a handkerchief.

"What did you think they would have done when you couldn't open up that vault?"

"Oh, I could have had it open several times but I had to stall for time."

Rand was dumbfounded. "*How* and *why* did you achieve the skill of opening a safe?"

"The circus. Will you help me to my feet, now? I need to go see about my dad. Did you see him?"

"Yes, he's the one who told me they took you to the bank. He was alive when I left him. I had someone go for the doctor and someone stay with him . . . But, Josie, don't change the subject. *How* do you know how to open a safe?"

"I'll tell you all about it later. Let's hurry and check on Dad."

As Josephine Fisher hurried out the back door with Rand in tow, she asked, "Have you ever been to a circus?"

"No, I can't say as I have."

"Well, then I have a *lot* to tell you but it will have to be later."

Chapter 19

RAND AND JOSIE HURRIED to the sheriff's office. They were glad to see the doctor there, who had everything under control. Those who had gathered made way for them to get through the door just as they were carrying Mr. Fisher out on a stretcher.

"You men go easy with him," Dr. Mayfield was saying. "I want you to take him to my office where I can keep an eye on him tonight." Dr. Michael Mayfield spotted Rand and a big grin spread across his face. "Rand, you son-of-a-gun! I heard you were in town." They gave each other a manly back-slapping hug. "Come along with me. I need to keep up with these men and open the door to my office."

Josie stayed by Rand's side, surprised that the men obviously knew each other quite well. "How's Dad doing?" she asked.

"Looks like he took a couple of hard blows to the head and he may have some broken ribs. I'm encouraged though, since he's been talking to me." He looked at Josie. "He's been asking about you, young lady. How are you doing?"

"I'm doing fine now, thank you. It's Dad I'm worried about."

"We'll take good care of him and leave the rest in God's hands"

Rand left Josie at the doctor's office and hurried back to the sheriff's. The last few days were taking a toll on him and he was bone tired, but he pushed himself, knowing the job was almost done. He wanted to find Val first of all.

"Hey, Rand, how is George Fisher doing?" Val asked.

"He's alive and the doctor was encouraged cause he's talking. Are you up to helping me with some things?"

"Sure, just tell me what you need."

"I need to locate the banker's house to tell him what happened. He can figure out a way to secure the back door of the bank. While I do that, can you find some men to help you haul the bodies in the bank to the undertaker?"

"I can take care of that," Val assured him.

"I guess the mess in the back cell and the bank can wait until morning to be cleaned up. Do you know where they keep the key to the door here at the jail? I'm going to lock it up tonight since we don't have any prisoners."

"There's a bunch of keys on the wall over there behind the desk. I imagine one of them will lock up the place."

After securing the sheriff's office, locating the banker, and taking care of Ducky, Rand stopped back by the doctor's office. He stepped in to find Emily, Mrs. Fitzpatrick, and Nicholas Clench, along with Josie, listening to the doctor. "I've stitched up his head and wrapped his ribs. For tonight I want him to be very still. I want to monitor him close tonight so you all can go back to the hotel and get some sleep."

Josie looked stressed. "I don't want to leave my dad, Dr. Mayfield. Can't I stay with him?"

"Not tonight, Josie. If your father does well tonight then tomorrow maybe you and my nurse can stay with him tomorrow night. There's a bed in the next room here that you can stay in tonight, if you want to. If there's any change or he asks for you, I'll wake you."

"Thank you, Dr. Mayfield. Can I go in now and say good night to him?"

"I think that would be a good idea, but only you, Josie. Sorry, but the rest of you should go on and get your rest."

Rand was hoping to have a few minutes to talk to Josie alone, but it didn't look like that was going to happen so he left with the others and went back to the hotel. Rand stood and stared at the bed in his room for a few moments. *I don't even care if I need a bath or I didn't get to eat supper. That bed is calling me and I'm going to answer and worry about my other problems tomorrow.*

"Hey, Emily, what are you doing here?" Josie was surprised to see her friend back at the doctor's office.

"I woke up early and just kept thinking about you, so I decided to come and see how you were doing. How is your father this morning?"

"I'm not sure yet. Dr. Mayfield is still in there with him. I'm waiting for the doctor to come out and tell me if Dad can have anything to eat or drink."

"Have you seen him at all since we left last night?"

"Just for a short time earlier this morning. He seemed to be alert and talked with me a little. He wanted to know what happened at the bank."

"I'm so glad it's all over! What a terrible ordeal to have to go through. If it hadn't been for you and Rand I don't know what would have happened. Thank you, Josie, for what you've done."

"You're welcome, but I know you would have done the same for me, Emily. That's what friends do, they help each other."

Dr. Mayfield interrupted their conversation. "Hello, Emily, how are your injuries doing this morning? Your leg and arm?"

"A lot better, thanks to your nurse and her ministrations. The hot soaks and salve have really helped my leg. It's healing just fine."

"I'm glad to hear that. I have a proposition for you two ladies."

Josie looked curiously at Dr. Mayfield. "What is that?"

"Your father seems to be doing well this morning and I am in need of coffee and breakfast. If you don't mind, I'm going to leave the door open to the room where he's resting, and go get some breakfast. You two can sit out here and chat, but if he starts moving around very much or acting like he's distressed, get someone to come after me. I won't be gone long, so everything should be all right."

"Sure, we can do that, Dr. Mayfield. You go ahead, we'll be just fine," Josie told him.

After the doctor left, Josie looked into her friend's eyes. "Now tell me how you really are doing? I can tell you're trying to hide just how badly you're really hurting."

"You may be sorry you asked because I'll cry if I talk about it very much. Once I get started crying I have a hard time stopping."

"Oh, well, what's a few tears between good friends," Josie said.

"If you really want to know, I'm confused, and I don't quite know what to do with this ache in my chest. I know Peter had feelings for me, or I *thought* he did. If he really cared for me at all, why would he just leave without saying goodbye? I just can't settle that in my mind."

"I have a feeling that it would have been too painful for him to face you with a goodbye. Also, Peter may have walked away without a word trying to make it easier for *you* to let him go, because . . . he loves you that much."

"That's a funny kind of love!"

"I don't think so. If you truly love someone you want the best for them. Peter probably worries that anyone he gets involved with would eventually become hurt because of his scars. You heard how awful those outlaws were to him. Don't you think that hurt him deeply to be called *freak* in front of you? He's just learned to walk away. Really, Emily, put yourself in his place. Would you be able to let Peter go if it was best for him?"

"I guess I'm just selfish. I love Peter so much that I don't want to live without him. I've considered going to his mountain and staying there with him." Josie started to protest, but Emily held up her one good hand to stop her. "I know, I know! I wouldn't be happy living like that year after year. But I don't think he's happy there either."

"Emily, let's pray about it. Let's pray that God will give us a solution or He'll give you the strength to let Peter go if it's best for him."

"Pray?" Emily's eyes grew large. "You mean right *now*, out *loud*?"

"Yes. Don't you pray, Emily?"

"No . . . I mean, yes." Emily dropped her head as a tear slid down her cheek.

"Oh, stupid me!" Josie said. "I didn't mean to make you cry. I shouldn't have said that like I did."

"No, it's not that. You just made me remember the one time I really *did* pray." Another tear made its way down Emily's cheek.

"What happened?" Josie asked.

"When we were at the cabin, the outlaws forced Peter to go to town with Carl to demand the ransom. I begged God to keep him safe. I hadn't even thought about it until now but he answered my prayer, Josie. He kept Peter safe! I'm so ashamed I didn't recognize that sooner."

Josie pulled her handkerchief from her pocket and handed it to Emily. She had a smile on her face when she spoke again. "That's wonderful, Emily. I know we don't always get what we want when we pray but God does hear our prayers, and he wants the best for us. You can thank God for answering your prayer now."

"I want to pray. But I don't really know how," Emily sniffed. "What do I say?"

"You pray the same way you did in that cabin. Prayer is just talking to God."

Josie prayed a simple prayer asking God to give them an answer about how to help Peter and to give Emily peace. She prayed that God would help Emily see what was best for her and Peter. She then gave Emily time to voice her own prayer. While Emily prayed, Josie was saying her own private prayer. *Heavenly Father, thank you for this dear, sweet friend and what you are doing in her life. Help me to be a good example to her.*

Chapter 20

WHAT DID I GET myself into! After his eventful week, Rand had slept late and let himself enjoy a nice hot bath before going down to breakfast. *I must be some kind of a romantic fool to let myself get into this predicament. Maybe I should go check on George Fisher and have a good long talk with Josie while I'm there. Maybe we can come up with something.* With a plan, of sorts, Rand hurried to shave, get dressed, and head downstairs to have breakfast.

Halfway through his meal of beef steak, eggs, biscuits and gravy, Rand heard a familiar voice. "Eating breakfast late this morning, aren't you?"

"Good morning, Josie. How's your father doing this morning? I was thinking of going to the doctor's office and seeing you when I finish here."

"The doctor thinks he's going to be fine. He still wants to keep an eye on him for a couple more days. He has orders to be still and take it easy which doesn't make Dad happy."

"I'm glad he's doing better. Do you have time to sit and talk with me?"

"Sure, I can sit a few minutes with you. Let me take this tray of dishes back to the kitchen. I'll be right back."

A couple of minutes later Josie was back. Rand pulled out her chair for her. "You look mighty pretty today."

"Why, thank you, Rand. You look rather handsome yourself. It's amazing what a good night's sleep can do for a person."

"You're right about that."

Rand, all of a sudden, felt uncomfortable. *How in the world do I start this conversation? I guess the best thing to . . . ."*

"The best thing to do, Rand, is to go ahead say what you want to say, or ask what you want to ask. I can tell you have something on your mind." Josie smiled at his unease.

"If you only knew, Miss Fisher, I have so many unanswered questions I want to ask you, but there's one thing I really need help with, and I need to make a decision right away."

"I can't imagine what you think I could advise you about. You've got me really curious now. What would you like for me to help you with?"

"It's about Emily, and I figure you know her pretty well by now. The two of you have become pretty good friends."

"I guess we have, but what do you need to know about Emily?"

"Well, how does she feel about Peter?" Rand looked more than a little embarrassed.

"I can't believe it, Mr. Trinity. You are asking me about affairs of the heart. This is a side of you I haven't seen. You must be a real romantic."

"It's a simple question, Josie. Can you tell me or not?"

"I'm just teasing you. Don't get all upset with me. I think it's rather sweet that you care, although, I'm not sure there is anything that can be done now. I will tell you that Emily is miserable. She loves Peter but is having a hard time understanding why he just up and left without a chance to say goodbye. She feels sure Peter loves her but thinks that she would soon grow tired of being tied to a freak. But, oh well, it doesn't matter now cause Peter is gone and doesn't want to be found."

"That's just it, Josie, he's not . . . ."

Josie started to giggle. The word *freak* had triggered a memory. "That's it! Why didn't I see it before? Oh, how I *wish* Peter was here!"

"That's what I've been trying to tell you. He *is* here."

Josie leaned forward, looking intently at Rand. "What do you mean? He's here in town? Where? How?"

"I might have stretched it a little, but I told him I might need him for the trial when the judge gets here."

"But *where* is he?"

"In the train car that Nicholas Clench and I rode in when we came to Cheyenne. I can't let him stay there any longer because now that all the gang of outlaws are dead, there won't be a trial. I know he cares for Emily. I just don't know how to help him."

"I have an idea, Rand. What are you doing the rest of the day?"

"I don't have anything I have to do until later this afternoon. Someone slipped a note under my door from Dr. Mayfield. I'm expected at their house this evening for supper."

"Then we'll have plenty of time. Will you come to my house in about an hour? I'll want you to take me to see Peter."

"Can you tell me what you're going to do?"

"If you don't mind, I'd rather wait and see if I have what I need first, then I'll explain to you and Peter at the same time."

Rand looked skeptical. "If that's the way you want it, but I hope it's a good idea. It will take a lot to get Peter to change his mind about going back to his mountain. I'm not even sure he'll talk to you."

Josie got up to leave. "You are one special man, Rand Trinity. I'm so excited I could *bust*! See you in an hour."

God, you are so wonderful. Thank you so much for giving me this inspiration. Josie was on her way to the little house close to the telegraph office that she and her father had been living in. *Please prepare Peter's heart to be receptive to my idea.*

It took Josie almost the full hour to round up all the things she needed. Then she sat in a rocking chair by the front window watching for Rand. Her heart sped up when she saw him walking toward the house. The memory of their one and only kiss lingered on the fringes of her mind as she watched his face come into focus. She had found it almost impossible to keep her emotions under control when she dwelt on the sweetness of the moment. *God, please help me to understand my feelings for Rand. I've never felt like this around any other man in my life. Is it just friendship . . . or is it more?*

Josephine flung the door open before Rand could knock. "Come on in. I'm going to need some help carrying this stuff over to the train car."

Rand stepped into the small front room of the house and noticed a tidy, well-kept room that was light and comfortable looking with rugs scattered around and lace curtains at the windows. "What do you want me to carry?"

"If you can carry that box on that chair by the door, I'll carry this sack." Josie held up a flour sack that was half full.

"Is this all?" Rand asked.

"Yes, for now. I'll need to talk with Peter and figure out if I need anything else, but I think I've got enough here to convince him of what I have in mind."

Rand gave her a skeptical look. "It scares me to death to think of all the things you've got in that mind of yours, Miss Fisher, but let's go. I'm dying to know what you have in mind for poor Peter O'Donnell."

Josie just grinned at him as they started on their way. "I'm really excited about this, Rand. Emily and I prayed this morning that God would give us a solution to help Peter or that He would give Emily peace about Peter going back to his mountain."

"And you think what you have in mind is God's answer to your prayers?"

"I really do, Rand. I truly hadn't thought very much about the circus in some time."

"There's that *circus* thing you keep talking about. When are you going to tell me what all the circus stuff means?"

"In about five or ten minutes."

All was quiet as they stepped up on the stairs of the train car. Rand knocked and called, "It's Rand."

The door slowly opened and Peter stood just inside with the hood of his cape up over his head and part way over his eyes. "Hi, Peter," Rand greeted him. "I've brought some news and a friend with me. How are you doing?"

Peter stood unmoving for a few moments. "I'm doing all right, Rand. Who is this with you?"

Rand looked confused. "Oh, I guess you haven't actually met Josie yet. Peter O'Donnell meet Josephine Fisher."

Peter nodded at a smiling Josephine then quickly turned to Rand. "I don't know why you've brought her here but I don't think this is a good idea, Rand."

"Sorry, Peter. I know I told you that you wouldn't have to see anyone but I felt strongly that you should hear Josie out. She's a friend of Emily's and has something she wants to tell you. Just so you know, you will now be able to do or go anywhere you want because all of the outlaw gang are dead and there won't be a trial. I'm asking you as a personal favor to listen to what Miss Fisher has to say."

Peter stepped back and motioned for his guests to come in. "I'll listen to what Emily's friend has to say and then I'll be on my way."

The three moved into the sitting area of the car. Rand and Peter stood looking expectantly at Josie who didn't hesitate to take charge. "I want to tell you a little about myself first, so if you two gentlemen will sit down I'll start my story."

Neither of the men said a word. They both sat in the chair that was nearest them. Josie stood quietly for a moment with her eyes closed then looked up with a strange expression on her face. "Some of this is painful for me, so don't be surprised if I cry a little. I haven't talked about my mother for a long time and it will be good for me to tell you about her. My mother had a beauty that caused people to stop and stare. She had inner qualities that shone from her eyes and a smile that lit up a room, and she was a trapeze artist for the famous Kingston's Circus. That's where Dad met her. He did a lot of the labor for the circus, like putting up the big tents, and then he got interest in clowning. He learned from some of the best and became a remarkable clown. He was always a hit with the crowds.

"Mom and Dad fell in love, got married, and a year later I was born. I was raised in a circus family. I don't say the word *family* lightly, because that's what we were. I was taken care of by my circus family and learned from everyone. As I grew up I became part of the different acts for the big shows in the evening. I started with clowning with my dad. Those were some of the best times of my life. When I was twelve . . . ." Josie paused and took a deep breath, "my mother fell from the trapeze during one of the shows. I never missed one of her performances if I could help it, and I was there for that one. For some reason that no one could explain, one of the ropes broke on her trapeze and she died from the fall. I had been learning trapeze acts from Mom, but after her death, Dad forbade me to have anything to do with the trapeze."

Josie paused to take a deep breath and Peter spoke up, "I'm sorry for you, Miss Fisher. I've lost family too, but I don't see what that has to do with me."

"You will in a minute, Peter. You see, the circus ran little side shows all during the day and night, all manner of entertainment and foods from dancing girls, popcorn, candied apples, strong-man exhibitions, the largest women in the world, the tallest man in the world. You name it and at one time or another you could find it in the circus.

"There was one part, though, that took me a long time to learn to love and that was the freak shows. That's what the circus called them. The hawkers would call to everyone to come see the freaks of nature. I was afraid of the people who everyone called a freak."

Peter stiffened and jerked his head up straighter. "I hate that word! No one should ever be called a *freak*."

"I know, Peter, I hate the word too. But the people I came to admire and love the most were in that part of the circus. Those wonderful people were making the best of what they could not change. Believe me, they didn't like being called a freak either but they endured it because the circus gave them freedom and kept them out of institutions.

"I'll tell you a little secret." Josie grinned mischievously. "We worked at making them look uglier and scarier than they really were. That's what people wanted to see. More than anything, being part of the circus gave them family and friends who understood what they were going through. All the cruelty and names hurled at them, they endured for each other. I learned to love them and spent as much time as I could with them."

Rand was shaking his head. "Josie, please don't tell me you're going to try and talk Peter into joining a circus!"

"No, not at all, Rand. Peter doesn't even begin to have the problems these people had. How long has it been since you looked in the mirror, Peter."

"I only looked at myself one time after the accident and refused to have a mirror anywhere around after that. Those horrid red scars were about the ugliest things I had ever seen."

"They were ugly right after your accident but I didn't see any red scars when those outlaws pulled your hood down and exposed your head. You had scars, sure, but they were not that bad."

Peter looked shocked. "When . . . when . . . did you see me with my hood down? You weren't there when those outlaws did that!"

"Oh, but I *was* there. Do you remember that dirty, obnoxious kid named Joe, who showed up and wanted to join the gang?"

"Of course I remember him but, what's he got to do with anything?"

"That was *me*, Peter." Josie paused to let that sink in.

"I don't believe it." Peter turned to Rand with an incredulous look. "Is she telling the truth? Did you know that kid was a woman?"

"She's telling the truth, and no, I didn't know it was a woman until she got close enough for me to see her eyes. She's the one who saved my life. I didn't know what she was going to do to save me, so I was praying hard that she knew what she was doing. When she threw that knife it was a perfect throw. It hit the rope where it was tied around the limb they had me stretched out on."

"Sorry, but it was not a perfect throw," Josie interjected. "If I had thrown it perfectly it would have cut the rope clean through. I was a little out of practice and there was a tiny thread of rope left. It was your weight that caused it to break."

Rand's forehead wrinkled in a scowl. "You never did tell me how you learned to throw a knife like that."

"Dad and I were always trying to come up with a new act for one of the side shows. After Mom died, we practiced until we got good enough to do a knife throwing exhibition. Dad would put me against a backdrop and throw knives around my body. I finally got good enough that he would let me throw knives around him. We did another show that was a fast draw and accuracy contest. I loved showing up all the men."

"I just bet you did," Rand said with a chuckle. "I'm ready to hear where you're taking us with this, and I'm sure Peter is too."

"Sure, I'll get to the point. Dad and I became expert makeup and disguise artists because of the clowning and helping the others with their makeup. We used a lot of makeup on the ones who were in the freak shows also. I can disguise myself in many other ways besides a young boy." She looked at Peter. "Your little old scars are nothing! And I want to teach you how to cover them and be able to live a normal life. Will you give me a chance to do that, Peter? I don't see as you have anything to lose and you might find a life you never dreamed you could have."

Chapter 21

ETER WAS STUNNED. SEVERAL times he looked between Josie and Rand. Finally his gaze rested on Rand. "I don't know what to say. What do you think, Rand?"

"I agree with Josie. What do you have to lose by letting her show you what she can do? I figure she knows what she's doing because she's fooled me *twice*." Rand's eyes locked on Josie's. "But I can tell you . . . it's for *sure* she won't fool me again." He looked at Peter. "Besides, if you like what she does, you win. If you don't like it you can go on your way."

Peter looked skeptical but he nodded at Josie. Inwardly, he was a man struggling for strength. *God, please help me. Give me the courage to face my future.* Rather subdued, he answered, "All right, you've got your chance. What do you want me to do?"

Josie looked relieved. "First, I want you to take off your cape and shirt."

"Why do I need to take off my shirt?" Peter protested. "I don't feel right being undressed in front of you."

"Special circumstances require a little impropriety at times. If it makes you feel any better, I've seen men's chests before. A lot of the workers and performers of the circus went without shirts during the hot seasons and sometimes during performances. It won't bother me and I don't want you to let it bother you, because I need to see the extent of your scars, especially on your neck."

With a big sigh of resignation, Peter lowered the hood and took off his cape and shirt. He laid them across his lap as if he might need them in a hurry. He didn't look at either Josie or Rand but focused on some spot across the room.

Josie circled the chair Peter sat in, then went to the box she had brought. She rummaged around until she found what she wanted. "Here they are. I'm going to hand you a mirror and I want you to look at yourself because I want to point out a few things to you."

Peter's actions showed his reluctance to look in the mirror. Rand felt sympathy for the man when he noticed that Peter's hands shook as he reached out and took the mirror. "I really don't want to see myself. Do I have to do this?"

"Yes, Peter, it's important. Let me prepare you. You are going to see mostly a bald man. You have tufts of hair on the right side of your head which makes you look strange, but we can take care of that. The left side of your head has the most damage on it because your ear on that side was mostly burned off. I bet you threw your arms around your face to protect it."

"Yes, of course it was instinct, I suppose, to protect my face."

"Your face is still very handsome. Now, I want you to look at that face right now. Look in the mirror but only look at your facial features, eyes, mouth, chin, and forehead."

It was silent in the train car as Peter lifted the mirror and stared into the shiny object. After a few moments, Josie asked, "What do you see?"

"I see my face," he said unhappily.

"No, you don't. You see a man with a long, scraggly beard who is trying to hide behind that beard and a hooded cape. That is not the real you. Look at me, Peter."

Obediently, Peter looked in Josie's eyes. She deliberately held his gaze and tried to read what she saw there. After dropping her eyes, she finally spoke. "What I see when I look at the real you, is a man who has been deeply wounded in body and spirit. A man who is afraid to fight or hope. I want you to tell me right now if you are going to be a man who is willing to fight this fear. I don't think you're a coward. Look at what you've been through to save Emily. Before your accident when you stood in front of hundreds of people and sang, it took a lot of courage. As far as I'm concerned, it takes more courage to face the wild world on that mountain you plan on living on year after year, than anything I've mentioned. The loneliness would be more than I could bear."

Josie looked intently into Peter's eyes once again. "Well, what is it going to be? Are you willing to learn what's necessary to live in this crazy, exciting world again? Or are you going to live in fear and hide on your mountain?"

"I don't think you understand what I've been through," Peter said. "But you're right about some of the things you mentioned. I know I'm not a coward but after a while, the battle got so big I think maybe I just grew too weary to fight the overwhelming obstacles that were being thrown at me. I didn't have anyone but God to turn to and it seemed as if God was deaf to my pleas for help."

"He wasn't deaf," Josie replied. "He heard every prayer you prayed and whether we understand or not, God has been with you through everything you've had to face and He's not finished with you yet. Now, do we go on . . . or do I leave?"

Peter breathed in deeply and let it slowly escape. "I want to fight and live like everyone else. I want to sing again, love again, and explore the world with the one I love. But what if it doesn't work?"

"Then you will have tried and given it the best you could. That should be worth something."

"Yes, I'll know I tried. What do we do first?"

"Off with the beard and the hair on the right side of your head. Do you want me to shave it or are you up to doing it? I brought all the things you'll need if you want to do it yourself."

Peter looked a little indignant. "Of course I'll do it myself."

"Good for you. I need to go and check on my dad. Dr. Mayfield's nurse has been with him since this morning, so I need to check in and tell her it'll be a little while before I get back."

Josie scowled at Peter. "Promise me you'll be here when I get back."

"I promise."

Rand had been quietly sitting back watching the interaction between Peter and Josie. He now grinned and told Josie, "If he even looks like he's going to take off, I'll handcuff him to something solid."

Josie headed for the door." That will work, see you shortly. And, Peter, don't panic when you see your naked face. It will look different than you remember but I'll fix you up." With that said, Josie smiled at the two men and was gone in a flash.

The men stood in the middle of the car, gawking at the door that Josie had flown out of. They were completely still until Peter said, "Rand, what just happened?"

Rand, still looking at the door, answered calmly, "Oh, you just got hit with a 'Josie-storm' is all. She moves like a tornado and has the power to send you flying. When she's gone, if you're still alive, you just have to pick up the pieces and go on. Other than that, I haven't decided what I think of the Josie-storm."

Rand couldn't help but let go of the mirth he had inside. His chuckle built to an all out belly laugh that was so contagious that Peter caught on, laughing so hard he doubled over and had to sit down. Their roaring laughter went on to the point that Rand started to feel embarrassed at the spectacle he was making. "I'm sorry, but I can't stop!" His gut was starting to ache when he looked at Peter and started to say something, and they both started another round of laughing.

Finally, Peter managed to somehow pull himself together. "Man, I haven't laughed like that in ages. No, I have *never* laughed like that! It felt good to let go, but I better get this hair off my face before the Josie-storm comes back and removes it herself." He laughed again but only a short burst. "Would you mind finding some scissors and cutting these few patches of hair off the right side of my head?"

"I've never cut a man's hair before but I don't know why I can't get the job done. Do you want me to cut it before or after you shave?"

"Go ahead and cut it now, then I'll shave."

They grew serious as they tackled the job of removing all the hair from Peter's head and face. Rand felt pride in the woman who had stormed into his life a few days ago. *What a woman! She's smart, brave, creative, pretty, bossy, and gives herself to help other people. Oh yeah, I forgot something important. She's got soft, sweet lips.*

Peter startled Rand out of his thoughts. "Would it be rude to ask what that big grin on your face is all about?"

Rand hadn't noticed that Peter had been watching him through the mirror. "I don't know about rude, but I'm not going to tell you. Some thoughts are meant to *stay* private." A little later, Peter was staring intently into the mirror he had used to shave. "What are you thinking, Peter?"

"Miss Fisher was right. It's still an ugly sight but it's not as bad as I remembered." Peter turned to face Rand. "Thanks, Rand, for being here with me. I don't know how this will turn out but I want you to know that I appreciate your friendship."

They talked like old friends until a knock came at the door. Rand opened it to find Josie standing there with a pitcher of milk and a large sack. "Are you two hungry? I brought some sandwiches and a pitcher of milk." She didn't have to ask twice. In no time, they had eaten their fill and were wiping their mouths.

"What do we do now?" Peter asked.

Josie smiled. "I make you *handsome*, is what we do now."

"You've got your work cut out for you," Peter winced, "so you better get started."

Rand watched in fascination as Josie worked on Peter. After trying several wigs that transformed Peter's appearance almost magically, she chose a dark brown wavy one that was short in the front and longer in the back. The long hair covered the scars on Peter's neck. A white shirt paired with a fancy dark brown suit jacket almost completely finished covering the scars. Josie undid the top two buttons of the shirt and wrapped a white silk scarf around his neck. The scarf hid the rest of the scars. "What do you think, Rand?"

"It's remarkable, Josie! You've changed his looks drastically. He looks like a wealthy gentleman. Where did you get all the wigs?"

"These are Dad's wigs. We know an expert wig maker in New York that fashions all our wigs. This one really works nicely for you, Peter. When you can, you need to go to New York and have some especially made for you. This one will work for now but the wig needs to be a fit for your head. You would be amazed at what Mr. Langston can do."

"Can I look at what you've done to me now?" Peter asked. "It's hard to sit here and listen to you and Rand discuss my looks and not see what you're talking about."

"Yes, I'll let you look now but there's one place I'm still deciding what to do with. I'll show you a couple of different options and let you decide which one you want to use for now."

For long moments, Peter stared into the mirror. "I can't believe that is really me! It feels so peculiar to look at this stranger in the mirror."

"It'll take a little while to get used to but right now I want you to look at your left eye. There where the scars pull at the corner of your eye is the area I was talking about. Your face is rather white because of your beard and wearing the hood up on your cape all the time. If you allow the sun to tan your whole head, those scars will not show up as much. Or, if you like, I can show you how to mix a cosmetic that will make your white skin look more like a man of the outdoors. Then, there is one other trick I have."

Josie went to the flour sack and dug around until she found what she wanted and took it over to Peter. "What is that?" he asked.

"It's an eye patch. I've cut this one especially for you. I've made it wider on the left side to cover the scars. You'll need to have a proper one made if you decide to use an eye patch. There are a couple of problems, though, that you need to think about if you go that route. One is, learning to use only your right eye when you're out and about, and that can be a little tricky. Of course you wouldn't have to wear it all the time. Dad found that the patch draws attention. People seem fascinated by anyone wearing one. I think it gives an air of mystery, especially with women." Josie had continued to put the patch in place while she talked. Finished, she stood back to admired her work. "Oh my, Mr. O'Donnell, you look marvelous! Go ahead and look."

A quirky little grin appeared on Peter's face when he lifted the mirror to see himself. He tried several times to speak but his voice was choked with emotion.

Josie put her hand on his shoulder. "Don't try to talk right now. Give yourself time to think about all of this. You need to know that wearing a wig can sometimes be uncomfortable, especially when it's hot. Mr. Langston can teach you all there is to know about wearing a wig. When you get used to it you won't even know you have it on.

"Also, you will need to have a tailor make your jackets and shirts fit just for you. With the right kind of shirt, you won't need the neck scarf. You are close to Dad's size and height, so I'll only need to take in, just a little bit, the pants that go with this jacket. I can do that tonight while I sit with Dad in the doctor's office. I want to come in the morning and completely fix you up from head to toe. Then you and I will walk the town, go in the stores, then have some lunch. I want to be with you the first time you go out so I can coach you on any problems or questions you might have.

"The day after tomorrow is Sunday and I'm inviting you and Rand to come to church. You'll be on your own to get ready if you decide to come. Be a tad late and sit in the back. That will give you more time to adjust to socializing again.

"Your boots will be fine but if you want to, we can shop tomorrow and see if there's some in town that look dressier. That's up to you, but I want you to be completely comfortable with how you look.

"Now, I've given you a lot to think about. So tell me if you like what I've said so far and want to continue."

Peter waited several moments to respond. When he did, it was with gratitude and sincerity. "Miss Fisher, you have opened my eyes to so many possibilities that I had never thought of. *Yes*, I want to continue. *Thank you* doesn't even begin to say what I feel."

"A thank you is enough, Peter. You can't know the joy it gives me to be able to help you. I'm going to go now. I have to get back to the hotel and make pies for tonight and tomorrow. I promised Dad a peach pie with his supper tonight. I'll leave the wig and eye patch here with you but I'll need to take the clothes and make sure they're pressed for our time out on the town tomorrow.

"And, I want you to know that Emily will probably be in church with me on Sunday morning. I think it will be best if you don't reveal to her who you are when there are a lot of people around. I honestly don't think she'll recognize you at all, but if you're ready, maybe Sunday afternoon we'll figure out what to do. Do you have any questions?"

"I'm overwhelmed at the moment and can't think of any questions right now."

"Good, I'll see you in the morning."

Rand stood and picked up the box he had carried over. "I'll leave too, Peter. I'm expected to ride out to a friend's house for supper tonight, but you'll get your supper as usual. Is that working out all right?"

"Yes, thank you. The meals are left by the door just like you said they would be."

"Good, I'll try and come with Josie in the morning, if that's all right with you two."

After their goodbyes, Rand walked Josie back to her house. He set the box on a chair by the door and turned to Josie. "Miss Josephine Fisher, you are one incredible woman." He kissed her on the forehead. "I've got to get Ducky and head on out to the doc's house. I'll see you tomorrow."

Chapter 22

THE NEXT MORNING RAND found himself in the best mood he had been in since he couldn't remember when. His relaxed time with Peter, the laughter, watching Josie work her magic on Peter had him singing to himself as he prepared to go down to breakfast. His time with family and friends at Dr. Mayfield's ranch had been the perfect end to the day. It worked out that he got to have breakfast with Mr. Clench and Mrs. Fitzpatrick. Emily joined them half way through the meal. Mrs. Fitzpatrick beamed at her granddaughter. "You look lovely this morning, Emily."

"Thank you, Grandmother. Hello, Rand, how are you this morning?"

"Fine. I've had two cups of coffee and I'm finishing off a good breakfast. What more could a man ask for?"

"Did Grandmother invite you to our special '*thank you*' dinner tomorrow afternoon? I think we are all going to church with Josie in the morning then around two, Grandmother has planned a special meal here at the hotel for a few of us."

"Oh dear, I forgot to tell Rand about it." Mrs. Fitzpatrick apologized. "I'm sorry; I do hope you can come, Rand."

"I'd be pleased to join you," Rand answered.

"Oh, good," Mrs. Fitzpatrick happily replied. "What are your plans for the day, if you don't mind me asking?"

"I'm going to spend some time with a friend and do some shopping for some church clothes. How are you going to spend the day?" Rand asked.

Mr. Clench answered, "I've rented a buggy and we're going to go for a ride along the river. I think my ladies need an outing to get some fresh air. They've been cooped up in the hotel for several days now."

"You will be careful, won't you?" Rand cautioned.

"Yes, we're not going far and won't be gone very long. The ladies want to get ready for tomorrow."

"I'll probably see you later today then." Rand excused himself and headed out the door, anticipating spending the day with Peter in his new life adventure. *This is going to be fun. Anyway, I hope it is. I'm going to miss Peter when I leave. I wonder what he will end up doing.* Rand shook his head and chuckled out loud. *Who am I kidding? I'm going to miss Josephine Fisher more than anyone. I wish I could have more time with her, but I don't suppose that will happen. I need to send a telegram to the main office as soon as George's replacement gets here. I don't have any idea what I'll be doing next.*

At the railroad car, Rand tapped on the door. He recognized Josie's voice, "Come on in, Rand, we're just about ready."

Rand stepped in, took one look at Peter all decked out in his finery, and whistled. "Man, you look like some of those rich folks I've seen back east. Are you sure you want this rough looking cowboy to go with you?"

"Are you kidding?" Peter quickly replied. "I'm going to need you and Josie to help me get comfortable around people again." He was thoughtful a moment then confessed what was bothering him. "It's hard to explain, but in my mind I still see myself with those ugly red scars, like they were after the accident."

Josie looked at him and smiled. "I'm going to be pleased as can be to walk the town with two handsome men. Let's get going."

The three stepped down off the platform at the back of the train car and Josie moved in between them. They both offered her their arms and she hooked a hand in each of their elbows.

Peter was the first to speak. "While we're walking can we talk about Emily? I'm feeling somewhat guilty for leaving her out of this."

"Don't feel guilty, Peter," Josie said. "Emily has had so much hurt lately. Her mother and father died in that train wreck and that was enough to send anyone into depression. Her injuries are healing nicely, but it still takes a toll on a person when they go through something that traumatic. The hardest part for her has been finding you, Peter, and then having you walk away. She knows in her *mind* that you did it to protect her, but her *heart* is having a hard time accepting it. She knows that she has to let you go."

The trio started seeing familiar people as they strolled along the boardwalk. A lot of them knew Josie and the whole town was getting to know Rand since the chaos at the sheriff's office and bank. Rumors and stories spread like wildfire in a town like Cheyenne. Josie kept them moving along by waving or nodding a greeting instead of stopping to chat. She kept up her conversation as they enjoyed their walk.

"I don't want Emily to get hurt again like that, Peter. You may decide you want to go back to your mountain. I want you to be *sure* of what you are going to do before we let Emily know you're still here."

"That's fair enough, but I can't imagine me wanting to go back to that life. You've opened my eyes, Josie, and last night my mind exploded with all the possibilities. There's the hardware store. I'd like to go in there if you two don't mind. The owner has been a friend and is the one who saw that my supplies got on the train. He's holding my money for me and I would like to look at some boots."

As they left the hardware store, Josie told them about the dinner that Mrs. Fitzpatrick and Emily had planned. "Are you going to be there, Rand?"

"Sure, I'm planning on being there."

"Good. Mrs. Fitzpatrick has been telling different ones that it's a thank you to all the people who helped find Emily. But actually, it's a surprise birthday party for Emily. She appears to have forgotten all about her birthday so don't let the cat out of the bag! What would you think about Rand and me surprising Emily by presenting you to everyone?"

"Wow! I don't know," Peter said. "Do you think that's a good idea?"

"Well, I think it's a wonderful idea. Yes, it will be a shock but I can't think of a more wonderful birthday present to give to Emily."

"If you think it's all right, I guess I'm fine with it."

"How do you feel about that idea, Rand?" Josie asked.

"Why don't *you* present Peter as your birthday present. I didn't do anything," Rand protested.

"Oh, yes you did. You're the one who talked Peter into coming back to town."

After a thoughtful moment, Rand agreed. "All right then, but don't make a big deal about me, please."

Peter got excited about the turn of events in his life. "Will you help me pick out a birthday present, Josie?"

"Yes, I will, but if you two can manage without me, I need to go check on my father and do a few more errands. I think Dr. Mayfield is going to let Dad go home to sleep in his own bed tonight, since he is doing so well."

After Josie helped Peter pick out two beautiful combs for Emily, she left the men to fend for themselves.

"I've got to hurry if I'm going to be ready," Josie mumbled to herself. She dearly loved being in disguise. There had been a lot of dangerous times when she was on a job, but this was going to be fun since she knew she wasn't in any danger. She had stopped at the doctor's office and spoke with her father, informing him of what she was going to do. She also confirmed with the doctor that her father was doing well enough to go home that afternoon. But he had to follow all the doctor's orders and take it easy for at least another week.

Josie was in high spirits when she arrived at her home. There was one trunk in particular she needed and she knew exactly where it was. After getting the trunk and dragging it into her bedroom, she began to transform herself into a little old lady. She ironed the wrinkles out of the old fashioned dark blue dress, that had a high neckline and a collar edged with white lace. The sleeves were long and had cuffs of the same white lace. She tied on the padding used to alter her figure and stepped into the dress, pulling it up, then buttoning the dark blue buttons up the front. A careful appraisal in her full length mirror caused a grin to spread across her face. "*Perfect,*" she announced. "Now for the wig."

Heavy stockings, dark clunky shoes, white powder to make her look pale, white gloves, a shawl, a cane, and a hat on top of the gray wig almost finished her costume. *One more thing . . . where are those glasses? Here they are!* Josie placed the thick lenses on her nose and pulled the netting over her forehead. She giggled as she looked at herself. *With these glasses, Rand can't look into my eyes. That would be a dead giveaway for sure.* Practicing her slow shuffling walk, hunched over the cane for support, sent a shiver of excitement down her spine. She had practiced long hours after watching and imitating a neighbor, about a year ago. The lady was almost eighty eight and had been the perfect example for Josie to mimic.

"Ready!" she finally said. "Now, let's see if I can fool two young men."

Josie shuffled her way down the boardwalk. Rand was going to take Peter to a café several blocks away, where Emily and her grandmother were not likely to be. Josie had timed her walk perfectly to when the men walked out of the café, she would be in place.

There they are!

Using her cane for balance and slightly stooped over, she stepped down to the dirt road just as a wagon came toward her. She didn't hesitate but kept going as if she didn't see the wagon. *That wagon will make it look more realistic.*

For a moment, Josie thought the men might hurry on past and mess up her act, but then Rand noticed and yelled at her as the wagon rumbled closer. "Hey, lady! Watch out for the wagon!"

Josie drew back as if frightened and dropped the bag she had in her hand. All manner of things rolled out of the bag and in all directions; several balls of yarn, knitting needles, scissors, and numerous other paraphernalia that women were known to carry.

Rand ran into the street after the wagon passed by. "Are you all right?" he asked.

Peter was right behind him and began picking up some of the items that had fallen out of the bag.

"My, oh my. *Clumsy* is what I am," Josie stammered in a raspy whisper. "My eyes are not as good as they used to be, but to tell the truth, I wasn't paying attention to where I was going. I was just worried about a friend of mine." She looked around, all confused like. "I should have been paying attention to where I was going."

"Here you are, ma'am." Peter handed her several of the objects that had fallen out of her bag.

Two more wagons were coming from different directions, trying to get around the three seemingly crazy people in the middle of the road. Rand got impatient with one man who began yelling at them. He glared at the man and held out his hand to signal *stop*. "Hold your horses!" he shouted. "Or I'll arrest you and throw you in jail for being a nuisance!"

The man started to return a barb of his own but seemed to think better of it when he realized who Rand was. "Sorry, Marshal, take your time."

"Let me help you to the boardwalk, ma'am." Rand handed the lady's bag to Peter. "Will you get the rest of her things before we all get run over?" Rand took hold of Josie's arm, and gently led her to safety. "There now, Peter will have all your things gathered up in just a minute."

Josie watched unobtrusively as Peter struggled to find everything with only one good eye. *Good for you, Peter. You're doing just fine.* To Rand, she said in a shaky voice, "I didn't mean to be such a bother."

"It wasn't any bother, ma'am."

Peter joined Rand on the boardwalk. "Here you go. I think I got everything."

"What nice young men you are to this old lady. How can I ever thank you?"

"Don't worry about a thing. We were glad to help." Rand smiled into the thick glasses. "You said you were worried about your friend. Does this friend live here in town?"

"Oh, yes, he lives here in town and runs the telegraph office. My grandson told me he was seriously hurt when some outlaws beat him up. Poor sweet Josephine. I've come to help her take care of her father."

Rand almost choked at the thought of this fragile old lady taking care of anyone. He thought she might be on the verge of tears when she started sniffing. "Are you talking about George Fisher?" he said as he handed her his handkerchief.

"Thank you," she sniffled. "Why, yes, do you know him?"

"Yes, I know George. He's at the doctor's office but I think they're going to let him go home this afternoon."

"That is indeed good news. Could I impose on you two to see me to the doctor's office? I'm feeling a little tired."

Peter and Rand both agreed at the same time that it would be no trouble at all. Peter offered to carry her bag. "If you'll let me take your bag, you can hang on to both of us and we'll have you there in no time."

The three walked painfully slow toward the doctor's office as Josie kept up a running dialogue, mostly with herself. At one point, she giggled and said, "I haven't had this much attention in a very long time. Makes me feel like a young girl again."

The men were enjoying themselves and smiled at each other over the sweet, fragile, little old lady's head. They finally got to the doctor's office and stepped into the room where George Fisher was. He called to the trio, "Is that you, Mrs. Simpson? Where did you find those two young men to escort you?"

"Just found them out on the street, George. How are you doing? I've come to help Josie take care of you tonight."

"You shouldn't have bothered, Mrs. Simpson. We would have gotten along fine."

"Maybe, maybe not. Joel dropped me off at your place and will be back for me in the morning. So you're stuck with me until then. When you weren't at your house, I started walking. Just about got run over but these nice young men rescued me."

Rand shook George's hand and introduced Peter to him. "Glad to hear you're doing better today. Is there anything we can do for you?"

"Well, now that you mention it, I'd appreciate it if you two would go hire a buggy for me to ride home in. Doc doesn't want me walking that far, but it seems silly to hire a buggy just to take me across town."

Josie carried out her scheme perfectly. Rand and Peter hired a buggy and saw Mrs. Simpson and George to the house. On the porch, as they were saying their goodbye's, Josie finished her act with a promise. "I've just decided what I'm going to do to show my appreciation for all your help. While I'm helping Josephine take care of George, I'm going to knit my two heroes, nice wool scarves to keep your necks warm this winter."

Rand started to protest but then thought better of it. "That would be real nice, Mrs. Simpson. You take care now."

Chapter 23

"I CAN'T TELL YOU, RAND, how much I enjoyed yesterday with you." Peter smiled at his new friend. Since they were going to church and a party afterward, Peter had on a new suit, white shirt, and a string tie.

"Glad you did, Peter. I can honestly say I enjoyed it too. You know, I haven't had a good friend since I left home. My cousin, Aaron, was the best friend a man could want. We had a lot of good times working hard together, hunting and exploring the mountain wilderness behind our home. Now he's got a family, so I suppose those times are long gone."

"You're blessed to still have family. Mine are all gone. I've wondered if I still have family back in Ireland and think I might sail back there someday and see if I can find any of them."

"What do you plan on doing now, Peter?"

"I don't know yet what I'm going to do. A lot depends on Emily and how she feels about me now. I hope she can forgive me for walking away. At the time, I felt like I needed to make a clean break and get out of her way so she could go on with her life."

"Well, you'll soon find out. Did you have any trouble getting the wig and eye patch on?"

"Not too much. The eye patch was tricky. Does it look all right to you?"

"Yes, you look fine, Peter, and did a good job. A person would have to look real close to see any scars. Everything covers them very nicely. I'm somewhat jealous of the eye patch, though. Josie was right when she said it would attract women. The ones we passed in town yesterday seemed to have a hard time looking away. I even saw a few smiles aimed at you from some of them. You can't tell me you didn't notice."

Peter laughed. "Yes, I noticed. You got your share of women looking your way too, but I suppose you didn't notice, did you?"

"It'd be hard not to notice," Rand added, grinning. "I think it must be the red hair. You know what they say about red-headed cowboys, don't you?"

"Can't say as I do, so why don't you tell me."

"Let's see, it goes something like this. 'Listen good women to a word of advice, to catch a cowboy, you have to be clever and nice. In your pursuit of a cowboy lover, a redheaded one will love you forever."

"I think you're the one that's clever," Peter teased. He paused a moment. "I hear church bells in the distance. We better get going."

"Yeah, if we ride slowly, we shouldn't get there too early. We'll be able to sit near the back of the church. You ready for this?"

"Yes I'm ready. My nerves are working on me but I'm looking forward to going to Sunday services. It's been about two and a half years since I've had a chance to go."

"It hasn't been that long for me but I'm still looking forward to today."

Rand had brought an extra horse for Peter and they mounted up and started out. They made quite a sight trotting down the main Street of Cheyenne. A sign over the door of the church read: *Cheyenne Community Church*. All manner of conveyances were scattered around the perimeter of the yard. The day was bright and clear, only a smattering of light clouds in the sky. An old hound dog, lying in the back of a wagon, rose up just enough to watch the two men make their way into the church where the congregation was already singing a hymn.

They found a place to sit that was close to the back and someone handed them a hymnal after they got into place. Not wanting to draw attention, Peter and Rand sang along very quietly. During the second hymn, both men became very still and listened. Somewhere close to the front, two voices blended in beautiful harmony as the congregation sang, 'Fairest Lord Jesus'. No doubt about it, one of the voices belonged to Emily Fitzpatrick. But who was the alto voice that blended so nicely with Emily's soprano? Rand peered around people's heads to see who it was. *I should have known! It's Josephine singing. Is there anything that girl can't do?!*

During the second stanza, a hush fell over the sanctuary except for the two girls' voices. Josie faltered and looked around to see what had happened to everyone, but Emily kept singing, nudging Josie to keep on also. The song finally ended, ushering in a reverent stillness, and then the pastor spoke.

"I feel the presence of the Lord Jesus with us this morning. Josie and Emily have truly blessed us with their beautiful voices and have led us perfectly into the next song. You may stay seated as we join our voices with theirs in, 'Nearer My God to Thee'".

Pastor Reefer, as everyone called him, was a big man, his voice calm and gentle as he started speaking. "Would you all stand for the reading of God's Word? Open your bibles to 2 Peter 3:10-18 and follow along." After reading the text of his sermon and offering a prayer, the pastor spoke about the day of the Lord coming 'like a thief in the night', saying the heavens shall pass away with a great noise and the elements shall melt with a great heat, the earth also and the works that are therein shall be burned up.

"Now let's think about verse eleven. It's saying here that since we know all that is going to happen, what manner of people aught we to be?" Pastor Reefer continued through the scriptures carefully covering the attributes of a Christian life. All was quiet as he made a final point. "Since we know Jesus Christ is going to come like a thief in the night to take all believers to heaven to be with Him, I'd say, well, you better be ready! To give your life to Christ should not be something you put off for another day. As the scripture says 'today is the day of salvation.' Let's sing, 'Nearer My God to Thee', again, as our closing hymn. Please make sure you're ready to meet the Lord when He comes to take you home. Are there any announcements or does anyone have something to say before we close with the final hymn?"

"I do."

The congregation rustled with movement as they tried to find who had spoken. Emily stood and addressed the pastor, with a face full of determination. "I want to do what the bible says to do."

"In what way do you mean, Miss Emily?" the pastor smiled as he asked.

"Well, I've been reading my friend's bible and it says in the book of . . . Romans, I think it is, that if we confess about Jesus and believe in our hearts that God raised him from the dead, we can be saved and go to heaven. Anyway, it says something like that and I want to do it now. Is it all right if I do that now?"

"My dear lady, I see no reason why you can't declare your belief in the Lord Jesus Christ this fine day."

"Thank you. I would like very much to tell everyone what happened to me." The pastor nodded his permission for Emily to continue. "Most everyone probably knows that I was the only survivor on the train that was wrecked and robbed. Peter, the man who rescued me, asked me if I believed in God. During our capture by outlaws and during my captivity I came to realize I do believe in God and Jesus Christ. I believe that he died for me and I want to give my life to Him now."

Rand glanced at Peter who was intently watching and listening to Emily. *Wonder what he's thinking. Sure hope it all turns out good for him and that girl he loves.*

The pastor looked pleased. "You have courageously confessed your belief before men and that's important. Maybe there is someone else here who would like to confess their belief in the Lord Jesus Christ." A hush fell over the room as a shy, young girl about fifteen years old stood. "Wonderful," the pastor said. "Anyone else?" No one else stood so he asked Emily and the young girl he called, Daisy, to come up front and talk to him after they sang the final hymn.

Peter and Rand were the first ones to leave the building. Peter tugged at Rand's sleeve and motioned him over to the side of the yard. "Rand, I *have* to talk to Emily! This isn't right not telling her I'm here. What will she think of me?"

"I know you're anxious, Peter, but I think you should at least wait until it's more private. You don't know what her reaction will be and I don't think you want her embarrassed in front of a crowd. Besides, she's talking to the pastor now, anyway."

"Yeah, I guess. But I'm not going to wait very much longer. You know, I love her and I don't . . . ."

They were all of a sudden distracted by the sound of sobbing coming from behind a bush at the corner of the church. They approached cautiously and found a boy sitting on the ground, crying his eyes out. Rand squatted down in front of him. "Hey, little man, what's wrong?"

Two big brown eyes looked back at Rand with an expression of misery. "I need to find the Marshall, the one who can find people. Charlie told me he might be in church today. Charlie is my friend. Did you see the Marshall in the church?"

"Well, I'm a Marshall," Rand said. "Who do you need to find?"

The boy appeared to be about seven years old with dark brown hair that looked like it hadn't been combed for several days. His overalls were wrinkled and dirty. He rubbed his tear stained eyes. "His name is Jack. Will you help me find Jack?"

"My job is to help people and catch the bad guys, so I guess I can help you find Jack. Tell me about him. How old is he?"

The boy shrugged. "I don't know."

"Well, is he as big as you are?"

A crowd had gathered and some teenager laughed out loud. "It's his *dog*, Marshall. A black and white mutt of some kind. Toby, leave the Marshall alone. He's got better things to do than chase around after your silly old dog."

The boy called *Toby* jumped to his feet. "He ain't no silly old dog! He's my best friend." Toby looked up at Rand who was now standing beside Peter. "Will you still help me find Jack even if he *is* a dog?"

Rand smiled at Toby. "You know, I think a boy's dog is very important and I would say it's my duty to help you find Jack. Where's the last place you saw him?"

The heartwarming smile from Toby showed two missing front teeth. "Last time I saw him was before I went to bed last night. Mrs. Redden won't let him come in the house so he sleeps in a box by the back door. He wasn't there this morning and I can't find him anywhere!"

A woman in the crowd came closer. "Where is Mrs. Redden, Tobias? She didn't come to church today."

"No, I don't think she feels very good," the tyke answered. "She just stays in bed and sleeps. She won't wake up. She must be real sick to stay in bed. She ain't woke up for two days."

Alarmed, Rand glanced at the lady who had spoken to Toby. "Do you think you could get the minister and a couple of women to check on Mrs. Redden?"

The woman nodded, already turning away. "Of course, we'll go right now."

Rand turned back to Toby, who was staring and scowling at Peter's eye patch. "Is he a pirate?" the lad asked, his face scrunched with suspicion.

Rand couldn't help but smile. "This is a friend of mine. His name is Peter O'Donnell. I guess you'll have to ask *him* if he's a pirate."

The moment Rand heard a sharp gasp from behind him, he realized his mistake. *Oh no, me and my big mouth!* He turned to find Emily glaring straight at Peter.

"Emily . . ." Peter started toward her, tried to reach her through the crowd. "Please, let me explain . . . It's not what you think."

Emily took a step back and then another. She could only gape at the handsome stranger who was said to be Peter O'Donnell. "Peter," she stammered. "No . . . no, you're *gone* . . . You . . ." Hurt and confusion clouded her face as she turned and fled to her waiting carriage and the safety of her grandmother.

Josie reached out to Peter, stopping his advance toward the carriage. "This is my fault, Peter. Let me talk to her and explain. I think she will listen to me. I hope so, anyway."

Peter could only nod. "Then go, Josie. *Make* her understand. Please!"

Before Josie turned toward the carriage, she pointed her finger right in Peter's face. "Don't you *dare* leave town! And both of you better be at that dinner party or I'll find you and make you wish you had never been born!" She whirled around and rushed to the carriage.

Rand took a deep breath and let it out slowly. He clapped Peter on the shoulder. "I'm sorry, Peter. Looks like another Josie-storm has hit. Are you up to helping me find Toby's dog? We should have time to hunt it down before the dinner party and we don't *dare* miss that. I think she meant every word she said, and I'm not sure we would survive the next storm!"

Chapter 24

"WHAT DO YOU MEAN it's your fault? Are you telling me that you *knew* Peter was still in town?" Emily dabbed at her red eyes, still full of confusion and anger.

"Yes, I've known he's in town and it's my fault we kept it from you." The look on Emily's face made Josie squirm. She was definitely guilty and wanted desperately to explain the rationale of her actions. "When I tell you why, I think you'll understand, and hopefully forgive me."

"I'm listening," Emily bristled. "Although I can't imagine why someone I thought was a friend would keep something like that from me."

"It's *because* I'm your friend that I asked Peter to wait before he talked to you."

"You mean Peter *wanted* to come to me? It wasn't his idea to stay away?"

"That's right. He felt really bad for not letting you in on what we were doing."

"Oh, Josie, you better start from the beginning and tell me everything. This is very confusing."

Josie was aware that Nicholas Clench and Mrs. Fitzpatrick were listening from the front seat of the carriage as it swayed and bounced down the road through town. She also noticed that Nicholas was driving randomly with no particular destination in mind. Nicholas and Cecilia would glance at each other from time to time but kept silent, letting the girls talk things out.

Josie sighed, settled back in the seat, and started her story. "Do you remember that Rand left the morning after you were rescued, to try and find the outlaw that got away?"

"Yes, I remember."

"Well, he happened to run into Peter that day when he came across a wagon train headed west. Peter had hitched a ride on that wagon train to get back to the mountains. Rand told him that since he was still close to town, he wanted Peter to come back to Cheyenne in case they needed him as a witness when the judge came to town. He also told him that he wouldn't have to see anyone unless they needed him to testify. So Peter came back and Rand hid him in Mrs. Fitzpatrick's train cars, you know, the ones on the side rail, and arranged for meals to be brought out to the car."

"So, that's where he's been. I was wondering."

"Yes, but when all the outlaws were killed, Rand knew he had to let Peter go. That's when I found out what Rand had done. He confided in me that he was going to have to tell Peter he could leave, but he just couldn't figure out how to help get you and Peter together. That's when it came to me."

"When *what* came to you, Josie?"

"Remember when we prayed at the doctor's office about what to do about Peter?"

"Yes, I remember quite clearly."

"I think it was because of that prayer that the answer came to me."

"Go on, then, and don't leave *anything* out."

Josie could see that some of Emily's hurt and anger had turned into eager anticipation, so she told Emily everything else including being raised in a circus family atmosphere and that she and her father were special agents for the Pinkerton Agency. "So, you see, I didn't want you to be hurt again if Peter didn't want to come back into a life with wigs and special clothes. It will be quite an adjustment for him. But I think he's doing it, mainly for you, Emily."

Emily sat quietly for a full minute before she spoke. "I'm sorry I was angry with you, Josie. I think I understand now. But whatever do we do now?"

"We go get ready for a dinner party. Rand and Peter will both be there."

"Are you sure? Peter might not come, now."

"Yes, I'm sure. Peter wants to be with you as badly as you want to be with him. Besides, I threatened to hunt them down and make them sorry if either of them didn't show up."

Cecilia Fitzpatrick spoke for the first time since they had gotten into the carriage. "Nicholas, take us to the hotel. We have a party to get ready for!"

"I'm so nervous, Rand, my hands are shaking. You go in first and see if it's safe for me. I don't want to cause Emily any more stress than I already have."

Peter and Rand were on the boardwalk in front of the hotel. Rand turned to grin at Peter. "Man, I don't blame you for being nervous. I'm nervous myself, but I don't want to face Josephine Fisher's wrath by not showing up. Let's go in *like men* and show them what we're made of! Besides, I think Emily would help Josie hunt us down and make us sorry we were ever born if we don't make our appearance. I have a feeling that *together* those two women would be a mighty force to reckon with."

"You're probably right. Well, let's get it over with. Might as well face our fate now."

The men entered the hotel and were immediately greeted by a heavenly aroma. "Ah . . . It sure smells good in here. I'm glad you talked me into staying," Peter said.

A hotel maid appeared as soon as the door shut behind them. "Right this way gentleman. Mrs. Fitzpatrick reserved the entire dining room for this afternoon party. We've never had anything so elegant here before. It's just wonderful!"

The dining room was a beautiful sight. A long table with pristine white cloths held white tapers and colorful spring bouquets on each end and in the middle. Each place was set with gleaming silverware and yellow colored napkins in a fancy fold. Across the room by the fireplace sat George Fisher in one of the comfortable padded chairs. He waved them over.

"Come on over here, you two. I have my orders that I have to stay in this chair and rest, so I need company. That's the only way Josie would let me come." George waited till Peter and Rand seated themselves, then leaned toward them and whispered conspiratorially, "Actually, she said if I didn't take it easy she would throw the peach cobbler to the hogs and I wouldn't get any. So, here I sit until I get my fill of cobbler, then we'll see what happens. I'm tired of just laying around."

Rand laughed at George. "I hope that means you're feeling well and on the mend."

"Sure enough, I am. I had a bad headache yesterday, but today, I'm doing a lot better."

Nicholas Clench entered the dining room and made his way over to the men. "I'm glad to see you all here. Oh, there is Valentine coming in. Come on over here, Mr. Matson. Let's all make ourselves comfortable. The women will be down . . . who *knows* when they'll be down!"

Rand had to fight his emotions to keep from laughing at Val. He wore a new suit of clothes, had a haircut, his beard trimmed, shiny polished boots, and acted like it was an everyday occurrence to be at a fancy party. "I almost didn't recognize you, Val, with you all 'gussied up'."

Val, who had sat beside Rand, responded solemnly, "I'll have to admit it's been a while since I got all 'fanci-fied' for a party."

"Looks like our last two guests have arrived." Nicholas stood. "If you men will excuse me I'll bring Dr. Mayfield over and send his wife upstairs with the women. Then we'll introduce Peter to everyone. I haven't really been introduced properly, myself, so sit tight until I get back."

Half an hour later, the men stood when a flurry of chatter and rustling petticoats were heard descending the stairway. "Brace yourselves, men, you're in for a special treat, but be steady and prepare for an onslaught of feminine intrigue!" Nicholas Clench spoke quietly so just the men heard that comment. Then he put a charming smile on his face, turned on his heel, and led the men to the ladies who were coming into the dining room.

"There you are, ladies, and I must say it was well worth the wait to behold such beauty."

Cecelia Fitzpatrick beamed at Nicholas. "Thank you, Nicholas. Are you men ready to sit down to eat?"

"Have you ever known me to *not* be ready to eat?" Nicholas answered.

"You're right. I don't know why I even asked. While you get everyone seated, I'll go tell the kitchen staff to bring on the food."

While Nicholas coordinated the seating, Emily turned toward Peter. He stood frozen to the floor as she made her way over to him. "Peter, I would like for you to sit next to me," she said, as if nothing had ever transpired between them. "That is, if you don't mind."

Peter stood mute, staring at this beautiful woman. He had been around important and famous people in his short life on the stage and didn't consider himself shy or quiet, but for the first time in his life, he couldn't think of a thing to say. His mouth was so dry his tongue stuck to the roof of his mouth. "I . . . well . . . I . . . mind?"

"Are you all right?" Emily asked. "Do you or do you *not* want to sit next to me?"

"No! I mean, *yes*! I mean . . . No, I'm not all right and yes I want to sit next to you."

"What's wrong, Peter, are you ill?" she said with alarm.

He knew he sounded like he'd lost his mind but at the moment he didn't care. Emily Fitzpatrick was only a few feet away, wearing a beautiful yellow gown, the shade of his mother's favorite roses at the farm where he had grown up. Her black hair was piled on top of her head with ringlets framing her face. Pearls were entwined in her hair and a string of them were around her slender neck. Peter finally did find his voice but what came out of his mouth was nothing but eloquence.

"Emily Fitzpatrick, you are a vision of loveliness. I knew you were a beautiful woman, but right now you take my breath away! The only food I need is to feast my eyes on your beauty. I would gladly sit anywhere you asked as long as I can memorize your gorgeous face and gaze into your enchanting eyes."

The room had grown quiet as everyone listened to Peter's declaration. Now Emily was tongue-tied. She stood speechless and unmoving as if a spell had been cast upon her.

Val broke the spell. "Well said, young man. Those were mighty pretty words and I agree. Every woman in this room is a feast for the eyes. *You* may not need any grub, but I'm starving, my stomach needs more than eye food!"

Everyone laughed and the party was underway. The food was delicious and the conversation around the table covered many topics. Josie asked Peter and Rand if they had found Toby's dog and was relieved when they said yes. "I'm so glad you found him. That little boy has lost so much these last few months. He was the only one in his family who lived after an outbreak of cholera on the wagon train they were with. Mrs. Redden agreed to keep him until some of Tobias's family could be found. She was elderly, but seemed to be pleased to have Tobias stay with her. She told some of the women that he was a big help to her." Josie searched Rand's face when she asked, "Mrs. Redden was dead, wasn't she?"

"I'm afraid so. We think she probably died in her sleep a couple of days ago. The pastor took Tobias home with him. I wish you could have seen the look on the little guy's face when the pastor told him that Jack could come in the house and sleep in the room with him."

Val asked George about the new man in the telegraph office. "Does that mean you'll be leaving, George?"

"I suppose so, Val. I'm not sure just when. The new man is bunking in the office until Josie and I find out what we're supposed to do next. I figure we'll be getting our orders soon.

What do you think the town will do about a sheriff, Doctor Mayfield?"

"The town council will meet next week," the doctor answered. "They'll decide what to do then, but in the meantime the young deputy sheriff is doing a good job. We just need to find him some help real soon."

The conversation flowed smoothly until everyone had eaten their fill and Nicholas stood to get everyone's attention. "This has been a most enjoyable day and Cecilia and I want to thank you for coming. First, I want to tell you that Cecilia has agreed to be my wife and we will be married as soon as we get back home."

This announcement created a stir of excitement as everyone clapped and voiced their congratulations. Nicholas finally held his hand up and called for silence. "The next thing I want to do is express our gratitude to those of you who were instrumental in finding and bringing Emily back to us safe and sound. We count you as our friends and will be forever grateful for all you've done for her."

Cecilia stood and moved closer to Nicholas. "I agree this has been a wonderful day but it is not over yet. There is one more thing we are going to celebrate today and that is the twenty-second birthday of my granddaughter!"

Emily's reaction was what everyone had hoped for. Total surprise. "Is it . . . I didn't even . . . think . . . are you *sure?*"

The guests burst into laughter as a birthday cake was brought in at that moment and the room was filled with birthday wishes. Peter got up and stood behind Emily's chair to make room for the cake to be placed in front of her. *She's twenty two years old, now I won't have to ask her age. Just find time to talk to her alone. She's been awfully quiet during the meal, I'm not sure what that means but I intend to find out. God, prepare my heart for our conversation and give me wisdom to know what to say and do.*

Mrs. Fitzpatrick got everyone's attention again. "Molly is going to put the cake on the dessert table along with some of our Josie's wonderful pastries, so help yourself. Please stay as long as you like. We look forward to visiting with everyone and getting to know you better. Now, let's move over to the comfortable chairs by the fireplace and let the ladies in the kitchen clean up the table."

Rand stood and helped Josie out of her chair. He whispered in her ear, "There wouldn't happen to be a chocolate cream pie over on the dessert table, would there?"

"I guess you'll just have to go over and look for yourself," she whispered back, standing closer than necessary. "But remember, I only fix special things for the people I care about."

Valentine drew Josie's attention away from Rand, but she watched from the corner of her eye and saw Rand walk casually over to the table loaded with desserts. He turned back toward her with the biggest grin on his face. "Val, let's go over and get a piece of that birthday cake."

Val offered his arm. "I'd be pleased to walk you over and see all the sweets you made. I'm sure I can find something I like."

Val's attention was soon taken up by one of the serving ladies and a big piece of cake. Josie scanned the room, her heart light and happy. She watched Rand take a big bite of chocolate pie, close his eyes, and lose himself in the taste of something heavenly. He opened his eyes and looked straight at her, winked and went for another bite.

At that moment, a server hurried over to Rand, poured him a cup of coffee and discreetly handed him a piece of paper. Rand reluctantly put his unfinished pie on the table by his chair. He unfolded the paper and quickly read what was there, folded it again and put it in his shirt pocket. He tried to act nonchalant but the scowl on his face said the note was serious. Josie knew he was trying to cover up bad news when he pasted on a smile and acted like nothing was wrong. She started toward him but Emily caught her arm.

"Josie, Peter and I are going to walk and get some fresh air, maybe watch the sunset. Grandmother suggested that you and Rand might like to join us."

Chapter 25

"Look at those two," Josie said. "I would really like to hear what they're saying to each other. It's nice they finally have time alone to share how they feel." Emily and Peter were walking ahead of Josie and Rand. "I think they're going to be all right, Rand. Don't you think so?"

"I think it might be a safe bet since he's been holding her hand and she hasn't objected."

"She's a beautiful woman and such a good friend. I hate to think of us going our separate ways, but it's going to happen real soon now. In a couple of days the pastor will go with them to the gravesite where her mother and father are buried. The grave marker was put in place sometime yesterday. I suppose they'll be leaving after that."

"Have you heard where you and your father will be going now?" Rand asked.

"Not yet, although I'm sure we will be hearing from the main office soon and going back east. Dad and I are not typical agents. Actually, I'm not even an agent, but they know I help Dad when he needs it. We're more like . . . undercover spies. We go into a situation and get information to help the other agents. The new telegraph operator is bunking at the telegraph office until we leave, then he'll move into the house we've been staying in." Josie stopped and turned toward Rand. "What about you?"

"Oh, I suppose I'll be leaving soon too."

Josie stopped and frowned. "Rand, out with it! What was in the note Molly handed you? I could tell by the look on your face it wasn't good news."

Rand smiled. "I don't think I've told you how pretty you look tonight. I love that color of blue on you. It makes your eyes glow and your hair looks nice done up like that."

"Stop it, Rand. What did it say? Are they calling you back east?"

Rand didn't speak right away. He looked over Josie's shoulder at the dark clouds forming in the west. "I guess you could say I've got my orders."

"Well?"

"Well, what?"

"You know *what*. What did it say?"

"Maybe I don't want to say right now. It's something I need to think about."

"Can't you share it with me and we can talk about it? Maybe I can help, or maybe you don't trust me yet."

"It's not so much a matter of trust, Josie. It's your eagerness to help that worries me. I don't think I could live with myself if I pulled you into a dangerous situation again and you got hurt, or *worse*."

"Does that mean you care for me . . . just a little?" The quirky smile on her face told Rand she was teasing.

"You know very well that I care for you *more* than just a *little*. That's one of my problems. I care too much." Josie eagerly waited to hear more. "I've never even been tempted to get involved in a relationship with a woman until now. I've seen at least three marshals killed in the line of duty and leave a wife and kids. One man was crippled for life and can't take care of his family. I swore I wouldn't get married and have kids because I've seen firsthand the pain it caused those families. I don't want to do that to you. Besides we don't have time to figure out if we were meant to be together. Our lives will be going in two separate ways, real soon now."

"You sure don't give a woman much credit, Rand. The right woman would understand the risks of marrying a lawman. She might even be a great help."

"You might be right, Josie, but I've got bigger problems to deal with and can't think about something as serious as that right now."

"I understand, but I promise if you share your problem with me I won't get in the way or do anything without your permission. I just want to help."

"I was hoping you didn't see me get the note." Rand took a deep breath and slowly let it out as he reached into his pocket for the note. Reluctantly, he handed it to her.

Josie silently read:

Dangerous outlaw sighted getting on train in Ohio. Headed your way. Train arrives Monday afternoon. Arrest on train. Escort back to main headquarters on eastbound train Tuesday. Hire one man to help bring him back. Look for likeness on poster at local sheriff's office. Warning, killed six men, two marshals. Name, Charlie Lancaster, AKA, Cutthroat Charlie. May have brother in Cheyenne area.

Josie refolded the telegram and handed it back to Rand. They were silent as they continued their walk. A full five minutes went by before Josie spoke again. "Do you know what you're going to do?"

"Not yet, but I need to talk to Deputy Jones and get a hold of that wanted poster. Sounds like they expect the brother to be around somewhere in this area and cause trouble. I've already made up my mind to ask Valentine if he'll help me get the outlaw back east. I'll try and catch him before he leaves the party, so I'd like to head back to the hotel now, if you don't mind."

"Sure, I understand. Let's get Peter and Emily's attention and head back."

"Josie, I want your promise that you'll keep this quiet. I'm not going to tell Peter and I don't want you to tell Emily or your father. He doesn't need to get mixed up in something like this yet. I just can't let it get out what I have to do. If the brother here got wind that a U.S. Marshal was getting ready to arrest his brother on the train, there's no telling what he might do."

"Is there any way I can help?"

"If you can come up with some way to keep the towns people away from the train station tomorrow that would be a great help. The least amount of people around, the better it'll be for me."

"I'll pray about it and come up with some . . . you know, I already have an idea."

"That was fast! What's your idea?"

"I've been thinking of asking Emily and Peter to sing for us, but instead, I'll ask them if they'll give a free concert at the church tomorrow afternoon, for the whole town. That will get almost everyone to the opposite end of town away from the train station."

"You know, that just might work! Smart girl! If you can set that up it would take a heavy weight off my shoulders. Let's head back." Rand whistled to get Peter's attention and motioned that they were going back to the hotel.

Sometime later, Rand approached Josie. "Val has agreed to help me and we're going to go now and find the deputy. Will you meet me here for an early breakfast? I'll need to know how your plan goes."

"Yes, I'll be here around six. I haven't been able to talk with Emily and Peter yet, but I will before long."

"All right, see you in the morning. And Josie, you really do look beautiful. The prettiest girl in town tonight."

Josephine Fisher's smile was radiant. And, while the smile was there, her heart was in turmoil. *Oh, Rand, what are we going to do? I don't think I can stand to see you walk out of my life.*

"Good morning, Rand. You ready for a cup of hot coffee?" Josie had been watching for Rand to get there. He seated himself at a table close to the kitchen door.

"Good morning, Josie. Coffee sounds real good. How long have you been here?"

"Not very long. You look tired. Didn't you get any sleep last night?" She placed a cup in front of Rand and poured it full of steaming coffee.

"Oh, I guess I got enough. Did you talk to Peter and Emily?"

"Yes, I did. I'll tell you all about it but let me get your order in so it can be cooking."

"Wait, what I'd really like is a piece of that chocolate cream pie if there's any left. Maybe I'll feel like eating more later."

"I'll go check and be right back." Josie returned with a large piece of the pie and a cup of coffee for herself. She placed it in front of Rand and sat down across from him. "You were lucky, that's the last piece of that pie."

"Thanks. It's just what I need to start my morning. Aren't you going to have something to eat?"

"Not right now," Josie said around a yawn. "I was up later than usual talking to Emily and Peter. He was reluctant at first but we finally got him to agree to the concert this afternoon. He got into the spirit of performing with Emily once we started planning. The afternoon train usually comes in around four o'clock if there's no problems. I know a couple of teenage boys who will get the word out about the special performance at four o'clock at the church. It's short notice and not the best time of day, but I'm guessing anyone who's in town or lives close will be there."

"That should work. Thanks, Josie. Is four o'clock the regular time for the train?"

Josie eyed him carefully as he scooped pie into his mouth. "Are you really all right, Rand? I just told you the train times, not thirty seconds ago. Maybe you didn't get enough sleep. Anyway, I'm really looking forward to the concert. How did you and Val do last night?"

"Val took me to the deputy's house and we clued him in on what's happening on the way to the sheriff's office."

"Did you find the wanted poster?"

"Yeah, at first I was afraid he didn't have it and that could be bad for me, but we finally found it at the bottom of the pile. The man looks older than I thought he would be."

"Do you have the poster with you?"

"No, I left it at the sheriff's office. Val and I studied it and tried to come up with different ways he might disguise himself. The best way to recognize him is by the lobe of his left ear. It has a fair-sized nick out of it. He's probably about sixty years old and slim. If you get a chance, drop by the sheriff's office and take a look at it."

"I'll do that."

They sat in comfortable silence as Rand finished his pie, both lost in their own thoughts until Rand wiped his mouth with a napkin and leaned back in his chair with a contented sigh. "That was good! Just what I needed this morning."

"I'm glad you enjoyed it. What are you going to do now?"

"I'm going to meet up with Val. He stays with his friend who owns the livery stable when he's in town. We're going to the smithy's to get him working on some good heavy shackles for when I take Charlie Lancaster back east. I'll shackle him in a freight car to keep him away from passengers."

"That's a good idea. Are you going to use any other men besides Val and the deputy to arrest the man?"

"I don't think so. The three of us should be able to get the job done if everything goes like I hope it will. I'll arrest the outlaw, put him in jail for the night, and be on the east-bound train in the morning."

"What about the outlaw's brother?"

"I don't know, Josie. I'll just have to handle that one if or when he shows up. He may not even be anywhere around and it's entirely possible that Charlie Lancaster got off the train somewhere back down the tracks."

They were silent for a few moments, then Josie, looking worried, asked, "Will we see each other again, Rand?"

He searched her shimmering blue eyes as if trying to find some answer in them. "I honestly don't know, Josie. I would like it very much if we did. Where do you and your father live when you're not on a job?"

"We have a beautiful place outside of Williamsburg, Kentucky, along the Cumberland River. Dad and I love going back home. We don't get to spend a lot of time there, but it's a great place. If you ever get in that part of the country will you look us up?"

"I'd like that." Rand reached across the table and placed his hand over Josie's hand. "If I get *anywhere* in Kentucky I'll make sure to look you up." He reluctantly removed his hand when two cowboys came into the dining room and sat at a table by the window.

Josephine smiled sweetly at Rand. "Please do, I'd love that." They both stood. "I need to get to work now, but Rand, if you think of any way that I can help, leave me a message at the front desk here at the hotel. I'll check it several times today."

"Thanks for helping with everything you've done so far."

Rand watched as Josephine made her way to the table where the two cowboys were. A pang of jealousy hit him in the gut as he watched the cowboys smile and flirt with her. *I have no right to jealous feelings when it comes to Josephine Fisher, but man, it's there and I don't like the feeling!*

Chapter 26

RAND KEPT BUSY AFTER leaving the hotel. He found Valentine and they went to the blacksmith together. He explained to the smithy what kind of shackles he wanted then left him with a warning. "Mr. Hastings, it's important that no one knows I'm going to arrest an outlaw coming in on the train this afternoon. That man has a brother who might be in this area and if he got wind of it, he might cause all kinds of trouble."

"Don't worry about me, Marshal. I'll keep it to myself and these shackles will be ready for you by the end of the day. Good luck to you. Glad you'll be hauling this one out of town and back to prison where he belongs."

"If all goes well that's exactly what I intend to do." Rand turned to leave. "Come on, Val, let's go to the sheriff's office and see that deputy. I want to check out the jail cells before I put anyone in them. Then we'll all three go down to the train station and talk to the ticket agent and the new man at the telegraph office. They'll be close enough to the action that I'll want them to be prepared if anything goes wrong. Can you think of anything I might have forgotten?"

"You've about got it covered, except I've been thinking that you should send a telegram to the station back down the tracks and find out how many passenger cars and passengers are on that train. If there's just one car that would be good, but if there's two or three cars we'll need to change our plans."

"Good idea, Val. That information will be valuable. I don't want anything to go wrong or innocent by-standers getting hurt."

After checking out the jail cells at the sheriff's office, the deputy accompanied Val and Rand to the train depot and telegraph office, where Rand sent a telegram asking the number of passenger cars and how many people were traveling on that train. He read the answering telegram aloud to the others.

"Two passenger cars. Ten men on the first car, two have wives with them. Two families traveling in the second car with seven children. Train running on time."

Rand groaned. "Man, I was hoping there wouldn't be any kids on that train."

Val slapped Rand on the back. "That won't be so hard. Since the deputy here has more authority than I do, I'll take the car with the children and keep them inside and out of the way till you signal that it's safe. You and the deputy can board the first car and find our outlaw."

"All right, Val, that's as good a plan as any I could come up with. What do you think, deputy?"

"I like it, but are you going to take the lead when we board the first car?"

"That's my job. You just back me up and be ready for anything and maybe we can get this done without anyone getting hurt."

The three men shook hands and the deputy left for his home. "Well, Val, we're about as ready as we can be. Why don't we go get some lunch at the hotel?"

"You go ahead, I need to get a bag packed so I'll be ready to go. With both of us spending the night at the jail I won't have time to do that in the morning."

"Good idea, I need to do the same. Come on over to the hotel about three o'clock and we'll walk back over together."

"Sounds good. I'll see you later."

Walking back to the hotel, Rand felt his stomach tighten up. *Maybe I'll skip lunch and just go up to my room, try to relax for a while. . . . Who am I kidding? I'll be nervous until four o'clock and the action starts.* He stopped at the front desk of the hotel. "Will you have someone in the kitchen bring a sandwich and coffee to my room?"

"Sure, Mr. Trinity. Do you want any particular kind of sandwich?"

"No, it doesn't matter. Whatever they have on hand will be fine." At the top of the stairs, he ran into Peter and Emily.

"Hi, Rand," Emily greeted him. "Where have you been all morning?"

"Oh, no place in particular, just here and there."

"Do you want to go with us over to the church? Josie has been there since after her shift at the café getting set up for the concert. She has a couple of men building a small platform, said there will be too many people coming and they won't all fit inside the church so we are having it out on the grounds."

"Thanks for the invite, but I've got something to do here at the hotel. If I get a chance I'll come on down to the church in a little while and see if I can help."

"Good, I'm so excited. This is going to be so much fun, isn't it, Peter?"

Emily looked up at Peter for his response. "Yes, I believe it is going to be a lot of fun. I'll have to admit I had my doubts at first, but after all the planning I think we've got quit a program to put on. You are coming, aren't you, Rand?"

"I don't want to miss one minute of your concert. Having to arrest an outlaw is the only thing I can think of that might keep me from making it for your first performance together."

At least I didn't lie. I don't want to miss it, and would love to be sitting with Josie for the whole thing. The memory of his hand on hers at breakfast came flooding back. *Yeah, I might even hold hands with her and not care a lick if everyone saw it.*

Back in his room, Rand paced, ate half of the sandwich, and prayed. He stretched out on the bed and lamented. *I'm going to miss this bed. Never have slept on any bed as comfortable as this one. Don't suppose I ever will again either.* Rand closed his eyes and went over all the plans he had made. Trying to cover every scenario of what might happen; he decided there was nothing more he could do.

A knock on the door caused Rand to sit straight up. *Can't believe I went to sleep.* "Who is it?" he called out.

"It's Val. You ready to go?"

Rand opened the door. "Yeah, I'll be ready when I splash cold water on my face. I guess I dozed off."

"I don't know how you stay so calm," Val commented, shaking his head.

"I don't stay calm. Don't suppose it shows on the outside but I'm always uptight on the inside until it comes time to act. It's hard to explain, but when I step out to do my job it's like a calm resolve comes over me to do what I need to do to get the bad guy and put him away. Seems to me like it's

God's way of letting me know He's with me. Some might think it's a crazy way to think, but that's how I see it."

"It doesn't matter what anyone else thinks, you just keep believing that way."

The special concert started right on time. A large crowd had scattered across the church yard, sitting in family groups on blankets. A few had backed their wagons to the edge of the yard and were making themselves comfortable sitting in the backs of the wagons. The benches that had been brought out of the church and placed in front of the platform were full. Even though some rough looking characters were mixed in with the crowd, the atmosphere was charged with excitement over a community gathering.

The pastor prayed, introduced Peter and Emily, then stepped down to take his seat. Peter escorted Emily up on the platform and immediately they took command and captivated the audience. Singing a couple of lively songs, the duo had everyone grinning and clapping along with them. Josie was amazed how attentive and involved the crowd had become. Peter invited the children to come and sit on the ground in front of the platform as Emily stepped down and sat by Josie. He told a story of a leprechaun who lived in the woods in Ireland. This mischievous leprechaun liked to scare the children who lived at the farms around the woods. As Peter wove his Irish tale the children sat spellbound, hanging on to every word. He ended by singing an Irish tune that went along with the story. Emily, not taking her eyes off Peter, whispered to Josie, "Isn't he wonderful?"

"I think you're both wonderful," Josie whispered back. She was struggling with wanting to be in two places at once. Though enjoying the concert immensely, she heard the train whistle in the distance announcing its arrival and her heart spun into turmoil. *Be safe Rand. I will stay here because I promised I would help by staying away, but it's harder than I thought it would be. I so want to be with you. God, please keep Rand and the men who are helping him to be safe. Don't let anything happen to him, please!*

"There's the whistle. Are you two ready?" Rand looked at Val and the deputy.

"I'm as ready as I'll ever be but then I've got the easy part," Val commented.

"Don't get too relaxed, Val. I need you to be ready for anything," Rand warned.

The deputy chuckled. "You may have the *hardest* part, Mr. Matson. Seven kids can tie a man in knots in no time."

"You might be right. I hadn't thought about all the young un's, but I figure I can handle that many."

Rand opened the door to the depot. "It's pulling in, let's get in place." Rand, Val, and Garth Jones had been waiting inside the small depot along with the ticket agent. "Remember, no one gets off the train until I get a good look at every one."

Once outside, Val headed straight for the second passenger car, the deputy went to the back of the first car, and Rand quickly made his way to the door at the front of the first car.

He stepped into the car just as people were starting to move around. "I need your attention, please!" he said in a loud voice. "Would you all please sit down?"

The passengers turned in his direction with questioning looks. The Porter who was in the middle of the car helping a lady with a bag frowned at Rand. "Who are you, sir, and what do you think you are doing giving us orders? Is this a holdup?"

Rand flashed his badge that was on his shirt under a vest. "I'm U. S. Marshall, Rand Trinity, and I need to get a good look at each of these passengers."

"Well, yes, sir. In that case we'll just do like you say. Everyone sit down and let the marshal do his job."

"Thanks, it won't take long." Rand made eye contact with the deputy sheriff who was standing by the door at the back of the car. The deputy nodded that he was ready.

Rand glanced at the ten passengers and located only one man sitting at the back of the car that was even close to the identity of the escaped killer. There was a dirty brown cowboy hat pulled down over his eyes and he was looking out the window.

Rand kept his face neutral and spoke to the man closest to him, then moved to the couple sitting across the aisle. As he made his way toward the back, he made a decision. *I need to get these people off the train. The closer I get to the last passenger in the brown hat, the more I'm convinced he's our man.*

Never turning his back on the suspicious man, he said in a loud voice, "Everyone that I've spoken to please go ahead and get off the train."

The porter could be heard ushering people off the train. Then the deputy nodded. "That's it, they're all off the train now."

"Would you please tell me your name," Rand said to the only man left. He was surprised as the man slowly got to his feet and pushed back his hat. Rand was tall, but this man had a couple of inches on him and probably thirty pounds heavier.

"Name is Jim Sanders. What's this all about, marshal?"

"It's about an escaped convict by the name of Charlie Lancaster. Would you remove your hat and pull your hair back?"

"Why would I want to do that? You need to back off, marshal. You've got the wrong man."

"If I've got the wrong man then you won't mind doing what I asked. Take your hat off and pull your hair back away from your face."

With an insolent smile the man reached for his hat.

Rand drew his pistol in a flash. "Take it nice and easy. No sudden moves or you're a dead man!"

The man kept his sneer in place as he pulled his hair back, revealing a nick in his left ear lobe.

Rand nodded at the deputy. "It's him."

"All right, marshal, I suppose you got me. Are you *sure* you can handle what you got?" He laughed, a low and menacing growl. "You don't look old enough to be away from your mama's lap."

Anger flared in Rand for a moment but he tamped it down and showed no reaction to the man's barb. "Move slowly and put your hands behind your back."

The deputy pulled a short length of rope out of his pocket and with a nod from Rand tied the man's hands securely. "Let's take him out this back door and out behind the depot. We'll walk him to the jail."

The transition from the train to the sheriff's office went smoothly. The streets were relatively quiet, thanks to the concert. Only a handful of people stopped to watch as Rand and the deputy marched the man down the street and entered the jail house. Val followed a ways behind watching the roof tops and alleys between buildings.

The prisoner was soon locked up but Val asked, worry in his voice, "What are you thinking, Rand? Something's not quite right."

"I agree, Val, it was *too* easy. He didn't seem worried at all. I watched the whole way and he didn't seem to be looking around for anyone. Didn't even try to get away. Just let us up and take him to jail." Rand stood shaking his head and thinking deeply.

"What are you going to do now?" Garth wanted to know.

Chapter 27

WORD SPREAD QUICKLY THAT the marshal had arrested a dangerous criminal. Josie was tied up with all the details of putting the church in order and seeing that the church yard was cleaned up and ready for the next service on Wednesday evening. After checking if she was needed at the hotel she hurried home.

"Is that you, Josie?

"Yes, it's me, Dad."

"Come in the kitchen and talk to me. I warmed up the stew for us."

"I'll be there in a minute. The stew sounds good. Thanks for heating it up."

When she entered the kitchen a short time later Josie smiled at her father who was patiently waiting at the table with two bowls of steaming stew and plate of sliced bread. When Josie sat down they bowed their heads and her father said a prayer, blessing their food. When he finished the prayer he looked at Josie. "All right, I want to hear all about it, and don't tell me you didn't know what was going to happen. I know you too well for you to deny it. Why didn't you tell me, so I could help?"

"I would have told you, Dad, but Rand made me promise not to tell anyone. Rand tried to hide it from me too, but I happened to see Molly give him the telegram. I pulled it out of him, but he didn't want you put in any danger so soon after you got beat nearly to death. I'm thankful he cared, and believe me it was hard not to tell you. It was harder for me to stay at the concert and not run down here and see if I could help. Have you talked to anyone?"

"Not really. Nicholas Clench and I stopped by the sheriff's office but there were other curious people hanging around so we didn't bother Rand. Garth wouldn't let anyone in the office anyway. He stood outside and told people to go on home. I was feeling pretty tired by then so came on back home and took a nap."

Josie could see the strain on her father's face. "Are you all right, Dad?"

"Yes, I'm fine. I still get tired pretty easy, but that gets better every day that goes by."

"I'm glad. How did you like the concert?"

"It was great. Those two put on quite a show."

"Yes, this town has never seen anything quite like that, and is not likely to see anything like it in the near future."

There was a pause in the conversation as father and daughter ate their meal. When Mr. Fisher pushed his bowl to the side he asked, "What now? You're going to go see him aren't you?"

"I can't keep anything from you, can I?" Josie smiled at her father. "Yes, I need to see him. He'll be leaving on the morning train. That will be a busy time for him, and I don't want to distract him because he'll have so much on his mind. It's going to be dangerous. Charlie Lancaster has a brother that might be in this area, so Rand will need to be alert."

"I hadn't heard that. When we go down to the office, I'll see if he might need me in the morning."

"We?"

"Yes, and no argument, I'm going with you. Don't worry; I'll give the two of you a little privacy to say your goodbyes. He's a good man, Josie."

"Yes, he is." She put the bowls in the wash pan. I'll be ready in about an hour."

Darkness had settled. Noises from the establishments at the rowdy end of town could still be heard. Laughter, loud voices, and piano music were evidence of life after dark. Rand had put a dark wool blanket over the only window in the sheriff's office to conceal movement in case someone got a notion to shoot through the window at him or Val. From the desk of the previous sheriff, Rand pulled out paper and ink that he had seen earlier and started to write by the light of the one dim lantern that sat on the desk.

Dear Josie,

What do I want to say to Josephine Fisher? Maybe it's crazy to even try to write down what I'm feeling. Especially since I'm not sure what it is that I'm feeling. I've never known anyone quite like her. I need to write something, since I won't be able to say goodbye tomorrow. Anyway, I won't be able to say goodbye like I want to.

Rand picked up the pen, dipped it into the ink, and had it poised over the paper when a light tapping sounded at the door. He was so engrossed in his thoughts it startled him for a second. *Man! I didn't even hear them walk up on the boardwalk. I've got to do better than that or I'll get myself killed, and maybe Val, too!*

Stepping to the side of the door, Rand spoke quietly. "Who's there?"

"It's George Fisher, Rand. I'd like to speak to you for a minute. It's quiet out here and no one is around."

Rand unlocked the door to let George enter and was surprised when Josie quickly slipped into the office first with her father right behind her. "Hi, you two. Is something wrong?"

"No, nothing is wrong except my daughter was going to come over here by herself and I insisted on escorting her. Where's Val? I thought the two of you were going to be here together tonight."

"He's here. There wasn't any reason for both of us to be awake all night so we're taking turns staying on watch. We're using the first bunk right inside the door to the cells. Lancaster is in the last cell on the left."

"Do you think Val is asleep yet?"

"I'm sure he's not because I don't hear any snoring. It hasn't been that long since he went in there, anyway."

"I'm going to go check and see for myself. I'd like to talk to him for a few minutes if that's all right."

"That's fine with me. I'm sure he'll fill you in on everything."

George left the door slightly ajar as he went back to find Val. Rand smiled, a mischievous gleam in his eye. "Do you think he doesn't trust me with his beautiful daughter?"

"I'm quite sure it's not *you* he doesn't trust. He knows his daughter all too well."

They stood looking into each other's eyes for the longest time. Josie was the one who broke the silence. "I just had to come and say goodbye in person. I know you'll have your hands full tomorrow. I hope you don't mind."

"I don't mind at all. As a matter of fact, I was just starting to write you a note, but was having a hard time finding the words I wanted to say. Seems like time is against us right now."

"I know what you mean, but let's pray God will grant us the time we need in the near future if that's what His will is for our lives."

"I like that idea." He stepped a little closer to Josie. "Let's don't waste these few minutes your father has given us talking about things we can't change. I have something else on my mind."

"Oh? And what is that?"

"I'd rather *show* you than tell you. It's something I haven't been able to stop thinking about ever since we shared that kiss while watching the outlaw's cabin."

Josie just smiled and in two steps, Rand had Josephine Fisher in his arms. They gave and received kisses that spoke more than words ever could. Finally, Rand pulled away enough to look into her upturned face. "My feelings for you are mighty powerful, Josie," he whispered.

"I know." Her eyes were shimmering in the dim light of the lantern. "What are we going to do?"

"We are going to do what you just said. We'll pray for time to be together in the near future. And I mean, *near* future."

"Did I say that?"

"Yes, and it was good advice. By the way, thanks for the help you gave me in getting the concert set up. It worked perfectly and the area around the train station was quiet." Still holding Josie snuggly in his arms, Rand asked, "Will you tell me about the concert?"

"It was *wonderful*, Rand! Those two did a beautiful job. You would have thought they had been performing together for years; they were such a huge hit! The most amazing part was at the end of the program. Peter had Emily sit on a chair on the stage, and he asked her to sing the love song she had written for him. I think she truly was surprised by that but she sang to him like he was the only one in the world. Like it was just the two of them alone in their secret hide-away. When she finished singing, Peter set the guitar aside, got down on one knee in front of her and sang to *her*. He had added his own verse at the end of the song. Emily had to wipe tears from her eyes several times, along with a number of the audience who were dabbing their own eyes. Oh, Rand, it was so wonderful! Would you believe he proposed to her right there in front of everyone?"

Rand chuckled.

Josie pulled back so she could see his face. "Did you *know* he was going to do that?"

"Well, not exactly. He mentioned it, but the last time we talked he hadn't made up his mind yet."

Josie considered that for a few moments. "It's awfully fast, but if you had seen them singing to each other . . . I don't see how anyone could doubt their love."

"Peter is a level headed man. He told me he would make sure they had a long enough engagement for Emily to be sure she wanted a life with him. By the way, what did she say?"

"Are you kidding! She threw herself in his arms and said *yes*! Scared me for a minute. I think she almost knocked Peter's wig off. That wig doesn't fit him like a specially made one will."

"Will you tell them I'm sorry I missed the concert but they helped me tremendously by keeping the town people out of the way."

"Yes, I'll tell them. But, Rand, we only have a few more minutes until Dad comes back in. Will you hold me until then?"

"There's nothing I would like more." Rand took Josie in his arms again, gently kissed her, and held her until her father stepped back into the room.

"It's time for us to leave, Josie."

Chapter 28

"HAVE WE COVERED EVERYTHING, Val?"

"As near as I can tell, we're ready to go."

"Good, I know there are things that will come up that we haven't thought of, but the important things are covered. Don't be afraid to speak up if you feel uneasy about anything. And Val, thanks for helping me with this. There aren't very many men in this world that I would trust like I do you."

"I'm mighty glad to do it, Rand. We'll get this job done, then you can go find that gal you was dreaming about last night. You was talkin' in your sleep, you know. I think what you said was, 'Kiss me again, you *sweet thing.*'"

"I don't talk in my sleep and you know it, you old goat! Why don't you go and order breakfast for the three of us."

"All right, if you say so. Do you want me to go to the train station and see if the train is on time?"

"No, it's a little early for that. This may be the last chance we get to eat a good meal for a few days, so we'll take our time and enjoy it. Order *plenty,* I'm hungry this morning!" Rand paused and eyed Valentine. "And, Val, be safe out there. Keep an eye out for trouble."

"You bet I will."

Valentine Matson returned a short time later, after placing an order at the hotel kitchen. Rand unlocked the door and let him in then quickly bolted the door again. "It's real quiet out there this morning," Val said. "I suppose word has gotten around that we'll be puttin' that varmint in the cell back there on the train."

"Let's just hope it stays quiet."

"Yeah, at least until we get to eat our breakfast. I hope you're real hungry cause I ordered *big* just like you told me. They were going to send a couple of ladies down with the breakfast, but I told them to find some men to do it and keep the ladies inside out of the way."

"Good thinking, Val. I wish I could keep Josie out of the way too. She has more courage than most men and she worries me to death."

Val chuckled. "You got that one right. She's got more spunk in her than I've ever seen in any young woman I've known and I've known quite a few in my time. It's going to take a strong man to keep her in line but he'd be one mighty lucky fellow to lasso that filly."

The two friends talked until a loud knock sounded at the door. Two men stood just outside with large heavy trays of food. After taking the prisoner his share, Rand and Val didn't waste any time digging in and polishing off most of the food on the trays.

A few moments later, Rand took out his pocket watch, checked the time, then sighed deeply. "It's time to go get the wagon. I hate to make you do all the running, but I feel responsible for all of this and feel like I need to stay with the prisoner."

"I don't mind doing the running. It beats sittin' in a chair watching the time go by. I'll just go get the buggy, stop by the blacksmith shop and load what we need from there. I already put out bags and bedrolls in the wagon."

"Did you get plenty of ammunition?"

"Yep, just like you asked me to."

"All right then, let's kick the plan into motion."

Rand watched out the window observing the activities that were beginning to take place in town. He noticed Val had been right about the number of people out this morning. About an hour later, Val drove a wagon right up to the door. He had the blacksmith on the wagon with him.

"I just now checked with the ticket agent," Val said. "And he said the last message was the train is running early. Did you know this is the first east bound train since the track was torn up by those outlaws?"

"No, I didn't, but I'm glad we're going to be on it. I'd hate to travel by horseback all the way back east with this man."

"Yeah, I don't think I would like that either. Do you want the shackles put on that weasel right now?"

"Yes, let's get him shackled now then you and Bob can go wait for the train."

Rand was pleased with the job the blacksmith had done. He explained the mechanism to Rand. "When the train comes in I'll attach this bolt with this iron ring to the main support on the train car. It will probably be the corner support and when you slip this long heavy chain through the ring over the hand shackles and down through the ankle shackles, I'll hook the two ends of the chain together and I promise you this man won't go anywhere. Also, you'll need another blacksmith to get these shackles off." The blacksmith looked at the prisoner. "Mister, the less you move around the better it will be on you." The prisoner, for the first time, truly looked worried. "Put your hands out in front of you," the blacksmith ordered.

"I'd rather die than be shackled up with those chains," the prisoner snarled. He suddenly grabbed the blacksmith by the front of his shirt and shoved him as hard as he could toward the door of the cell where Rand was standing guard with his weapon in hand. In the next moment, Rand was on the floor with Bob Hastings on top of his legs, his pistol knocked loose and out of reach. The prisoner then jumped over the two men on the floor but the blacksmith had quickly rolled off of Rand and grabbed the leg of the prisoner, yanking him to the floor. Rand was on top of the prisoner in a flash, but Charlie Lancaster wasn't about to give up without a fight. A wild wrestling match ensued with a few blows landing here and there, but Rand's youth and experience soon enabled him to subdue the prisoner. The ruckus had brought Val running in from the front office and it took all three men to hold Charlie Lancaster down to get the shackles on his wrists and ankles.

Val quickly tired of the vile cursing coming from newly shackled man. "Mr. Lancaster, if you don't shut your mouth, I'm going to take off my dirty socks and stuff them in your mouth with a gag to hold them in there!"

"Well, I'm glad that's done," Rand said, wiping blood off his lip.

"Sorry I let him get the jump on me, Marshal," Bob Hastings apologized.

"Don't worry about it," Rand answered. "It was more my fault than yours. I should have known he'd make a move like that. You did a good job, Mr. Hastings. What do I owe you?"

"Not a thing, Marshal. This one's on me. I'm glad there was a lawman around to take care of that gang and arrest this criminal. If we're going to have a decent town we need good lawmen. I'll go with Val now and when that train comes in, it won't take me long to attach this special bolt and ring to the car."

"Val, go ahead and take Mr. Hastings to the depot and wait for the train."

When Val and Bob Hastings came back, Rand stepped out on the boardwalk and looked around. He was glad to see Deputy Garth Jones with Val and Bob. The deputy jumped down from the seat of the wagon.

"Good morning, Marshal. I thought I'd better let you know that I have about twenty men all along the road to the depot. Ten on one side and ten on the other and they'll be watching for any trouble. They're all carrying rifles in plain sight and every one of them is on the boardwalk or the ground. If you see anyone suspicious in windows or on the roofs, they're *not* one of our men."

"Thanks for the extra help, Garth. Val is going to drive and I'll be walking behind the wagon. Would you like to walk with me?"

"Sure, I'd be happy to."

The two lawmen escorted the prisoner out to the wagon and loaded him in the back. "I don't know why you needed so many men to look after one little old man," the prisoner growled. "All shackled up like this, I'm not likely to go anywhere."

Rand ignored the man's comment and motioned for Val to start the wagon forward. The walk to the train was uneventful, but Rand knew he couldn't relax just yet. He checked out the train cars and saw there were three passenger cars toward the front followed by four freight cars. Rand, Val, and the prisoner were going to be in the last car.

"Val, you and Bob go in first and be ready to . . . ." Before Rand finished his sentence, he heard a familiar voice calling from across the street.

"Yoo-hoo, Marshal Trinity! Wait up a minute!"

Rand couldn't believe his eyes. Josie was running toward him. "What are you doing, Josie? Go back home!"

She ignored his demand and ran right up to him while the other men froze in their tracks, all gawking at the pretty Josie. "I just *had* to bring this little package for you to take with you," she said sweetly. "It's just a little reminder of your time here in our town." She handed him a package wrapped in plain brown paper. "I wrote my name and address right *here*," she said as she tapped the package with her finger.

Rand stared at the package, reading an urgent message where Josie had tapped her finger. He finally looked back at her. "Thanks, Josie. It was thoughtful of you to think of me."

"You're welcome. Have a safe trip. Goodbye, Marshal."

Josie quickly left the same way she had come. *Bless you, Josephine Fisher. You did it again.* Rand stood a moment, then made a decision on how to handle the new situation that Josie had put in his hands. *I don't want these men in more danger than they are already in. I've got to get them away from this car.*

Rand handed the package to Val, making sure the message was facing him. "Val, will you hold this package a minute?"

Val took it, glanced down at the writing then handed it to the deputy, nodding to Rand that he understood what was expected of him. Signaling to Bob, Val quietly told him to take cover behind the wagon, then he and Garth got into position to back Rand up.

Scanning the area, Rand was pleased to see men around the perimeter of the depot with rifles in hand. *If it is Charlie Lancaster's brother in this car, he's not going anywhere. Now if I can just get him to come out without anyone getting shot.*

With a quick glance inside, Rand could see that one end of the car was piled with stacked freight boxes and the other end was where their gear was and where they would be riding. *No place to hide except behind some of the freight.*

There wasn't much cover for Rand, but he used what was available, standing with his back pressed against the door of the car. Facing the freight area, he called out, "Come on out! We know you're in there and you don't have a chance! Throw your guns out and make it quick!" There was no response. Rand tried again. "Don't be foolish. If you are someone just trying to get a free train ride, we won't shoot, we'll let you get off and leave. But, you better make yourself known *right now* if that's the case."

Still no response. "If you're a Lancaster and trying to help your brother, listen and listen carefully. You haven't done anything wrong, *yet*. I didn't find any wanted posters on you so don't make it worse on yourself. There are more than twenty armed men outside this car and it's impossible for you to get away."

The silence told Rand it was Charlie Lancaster's brother hiding in the back. "I'm a patient man, but your time is about up, Mr. Lancaster. Make up your mind right now or get filled with lead!"

"All right," a voice answered. "Don't shoot, I'm coming out!"

"Your gun comes out first," Rand ordered. "Put it on the floor and push it out." A rifle came sliding out from behind the crates. "Now your pistol."

"I don't have a pistol," the hidden man said.

"Come out then with your hands high in the air. No sudden movements. I don't want to mistake any quick movements in the wrong way."

Finally, a man came out from behind the crates. He was almost identical to his prisoner, Charlie Lancaster, but was dressed nicely, like a fancy gambler, and was thinner. "Val, bring the prisoner on up here. Deputy, get this new one tied up. Be sure to check him thoroughly for other weapons. A lot of his kind likes to hide those little derringers up their sleeve."

After Deputy Jones tied the hands of the new prisoner and checked for hidden weapons, the two brothers came face to face.

"Hi, John, it's been a long time," said Charlie Lancaster.

"Yeah, I tried, brother. I guess we gambled and lost this one."

"Enough of the family reunion," Rand said. "Deputy, keep him covered while Val and I help Bob chain our prisoner to the car."

In about half an hour, Rand and Val stood at the door of the freight car looking out at the group of men who had backed him up.

Deputy Jones asked, "What do we do with this one?"

"Are you sure you got all hidden weapons he might have?" Rand asked.

"Yes, found his hide-away derringer and two knives."

"Good, he's all yours. Just hold him long enough for the train to get far enough away that he can't catch it. Then let him go. If he gives you any trouble, hold him until the judge comes to town and charge him with interfering with the duty of a U.S. Marshal."

Rand smiled and spoke loudly so all the men hanging around the depot could hear him. "I want to thank you and all the men here who helped me today. It's a good thing when the people of a town stand behind the lawmen trying to protect them. Thanks to all of you."

"Thanks to *you*, Marshall Trinity," said Deputy Jones. "I'm proud to have worked beside you. Watch yourself and have a safe trip."

Rand's eyes swept the group of men in the area of the depot building. He smiled and started to turn when he spotted Josie standing on the porch of her home. Emotions flooded him at the sight of her standing alone watching him leave. He quickly turned to Val. "Will you be all right for a few minutes, Val?"

"Sure," said Val, following Rand's line of vision, a big grin on his face. "This varmint here isn't going anywhere, so go do what you've a mind to do."

Rand jumped to the ground and all eyes were on him as his long legs quickly took him across the depot yard and up on the porch of the Fisher house. For a moment, he stood directly in front of Josephine Fisher, just taking in the sight of her pretty face.

"Josie?"

"What is it, Rand?" Her shiny blue eyes were full of questions, longing, or something else Rand couldn't quite define.

"It's tearing me up inside to leave you here."

"I know, Rand, but it can't be helped. You have a job to do and I understand that. One of the things I love about you is your integrity and honesty to do what's right and finish what you start."

"I'm glad you understand, but I want you to also understand I *am* going to Kentucky and getting you as soon as I can. Will you wait for me?"

"Are you asking me to marry you?"

"I guess that's exactly what I'm asking. We'll work things out. I love you, Josephine Fisher and can't think of anyone I would rather have by my side and live to be an old man with."

Rand didn't wait for Josie to answer. He pulled her into an embrace and kissed her with all the longing he felt in his heart. When Josephine returned the kiss with passion, Rand knew he had his answer. The two on the porch were oblivious to the blowing train whistle and the cheers and calls from the men watching.

As Rand made himself step away and turned to leave, Josie stopped him. "Rand?"

"What?"

Her parting smile was one Rand would never forget. "I love you, too, and I'll be waiting. Just don't make me wait too long. I hate to wait."

"I'll find the fastest horse there is and be there before you know it."

Rand dashed off to the train car and Val gave him a hand up. "Well done."

Rand leaned out the door of the train and signaled the engineer to move out. In moments the train jerked forward. Rand stood at the doorway and watched the town slip away. He caught sight of the Fisher house and a Josie standing on the porch. She lifted her hand in a gesture of farewell. He returned the wave, but was keenly aware of emptiness in his heart as the house faded away. When the town was a dot in the distance, his eye caught sight of the package Josie had handed him. He picked it up and sat down on the hay that Val had put on their end of the car to sleep on. He read the note again.

Danger. Man climbed in train car after Val left. Looks like brother.

"Pretty clever, isn't she?" Val commented.

"I can't deny that."

"Go ahead and open the package. Let's see what she put in it."

"It's probably nothing. Just her way of getting me the message, but I'll open it just to make sure."

Rand was wrong. In the package was his freshly ironed handkerchief and a rusty-red colored knitted neck scarf that would look nice with his red hair. Before he could make sense of what he was looking at a note fell out of the scarf. He read the note to himself.

> Dear Rand,
>
> I wanted to return your handkerchief you loaned me when you and Peter helped me across the street. And here is the neck scarf I promised to knit to keep you warm this next winter. Wear it and think of me.
> Love,
> Josephine Fisher

Rand sat dumbfounded for the longest time, staring at the scarf and handkerchief. Val was dying of curiosity. "What is it, Rand? What did she say?"

Rand chuckled out loud. "She did it again, Val. She fooled me *again*." Rand then took the scarf and wrapped it around his neck. Thinking he would find the fragrance of roses he had smelled on her hair, he buried his face in the scarf and inhaled deeply . . . then lifted his nose, a puzzled look on his face. All of a sudden he broke out in riotous laughter. Trying to gain his composure, he blurted out in spurts, "How . . . does she . . . do it?"

"Do *what*?" Val demanded, frustrated with curiosity.

"I don't know how she does it but she continues to amaze me."

"What did she do?"

"The scarf?"

"Hot spit, Rand, what about the scarf?"

"The scarf smells like chocolate cream pie!"

Part 2

Make Believe Meadow

Chapter 1

"MA, WHERE ARE YOU!?"

"I'm on the front porch." Anna Summers dropped the shirt she was mending into her lap and looked up with concern as her fifteen-year-old daughter hurried out on the porch, mumbling around a piece of bread she had grabbed off the kitchen table.

"Ma, you've got to come with me! There is a man . . . I think he's hurts bad . . . uh, maybe even dead by now!"

"Beth Ann, slow down and start over. I can't understand what you're telling me with your mouth full. Start at the beginning. Where did you ride today? You didn't go farther than your pa said you could ride, did you?"

Perplexed, Beth Ann flinched as she knew guilt was evident on her face. She knew her mother could read her like a book and she didn't want to lie. "Oh, maybe a little, but I was all right. That's not what's important. That man might need help."

"What man are you talking about?"

"I don't know who he is. He was just lying there on the ground. I didn't see any blood, but I could see his chest moving up and down, just slightly though. I was nervous about getting too close."

"Thank goodness you used your head and did the right thing. How long will it take us to get to this man?"

"An hour if we really hurry." Under her breath she muttered, "Maybe more."

"That far, Beth? You would be in real trouble if your pa knew."

"Don't tell him and he'll never know. He keeps us like prisoners way up here in these mountains. What am I supposed to do, sit in this cabin all day?"

"Never mind that now. I'll change into riding clothes. You go saddle my horse, or do we need the wagon?"

"It'll have to be horses. We'd never get a wagon where we're going. Besides, Fred took the wagon for supplies. He won't be back until late tomorrow."

Beth Ann Summers dashed toward the barn and Anna Summers hurried into the house, tossing her sewing on a chair by the door. While she dressed for riding, her mind raced through the items she might need.

A short time later, Beth Ann hurried through the back door of the house. "Are you ready, Ma? Bell is all saddled and out back with Star."

"Yes, I'm getting an extra blanket in case we need it. Get that flour sack on the kitchen table and tie it on Bell. I'll be right out."

Anna Summers loaded the rest of her things on her horse. "I've been thinking the two of us needed to go for a ride again, but I didn't mean for it to be this way." She mounted her horse and smiled at her daughter. "All right, I'm ready. You take the lead, Beth, but don't get in too much of a rush. We have time to check on this man and still get back in time to take care of chores before nightfall."

Mother and daughter didn't waste any more time talking; they rode out of the hidden valley they called home for close to five years. Anna's mind kept recalling her daughter's words. *She's right, we are prisoners. I've got to get her out of here before she figures out just how much of a prisoner we really are.* Her next thoughts were even more chilling. *She's almost sixteen and I don't like the way a couple of the men are watching her. Even her father is noticing her as a young woman. I don't think he would ever hurt her . . . but . . . he might . . .* Anna felt a shudder run through her body. *It scares me to think what he would do to keep her here. No one takes what belongs to Dean Summers! No one! Unless he gives it.*

Beth led the way, zigzagging through beautiful heavily wooded areas and small glades that still had a few wild flowers showing their colors. The trees hadn't yet exhibited their brilliant red and gold of fall, but there was already coolness in the evening air. It wouldn't be much longer till winter. Anna knew before winter came to the mountains she needed to get Beth Ann out of Dean's hands. She just hadn't figured out how.

Beth had been following a narrow trail at the base of a cliff. As she came to a wide spot in the trail, she slowed her pace and Anna rode up beside her. "We're almost there, Ma. I've been thinking we should leave the horses here. There won't be room for us and both horses where he's at. Let's take our rifles and check things out. It's not that far and I can come back for what we might need."

"All right, but let me go first."

In a few moments, Anna got a glimpse of an arm laying partway on the trail. She stopped and scanned the area for danger.

Beth's quiet voice, close to her ear, gave her a start. "How do you suppose he got there, Ma?"

"Let's get a bit closer and maybe I can figure out more. Keep your rifle ready in case he tries to pull something." Making sure there was no immediate danger, Anna made her way to the stranger. He looked relatively tall, with silvery gray hair and a neat mustache the same color. She guessed his age to be fifty or so. He was dressed like most cowboys, only different somehow, but she couldn't quite figure out how. There was just something about him that made her think he was an important man. A man of strength and character.

"Beth spoke quietly again, "Looks like he's still out cold. I don't think he's moved an inch since I found him. He's alive, isn't he?"

Anna took a deep breath, got down on one knee and touched the man's shoulder. She shook it gently. "Mister, can you hear me?" She could feel the warmth of his body but there was no response.

Beth got down beside her mother. "Do you see any blood? Do you think he was shot?"

"There's a small amount dab of blood under his head." Anna looked up. "You know, I think he must have fallen from that ledge up there, hit his head on the way down . . . maybe, yes, there's a rock under his head. I wonder if he has any broken bones."

Anna checked the man's arm that was stretched out on the trail then reached across his body and felt the other arm. The light-weight jacket he was wearing slid away and both Anna and Beth gasped, then froze at what they saw. One of the tiny shafts of light that filtered through the tree overhead created a small burst of light on a U.S. Marshall's badge.

"Oh no, Ma, what are we going to do?"

Anna didn't answer immediately but when she did, her voice was harsh and troubled. "I don't *know*, Beth! I've got to *think!* Let me think." She finally looked at her daughter and saw the hurt in her daughter's hazel eyes. "I'm sorry, honey, I didn't mean to sound so angry. It's not *you*. I just didn't need this kind of trouble. But we'll figure something out. Will you go get the canteen and the cloth that's in the sack on my horse? Then look around and see if you can find the man's horse. He has to have a horse here somewhere. Maybe up above us."

Beth left and was back very quickly with the water and cloth. As she turned to leave again, her mother stopped her. "Beth?"

"What, Ma?"

Anna smiled to soften her words. "Please be careful. I don't want anything to happen to you."

"I'll be careful, don't worry."

Anna was surprised when Beth came back in a short time. "I didn't have to go find his horse, Ma. His horse found Bell and Star. I tied him up with them."

"Is his horse all right?"

"As far as I can see he looks great. He's a big dapple gray gelding. I rode Star up above and saw where the man fell, but it doesn't make any sense *why* he fell. Looks like he just dropped off his horse to the ground and rolled over the cliff." Beth watched her mother finish cleaning off the blood from the marshal's head. "What are we going to do with him, Ma?"

Gently, Anna laid the man's head back on the ground and stood facing her daughter. "We've got to move him and I'll need you to help me. You do understand we can't say a word of this to anyone. No one must ever know where we've put him."

"Where are we going to take him?"

"Remember that old cabin we ran into this summer, the one that was in a pretty alcove to the west of the house? It's hard to see and not too far from our place."

"Ma, that thing is about to fall apart. I'm not sure it would be safe."

"It has stood this long and is probably a lot sturdier than it looks. We don't have much choice anyway. It will have to do. Our biggest problem is getting him there. I'm not even sure we can get him on a horse."

A deep masculine voice startled both of the women. "I can probably do it if you two ladies will help me."

"Oh, thank goodness you're awake." Anna went down on her knees beside the marshal again. "You hit your head on a rock when you fell. Are you sure you can get up?"

"I won't know until I try," the marshal grimaced. "When my head quits spinning I'll give it a go."

"You took quite a fall. Are you hurt anywhere else?" Anna asked.

"My hip feels like it's on fire." The marshal shifted his weight. "That's part of the problem, landed on my pistol when I hit the ground. I don't think my hip is broken though, probably just bruised. Sure hope my pistol isn't broken either. I've had it a long time and wouldn't feel right without it."

"You should be more worried about yourself than some stupid gun!" Anna said, irritated.

"You're right, lady, but a pistol can mean the difference between life and death if you're a lawman. And I'm worried more than you know about the state of my health."

"Sorry I spoke so harshly," Anna said. "You've just brought trouble to me and my daughter that is going to be difficult to deal with."

"No, I'm the one that's sorry, but I'm going to need your help at least for today. I'll try to not be a bother after that. I think I'm ready to try and get up now."

Anna slipped her arm under the man's neck and helped him try to sit up. Half way up he sucked air in through his teeth and moaned. "Lay me back down, I'm not ready yet."

She did as he requested and waited. She could feel the anxious presence of her unusually quiet daughter standing behind her. "Beth, wet this rag again for me."

Beth dashed some water from the canteen on the rag and handed it back. Anna cooled the face of the marshal. "You're as white as a ghost, mister. Are you sure you're up to this?"

"I'm not sure of anything right now. I think we moved too fast that first time. Made my stomach roll over. I'm ready to try again. Let's just go slow and easy."

The second attempt got the marshal to a sitting position but he leaned heavily on Anna. A long low rumble of agony came from deep within the man's throat. "I hate to tell you this but I'm afraid my leg is broken. It's throbbing like thunder right now."

"Which one?"

"Right leg between the knee and ankle."

"I'm going to lay you back down and check it out," Anna said.

The marshal and Anna made eye contact. Their faces were close enough he could have kissed her if he'd wanted. Instead, he whispered, "Go ahead and do what you have to do. I appreciate it, Mrs. . . . ."

"Anna. Just Anna."

With Beth helping, Anna did what needed to be done, just as the marshal said. She felt him stiffen, fighting the pain, then slip into unconsciousness when she straightened the broken leg. Beth helped her with the splint. "It's crude, Beth, but it will have to do. I'll wash his face and see if he'll come around. Bring his horse here while I rouse him again."

When the marshal rallied again and after a small sip of water the three managed the task of getting him into his saddle. The gray gelding seemed to sense the seriousness of what was happening and stood quietly. Beth told her mother, as they were getting ready to leave, "I know a shorter way to get to that cabin. If you'll help him, Ma, I'll lead the way."

"Go ahead, then. I'm glad you know the trails like you do. Take it easy though. If he falls off his horse I'm not sure we could get him back on again."

After a number of stops to make sure the marshal was secure in his saddle, they finally reached the old dilapidated cabin. "Beth, come take my place and hold him on his horse. I'll hurry and make a place to put him in the cabin."

An hour later, U.S. Marshal, Lance Chambers, watched as the two women rode away. There was no door on the cabin. It had fallen off the leather hinges long ago. "Well, God, I'm not sure why you let me get in this predicament. But, I suppose you'll help this fifty-one-year-old man through this mess, like you've helped me through all the other messes I've been in."

Even though his head was pounding and ached ferociously, Lance glanced around and took stock of his surroundings. *What more could a guy ask for? I've got a roof over my head, saddle bags within reach, canteen of water, my rifle, and a blanket to cover this body that aches from head to toes. Those two women surely saved my life and I'm grateful. But I wonder how involved those two are with the gang I'm after.* Lance tried to ignore the thoughts that crowded into his mind, but it didn't work. They crowded their way in anyway. *It's been so long since I've been that close to a woman, I plumb forgot how soft and sweet smelling they can be.*

As the long night of misery stretched out before him, Marshal Chambers began doing what he knew was the only thing that would see him through the night; he started praying and quoting scripture.

Chapter 2

"JUDGE CRAMER, THERE'S SOMEONE here to see you."

"Who is it, Samuel?"

"He must be the extra marshal you asked for. Says his name is Rand Trinity."

"It's about time! Send him in."

Judge Cramer heard his clerk in the hallway telling the visitor to 'go right in'. He was aware of footsteps approaching his desk and felt the presence of a person standing before him, but kept his head bent over the papers on his desk, not looking up until he had signed off on the document he had been reading.

Rand Trinity stood quietly waiting for the judge to acknowledge him. A musty smell of age and the lingering odor of cigar smoke hung heavy in the room. Finally, the judge looked up at the man who stood respectfully before him. He found a tall, red headed, young man with a cowboy hat in his hand. He was nicely dressed, lean and muscular, and didn't even flinch as the judge sized him up. Rand Trinity could almost read the judge's mind and was enjoying the moment, as if he knew what was coming next.

"You *can't* be the U.S. Marshal I sent for. Who are you and what do you want?" His voice was edged with irritation.

"I'm Rand Trinity, U.S. Marshal, sent to report to you. I was told you would inform me what you needed when I arrived here in Lexington."

"I need a *man* not some *kid*! I need someone with maturity and experience. You'll have to go on back to where you came from and I'll wire Washington, have them send someone else. I don't have time to nursemaid some beginner."

"Sorry to disappoint you, Judge Cramer, but there is no other marshal who could come right now. I just finished my last assignment and they sent me here. As I understand, the matter here is urgent and since I'm here why don't you let me help. It may take weeks before there's another marshal free to help you."

"Blast it, what's a man to do!?" Red faced, the judge looked ready to explode.

"Sir, are you a believer in the bible?" Rand asked quietly.

"What kind of question is that? Of course I believe the bible. My grandfather was a preacher and I was raised with the teachings of the bible. I've got news for *you* if you think you're going to teach me something from the bible."

Rand was calm when he answered, "No, not teach you, but maybe remind you of what Paul said to Timothy about not letting any man despise his youth. I've wanted to be a lawman since I was fourteen and my father was killed by some no account gang robbing a train. Those men were never brought to justice. I've spent the last few years learning the law and riding with some of the finest marshals in this country. A man has to carry his own weight after a while. I've had a couple of assignments that I've carried out successfully on my own. I would ask that you not look down on me because I'm young but let me help you. Let me do what I've been trained to do. And if I was honest, which I am, I'd say it's what I know God wants me to do."

The judge pulled his eyes from Rand's face and stared out the window for a few moments, then looked back at the young marshal. As he faced Rand again, he conceded. "All right but if you feel this isn't the right assignment for you, I want you to tell me right up front, so we don't get you killed and waste a lot of time."

"That's a promise, Judge Cramer. Just tell me what to do."

Judge Cramer removed his spectacles, laid them on the table and rubbed the bridge of his nose for a full minute before he began. "Have you ever met Lance Chambers?"

"Sure. I spent some time with him a couple years back. Tracked a lone outlaw through the hills of Tennessee with him. In the middle of the night the outlaw had gotten the banker and his wife out of bed and forced him to open the vault at the bank while holding a gun to the wife's head. He took the money then shot and killed both the banker and his wife."

"Are you the one that was with him? He told me about that. Said this new kid marshal who was riding with him was better at tracking than he was. Learned it from his Arapaho friends. That was you?"

"Guess I'm the only one it could be. I learned to track from my Arapaho friends in the Dakota Territory where I lived on a ranch with my uncle. I don't know about being better at tracking, but we made a good team. Marshal Chambers called me *kid* all the time to annoy me. But the truth is, I learned a lot from him on that assignment. He's not only a top notch ranger but as Godly a man as I've ever met."

"Maybe they sent the right man to me after all." The judge stood up and paced the floor a few moments. "Lance Chambers is the best friend I've ever had. I'm afraid he's in trouble and is either dead or in need of help. My problem is . . . I feel responsible."

"Why would that be?" Rand asked.

"Because after a couple of months of investigating, he came to check in with me. He said he thought he had an idea of how the gang was working. Then right here in front of me he had a spell with his heart. Scared me but he wouldn't let me call a doctor. Said he'd already seen one and there wasn't anything that could be done. He said he's only had a few of the spells and that they don't last long. I tried to convince him to let someone else handle this and that he should retire. Ha! Like talking to a brick wall. But he did tell me that this would be his last job and begged me not to say anything so he could finish what he started."

Rand shook his head. "I sure hate to hear that. We need men like him in this country. Tell me more about what he was working on."

"Marshal Willis Russell is tied up with the proslavery group that are terrorizing blacks and black sympathizers in the counties north of here, so he couldn't help me. Bunch of cowards if you ask me. Hiding under sheets and masks to frighten and kill innocent freed blacks and abolitionists. Anyway,

I asked for Lance to come and help us with a rash of robberies we've had over the last couple years. Our local lawmen couldn't seem to get a handle on who or how the robberies were happening. So I asked for help."

"I know of the Ku Klux Klan," Rand responded. "Does Marshal Chambers think they're responsible for the robberies?"

"No, he never linked the KKK with the robberies. He did figure out that it's a gang that is working out of the mountain country to the east of here. A few months ago he got a tip from a man who was in the area of a train robbery. He told Chambers he saw a group of five men bunched together not far from where the robbery took place. He said they seemed to be getting instructions then they split up and went in five different directions.

"Lance checks in with me from time to time and lets me know anything new. Three weeks ago he came by and said he tracked two of the men that left that group. And eventually both men headed east into the mountains. Lost the trail of the first man and the weather wiped out the tracks of the other one. Some old timer up that way told Lance he'd seen one rider up on Turkey Trot Ridge but other than that it had been real quiet and that's the way the old timer likes it."

Rand Trinity gleaned as much information from Judge Cramer as he could then asked about a place to spend the night. "Since you said it was urgent I came by train. I'll need a place to stay tonight, a good horse, packhorse, and supplies for a couple of weeks. There's plenty of time this afternoon to gather what I need and I'll leave first thing in the morning."

"Sounds good but you watch yourself! They're a crafty bunch of outlaws to fool so many for so long."

A few hours later, Rand Trinity turned and took a long look at the sunset as he stood on the porch of the boarding house the judge had sent him to. Mentally, he went over all of his preparations for leaving in the morning. Satisfied that he was ready, he let his nose dictate the next move. Food! The smell of something good led him inside for what he knew would be his last good meal for a while.

Later, when Rand excused himself and went to his room, he took off his boots, and stretched out on the bed. The first thing that hit him was disappointment, but he shook off the feeling knowing he had a job to do and a man's life might be at stake. *Sorry, Josie, I tried to see you! When I get through with this job I'll make sure nothing keeps me from spending some time with you. I miss your incredible spirit. Might as well face it, I miss everything about you.* This thought immediately brought up a mental picture of the young woman, Josephine Fisher, who he had been unable to get off his mind for the last couple of months. The memory of her wavy honey blond hair, her blue sparkling eyes, and their last kiss brought a slight smile to his face. Rand mentally went over the letter he had posted that afternoon.

Dear Josie,

I am writing this letter to let you know I will be delayed in coming to see you. I was called in on an urgent need in Lexington. I'm not sure how long it will take to finish this assignment but be assured I will be coming to see you as soon as I can.

I hope you and your father are doing well. I delivered my prisoner and had to make a trip to Washington for reports and updates. My thoughts have been of you since I last saw you. There are so many things I want to share with you. We have plans to make. Tell your father hello for me.
Hope to see you soon.
Thinking of you,

Rand

Sleep and sweet dreams claimed him but the gray of early morning found him jolted out of a dream that left him in a cold sweat and with a dry mouth. Rand swung his feet to the rug by his bed and tried to shake off the dream of a gunman holding Josephine prisoner, a gun pointed at her head. In his dream he felt frozen, unable to move.

"I wonder what brought that on," he mumbled to himself.

After slipping on his pants and shrugging into his shirt, Rand walked to the window, drew the curtains aside and looked out at the mostly dark quiet neighborhood. He heard a rooster crow and a dog bark somewhere close by. *I might as well get going.* Before he moved from the window another thought came. *Josie, be safe, don't get yourself into trouble.* Rand chuckled softly. *Now that was a crazy thing to say. Unless you've changed in the last few months I'm sure there is something exciting going on wherever you are.*

Lance Chambers gritted his teeth as he rolled carefully to his left hip, facing the wall of the hideaway cabin where Anna and Beth Ann had put him for the night. *What a miserable mess I'm in. At least it's starting to get light outside.* Lance couldn't remember much about the ride to the cabin but he felt it was in a heavily timbered area. There had been noises of small creatures during the night but the sound of his horse, Slate, chomping grass close to the cabin had been reassuring. Prayers, scriptures, and fireflies had kept him occupied for a while, but as night encompassed the cabin, his life became one black hole of misery.

Startled awake, Lance lay still trying to identify the sound that had penetrated his groggy mind. *I must have dozed off.* His back was to the doorway, but hearing a nicker from Slate told him what the noise had been. "Sorry, Slate, I know you need water." Lance turned his head toward the doorway. "Give me a few more minutes and I'll try to figure out something." Slate shook his head and nickered again. "All right, I'm on it." Lance placed his hands on the board next to the wall and slowly began pushing himself up, first to his elbow then to his left hip. The board holding his weight was loose and moved slightly. Beads of perspiration broke out on his forehead when he finally made it to a sitting position. Every muscle in his body protested, his head pounded from the exertion and his leg was one dull ache. *I feel like I've done a hard days labor just trying to sit up.* Lance filled his lungs with crisp morning air and slowly let it out. *What I wouldn't give for a strong cup of coffee and a warm fire.*

Slate was watching him curiously as if he was waiting for his master's next move. "Don't look at me that way. I'm doing the best I can," Lance grumbled to his horse. "I need a crutch." With one quick perusal of the cabin, Lance knew he was probably going to have to crawl to his horse. A sudden thought came to mind. "Maybe the loose board will work." The board was definitely loose and was about the right length. "Now, if only I have the strength to pull it up."

Lance was surprised when the board only had one rusted nail holding it down. He lifted it right out of its place on the floor. He was even more surprised at what was underneath the board. The significance of what he had discovered didn't take long for him to realize he might be in trouble. "I've got to get out of here before someone finds me. I'm certainly in no shape to defend myself."

The sound of approaching horses left him no time to plan. He dropped the board back into place and grabbed his rifle, waiting, hoping it was Anna and her daughter.

Chapter 3

"Ma, I wish you would tell me what we're going to do with the marshal," Beth Ann groused to her mother as they approached the cabin.

"I will tell you at the same time as I tell the marshal, Beth. I don't want to have to tell it twice. It took me most of the night to make up my mind, but I'm determined to make my plan work for all three of us. You and I are going to have a long talk tonight; there are some things I need to tell you. So be patient with me until then."

"All right, I'll try. But you know how hard it is for me to wait."

"I know but it won't be long now. Let's go in and see if the marshal is still alive."

Anna and Beth approached the cabin, Anna calling out, "Hello, the cabin!"

"Come on in, I won't shoot you," Marshal Chambers answered.

Beth pushed the marshal's horse away from the door and the two entered slowly. Surprised to see the marshal sitting up, Anna thought he might be doing better than when they had left him. But a closer look and she knew that wasn't the case. "How are you this morning?"

"That's a good question I just don't know how to answer at the moment. I can say I'm still alive. A body could say that's a good thing, but being alive can hurt awful bad at times. You wouldn't happen to have a cup of hot black coffee in your pocket, would you?"

"No, I'm sorry. I did bring you something to eat, though. Do you think you can scoot back against the wall and eat a bite? We need to talk while you eat."

"I'll give it a try."

"Do you need me to help you?"

"If you'll help that no good leg move along with me, I can do the rest."

With a great deal of effort, the marshal managed to move back against the rough log wall. Anna's heart wrenched to see the pain the movement caused the marshal. His face was a sickly pale gray when he leaned his head back to rest against the logs. "I'm sorry. I wish I could have done better for you yesterday."

"Don't worry about it. I appreciate what you've already done."

"I'll get the food I brought for you and we can talk."

"Thank you. Is there a place your daughter might take Slate for some water? He's been fussing at me about needing a drink."

"I suppose Slate is your horse?"

Lance gave her a lopsided grin and a nod in answer.

"Sure, there's a spring out back a short ways. Beth, will you take care of the marshal's horse while I get his breakfast?"

"I'd be glad to. Just don't tell anything until I get back," Beth warned.

"Well, then, get a move on and hurry back."

Anna scooted Beth out the doorway ahead of her, got the flour sack off her horse and went back into the cabin. She handed the marshal a cloth-covered bundle from the sack. "Please don't ask a lot of questions when Beth gets back. I'll explain more to you later."

"All right, if you promise to answer all my questions later. And be warned, I've got a lot of questions."

"I'm sure you do and I'll do my best to answer them."

"It's a deal, then." The marshal looked at his cloth wrapped breakfast. "What did you bring me?"

"Not much. Just an egg sandwich and a jar of milk."

"Sounds like a feast to me!" The marshal bowed his head before he unwrapped his breakfast. It took a moment for Anna to realize he was saying a prayer.

She quickly looked away as tears threatened to fall. *I've forgotten how to pray. God probably wouldn't listen to the prayers of someone who's done the things I have.* Anna looked back at the marshal and saw he was watching her.

"You all right?" he asked.

Anna cleared her throat. "Yes, I'm fine."

"Sorry I don't have a chair to offer you, but this sandwich will go down a lot better if you wouldn't stand over me. Can you sit down here with me?"

"Sure, I don't mind. I'm all dirty anyway from morning chores."

"My saddle blanket is over by the door with my saddle, if you want to sit on that."

"Thanks, but I'll be all right." Anna sat a few feet away from the marshal and leaned back against the same log wall that he was leaning on. *How am I going to do this? And what if he won't help me?* The room fell into an uncomfortable silence as Anna waited for Beth to get back. She didn't have to wait long. Beth rushed back into the cabin all breathless with ruddy cheeks.

"I'm back! You didn't talk about anything important did you?"

Anna gave Beth a nervous smile. "No, we haven't talked yet. Come over here and sit down by me. We need to give the marshal time to eat."

Beth plopped down on the floor close to her mother, crossed her legs and propped her elbows on her knees. She stared at the marshal for a moment. "What's your name, mister?"

"Beth, please use some manners," Anna scolded. "The marshal will think you haven't been taught a thing."

"Sorry, I just think its awkward calling him marshal all the time."

Lance set his half-eaten sandwich down and took a long drink of milk. "She's right," he said with a smile. "My name is Lance Chambers, U.S. Marshal. I'm surprised you two came back this morning. I meant it when I told you your help yesterday was appreciated and you didn't need to do anything else for me."

"I know, but I couldn't leave you like this and feel good about it. It just wouldn't be right to leave anyone in your condition to fend for themselves." Anna chewed on her bottom lip a moment then blurted out, "Besides, we need *you* as much as you need us!"

Beth scowled at her mother. "We do?"

"Yes, Beth, we do. I can't answer all your questions right now but I will tell you all you need to know later this evening after we get the marshal . . . er, Mr. Chambers, settled."

It was the marshal's turn to scowl. "How and where are you going to *settle* me?"

"We are going to move you to the house. I've thought long and hard about it and that's what we are going to do until you get stronger."

"I don't think Pa is going to like that," said Beth, still frowning.

"He won't know. If we're careful he'll never know there's anyone else in the house."

"You mean you're going to hide him?" Beth's eyebrows rose slightly. "Where?"

"The storage room in the attic. I've already fixed a place for him. The men never come in the house and your pa never goes upstairs. The only thing up there is your room and the storage room."

Lance was shaking his head. "I don't think you thought as long or hard as you needed to. How in thunder are you going to get me up to an attic? I think a better idea is for you two to help me saddle my horse, get in that saddle, and ride away from here."

"How far do you think you'll get, alone and in your condition? When I first came in here you were as white as a ghost, just from sitting up. It's a long way to anywhere from here. Besides I told you I need *your* help. I need you to get well enough so you can help me and Beth get away from this place. I'll help you and you can help me. I'm not saying it will be easy, but there is no way we can take care of you from here or anywhere else I could think of. Anything we do would draw suspicion from Dean and the other men, but Beth and I can move freely around the house."

"Who is Dean?" The marshal asked.

"Dean is Beth's pa."

"Is he the one who runs the outfit around here?"

"Yes." Anna looked from Marshal Chambers then to her daughter. They both had worried expressions on their faces, but seemed to be thinking over what she had said.

Beth spoke first. "Ma, why can't we just leave? There's a lot I don't understand but I'm smart enough to know that things are not right with Pa and the men. Are they outlaws, Ma? Is that why the marshal, I mean, Mr. Chambers is here?"

"You'll have to ask him that question, but I suspect that's what he's here for."

Beth didn't ask, but the question was on her face when she looked boldly into his eyes. He answered, "I'm not going to lie to you, young lady, because what your mother is suggesting is going to be dangerous and you need to know the facts. I'm after a gang of thieves and murderers who have been working the state of Kentucky for a few years now. The search has led me here. I'm in no shape to tackle the job of arresting one man, let alone a gang of men. I have no doubt if they happened to find me anywhere around here they will kill me. You'll have to ask your mother what they would do to the two of you for helping me. She knows what the situation is here better than I do."

Beth looked at her mother for the answer. Anna took a deep breath and looked down at her hands when she answered. "It wouldn't be pretty, Beth. I'm sure he would kill me. I don't know what he would do about you, though." Anna looked into her daughters eyes. The confusion and pain she saw was more than she could handle. Tears were threatening but she didn't want to fall apart in front of the marshal. "I'm so sorry, Beth. Please, I need you to trust me right now because we don't have time for the whole story. I promise I'll tell you everything when we get Mr. Chambers to the house and taken care of. We need to do this *right now* because we don't know when the men will start coming back. Fred will be back late this evening or first thing in the morning. It's just you and me now, and we have to work together on this."

Beth quietly responded, "All right, Ma, I trust you, but will hold you to your promise to tell me everything later today."

Lance Chambers watched mother and daughter embrace. He heard Anna say quietly, "Thank you, Beth, for your trust. I love you more than you will ever know." The scene was heart- wrenching and he felt there was more pain to come for the two women.

I wouldn't want to be in Anna's shoes. I can't imagine having to tell your daughter her father is a thief and murderer. Lance remembered what he had found under the board he was sitting on. *I've got to find out how much Anna knows and how deep she's in with the gang.*

"You need to know that I won't leave without the money," he casually commented.

Anna's puzzled look gave him hope. "I don't care if you take your money," she said. "We don't intend to rob you of your money, marshal."

"I'm not talking about *my* money. I don't have enough money on me to tempt even a poor thief. I'm talking about the money that's hidden right here in this cabin."

Lance watched Anna and Beth glance in every corner of the cabin. "What are you talking about? There's no money here. I don't think anyone even knows about this place. It's so hidden with all the trees around and vines growing on it, you can barely see it from the outside. Are you teasing us?" Anna challenged. "That's a funny way to joke around."

Lance was sure from their reactions that they didn't have a clue about the hidden money. "No, I'm not teasing, and someone does know about this cabin. There is money right under this board." He rapped on the board with his knuckles. "At least four of the bags have Wells Fargo Bank on them."

"I don't believe you," Anna accused. "If there are bags of money under that board, *show me!*"

The marshal tugged the board out of place and laid it beside him. Mother and daughter moved closer and peered down into the hole. They both gasped. "Ma, there *is* money hidden down there!" The hole contained a wooden box the length of the board along with sacks in a variety of sizes.

"How much is there?" Beth asked.

"I don't know," Lance Chambers answered. "I only found it a moment before you and your mother rode up. I was looking for something I could use for a crutch and the only thing I could get my hands on was that board." He looked at Anna. "We do need to get away from this cabin as soon as we can."

"Shouldn't we leave the money here? They might come for it and when it's gone they'll know someone was here." Anna's voice carried a tremor as she spoke.

"No, we'll take it with us. Even if they come here to get the money or put more in they'll know someone has been here. There's enough evidence outside from the horses to prove that. It's something we'll have to risk. If I leave it here they'll know someone was here and move it to another hiding place and I may never recover it. I can't take that chance."

Anna nodded. "I understand, but it does complicate things more. I can't let anything happen to Beth."

"Let's go while I still have some strength left in me. Beth, would you mind going out and finding a rock big enough to pound the nail out of this board?"

"Sure, I'll be right back," she said, dashing through the doorway.

"Anna," the marshal said when they were alone.

"Yes, what is it?" Anna asked, turning her eyes on his.

He looked into those troubled eyes, wincing at the pain he saw there. "I don't want anything to happen to you or Beth. I'll do my best to protect you and get all three of us out of here."

"Thank you," was all she could manage to say.

The women worked quickly to saddle the marshal's horse and load all the money sacks. Some sacks were stuffed into saddle bags while the sturdier ones were tied on with ropes. Frustrated over his helplessness, Lance Chambers saved his strength for the ride ahead of him. He couldn't do more than sit and watch mother and daughter work. They both looked to be somewhat over five foot, and were dressed in men's pants and shirts, the shirts tucked in with leather belts at their waists. Worn cowboy hats and boots had them looking like ranch hands. Anna was an attractive woman whom Lance figured to be around forty years old. Intertwined in the gray of her hair were dark reddish colors, pulled back with a ribbon and fell to the middle of her back. She was feminine from head to toe with delicate facial features, but her hazel-green eyes showed strength born from pain.

Beth looked a lot like her mother in height and build but her hair was different; dark brown that waved and curled down to her waist. He hadn't figured out the color of her eyes yet.

"You ready?" Anna's question startled Lance from his musings.

"Yes and no," he answered honestly. "I feel pretty worthless watching you two do all the work, but after eating, I feel somewhat stronger. Let me see if I can get up off the floor. Will you hold that board up for me, Beth? I'll use it for support on my right side and Anna, if you'll support me on my left side; I think I can get up."

The ride to the house wasn't as bad as Lance thought it would be, but dismounting and climbing the stairs into the house and up to the attic was extremely difficult. By the time he had lowered himself to the pallet on the floor, his head pounded with every beat of his heart, a cold sweat bathed his face and he felt as weak as a kitten.

"Thank you, ladies. I'd be in a mess without your help."

"We're going to hide everything you have up here, including your saddle." Anna scanned the room. "That empty barrel by the door will work to hide the money sacks. We'll find something to put on top of the sacks."

"What about my horse?" Lance asked.

"Beth can take him to the corral with our riding stock after she brushes him down real good and gives him some oats. We'll just say we don't know where he came from, that Beth found him up on the trail. That will work for now."

Beth grinned. "That won't be a lie. I *did* find him up on the trail. I just won't mention what else I found up on the trail," she giggled.

"By the way, did either of you happen to see my hat anywhere?" Lance asked.

Beth looked at her mother then at Lance. "I don't remember seeing a hat. Did you see one, Ma?"

"No, but you didn't have one when we took you to the cabin. It must still be up the mountain where you fell. Beth, maybe you should ride back up there and see if you can find it. We don't want any evidence of someone being around."

"Should I go right away?" Beth asked.

"Help me get everything up here first then go take care of the marshal's horse. After that you can go look for the hat."

Beth helped lug everything to the attic. Then Anna said to her, "I can finish this up now. You go on and take care of the horse then ride back up the mountain. While you're there try to brush away any evidence from us, kick dirt over the blood on the ground. And Beth, please be careful. I don't think the men will be back for a few days yet but if you do run into one of them it's important that you act normal. We'll talk more when you get back."

Lance waited until he heard the door downstairs close, then knew it was time for Anna to answer some questions. "Anna, I need to know how many men are working here. I've got to be ready in case of trouble."

"There are six men all together," she sighed. "Fred is the oldest of the bunch. He stays around here and looks after things while the others are gone. He went for supplies and should be back late tonight or tomorrow. Don't let him fool you. He may look old and weak but he's not, and is mean as they come. Then there's Dean, Dusty, Toby, Chigger, and Pete."

"Which one is your husband?"

"Dean is the one who's the boss of the outfit. He's Beth's pa, but . . . we're not married." Anna couldn't look Lance in the face but her next words were spoken with feelings that Lance couldn't quite figure out right away. Calmly, she said, "Beth and I are nothing more than his property to control and beat on when he's in one of his moods. Don't doubt for one minute that if he knew you were here and I helped you he would kill both of us."

Her next words were laced with hate and bitterness that was not hard to discern. "He might kill Beth too, but I'm afraid he will give her to Dusty who is his right-hand man. Dusty is quite a bit older than Beth and a real charmer, but when he's drinking he's like Dean and gets dangerously mean. He's been after Dean to give Beth to him as a bonus for his loyalty. Can you imagine!" she spat out. "Dean doesn't know that I heard him and Dusty talking about Beth out on the porch before they left a few weeks ago. Dean gave Dusty the go ahead to try and win her over, said he wouldn't stand in the way. I get sick thinking about it. That's why I've got to get her away from here. It doesn't matter if Dean kills me, but Beth doesn't deserve what I've gotten her into. You're my last hope to get Beth away from here."

The small musty room was quiet until Lance quietly said, "I sure could use a cup of hot coffee, Anna. Why don't you bring me and yourself a cup and we'll talk some more."

Chapter 4

ANNA BROUGHT TWO CUPS of coffee and a small plate of cookies up to the attic. Lance was sitting up, leaning against the wall. "Here, put this tray on your lap," she said. "It'll be easier for you. I really should get your things hidden and organized while we talk. You need to be resting so your body can heal up."

"I'll rest soon enough, but I have a few more questions for you."

Anna sat on an overturned wooden crate and took a few sips of her coffee. "What do you want to know?"

"Does Dean really beat on Beth?"

"Not much anymore. When she was younger I took most of his rage, but we both have learned what to do to keep Dean pacified and stay out of his way. When I feel Beth is in danger, I tell her she needs to finish her last chore and she knows to run and hide in the barn."

"Why do you stay with a man like that, Anna? Why haven't you just run away when he was gone?"

"That, Mr. Chambers, is harder to do than you know. I *have* tried several times to do that very thing. The first time I ran, he found me and slapped me around. The second time, he took a leather strap and beat me until I passed out. The third time, I felt desperate enough to ask for help. A friend helped me get away and hid me. I don't know how, but when Dean *did* find me . . . ." Anna's eyes were filled with a deep hatred. "I'm surprised I lived. Poor little Beth tried to take care of me. She was so small. Dean said I was *his* until he said I wasn't. Said there was no where I could go that he wouldn't find me and the next time I tried to leave him, Beth and I would end up just like my friend did. No one would ever find us, either. So . . . I learned to survive."

Lance shook his head. "That's tough, Anna. I'm so sorry."

"It's my own fault and probably what I deserve. I was so stupid and crazy, just looking for a good time. I should never have left my husband and son. He was a fine man."

Lance's eyebrows spiked upward. "You have a husband and son?"

"I *did*. But that was a long time ago, not important now. I have no idea where they are or if either one is still alive."

"What was your husband's name?"

"No, that doesn't matter now. Who would want a woman like me? Even God has turned his back on me because of the things I've done."

"I don't think you understand God if you believe that, Anna. Yes, there are consequences for the things we do but God would never turn his back on you. He loves you."

Anna didn't respond but got up and started organizing the room. Lance decided to turn the conversation to another matter. "Tell me about the layout of this place and how the gang works."

"The layout is simple enough. This is the main house. The men never come into the house. They come to the door once in a while if they need Dean. Most of their planning is done in the bunkhouse where the men stay. There's the barn and corral then the small pasture beyond that. Dean has mentioned a canyon a short distance north of here where he keeps three mares and a magnificent stallion, but I've never been there. It has a cabin and according to Dean, a lot of good grass for the horses. When the men are gone, Fred spends a good amount of time there. Dean and Dusty are obsessed with racing horses." Anna paused and looked around the small room. "That should do it. Is there anything you need right now?"

"No, I think you thought of everything. I'll be fine."

"Why don't you rest then? I'll go check on the stew and I think I know where I can find something better to splint your leg with. There is some laudanum around somewhere if you are having a lot of pain."

"Don't bother with the laudanum. I don't want to be drugged. My head isn't right yet and the leg aches a lot but I can handle that. Actually, I already feel better. The coffee was good and the cookies were a real treat. Thank you, Anna."

"You're welcome. I'll check on you in a while."

A few hours later, Anna checked on Lance for the third time. This time he was awake and sitting up. "Hi, did you have a good rest?" she asked.

"Yes, I'm happy to say I did. You fixed a right comfortable place for me up here."

"Good. If you're up to it, I would like to take a look at your leg and re-splint it. Then, I have a stew and cornbread ready to eat."

"All right, let's get it done! I've been smelling something good for a while now and was hoping I'd get to sample whatever it is."

"You can have as much as you want when I finish with your leg." Anna bent down to her knees. "I'd like to remove your boots and cut the bottom of your pant leg off. I've already ruined the pants when I had to splint your leg the first time."

"Sure, go ahead and cut it off. Just go slow and careful when you pull that one boot off. I'm not looking forward to that."

Anna nodded and went to work. After she finished, she looked at Lance's strained pale face. "How is that?" she asked.

Lance let out a long sigh. "It feels a lot better. You did a good job and it wasn't as bad as I had feared."

"How is your hip?"

"It's plenty sore like the rest of me, but I can put my weight on it now."

'That's a good sign." Anna stood and started for the door.

"Anna?" Lance said to her back.

She turned to face his kind eyes. "Yes?"

"You all right?" he asked, tentatively.

"Yes, I'm fine," she answered.

"Did Beth make it back?"

"Yes, but she didn't find your hat. I'm going to send her up here with a pan of warm water so you can wash up, then I'll bring you some stew."

"Have you talked to her yet?"

"No, I'll do that after we have our meal and do chores. I'm not looking forward to telling her what an awful ma she has. I'm afraid she'll hate me."

"You're doing the right thing, Anna. I'll be praying for you."

There was no response from Anna. She just turned and left the room.

A short time later, Lance heard Beth slowly making her way up the stairs. She entered the room balancing a pan of water with one hand and a towel wrapped around some unseen items in the other. "I thought I was going to spill the water half-way up the stairs," she said, putting the pan on the floor within Lance's reach and handing him the bundled items. There's soap, wash cloth and a comb wrapped up in this towel."

"Thanks, Beth. Did you have a good ride?"

"It was all right, but I didn't find your hat. Sorry."

"The wind probably picked it up and blew it to the next county."

"I guess you'll have to get a new one when you go to town."

"Yep, guess I will. I can't do without a hat to shade my eyes and keep the rain off my head."

"If you were out tonight you sure would need it. Looks like a storm brewing." Beth turned to leave, and then turned back. "Ma said for me to ask if you needed anything before she brings you something to eat."

Lance wanted to talk more with Beth. He could see the strain of the day weighting down her young shoulders so decided the time wasn't right. "No, not right now. I've got everything I need. If you get a chance, come back and talk to me for a while. I'm sure I'll get lonesome up here by myself. If you have some cards or checkers, maybe we can play a game to help pass the time."

"I don't know how to play cards and I don't have any checkers. The men play poker in the bunkhouse, but I'm not allowed in there."

"Don't worry about that. I'll teach you a couple of games I played with my daughter. It's been a while but I think I can remember the rules."

"You have a daughter?"

"Yes, and now a granddaughter, but she's too young to play cards. You ask your ma if it's all right."

"What are you going to ask me?" Anna said as she made her way through the doorway with a tray.

"Mr. Chambers wants to teach me a couple of card games that he played with his daughter. Would that be all right, Ma?"

"I don't see why not. Tonight might not be a good time, though, because we need to have our supper, do chores, then you and I need to have our talk."

"Oh." Worry, fear, and confusion clouded Beth's eyes for a moment. "I'm not sure I want to have a talk."

Anna put her arm around her daughter's shoulder and directed her toward the doorway. "I know for sure I don't, but it's something I've needed to talk to you about for a long time. We've always been there for each other and we're going to have to be even more in the days ahead.

"Maybe I should move north some."

Rand Trinity was talking to himself again. Being alone for days, talking to himself seemed normal. Or, talking to his horse, Sugar, which was a feisty young mare he'd rented in Lexington, seemed normal too. The pack horse was content to follow along with one of his own kind for company.

"After a week out here in these mountains I haven't found much of anything in this area. Maybe . . . if I . . . ." Movement caught his eye. He was in the trees but was sure he had seen something move down the hill a ways. He nudged his horse to get a better advantage of the area. *Probably just a deer or some other animal, but . . . ."*

Rand sat quietly and watched the area of movement until he was rewarded for his patience. *Well, I'll be, it's a woman! Must be a ranch or farm in this area.* He watched the woman's curious movements, realizing she was a young girl, and seemed to be looking for something. *What could she possibly be looking for around here? Berries or something like that, maybe.* After a while, the girl dismounted, picked up a small leafy branch and brushed the ground like she was trying to wipe away tracks. He'd done that many times and was sure that was what she was doing. Finally, she mounted her horse again and rode downhill. *I better find out what that young lady has to hide.*

Rand watched for signs of anything unusual as he made his way to where the girl had been. He dismounted a short distance away and walked carefully to where she had been sweeping the ground. *I guess she did a good job, I don't see anything out of the ordinary.* He spotted a gap on the soft edge of a drop off, and walked over to investigate. Looked like a clump of dirt had broken off when someone or something had gone over the edge. *Quite a fall from up here. I better go see if there's anything of interest down there.*

At the bottom of the drop off, Rand squatted on his heels and took his time to figure out the sign that was right before his eyes. *That young lady was definitely trying to cover something up. Right here, looks like she kicked dirt over something.* Rand plucked a short limb off a nearby bush and carefully dusted away the dirt from the ground where he hoped to find a clue. *Dried blood. I'd say someone fell from up above and hit his head on this rock. The rock I am looking at right now, that has . . . dried . . . blood on it.*

Rand stood and surveyed the area to see if he missed anything. He looked up at the ledge and noticed a color that didn't go with the surrounding trees and brush. There was something stuck in the branches of the tree about halfway down. *Ahh, blast it! I'm going to have to climb up there and get it.*

Twenty minutes later, Rand was on the ground holding a gray hat in his hands. *Thank the good Lord I've found your trail, Lance Chambers. I know this is your hat because of the braided hat band your daughter made for you. You wouldn't part with this hat for anything, so that means you're in trouble. That girl must know where you are or what happened to you, so I'll follow the girl.*

Rand took his time following the girl's tracks and eventually spotted smoke from a chimney. He tied the horses to a tree then dug out his field glasses. Making his way down to a hiding spot, he surveyed the area. A house and two other outbuildings were down in a meadow. He glimpsed the girl's horse tied at the back of the house. *So, this is where she came. There's a barn and another building, probably a bunkhouse. No smoke from that chimney.* In the fenced pasture were four horses. He stopped abruptly on a dark gray gelding. *That cinches it! I know Lance is here or was here. The only reason he would leave his hat and Slate is that he's hurt, sick, or dead.* That last condition seemed the most reasonable, but Rand didn't want to go there just yet.

After an hour of watching the area, the girl appeared from the back door of the house, took her horse and disappeared into the barn. *There has to be someone else there besides that young girl, but where are they? It's deadly quiet down there.* Moments later, another female came out the front door of house. Rand watched her walk briskly to the field, lead a milk cow to the barn, and disappear inside. *I don't like it. Something's not right.* Rand weighed his options and made up his mind. *After dark, I'll sneak down there behind the barn and snoop around some. I'm not going to make myself known until I get a look at the men of this outfit. There has to be some men. At least one, anyway. No one would leave two women this far out from civilization.*

As the light started fading, Rand walked back to the horses. He mounted and made a wide circle around the meadow and in the direction of the barn. By the time he reached the back of the barn it was dark and the wind had picked up bringing a spattering of rain. In the distance, a flash of light followed a clap of thunder. "Drat it, looks to be a bad one coming in. I'll be hanged if I'm going to get drenched when there's a perfectly good barn right in front of me." Rand led Sugar around the side of the barn that was farthest from the house and let himself in.

Letting his eyes adjust to the darkened barn, Rand found what he needed to take care of the horses. Three of the six stalls were being used by the milk cow and the two horses the women had been riding. Putting Sugar in one empty stall, the pack horse in another, he took the last stall for himself. He found enough food to ward off the gnawing hunger in his stomach and drank his fill from his canteen, then wrapped in his blanket and made himself as comfortable as possible for the night. *This is a lot better than being out in the wind and rain with lightning and thunder. I'll just have to be out of here before anyone finds me in the morning. I don't know . . . maybe I better just walk up to the door of the house and ask about Lance. On the other hand, I have a feeling something isn't quite right. I might be better off watching things around here for another day.*

Rand was mulling this over and considering the choices he had when the next thing he knew the distinct sound of a crowing rooster brought him fully awake. *I can't believe I slept so sound. I wonder what time it is.* Digging his pocket watch out of his pants he found it was too dark to see. Daylight was seeping through cracks in the barn but not enough to read his watch. *No matter, it's time I go to that house and ask some questions.*

As quickly as he could, Rand loaded the pack horse and was just tightening the cinch on Sugar's saddle when the barn door swung open. The girl he had seen on the hillside strode in, spotted him and came to an abrupt halt. Her face registered shock, then something like anger or fear. She stood glaring at him then stepped back a few paces, straightening her spine.

"Who are you and what are you doing in our barn!"

Rand nodded and smiled, hoping to diffuse her hostility. "Didn't mean to startle you. I just spent the night in your barn to get out of that bad storm we had last night. It was a gully washer. I was on my way to the house to pay for the night's stay and the oats I fed my two horses."

"Mister, you've got to get out of here . . . right now!"

Rand recognized fear in her voice. "I'll leave pretty quick . . . ."

"No! You leave *now*! It's dangerous for you to be found here." Her fear now shone in her eyes.

"I'm not going until I find out about a friend I'm looking for. That's his horse out in your pasture so I know he was here. His name is Lance Chambers . . . ."

"*He's* your friend?"

"Yes, is he here?"

The girl truly was frightened and kept glancing toward the road that led to the house. She fairly shouted at him, "I don't have time to tell you anything. You've got to get out of here *now*! Fred is coming up the road with our supply wagon. He'll be here any minute and if he finds you here, he'll kill you!"

Rand remained calm and steady "I'm not inclined to run when my friend needs help."

"You don't *understand*. Ma and I are helping him. We have him hidden up in our attic and we're taking care of him and his broken leg. If Fred or any of the other men know we helped a U.S. Marshal, they will kill all of us, even me and Ma! So, *please, please*, get on that horse and get out of here!"

"All right, but I won't be far away," Rand said with reluctance. He swung into the saddle and headed for the trees at the back of the barn.

Chapter 5

"HOW ARE YOU FEELING this morning?" Anna had just walked into the upstairs room with a breakfast tray for her hidden guest.

"It's amazing what good care, good food, and a night's rest can do for a person," Lance answered. "I'm actually feeling pretty good this morning, considering everything. Most important is my head is better. I don't get all light headed and dizzy as much when I move now."

"I'm glad. That's a good sign," Anna said, setting the tray down beside the marshal.

Lance noticed her red swollen eyes and figured she'd had a rough night. "Sit down and tell me how your talk went with Beth," he invited.

Anna sat on the overturned box and stared at the floor for a while before she spoke. Her voice was strained and full of emotion when she finally answered. "It was hard on both of us, but I didn't hold anything back. She knows everything now."

"How did she take it?"

"I'm not sure. She was so quiet and went to her room early. It's a lot for a young girl to take in and deal with."

"Did she ask questions?"

"Oh, yes, she had a lot of questions. The strange thing was she didn't show any emotion."

"I suspect the emotions . . . ."

Their conversation stopped abruptly as the front door of the house banged open then banged shut and Beth came running up the stairs. "Ma, there was a strange man in the barn!"

"What?" Anna gasped. "Where is he now, Beth?"

"I told him to get out of here. Fred was coming up the road with the wagon. I didn't have time to explain, just told him to leave right now because he was in danger."

"What did he say to that?"

"He didn't like it, but he left and said . . ."

A loud knock on the door downstairs brought Anna to her feet. "You stay here, Beth. I'll go talk to Fred. He's probably wanting to unload the supplies for the house."

As Anna left, Lance motioned for Beth to sit on the box her mother had vacated. "Tell me about your conversation with this stranger, Beth. What was said and what did he look like?"

"He said he was looking for a friend named Lance Chambers."

Lance's eyebrows arched a bit higher. "He knew me?"

"Yes, but I had to get him to leave."

"Did you say anything to him about me?"

"I told him Ma and I were taking care of you and your broken leg. I told him we had you hidden in our attic." Beth had an anxious look on her face. "I hope that was all right."

"Yes, you did fine. Tell me what he looked like."

"Well, he was a lot younger than you." Beth closed her eyes and thought a moment. "He was a very nice looking man, tall, and . . . he had red hair. He was holding his hat so I could see his hair real plain. He knew you had been here because he saw your horse in the pasture."

Lance leaned his head back against the wall with a big grin on his face. "Rand! It *has* to be Rand."

Beth watched curiously as the marshal continued to smile. "Who is that?"

"He's just one of our youngest U.S. Marshals, and in *my* opinion, one of the best. What else did he say to you?"

"Not much more than that. I could tell he didn't like it when I yelled at him to get out of here or we'd all be killed. He just said, 'All right, but I won't be far away.'"

"Good." Lance sighed with relief.

Anna came back just in time to hear Lance's last comment. "What's good?" she asked.

Beth answered excitedly, "The stranger is a U.S. Marshal and was looking for Mr. Chambers."

Anna rolled her eyes. "Wonderful! All we need is another lawman around with Fred here now and the others probably coming back anytime. Heaven help us!"

Lance fastened his eyes on Anna's and grinned. "The God of heaven is *already* helping us, Anna."

Rand was relieved that he'd found Lance still alive, but frustrated that the young girl had yelled for him to leave. *Ordered me around like I was her personal slave. I needed to talk to Lance, drat it! I don't know why I'm being so hard on her. She was obviously scared to death. Wish I could talk to her mother.*

By the time he found a place to watch the ranch, the clouds had rolled away and the sun was quickly drying out the ground. *Muggy. I sure could use a bath. If I sweat anymore I'll stink so bad they'll locate me just by the smell.*

Fred, the old man that drove the wagon to the front of the house, was interesting to watch. He unloaded supplies on the front porch and the women moved them inside. Then he stopped to unload supplies into the barn, then the bunkhouse. He worked in a quick efficient way. After unhitching the team of horses from the wagon he took them to the pasture. Rand saw the moment Fred spotted Slate. He gave Slate a going over then picked another horse and led him to the barn. He came out with the horse saddled and took off in a northeast direction. *I wonder where he's going. Guess I better follow him. Sure isn't any activity at the house. Maybe he'll lead me to the other men.*

Fred rode maybe close to two miles, then rode down into a narrow canyon. Rand found a trail that took him up hill and hopefully to the edge of the canyon so he could look down and see what would be of interest to the old ranch hand. He found just such a spot and looked over the edge.

Rand dismounted Sugar, found his field glasses and sat where he could get a good look. "What a perfect place to hide stolen horses," he mumbled to himself. *Small meadow, pool of water probably from an underground spring, and high walls to keep in a small herd of horses. That little shack doesn't look like much though.* Rand noted Fred's horse was the only one in front of the shack but Fred was in the meadow checking on the four horses that were grazing. *Those are fine looking animals down there. Looks like three mares and one stallion.* Rand took a longer look at the stallion. *Nice, really nice. Where did he get such a magnificent stallion? He sure doesn't like Fred, though.* Rand chuckled as he watched the big black stallion play his evading games with the old ranch hand. Fred finally tired of it and found a place under a tree and stretched out on the grassy ground, probably for a nap.

Rand began to worry about Marshal Chambers and the women in the house, so headed back in that direction. *With Fred in the canyon maybe I'll get a chance to get into the house and find out what I can do to help Lance.*

"Ma will be bringing you some lunch pretty quick," Beth told Lance. "And I'm going for a ride. Is there anything you need before I leave?"

"No, just remember what I said to tell my friend if you see him again."

"I will. I'll let him know everything that's happened since I found you and find out any plans he might have."

"Good girl. You be careful and don't take any chances."

Beth Ann had been busy with the morning's excitement and hadn't had time to think about all that her ma had told her the night before. She'd felt numb at first, like none of it was real. She couldn't figure it all out and fell asleep feeling bewildered and confused.

In the barn, Beth brushed Star, saddled her and rode toward her favorite spot where she would feel safe and could think. She had to go down the road that Fred had come to the house on. It was the only road leading to their house and some would say it wasn't a road at all. There was a creek to cross and that's where her spot was, a ways upstream.

"I wish I had someone to talk to," she mumbled to her horse. *A friend. If only I had a friend. If there really was a God in heaven he'd let me have a friend.*

Feeling irritated and bold at the same time, she let herself go for a moment as she walked Star to her safe place. "God, if you are really there, let me have a friend. I need a friend besides my ma." For a few moments it felt good to declare her want for a friend to God, but the feeling faded. *A person shouldn't talk to God like that. He might just strike me dead, but maybe I would be better off dead. I'm just a . . . .* Beth couldn't bring herself to speak the word aloud, a word she wasn't sure she even understood.

The small meadow by the creek welcomed her. She found her sitting-rock on the tiny sandy spot by the water. Shafts of light filtered through the trees, creating a shifting display of colors on the grass and wild flowers that hadn't yet faded. Flying insects danced in and out of the light shafts. Heavy moisture hung in the air as the sun warmed the damp earth. She often spotted a squirrel scampering from limb to limb, and listened to birds sing their songs. She enjoyed trying to figure out what they were singing about.

But today was different. Beth Ann had been told some disturbing information that was turning her life upside down. She didn't notice any of her favorite things. She tied Star to a bush, climbed on her thinking rock and let her emotions have their way. *Ma, what have you done to us? Why couldn't we have had a normal life, where I could go to school and have friends like other kids?* Beth wasn't one to cry but in her safe place, for the first time in a long time she let the tears come. Even welcomed them. A short cry later, she took her neck scarf off and wiped her eyes, but that started her crying again. "I'd be better off dead!" she moaned.

A voice came out of the blue. "I'm sorry, were you speaking to me? I couldn't quite understand what you said."

Beth's head jerked up to find a woman standing a few feet away; she had a tiny smile on her face that dispelled the fear Beth had felt for a moment. This petite woman was older than Beth, but just a few years so. Her hair was black, worn loose with curls cascading down her back. She wore a skirt and blouse in dazzling colors and her dangling gold earrings and bracelets sparkled in the sunlight.

Beautiful! She was beautiful! Beth wiped her eyes again and stared curiously at the woman. Finally, her voice worked. "No, I was talking to myself."

"Well, that's no fun," the woman said. "Is there room for two on that rock?"

"I don't know . . . maybe if I scoot over."

"How fun! You scoot over. I promise not to take up much room. If you start to fall off, I'll catch you. If I start to fall off you catch me."

The colorfully dressed woman settled on the rock right next to Beth. She giggled. "Now, we can talk to each other and won't have to talk to ourselves. What's your name?"

"Beth Ann. but most everyone calls me Beth."

"Oh, what a beautiful name. My name is Sarah. Most everyone calls me *Sarah*." She giggled at her own joke then put her arm around Beth's shoulders and squeezed. "We shall be great friends, don't you think?"

"I guess," Beth answered.

"What do you mean, you *guess*? Don't you want a friend?"

"Sure, everyone wants a friend."

"Tell me true, tell me sweet, say it loud, and please don't squeak, or I shall go away, my eyes are sure to leak."

"You can stay," Beth said in a hurry. "I would like to have you for a friend." She blew her nose again and stuffed the scarf in her pocket.

"We must make a pact then," the pretty lady declared.

"What do you mean? What's a *pact*?"

"It's kind of like an agreement or promise. I'll show you. Give me your arm." Sarah took Beth's arm and linked it with hers at their elbows. "Now, we must say together: 'We are friends, true to the end.' But be sure you *mean* it. Ready?"

"Yes," Beth answered. A slight smile was working its way onto her face.

In unison they said, 'We are friends, true to the end.' Sarah broke out in giggles and had Beth giggling too. "This is a lot more fun than talking to ourselves, don't you think?"

"Yes. I've never had a friend before." Beth's eyes clouded.

"Never?"

"Well, I have my ma, but I think that's different than a real friend."

"Look, Beth!" Sarah whispered and pointed to the sandy area across the creek. "See that tiny bird taking a bath? Do you ever think about being a bird and flying high in the clouds? Flying so high and free you forget all your troubles down here on earth."

"I've wondered what it would be like to fly like the birds," Beth admitted. "But never thought about getting away from my troubles by flying. That would be nice, though."

The girls were now talking in hushed tones. Sarah said, "Maybe you don't have any troubles."

"Beth groaned. "I've got troubles. I've got *big* troubles."

"Tell me about them. Maybe I can help."

Beth thought a moment and shook her head. "Its things I can't talk about."

"You can always tell a friend. A true friend won't tell anyone else. It will be their secret."

Beth didn't know how to start but the need to share her troubles compelled her into talking. Her new friend sitting beside her was so nice and easy to talk to. "My ma told me some things last night that I didn't know."

"Like what?" Sarah prompted.

"She and my pa never got married. My name is the same as my pa's, but her name is different even though she uses pa's last name. She was married before. Would that make me a . . .?" Beth scrunched up her nose and looked worried. "It's a bad word . . . I would be a . . . ."

"Wait!" Sarah interrupted. "Swallow it!"

"What?"

"Swallow the word," Sarah instructed.

"How do I do that?"

"Work up a lot of spit and swallow. Do it quickly!"

Beth Ann looked puzzled but did what Sarah said. "All right, I did it."

"Good! You must *never* let that word reach your tongue again. There are many words in this crazy world but you must never let a word *define* who you are. Let your heart and God teach you who you are." Sarah clapped her hands and giggled with delight. "Oh, I have a wonderful idea! I want to take you to Make Believe Meadow."

Beth's troubled shoulders lifted slightly. "Where is that?"

"Wherever I want it to be. We will go there tomorrow, but right now tell me more about your ma. You said she was married before?"

"Well, she told me she had a husband and a little boy, but then just left them. She said she was very selfish and foolish. I don't understand why she would do a thing like that."

"I don't know, Beth, but people make bad decisions all the time and then are sorry about them. Does she love you?"

"Last night I wondered, but in my heart I know she loves me. She cried and asked me to forgive her. We have always taken care of each other and when pa gets mad or drunk she always protects me."

"Does he hurt your ma?" Sarah asked gently.

"Yes. He slaps her sometimes now, but I remember a long time ago he beat and kicked her so bad she couldn't get off the bed for a long time. I was very young but I tried to take care of her. Ma said I was her little sweetheart. She even drew me a picture of a heart on a piece of paper. I still have it in my room."

"That was sweet. What about your pa? Does he love you?"

Beth's young shoulders lifted again. "I don't know. He's a bad man."

"What do you mean?"

"I shouldn't tell you anymore."

"Of course you should. I'm your friend now. Friends can talk about anything and will help each other."

The need to unburden herself was overpowering and Beth told her new friend everything she knew. Sarah took in all the information and was overwhelmed with the story. "So, you and your mother are hiding a U.S. Marshal who was hurt in a fall. There is another U.S. Marshal who came to find the one who was hurt and your pa's gang of bad men are coming any time now and would kill all of you if they found out that you and your ma helped these marshal's. Is that about right?"

"That's a short way to tell it. Where are your people?" Beth asked. "You should take them far away. It's not safe for them either."

"My people are camped a couple of miles down the road where it forks. We're in three gypsy wagons. You mustn't worry about us."

"Are you a gypsy?" Beth searched Sarah's face and took in her clothes and jewelry, as if seeing them for the first time.

"For now I am. I'm many things, Beth, but most of all, I'm your friend now and we are not alone. God is with us." Sarah hugged Beth then took Beth's hands in hers and prayed, "Heavenly Father, I ask for protection for Beth and all those around her. Give us your wisdom to know how to handle the situation we are in. Amen."

"I must go now, Beth. Promise me you will meet me here again tomorrow right after lunch time. I want to know what's going on. There may be some way I can help."

"I promise," Beth said with conviction.

"Good. Now you do what the marshals tell you." Sarah's heart was racing when she asked Beth what she was dying to know. "Do you know the name of the U.S. Marshals?"

"The older one is Lance Chambers, and the younger red headed marshal, Mr. Chambers called Rand."

Sarah hugged Beth again. "Thank you, my dear friend." She whirled around and called over her shoulder as she left, "See you here tomorrow . . . don't forget!"

Chapter 6

HIS PLAN TO GO down to the ranch house had to be put on hold when Rand found two new horses tied to the rail in front of the bunkhouse. He watched from his perch up the hill as the men unloaded their gear from the horses and carried them inside. *The girl indicated there was more than one man around here. That makes three in the bunkhouse now. I wonder how many more there are.*

Rand watched the two new men lead their horses to the pasture and felt a pang of anxiety as they spotted Slate. They talked by the fence for a while then one of the men shrugged his shoulders and headed back to the bunkhouse, the other man followed. *It sure enough won't be safe to try and get in the house now. I'll have to wait until dark.*

Shortly after the men disappeared into the bunkhouse, smoke came billowing out the chimney and the young girl who ordered him out of the barn came riding up the wagon road to the house. She rode to the back and tied her horse on the rail by the back porch. *I wonder where she's been.* Lack of information was frustrating him. *That's where I need to be, close to the back of the house and maybe I can get the attention of one of the women. They'll probably come to the outhouse sometime before they go to bed. I'll take my chances on that.*

Rand moved further back into the trees and slowly circled round to the back of the house. He found a place to stake his two horses where they could graze. *The girl's horse is gone. She must have put him in the barn for the night while I was making my move.* As the sun set and the valley shadows grew darker, Rand cautiously made his way toward the house just as someone opened the back door. He stayed hidden behind a tree. *Must be hot in the kitchen from cooking.* Moments later a gentle evening breeze carried the smells of supper to a U.S. Marshal who hadn't had a good meal for days. His mouth watered. *What I wouldn't give for a plate of whatever she's cooking. I smell fresh bread, roast beef, and apple pie. Maybe I'll get some before the night is over. Ha! Guess I can always hope.*

Night sounds stirred the air as Rand waited. He figured it was probably around nine o'clock when the two women came out the back door together. The younger girl was carrying a lantern. Rand was in place when they reached the door of the outhouse. He said quietly, "Don't scream, you're not alone."

Both women froze in their tracks.

"Who are you?" The older woman asked.

"I'm a friend of Lance Chambers and I'm a U.S. Marshal. I need to talk to Lance."

"All right, but you do what I tell you. Dean could ride in at any time. He often slips in after dark and it's dangerous to be anywhere around here."

Another bossy woman. "I understand, but it can't be helped. I need to talk to him so we can work out a plan to get him out of here."

"I won't argue with that but if he leaves, Beth Ann and I leave too."

"We'll work it out; just let me talk to Lance."

Anna told Beth, "Take the lantern and go into the outhouse. Marshal, you follow me. I'm not going to light a lantern until we get upstairs where Lance is. The men walk around at night and I don't want to have any light where you can be seen. Watch your step and be careful."

Rand followed Anna into the darkened house. As his eyes adjusted, he was able to go along with no problem. He saw her pick up a lantern off a table before they climbed the stairs. "The one on the right is my daughter's bedroom. This one is a storage room where Lance is." She opened the door and led the way into the room, quietly closing the door behind them. It was like a tomb as he stood in the darkness. "Lance, it's just me. I've brought someone who wants to talk to you."

Rand heard the strike of a match and the lantern flared to life. The brightness blinded him for a moment but he followed the woman to the back of the room where she lifted the lantern up and turned to Rand. "Here he . . ." She didn't finish the sentence. Like a statue she stood staring up at Rand, color drained from her face, wide confused eyes held his.

Lance broke the spell of the strange encounter. "Why you son-of-a-gun! It's about time you showed up to rescue me. Don't just stand there, come down here on the floor where we can talk."

Rand lowered himself to the floor and crossed his long legs. The men shook hands and talked like old friends until Lance remembered Anna still standing holding the lantern. "Anna, you can set the lantern down and sit with us?"

"I . . . I . . . Do you or your friend need anything? Maybe some coffee?"

"Sure," Lance answered. "I could use a cup of coffee if it wouldn't be a bother. You need anything, Rand?"

"To tell the truth I'm right near starved and would eat and drink anything the lady can find. Thought I might keel over from starvation just smelling your cooking, ma'am. Please don't go to a lot of trouble, anything will do."

Before Anna turned to leave she said, "I'll see what I can find. Beth and I will keep watch from the window for the men or for Dean coming home." She quickly left the room.

"Do I look that bad?" Rand asked. "I think I scared the woman to death. Her daughter sure wasn't scared of me when she ordered me out of the barn this morning."

Lance frowned. "I noticed it too. They've been good to me, Rand. She and Beth Ann have had it mighty rough here. I want to help them."

"Sure, we'll do what we can for them but I want to know everything that's happened. Tell me how you're feeling and what plans you might have."

Anna didn't think her legs would hold her up long enough to make it down the stairs. She was trembling and her legs felt like wet noodles. Beth Ann was sitting in the dark in a rocking chair close to one of the two windows in the front room. "What are you doing, Beth? You could go on up to bed if you want."

"I'm not ready, Ma. I'll just sit here and rock for a while. Pa may come riding in. I saw Pete and Chigger's horses in the pasture. That leaves Dusty and Toby. They could come in anytime too, but I know they wouldn't come to the house."

"You're right, and it's good for you to watch for trouble. I'll spell you in a bit."

"Ma?"

"Yes, what is it?"

"I'm scared. Do you think we'll get away from here?"

Anna could hear the fear in her daughter's voice. She picked up a small blanket off the divan and tucked it around Beth's shoulders. "Yes, we'll get away and go somewhere to make a new life for ourselves. I love you so much, sweetheart. Think about the places you would like to see and the things you want to do."

Beth Ann didn't answer so Anna went to the kitchen in the dark. She threw a few sticks of wood into the stove to heat up the coffee and warm the leftovers for the young man up in her attic. A young man whom she was sure she would have to reckon with sometime soon. *I just thought my troubles were almost over. I'm not sure my heart can take much more.*

"I was hoping I could get you out of here tonight, Lance." Rand had just finished devouring the food Anna had brought up and was on his second cup of coffee.

"There isn't anything I would like better but I don't think that would be wise. You can't be taking care of me out there in the woods. Anna said there are four men who ride with this Dean character who runs the show around here. There is one older man who hangs around the ranch and watches out for things. She said to not let him fool us. He's mean and capable of anything. That makes six men who are going to be all over the place and you can't be worrying about me."

"I've seen the older man. Followed him to a hidden canyon where there's a shack and meadow with a spring. There are three mares and a stallion there. The way they're tucked away in that canyon it wouldn't surprise me if they're stolen. That stallion is one fine piece of horse flesh."

"You're probably right. Dean has plans to buy a horse ranch somewhere around Lexington and raise race horses."

Rand shook his head. "We can't be worrying about horses now. I need to know how you're feeling, Lance. What do I need to do to get you and the women out of here?"

"I think in another day or two I'll be able to move around more. My head is doing a lot better. That was the worst of it. When I'd move, my head would swim and my stomach would do summersaults. You know, if I had something to use for a crutch that would help a lot. Do you think you could find something that would work for a crutch?"

"I don't know why not. It may not be pretty but I can find something that'll work."

"If we had a wagon we could cover and hide me and the girls in the back. That might work but as near as I can tell, there's only one wagon they use to haul supplies." Lance thought a minute. "Nah! Too many complications for that to work. The women would have to think of some reason to use the wagon and from what Anna says; she and her daughter are closely watched. They're held here almost like prisoners. That would put them in too much danger."

Rand was quiet a moment then came up with an idea. "Do you suppose there's a ranch somewhere in the area where I could borrow a wagon? I'd have to come up with a story about why I'm coming up here."

"That might work. You could say you were looking to buy a horse and thought they might have one they would sell you."

"I'll see what I can come up with tonight. I'll work on making you a crutch tomorrow; put it in the bushes behind the outhouse when I finish with it."

"As soon as I get the crutch I'll start practicing and getting used to moving around with it. At least my head is better. I couldn't do anything but lay flat on my back."

Just then Anna opened the door and stepped inside. "How are you two doing? Do you need anything else?"

Rand stood and handed Anna the tray his meal had been on. "Not for me, ma'am. That was mighty good eating and I appreciate you going to the trouble to feed me."

"I didn't mind at all. I've fixed you a sack of food to take with you when you leave."

Beth popped her head into the room. "Ma, I just saw one of the men ride to the bunkhouse. I'm pretty sure it was Dusty."

"All right, Beth, thanks for letting us know. You go on to bed now."

"I'll see you in the morning. Good night," Beth said as she closed the door.

"I better go now too," Rand said. "Glad we got a chance to talk, Lance. If you need to get a message to me, send it with one of the women when they go riding."

Anna said, "It will probably be Beth Ann. She gets out and rides every day. The men are used to her riding around the place. She has boundaries and can't ride too far, but it's the only pleasure she really has." Anna turned and took the few steps to the door. "I'll walk you out," she said to Rand. They stopped at the back door of the kitchen as Anna handed him the sack of food she had fixed. The urge to hug the young man in front of her was overwhelming, but she just touched his arm. "Please be careful."

Alone in the dark kitchen Anna was in a turmoil as to what she should do. *I have to know. I've got to talk to Lance and find out for sure. There is a chance I could be wrong, but everything in me is telling me I'm not wrong.*

At the attic door, Anna knocked lightly and let herself into the room. "It's me again, Lance. Do you feel like talking a few more minutes?"

"Sure, I'd enjoy the company. Come on over and sit."

Anna sat on the floor close to Lance so she could talk quietly and not bother Beth. "Did you and the young marshal come up with a plan?"

"We're working on it. Rand is going to make me a crutch tomorrow. He'll hide it in the bushes behind the outhouse. I need to start learning how to get around on the thing. You and Beth Ann need to be ready to move at a moment's notice. Make up a bundle of things you might need for a couple of days but only take the necessities. Maybe you could hide it in Beth Ann's room." Marshal Chambers was thoughtful a moment. "Rand is a good man and he'll come up with a plan to get us out of here."

"I . . . uh," Anna hesitated and looked down at her hands.

Lance watched her a moment. "What's wrong? Is there something bothering you?" Her worried look brought out a strong desire to protect this woman he had only met a couple of days before.

"There's something I need to know," she said in a whisper.

"Just ask. I'll tell you what I can."

"It's about the young marshal, you call him Rand. I was just wondering what his last name is, and what you know about him."

"Well, his name is Rand Trinity. I don't know a lot about his background except his father died some years back when he was a teenager. If I remember correctly, Rand and his father were traveling by train during the war. They were trying to get from the South to the North when the train was attacked and his father killed. Rand ended up in prison camp where a cousin found him and got him out of a prison hospital. The cousin took him out west and his uncle raised him on a horse ranch. He won't talk about his mother. All he's ever said is she abandoned him and his father when he was . . . ."

Pieces to the puzzle of Anna's life began falling into place. Lance paused and took a closer look at Anna's face. In the dim lantern light he saw a tear trickle down her cheek. There was so much pain and sorrow in her eyes he felt like crying too. Gently he touched her face with the palm of his hand and brushed away the tears that were falling freely now. "Is Rand your son?"

Anna nodded, covered her face with her hands, and quietly began sobbing. Lance pulled her into an embrace and held her while she wept. It took a while, but Anna slowly began to recover. She never moved from the comfort of Lance's arms, just started talking. "When I turned around and looked in his face it was such a shock I almost dropped the lantern. He looks just like Randal when I first met him, except for his red hair. I don't know what I'm going to do. Please don't tell him who I am. He must hate me and I don't blame him. I've ruined the lives of both my children. Anyone would tell you what a horrid person I am. I don't deserve to even be alive."

"Wait a minute. You're not going to talk like that around me. You're tired and have had a shock, but I'm here to tell you I know a great God and we're going to work all this out. Just not tonight. You need some rest and I need time to pray. God will show us what to do. You go get some rest now. We'll talk more in the morning."

Reluctantly, Anna made herself withdraw from the shelter of the marshal's arms. When she stood, the only thing she could think to do was apologize. "I'm sorry I dumped all that on you."

"I'm not one bit sorry, Anna. I'm glad I could be here for you."

"Thank you, Lance."

Chapter 7

ETH ANN WOKE LATER than usual. Tired as she was, sleep had been slow to come. As morning dawned Beth was reluctant to move out of the warmth of her blankets. So much was happening, but her encounter with the beautiful young woman in her little meadow was the strangest of all. *Could I have dreamed it? No! She was* real. *I know she was real, but where did she come from? Strange that she showed up right after I told God I needed a friend. Maybe He really did hear me.*

The thoughts of meeting Sarah again compelled her to get out of bed and dress. *I've got to get chores done so I won't be late to go for my ride. Let's see, I'll do my outdoor chores first. Then I have to help ma with the wash.* Sudden doubts dampened her excitement. *What if she doesn't show up? God please let her show up.*

Halfway through the laundry excitement started building in Beth Ann. "What is going on with you today, Beth? You're rushing through this laundry like you have an important date or something. Are you all right?"

"Yes, I'm fine. It's such a pretty day I'm anxious to go for my ride."

"Aren't you going to have something to eat before you go?"

"If you don't mind, Ma, I'll just get me something to eat when I get back."

"No, I don't mind. As a matter of fact why don't you go ahead and have your ride. There are only a few things left to hang out and I can finish that."

"Thanks, Ma."

"Please be careful, Beth. If at all possible stay away from the men."

"I will, Ma, see you later."

In a position to watch the bunkhouse and still be close to the back of the house, Rand had watched two men saddle their horses and ride out in the direction of the hidden canyon. *That leaves one man still in the bunkhouse. Probably the one that came in late last night is still sleeping.*

Earlier, Rand had found a perfect limb with a Y that would work for a crutch. As he watched the women do chores, then wash and hang out laundry, he smoothed out the rough places in the limb with his knife. *This should work. The mother, Lance called her Anna, I think, can pad the Y and make it more comfortable. Now to get it in the bushes behind the outhouse.*

Careful to stay hidden, Rand moved toward the back of the outhouse just in time to see the girl disappear into the house. He was as close to the clothes line as he dared to go when he spoke just loud enough for Anna to hear. "The crutch is ready. I put it where I told you I would."

Anna kept right on hanging clothes. "Thank you. I'll get it when it's safe."

"How is Lance this morning?"

"I think he's doing quite a bit better. He ate a good breakfast and is eager to try out the crutch."

"That sounds good. Does he need anything or have a message for me?"

"Not now. I'll come out several times during the day to check on the laundry. If you need to get a message to him tell me then."

"All right. You and your daughter be careful."

Anna looked up into the sky as if watching a bird. "Marshal, Beth is going for a ride in a few minutes. Will you keep an eye on her? The man in the bunkhouse named Dusty is trying to get close to her. He's a bad one and I'm afraid for her."

"Sure, I can do that. We'll have to make a move tomorrow. It's just getting too dangerous around here. If you can think of some way to use the wagon by the barn without causing attention, talk to Lance about it. I haven't come up with a workable plan yet, but if we're all thinking, we'll come up with something."

"I'll help all I can. I'm counting on you and Lance to get Beth away from here. It doesn't matter about me but promise me you'll get her far away from here."

"I promise I'll do everything I can."

Rand worked his way back to his two horses. He left the pack horse and saddled Sugar. The trees and underbrush were heavy but he finally found a trail that appeared to be parallel to the road Beth had ridden down. After about an hour, the bubbling gurgle of a stream caught his attention. He could hear underlying voices through the tumbling of the stream's water. The ride had been so quiet and peaceful, Rand was surprised to hear other people talking. *Is she meeting someone? I wonder what that girl is up to. I better find out in case she's up to something I need to know about.*

Leaving his horse tied to a tree, it didn't take long to slip behind some bushes and peek out at a small clearing next to the stream. He couldn't make much sense of what he was seeing. *What in the world! She's meeting another woman, a gypsy woman. Where did she come from? What could they be up to?*

Suddenly, the beautiful gypsy woman with black hair, tinkling bracelets, glittering necklace and earrings, began talking loudly, as if performing before a crowd. Rand was mesmerized as he watched the captivating gypsy lady clap her hands and twirl a couple of times while joyfully proclaiming, "Oh, we are going to have so much fun, my new friend!" She took Beth's hand and led her to a rock in a sandy area by the stream. "Are you ready to turn our secret place into a Make Believe Meadow?"

A slight grin worked her mouth as Beth shrugged. "I don't know. It seems kind of . . . childish."

"It doesn't hurt to dream or make believe once in a while, but it's not healthy to live in that frame of mind. We have to learn to cope in the real world and sometimes dreaming or make believe can help us see things in a different way. Will you trust me, Beth? There are some things I want you to see and some very special friends I want you to meet. It's all in our Make Believe Meadow."

"All right. What do I have to do?"

"Do whatever I do and just have fun. We can't live in Make Believe Meadow, but when you *do* get to go there, enjoy the experience. Now, let's hold hands like this." She took both of Beth's hands in hers. "Now close your eyes and circle to the right . . . *three times!*"

After the three circles, they were giggling like two little girls. "We're here now. Open your eyes. Remember what I told you yesterday about not letting a word define who you are?"

"Yes, I remember."

"Here in Make Believe Meadow you have choices. The first choice is: Do you want to be an ugly old witch with warts on your nose? Or do you want to be a beautiful princess? Choose quickly!"

"A beautiful princess," Beth answered immediately.

"Wonderful, a fine choice." Gypsy lady went to a sack sitting beside the rock. She pulled out a piece of red fabric and fashioned it around Beth's shoulders, who by now looked somewhat embarrassed. "Your *cape*, Princess Beth. Now you must have a crown if you are going to be a princess." Again, she dug into the bag and presented Beth with a tiara that sparkled like real diamonds glinting in the sun.

"Oh, how pretty!" Beth said, quite pleased.

"A pretty crown for a pretty princess." She placed the crown on Beth's head and had her sit on the rock as her throne. "Now, for your second choice: Do you want to have more friends? Or do you want to be alone?"

Beth Ann looked very serious. "I've always wanted friends but where can you find friends around here?"

The gypsy lady looked her in the eye. "We found each other, didn't we?"

"Yes," Beth said, nodding her head.

"There are more friends around our meadow than you know about. May I bring them out?"

Beth eyes cut a swath through the meadow. "Yes, I guess so," she said cautiously.

"Princess Beth, I want you to meet *Jessie*!"

Out of the bushes came the smallest man Rand had ever seen. *He's a dwarf!* Rand was totally swept up in the magic that was happening in the meadow. *I've never seen anything like this.*

The small man walked up to Beth like he was ten feet tall. "Princess Beth, I am so happy to meet you." He bowed elegantly.

Beth's eyes were as huge as saucers. *If she doesn't shut her mouth she's going to eat a fly.* Rand watched her with a grin on his face.

Jessie continued, "I have had to make choices in my life, Princess. I have been called many names, like ugly, dumb head, and the worst name, *freak!* One day I decided I didn't want to be any of those things. I wanted to be a brave knight, to fight and protect those who were in need. I want to be your friend, Princess Beth." He pulled a sword from its sheaf on his belt and held it high. "I pledge you my sword and my service as a knight." The man bowed again and sat down close to the rock.

"And now, Princess, I want you to meet Daisy." Rand thought Daisy was a little girl, at first. *I can't believe what I'm seeing. There are two of them.* The small woman was dressed in a simple yellow dress, holding something in her hands that was covered with a cloth. Rand strained to hear what she was saying, her voice being softer than the others. She curtsied. "I too am pleased to meet you, Princess Beth. Would you like to hear the story of my choices?"

By this time, Beth Ann had fallen completely into the spell of Make Believe Meadow. "Yes, please," she said, leaning forward a little. "I would love to hear your story."

The small woman was animated as she began to share her life story. "I was born into a family who was very rich. I knew I was different from the other women in our family but didn't think much of it until I heard my grandmother tell my father that I should have been put into an institution as soon as I was born, that the way I looked was an embarrassment to the family. I soon caught on that it was my mother who wouldn't let them send me away. She appeased the family by creating my own little world where they would never have to look at me or talk to me. I was given a great big room at the back of our large three story home. The room had a back door that led out into a garden with a fence that was so tall I couldn't see the outside world and they couldn't see me. My mother and a servant girl were the only people I ever saw. Mother taught me to read and write and helped me discover the world through books.

"As I grew older, my heart became restless. I didn't know what to do about it, so in my confusion I turned bitter and hateful. Life was not worth living. I just wanted my life to end!

"One day, the servant girl showed my mother a poster. She was excited about going to the circus with a friend. The poster was left on the table in my room, so when I was alone I read every word written about the circus. I was fifteen when I made my first choice all on my own. I was going to that circus or die trying! I would have to run away and walk a long distance to get there, but nothing was going to stop me.

"When I got to the edge of town I was very tired. I could see the lights and noise of the circus not too far away but I had to sit on a log to rest." Daisy giggled. "Really, I was afraid and had to work up the courage to keep going. The minute I stepped into the crowd of people, they started laughing at me and calling me names. One man threw something at me and told me to go back to the wagon where I belonged. I didn't know what he was talking about. I started crying and ran behind a tent. I was crying hard and knew I was too tired to walk anymore. That's when a man's voice spoke to me. It was such a kind voice that I didn't feel afraid. He sat beside me and said, 'What's the matter, little one?'

"I told him my story and he became one of my best friends. He took me to a large wagon that was part of the circus and introduced me to two other small people, just like me. They became my family."

Beth had to know, "Did your mother ever find you?"

"Yes, after a few days, but I had already fallen in love with Jessie. When I explained to mother, she cried, but understood. I made a choice to stay with Jessie and have never been sorry." Daisy beamed a big smile at Jessie and he returned it with love written all over his face. "I performed with the circus once in awhile, sang and danced, but what I wanted to do most of all is *cook*. I brought some honey cakes for you to sample. Would you like to try one and share the rest with your friends?"

Daisy uncovered the plate of cakes and held them out to Beth. The aroma was enticing. "Yes," Beth answered. "I would like one. They smell really good."

Everyone took a cake and chatted like they had known each other for years. Jessie pulled out a flute when he finished his cake and began to play a tune. As Daisy danced around the meadow, soon Jessie followed her. Beth and the gypsy lady talked and laughed while eating another cake.

Rand's mouth watered just watching the group eat the honey cakes. He had the strongest desire to go join the happy little group on the meadow. *Maybe if I join them they would share their honey cakes with me.* Preoccupied with his thoughts, Rand didn't hear the man sneaking up behind him. He froze when something jabbed him in the back.

"Put your hands up and turn around . . . real slow," the man ordered.

"All right," Rand conceded. *What an idiot I am. I got caught like a school boy. Dad would be ashamed of me.*

Marshal Rand Trinity turned to face his captor, but didn't expect his captor to be a *clown*, dressed in full costume, big red nose, white face with big red smile painted in place. And to top it off, a funny hat that didn't match any of the other parts of his costume. Rand glanced down and saw the man wasn't holding a gun but just a finger that he had poked in Rand's back.

The clown chucked. "She said you were in the area but I didn't believe her. How you doing, Rand?" The clown clapped him on the shoulder.

Rand couldn't get a word to come out of his gaping mouth and the clown laughed again. "You don't recognize me, do you?"

"No, I don't and I don't think it's funny! Who *are* you?"

"Well, not too long ago you knew me as George Fisher. Today I am Sebastian the Clown, but officially, my real name is Mitchell Morgan."

"George?" Rand practically gasped. "What are you doing here?"

"I don't have time to tell you the entire story because right now I'm helping Josie." George nodded in the direction of the meadow.

"Josie?" Rand turned back to scan the meadow. "Josie is *here*? *Where*?"

"That's her out there in the gypsy costume."

Rand didn't reply right away, just watched the meadow trying to understand what was going on. "George, none of this makes any sense. You all are in real danger being in this area. That girl's father and his gang are a bunch of thieving murderers and they're gathering at their ranch up the road."

"Yes, we know all about it, but Josie thought helping this girl was important."

"Helping her *how*?"

"You'll have to ask Josie about that. Yesterday, she found the girl crying and wanting to die. Seems she had just found out that her mother and father are not married and she's . . . well . . . she's illegitimate. That's hard on a young girl her age. Probably feels like no man will ever want her for a wife. You know girls think about those things. Josie is trying to help her realize she can make her life what she wants it to be." He paused a moment. "Josie is good with kids, Rand. She will make a wonderful mother."

Rand couldn't help but smile at the thought of Josie holding their baby in her arms. "Do you think she will ever be still long enough to become a mother or take care of a brood of little ones?"

"Don't worry about that. She doesn't talk about it very often but it's her heart's desire to have a home with a husband and children. She's never had stability with us moving around all the time. That's what she wants and that's what I want for her. Well, there's my cue. Stay here, Rand, until I call you. I'll do my clown part then call you to come out."

Sarah called Sebastian's name and the clown patted his own chest. Rand stepped back in surprise as a tiny brown ball of fur jumped into the clown's arms. "Meet Chico, Rand. I'll call you pretty soon now."

The miniature brown dog looked at Rand with a huge grin on its face. Sebastian bounded out into the meadow with his doggy companion. *Now I know I'm losing my mind! That dog just smiled at me. I've never seen a dog smile before.* His attention was drawn to Sarah as she said, "Princess Beth, this is Sebastian the clown."

Daisy interjected, "He's the man with the kind voice who was so nice to me."

Jessie added, "He's the man who taught me to be a brave knight and introduced me to Daisy."

Sarah smiled at Beth. "He's the man who taught me and helped me be the person I am today. He's special because he's my father. He made his choice long ago to be a clown. His passion in life is to entertain. Sebastian, you and Chico entertain the princess."

As the clown and the smiling dog did tricks and delighted everyone with their antics, Rand couldn't keep his eyes off Sarah. *Ah, Josie, you did it again! You fooled me again. I don't know if I can stand back here very much longer and just watch you. I want to hold you in my arms . . . And . . . .*

Sebastian leaned down and whispered in Josie's ear, as a squeal of delight erupted on the meadow. "He's here? Where is he?" Josie didn't wait for an answer. She called out, "Rand, where are you?" Right on cue, Rand walked out of hiding and into the meadow. He didn't have to walk far. Josie closed the distance between them, running and throwing herself into his arms. "Oh, Rand, I couldn't sleep all night just thinking about seeing you again. It was so hard to wait."

Rand nuzzled her ear, whispering, "If I had known you were anywhere around here you wouldn't have had to wait. Speaking of you being here, why *are* you here?"

Josie pushed back and smiled up at Rand. "Come with me. We need to talk, but first I need to finish what I started with Beth."

Rand joined the group as Daisy exclaimed, "Is this him? Is this your handsome red-headed U.S. Marshal?"

"Yes," Josie said, almost shyly. She clung to her man. "This is him."

"Why, he is *almost* as handsome as Jessie," Daisy boldly flirted and winked at Rand.

Everyone laughed and of course, Rand blushed. Then Sarah, the gypsy lady, took charge. "All right, everyone. Come make a circle."

Sebastian patted his chest and Chico jumped into his arms and into a small pocket sewn into the front of the costume. Only the dog's smiling face showed.

Everyone circled and looked at Sarah who smiled and spoke directly to Beth. "I hope you enjoyed Make Believe Meadow as much as I did, Beth. I will never forget it. I'm so glad God let us find each other and I hope you know He was here with us today. There was a reason we did this for you. We wanted you to see that there are others in this world who have had heavy troubles and have made choices that made them better people. Remember to not let words or hurtful people define who you are. Make your choices for your life with God's help." Sarah looked at the faces in her circle. "I love you all so much. I want to pray for you." She bowed her head and the others followed her example. "Thank you, God, for bringing us together today. I ask your blessings on each one of us, especially Beth, my new friend. We have things we must do in the next few days so please guide our plans and keep us all safe. Thank you again, Jesus, for your love. Amen.

"Well, we must leave Make Believe Meadow the same way we came in," Sarah continued. "Close your eyes and hold hands. Then we circle to the left, *three times!*"

Rand scowled at her. She tried to hide a smile and gave him a threatening look. "*All* of us must hold hands," she said again, looking right at Rand. At that moment, Rand couldn't deny Josie anything. So, feeling rather silly, he closed his eyes and circled three times to the left with everyone else. Then Sarah declared, "We are back! Open your eyes!"

For some strange reason, just for a moment, Rand felt like he had left a magical place and was back into the real world again. The realistic Rand pulled Josie apart from the others. "Josie, where is your group staying?"

"We have three gypsy wagons down the road where the road forks."

"You have *wagons?*"

"Yes, three of them."

"I think God just answered my prayers."

Chapter 8

"D O YOU THINK BETH will be alright, Rand? I feel bad sending her back there all by herself."

"She'll be fine getting to the house. It's what happens after she gets home that bothers me."

Rand was standing at the edge of the meadow with his arm around Josie's shoulder. Her father, Daisy, and Jessie joined them as they watched Beth ride up the road. Josie took a deep breath and let it out slowly. "I suppose she's been in her situation a long time and will handle herself fine with her mother's help. What are we going to do now, Rand?"

"Well, now that's a good question. First, I want to know what in the world you are doing here."

"That will take some time to explain. Let's go back to the wagons and Daisy and I will fix a nice supper, then I'll explain our situation. After that we can make plans to help get Beth and her mother out of danger."

"It's a bigger job than that for me, but you're right, we need to take time to talk and plan. "I have to go back to the ranch first and get my pack horse. Probably take me over an hour but I'll hurry."

"Can I ride with you, Rand?" Josie asked. "I don't want to let you out of my sight right now. I can help Daisy when we get back."

Rand looked at Josie with a crooked little grin. "I don't see why not but you've got to promise me you'll do *exactly* what I tell you. There are six dangerous men in this area and we all need to be on the alert." Rand frowned and shook his head. "On second thought, maybe it wouldn't be such a good idea, Josie."

She looked full into his face and into his eyes. Her startling blue eyes were his undoing and he groaned in feigned agony when she batted those eyes at him. "Please?"

Her father gave a mirthful snort. "You might as well give in now, Rand. When she turns those blue eyes on you it's hard to deny her anything. Besides, she can handle herself. Do you have your knives, Josie?"

"Yes, also my pistol."

Minutes later, Josie sat behind Rand on his horse, as they rode the narrow trail through the trees and brush. They were alert and watchful all the way to the pack horse. As they reached the meadow on their way back, Rand began to relax some and Josie slipped her arms around Rand's waist and leaned into him, giving him a tight squeeze. He felt the warmth of her body through his shirt and was pretty sure he felt her kiss his back. He turned and spoke quietly over his shoulder. "Now that's the kind of thing that makes it dangerous for you to be with me. With you so close and hugging me like that I lose all my concentration and can't think straight."

She hugged him again. "Are you sorry you let me come with you?"

"Oh, no! I enjoyed every minute with you. We should be fairly safe by now since we're on the main road. Still, you need to keep an eye out behind us."

"All right, I will. Do you have a plan?"

"I've given it some thought, but before we talk about anything else I still want to know what you and your father are doing here? And don't leave anything out, I want the whole story. Is it the Pinkerton's?"

"No, Dad and I don't work for the Pinkerton's anymore. I decided since I was going to be a married woman I should devote all my time to my husband. That's the way I think it should be. There just wouldn't be time to divide my life between a family and a job." She waited for Rand to respond and when he didn't, she continued. "Dad agreed and we both resigned. I hope you think I made the right decision."

Rand suddenly rained in Sugar. He listened a moment then quickly turned the horses into the trees. Spotting heavy brush and boulders big enough to hide behind, Rand guided the horses in that direction. As soon as he stopped, Josie slid off the back and pulled the pack horse in closer to her, putting her hand over his nostrils to keep him from calling to other horses. Rand did the same with Sugar and they stood quietly, listening.

A few minutes later voices drifted their way from the road. Rand started to signal for Josie not to talk then realized how foolish that would be. *Her dad was right; she knows how to handle herself. She knew what to do without being told. I'll have to tell her how proud I am of her.* Rand couldn't see how many were out on the road but it sounded like two men. He could pick up part of their conversation:

"You sure you don't want me to go back and chase off those gypsy people, Boss?"

"Nah, leave them alone for now. I just want to get home. I'm tired and I need a good stiff drink. Maybe tomorrow."

"I wouldn't mind having the horses those gypsies have. They were some of the best looking draft horses I've ever seen. If we get rid of those gypsies, can I have the horses?"

"Toby, I don't care what you do with those people or their horses, but you don't do nothing until I give you the go ahead. I don't want my plans ruined. This being our last job, I won't risk anything messing it up. In a few days we'll split the loot and go . . . ."

The voices trailed off. Josie didn't move until Rand did. He went directly to Josie, pulled her into his arms and kissed her. When he pulled away, she smiled up at him. "What was *that* for?"

"That's for *you* being *you*. I'm so proud of you and the way you handled yourself. I'm also glad you quit the Pinkerton's. I love you, Josephine Fish . . . What is your *real* name? I think your dad mentioned his real name is Mitchell Morgan. Is that your real last name, Morgan? What am I supposed to call him?"

Josie laughed. "Our last name is Morgan and most of our friends call dad Mitch." She said this very patiently like she was speaking to a child. Then a mischievous grin appeared on her pretty face. "Just call me Josie, because you're going to change my last name *soon*, I hope."

"You'll be Josephine *Trinity* just as soon as we can get some time to make plans about our future. Right now we need to get on down the road to your people. Who are they anyway? Come on, you can tell me as we ride."

Rand insisted that Josie ride in front this time. "I don't like you riding behind me. I want to look at you while you finish answering my questions."

On the road again, Josie said, "All right, what do you want to know first?"

"If you and your dad are not with the Pinkerton Agency, what are you doing here?"

"A wonderful old friend of dad's wrote him for help. He's like family to us and we couldn't turn down his plea. He has a horse ranch outside of Lexington with several quality race horses but his pride and joy is a stallion named Midnight Thunder. Midnight has won a number of races that has placed him in the top three race horses in the country. I haven't seen the horse but dad's friend, Phillip Dawson, showed us pictures of him. He is a magnificent creature! Midnight Thunder was stolen while they were transporting him for a race in Lexington. There were three men and a wagon with the horse. Two of the men were killed and the third was wounded and unable to tell them anything that would help with the robbery."

"I suppose your dad came up with the idea to travel as gypsies?"

"Actually, it was my idea. It made sense because as gypsies we could travel the country looking for leads. The wagon Jessie and Daisy have is set up like a tinker's wagon. Little Danny raises shire draft horses and has a fancy gypsy wagon that's quite impressive. You see, that's what the gypsies are famous for, selling kitchen utensils and all sorts of products for the household and selling horses like the draft horses. It's a perfect cover to travel to the farms and ranches. Jessie and Daisy have done pretty good selling their wares and Danny has an order for a pair of his horses. Our only lead was when we were visiting with a family this side of Lexington. Their thirteen-year-old boy told us he was out hunting in the hills back of their farm and saw two men leading a stallion as black as night. He said they were moving in this direction . . . so here we are."

"That explains what you're doing here, but who is Little Danny? I figure Daisy and Jessie are friends from your circus days. Is Danny another little person like them?"

Josephine giggled. "Quite the opposite. Little Danny is eight feet three inches tall and strong as a bear. He was part of the circus but when the owner of the circus decided to go back to tour in Europe, Dan didn't want to go across the ocean again. It petrified Daisy and Jessie to think of traveling on a ship. Dad and I didn't want to go, so we all left together and found places in Kentucky. Dan has his own place to the south of us and hired a young man to help him with his horses. Daisy and Jessie have their own place and live down the road north from us. We're all neighbors."

"Why do you all three have gypsy wagons?"

"Actually, two of them are Dan's. His people were gypsies. He told me once that because he was so big, he drew a lot at attention to their band and the gypsies didn't like it. So they sold Dan to the circus."

Rand shook his head. "People do dumb things, don't they?"

"Yes, they do." Josie was quiet for a while, thinking of Rand's mother abandoning her family and felt that was *worse* than dumb, but she didn't want to pass judgment. She wondered if Rand thought of his mother anymore. The subject was depressing. She continued her story.

"Dan tried his hand with sheep but didn't like it. He had a nice wagon to live in during that time and that's the one dad and I use. After we settled in Kentucky, Dan built, painted, and decorated the big fancy wagon he uses. Then he helped Jessie design and build the tinker's wagon. Jessie thought that would be a good thing for him and Daisy but it turned out to be dangerous for them. They were targets for the mean people in this world to harass because they were small. With Dan on this trip people keep their distance. Actually, Dan is kind and gentle with everyone, including animals. He dearly loves and spoils his horses."

"Sounds like you have some good neighbors, Josie. Is that your camp up ahead?"

"Yes, that's it. I'll leave you and dad to visit and make plans while I help Daisy with our supper. We'll have time to talk more later this evening."

With their stomachs full and the chores done, the group sat around the campfire to discuss their plans. Except for the heavy responsibilities weighing on his mind, it was one of the most pleasant evenings Rand had experienced in a long time. The most enjoyable time was after everyone headed for their beds and left him and Josie by the fire.

"I sure like your neighbors, Josie. That Dan is a fine man and Jessie and Daisy are pretty special people." They sat close, listening to night sounds, the fire crackling, horses cropping grass, a chorus of frogs and crickets filling the air with their music. "I can't stand the thought of any of you getting hurt tomorrow."

"We all feel that way, Rand. We can't turn our backs on people that need help, though."

"I know and I really do need the help. Promise me you won't take any unnecessary chances, all right?"

"I promise. We've made good plans but you know as well as I do that something could go wrong, there's always that chance. We'll have to do what the situation requires at the moment."

"Sure, I know. Your dad told me about how you all used the wagons to hide runaway slaves and take them through to Ohio. This isn't the first time you've played gypsy."

"Those were bad dangerous times but God took care of us then just like He will take care of us tomorrow."

"We need to get our rest so we'll be ready for tomorrow. Dan invited me to stay in his wagon. He's sleeping outside close to his horses. I think I'll bed down close to him."

"Rand?"

"What?"

"What did you tell Beth before she left this afternoon?"

"I told her to tell Lance and her mother to be ready to move quickly in the morning; That we were coming in to get them. I said don't take anything but the clothes on their backs, that they can come back after it's all over with to get anything important. And we will come right into the ranch yard and create a big commotion."

"Goodness, Beth, I'm glad you're home! You stayed out longer than you usually do. Are you all right?"

"Yes, Ma, I'm fine but we need to talk. I need to tell Marshal Chambers too, so let's go upstairs and I'll tell you both at the same time."

"All right. Sounds like you saw Marshal Trinity?"

"Yes, and he gave me the message."

"Let's hurry on up then. I need to start fixing supper pretty soon."

Beth hurried up the stairs with her mother on her heels. They knocked and entered the room. Anna sat on the box and Beth plopped down on the floor with her legs crossed in front of her. She blurted out, "Marshal Trinity and his friends are coming tomorrow morning to get us. He said we need to be ready to move quickly and not to bother taking anything with us."

"Wait, slow down," Marshal Chambers interrupted her. "Rand has some friends here? Are there other U.S. Marshals?"

"No, just a gypsy lady, a clown, and two little people. Oh, yes, and a tiny dog that smiles all the time."

Lance sat in stunned silence staring at Beth while her mother finally found her voice. "Beth Ann, what in the world are you saying? If you're trying to be funny, it's not working! You start from when you left the house and tell us everything you did today, and it better make sense."

Beth Ann sat there frowning for a few moments. "I guess I'll have to start with yesterday when I went to my favorite place to think about all you told me the other night. I was so confused, Ma. I just needed a friend to talk to. So I asked God to send me a friend. I started crying and didn't even notice when she came up to me, but there she was. Oh, Ma, she was so beautiful . . . and nice."

"*Who* came up to you?"

"A gypsy lady named Sarah."

"So, a beautiful gypsy lady just popped up out of nowhere. Really, Beth!"

"It's true. You've got to believe me."

"All right, continue your story and it better be good, because none of what you've said so far makes much sense."

Beth managed to get through her story. Anna and Lance glanced at each other, perplexed. "What do you think they're going to do, Lance?" Anna asked.

"I don't know but we better be ready anyway . . . ."

Just then, heavy boots tromped on the front porch; all three in the attic froze. The front door opened and closed, and Anna knew who it was. "It's Dean," she whispered. "Stay here, Beth, until I get him into the kitchen, then go to your room."

An angry voice rose from downstairs. "Anna, I'm home! Where are you, woman?"

Anna grabbed a towel that Lance had used. She quickly lifted the lid to the barrel where they had stashed the stolen money. She grabbed out a few apples she had put on top of the money and wrapped them in the towel.

"You better answer me, Anna!" Dean demanded. "I'm in no mood for games. I'm tired, hungry, and I want a drink."

"I'm right here, Dean," Anna said as she hurried down the stairs.

"What are you doing up there?" he growled.

"Just getting some apples from the storage room. I thought I might make a pie or that apple cake you like."

"Never mind about pie or cake, get me a drink!"

"You want it in the kitchen or the front room?"

The miserable man went rigid with impatience. "Wherever I am, is where I want it. Now get my drink!"

Before Anna could get to the kitchen, another set of boots sounded on the porch. Dean had not sat down yet so he jerked the door open. "What do you want, Dusty? I haven't even had time to sit. Can't it wait until after supper?"

"I don't think so, Boss. You know I wouldn't bother you unless it was important."

"All right, let's walk to the bunkhouse and I'll say howdy to the boys. You got any liquor over there?"

"Sure, we've got a couple of bottles going right now."

Dean walked out the door yelling over his shoulder, "I want *food* when I get back!"

Beth slipped down the stairs and found her mother in the kitchen. "It's going to be a bad night, isn't it, Ma?"

"I'm afraid so. Please stay out of the way as much as you can. Why don't you take care of your horse and milk the cow for me? Make sure the chickens are shut up before you come back."

"Sure, I forgot about Star. I'll hurry with the chores and come back to help with supper."

Anna reached out and pulled her daughter into her arms. "I'll be glad when this is all over, sweetheart. I'm so sorry you've been through so much."

"We'll be all right, Ma. We'll take care of each other."

"What's so important, Dusty?"

Dean and Dusty were walking toward the bunkhouse when Dusty stopped in the middle of the yard. Shaking his head, he told his boss some news that was sure to send him into a tail spin. "It's gone, Dean, every bit of our own private stash is *gone*! I went over to the shack this morning to put the thousand dollars with the other money . . . and it's gone! All the sacks, the box, everything, gone."

Dean's vocabulary at the news made Dusty take a step back. His boss had a foul mouth, but this was different than anything he'd heard before. "Who took it? Please tell me you looked around and found some sign of who was there and took it."

"Of *course* I looked around. Found some sign. There was at least two horses maybe three around the shack in the last few days. I could only identify one track for sure."

"Who was it, Dusty? I'll kill them for sure. We've worked too long and hard to save that much. You didn't let it slip to the men where you've been hiding the money, have you?"

"No, of course not. No one knows of that stash except you and me. The boys think what's hidden in the bunkhouse is all we've got. They're anxious to divide it and go their separate ways. It's been a long time and we're all ready to start new lives."

"I am too, but now I won't be able to start my horse ranch like I wanted to. Not without that stash of ours. Who was it, Dusty? Spit it out!"

"Anna's horse, Bell, has a funny marking on her left rear shoe. I would know it anywhere, but she may have just been around the shack and not found the money, cause there's been some other funny things going on around here. Fred found tracks up above the canyon where the horses are, and Chigger said there were tracks of two horses around the side and back of the barn. I think there's a stranger snooping around the place. I know you can't tell them we've been secretly hiding part of our loot, but come hear the boys out then you can tell us what to do and take care of business . . . *our* business."

After a good many drinks and hearing what his men had to say, Dean was fit to be tied. All right men, do whatever you need to do right away, then stay in the bunkhouse tonight. No matter what you hear at the house, stay away. Even if you hear gunshots. I'm afraid Anna has a man around and she'll pay dearly for crossing me. Dusty, give me about thirty minutes, then come on to the house and see if I have anything for you to do."

Every step Dean took across the ranch yard fueled his need to punish someone for his plans going awry. His need to control and dominate everyone and everything around him was a powerful force building inside. A force that made him want to *crush* someone. In his mind, Anna had a man around and they were plotting against him. *I'll kill her! And if Beth knows anything about it, I'll kill her too. There will be no mercy for them or the man who stole my money.*

Chapter 9

"ANNA!" THE HOUSE SHOOK when Dean shouted and slammed the front door.

Anna hurried from the kitchen, warning Beth with a look to stay put. "What is it, Dean? Is something wrong?" Rage was pulsing from every pore of the man's body. Anna had seen it before and she knew this could very well be the end of her.

"*Yes*, there is something *wrong*!" he yelled. "Where is Beth? I want her in here. I have some questions for you two."

"Beth is busy in the kitchen; can't I answer your questions?"

Anna knew it was coming and silently took the slap that had enough force to knock her off her feet. She hit the floor - *hard*. Beth came rushing to her mother's side. "Ma, are you all right?" Anna turned away from her daughter to hide her tears and the stinging pain from the slap. Beth jumped to her feet, facing her dad. "Don't hit her again, Pa! She didn't do anything wrong."

Beth managed to step back, avoiding the full force of her father's hand, but the hit was still strong enough to knock her into the chair against the wall. She flew out of the chair, in spite of his abuse, and stood facing her father again. "Don't *ever* hit us again! Do you hear me? Don't ever hit us again!" she screamed.

Dean's maniacal laugh chilled the room. He leaned down in Beth's face, cold eyes boring into hers. "And if I do, what're *you* going to do about it? Who's going to stop me from beating you both senseless?"

A booming man's voice thundered, "I will! If you ever touch either one of them again, I'll blow your head off!" His commanding tone broached no argument.

Dean turned to find the man at the top of the stairs with a pistol pointed at him. "Who are you, and what are you doing in my house?"

"I'm U.S. Marshal, Lance Chambers, and if you so much as *twitch,* it will be the last twitch you'll ever make."

Dean's hands clenched into hard fists. "You'll pay for this, Marshal. Might as well give it up now cause me or my men will kill you before this night is over."

Lance ignored the threat. "Very slowly, unbuckle your belt and drop it to the floor, then kick it away from you." Dean reluctantly complied. "Anna, get his gun belt. Beth, get the rifle by the door. Both of you hold your guns on him while I get down the stairs. Stand far enough away that he can't make a play for you and don't hesitate to shoot him if he even acts like he's going to move. He'd kill all three of us if he could, so keep your guns on him!"

Lance thumped his way down the stairs using the crutch and still holding his pistol ready. At the bottom, he asked Beth to hand him the rifle she was holding. He moved behind Dean and with the butt of the rifle, clubbed him over the head as hard as he could. Dean dropped to the floor. "Hurry, girls! Tie him up and gag him. I don't know how long he'll be out so you've got to do it quickly. I'm in no condition to fight him, so make sure he can't get loose." With Dean gagged and bound, Lance had the women drag the still unconscious man away from the door. "Sorry, you two had to do this, but it couldn't be helped. If you need to sit a minute, go ahead."

Anna shook her head. "I'm shaking, but I think I would do better if I stayed busy. Maybe some hot tea will calm me. Do you want anything, Lance?"

"A cup of coffee would be good. Beth, if you don't mind running up and getting my rifle, I'd appreciate it. I'll stay right here in this chair and keep an eye on my prisoner."

"It's getting dark. Do you want me to light a lantern?" Anna asked.

"No, it's fine. The men may be watching the house and it would be better if it was dark inside. Keep the lantern in the kitchen. That will be enough."

"What are we going to do about him?" Anna nodded toward Dean.

"Nothing right now. From what you've said, the others don't come to the house so we should be all right until help comes in the morning."

"I hope you're right. I'll go get your coffee."

"Thanks, Anna. I'm sorry I couldn't keep him from hitting you."

"We'll be fine. You saved our lives, you know. I'll never forget that."

Footsteps on the porch told them their night of excitement wasn't over. Lance lifted the rifle in readiness. "Be calm and answer the door," he whispered to Anna. "Invite him in, stay out of the way and let me handle it."

Anna rushed Beth to the kitchen then went to the front door. "Hi, Dusty. Do you need something?"

Dusty was all smiles. "Hi, Anna. The boss told me to come by, check in with him. Sure smells good in there. What's for supper?"

"Nothing fancy. Come on in, I'll get Dean."

Dusty stepped into the house, closing the door behind him. "Sure is dark in here. Want me to light a lantern?"

"No, we won't need one, there's light in the kitchen. You stay there and I'll get Dean."

Dusty stood in dim lantern light coming through the kitchen doorway. Suddenly a voice rose out of the darkened front room. "Stand real still, Dusty, put your hands in the air. You're under arrest."

Dusty was lightening fast, whirled toward the voice and went for his gun. But Lance was ready. One shot, through the heart, and Dusty was dead before he dropped in a heap on the floor.

Beth and Anna came warily into the room. "Is he dead?" Beth asked.

"Don't see how he could be anything but dead. Better check for sure, Anna. Beth, watch out the window and see if any of the men in the bunkhouse come to investigate."

"Dead as a doornail. What should we do with him?" Anna nodded toward Dusty's body.

"Cover him with a blanket and leave him there. He's not going to hurt anyone now, and this will all be over in the morning."

Lance thought it was strange that none of the men came to see about the gun shot. He was glad the rest of the evening was quiet, though. After eating a light supper with the girls, he told them, "You two should try and get some rest. I'd like for you to stay together, though."

"Come on, Beth, we'll sleep down here on my bed."

Lance thought they had retired when a short time later, Anna came back into the room. "Here's a blanket, Lance. Do you want me to take a turn watching?"

"No, I'll be fine, you go rest. I doubt I could sleep anyway." She turned to leave but he stopped her. "Anna, before you go, I want to tell you that no matter what happens tomorrow, I think you're a fine woman and . . . well . . . we'll talk more when this is all over."

"Thank you, Lance. I'll need to talk to you about what's going to happen to me."

"I can't say for sure since it will be up to a judge, but I'll do everything I can for you and Beth." His growing fondness for Anna squeezed his heart tight as he watched her resolutely walk back to her room. *She's one strong woman . . . but I want to take care of her.*

Rand felt uneasy when he moved into place behind the ranch house. *Why is it so quiet? That bawling milk cow is the only thing I can hear.* He continued to assess his surroundings, trying to determine what was making him so nervous. *There's smoke coming out the chimney of the house, but none from the bunkhouse. Maybe the men got drunk and are still asleep.*

The three gypsy wagons could be heard coming up the road. The plan was for the wagons to roll into the ranch yard with the last wagon pulling up right in front of the house. The first two wagons were to make such a commotion that all attention would be drawn to them. Then Rand would go through the back door of the house and get Lance and the two women out and into the last wagon where Daisy would be ready to hide them. *There's no way to change plans now, so I'll have to figure it out as I go along.*

As the last wagon rolled up to the front of the house, Rand dashed for the back door and let himself in. He was surprised to hear Lance call him. "Come in here, Rand. We're all in the front room."

Rand scanned the room and smiled when he spotted Lance sitting in a rocking chair by the fire. Anna and Beth were at the widows watching the commotion the others were causing. He couldn't see what was going on outside but they were certainly doing their part in making a lot of noise. "Looks like I'm a little late to the party," Rand said.

"Sorry, Rand, but we had to start earlier than planned."

"Is everyone all right?" Rand looked at each one, his gaze falling to the heap on the floor.

"Well, Dean over there in the corner isn't very happy. I figure the one covered with the blanket isn't very happy where he's at, either, but the rest of us in the house are all right. There is one thing that's been eating at me and that's the quiet bunkhouse across the yard. When I shot the one under the blanket none of the men came to investigate. It's been quiet all night and we haven't seen or heard anything from the other men."

"Yeah, that does seem strange. I noticed there wasn't any smoke from the bunkhouse chimney. I better get the attention of the others and call them in." Ever watchful, Rand stepped out on the front porch and whistled to the others, motioning for them to come to the house."

The little band of gypsy travelers crowded into the front room and were introduced to Marshal Chambers and Anna. Josie's father, Mitch, asked, "What's going on, Rand?"

"Marshal Chambers had to take care of these two last night." He indicated the body on the floor and the man tied up in the corner who was glaring in hatred at them all. "There are four others in the gang, but there has been no sign of them and no smoke from the chimney this morning. I'm going to go over and see if I can roust someone out of there. It's possible they took off in the night."

"I don't think so," said Anna as she watched out the window. "As near as I can tell, their horses are in the pasture, but I agree *something* is wrong."

Rand headed for the door. "I'm going to find out what it is."

"Wait!" Anna stopped Rand. "Let me go. I'll get the milk pail by the back door and head out like I'm getting the cow. They're used to me getting the cow and I can think of a reason to knock on the door and wake them. Maybe I can get a peek inside."

"Thanks for the offer," he told her. "But this is my responsibility. I won't send anyone into danger to do my job."

Mitch got into the conversation. "Don't get all uptight, Rand, but I'm going with you. You're not *sending* me; I am going because I want to back you up."

"I will go too," said Little Danny who had been sitting quietly on the floor. He wasn't able to stand up in the room without bending over."

Jessie was not to be left out. "Is there a door or window out the back of the bunkhouse?"

"Yes, there's a window," Anna told him.

"Then I will go to the back and make sure no one escapes out the window," Jessie said.

Lance Chambers chuckled at the look on Rand's face. "Well, Marshal, you have yourself a posse, and I won't be left out. There's a chair on the porch that I can sit in and help if I'm needed."

Rand knew determination when he saw it. "All right, if you all are sure, let's go. George . . . I mean, Mitch, you come with me. Dan, you make your way to the first wagon. Stay undercover unless you're needed. Jessie, we'll give you time to go out the back door and around the barn to the back of the bunkhouse, then we'll start the show."

A short time after Jessie left, the other men started for the door. Lance had instructions for the women. "Anna, you know what's at stake here and how dangerous Dean can be. All of you women stay away from him. If need be . . ." He looked at Beth and couldn't finish what he was going to say. "You women take care of each other."

Rand stood on one side of the bunkhouse door. He nodded for Mitch, who was on the other side, to bang on the door. Mitch banged. There was no movement inside. Rand shouted, "You men in there, come on out! There's no way for you to escape, so walk out with your hands in the air."

Still no movement or response from inside the bunkhouse. Rand shoved the door part way open. Only silence inside. Gun in hand, he stepped through the door ready for trouble. Mitch stepped up behind him and they both surveyed the room.

"Wow! It smells *bad* in here." Dirty bodies, liquor, stale food, and vomit permeated the air. Mitch stated the obvious: "They're all dead! What in the world happened to them?"

"There are only three here, Mitch, which means one is missing. Would you mind helping Lance over here? He needs to see this and we need to figure out what killed these three. I don't see blood anywhere."

"Sure, I'll get him and inform the others what we found."

Anna came to the bunkhouse to identify the men who were dead. Mitch found a container of rat poison and the story of what had happened became clear. She told them, "Fred is the one missing. Remember, Lance, I told you he's the one who stays here and takes care of the stock and cooks for the men."

"Yes, I remember. He's the one you said to watch out for."

"Yes, that's the one."

"Thanks, Anna. You might as well go on back to the house. You don't need to stay out here and see this mess any longer. Tell the women to stay in the house and let Jessie and Dan keep watch. I doubt that he's stupid enough to come back here but I won't take any chances."

After Anna left, Rand asked, "How do you see it, Lance?"

"I would say Fred poisoned these men last night with their supper and stole what he wanted from them. The rat poison in the cabinet by the cook stove points to that. The stolen goods in the bottom of that big box in the corner tells me that was where they kept their stash of stolen goods. What's left was too cumbersome for him to haul around, so he left that here. But, where would he go?"

Rand looked at Mitch. "That horse you're looking for, was there a reward offered?"

"Yes, a five thousand dollar reward. Why? What has that to do with this affair?"

"Well, if I'm right, I know where that horse is. When I first got to this ranch, I followed Fred to a box canyon a short distance from here. There's a stallion and three mares in that canyon and that stallion is solid black and one fine piece of horseflesh. If I'm right, Fred is going after the stallion *and* the reward."

Mitch answered, "We may be too late to catch him in the canyon if he left last night, but if he waited until this morning we might be lucky enough to find him there."

Rand started toward the door. "We need to hurry then if we have any hope of catching him before he leaves the area."

The three men went back to the house and Lance sat down on the porch chair. "You have no idea how much I want to go with you, Rand, but it would be foolish for me to try."

"I wish you could go too, Lance, but you're needed here."

Mitch was adamant, saying, "I'm going with him, Marshal Chambers. That horse is my job. If it's Midnight Thunder, I need to be the one to take care of him and return him to my friend. Rand and I will get the job done."

"I'm sure you will," said Lance. "Now go on before his trail gets cold."

Before Rand could even get his foot in the stirrup, Mitch stopped him. "There's one thing you need to take care of before we go."

"Oh, what is that?"

Mitch nodded toward the house. "Josie. You know if you don't tell her to stay here she'll be on our trail before we get to that tree up there. I'd ask her, but she'll obey you better than me."

"You're not playing fair, Mitch Morgan." Rand took his hat off and ran his fingers through his red hair then put it back on headed toward the house.

Josie came out the door before he set foot on the porch. "Are you and Dad going after Fred?"

"Yes and we need to leave now if we have any hope of picking up his trail. I'm not sure when we'll be back, but don't worry about us. I'm depending on you to help take care of things here?"

In the sweetest, sugary voice she could muster, Josie batted her sparkling blue eyes at Rand. "Of course I'll help here. You two be careful and hurry back."

Rand couldn't believe she would be so docile. It made him feel good down to his toes that she didn't argue. Aware of the fact that they were being watched, he gave her a quick kiss on the forehead and went for his horse. *Well, now, that was easy enough.* Rand looked back before they were out of sight. Josie was still on the porch watching. *Oh, shoot! I know good and well if she suspects I'm in trouble she'll be on my trail in a heartbeat. It was in her teasing eyes all the time.* Rand smiled as another thought came. *And, she knows . . . that I know . . . she'll do just that.*

Chapter 10

"H OW ARE YOU HOLDING up?" Josie found Anna working alone in the kitchen. Anna jerked and Josie realized she had startled her. "I'm sorry, didn't mean to scare you."

"That's all right. Guess I'm a little jumpy," Anna replied.

"After what you've been through it's no wonder you're jumpy. Seriously though, how are you doing?"

"Oh, I'm doing fine. It's strange being around people again. Speaking of people, where is everyone?"

"Daisy is showing Beth her wagon. Daisy will keep her entertained for a while. Let's see, after Dan hauled the body out of the front room and over to the bunkhouse, he said he was going to walk around and keep an eye out for any trouble. Marshal Chambers is visiting with Jessie in the other room. They're watching the prisoner and swapping stories."

The women were quiet for a while then Anna said, "I wish this was all over with. If Dean or Fred hurt any of you I'll never forgive myself. You have very nice friends, Josie. I'm so grateful you came along to help Lance and . . . Rand."

"Yes, I do have wonderful friends. Danny, Jessie and Daisy are like family to me and dad, and of course . . . I *love* . . . your son."

Anna slowly turned toward Josie, a look of surprise on her face. "You *know*? But, how could you possibly know?"

"From the few things Rand told me when we first met and what Beth confided in me, I figured it out."

"You haven't said anything to Rand?"

"No. I almost did last night but decided against it. He has a dangerous job to do here and I didn't want him distracted."

"Are you going to tell him?" Anna asked, worried.

"I'm not sure. Don't you think *you* should be the one to tell him and Beth?"

"Why can't we leave it like it is? They don't need to know. Beth and I will find some place to go and you and Rand can go on with your lives."

"Think about what you're saying, Anna. What if something happens to you? Beth will be all alone. Is that what you want for your daughter? Rand is her brother and I already care a great deal for her. She's going to need Rand, she'll need *family*."

Tears were starting to spill down Anna's face. "What if he hates me and wants nothing to do with Beth Ann?"

"That's something we'll have to deal with when the time comes. But don't underestimate Rand. He's a wonderful man. He's tough but he has a big heart too."

"You're going to tell Rand anyway, aren't you?"

"Yes. I won't keep secrets from the man I love, the man I'm going to marry. I'll be praying for you, Anna."

Anna wiped her eyes. "Now you sound like Lance. He's always praying about things."

Josie smiled. "I've just met Lance, and he seems like a fine man. I know Rand thinks a lot of him. I have an idea you think a lot of Marshal Lance Chambers, too."

Anna wiped her eyes again with the tail of her apron and went back to peeling potatoes. "I'm trying not to think about much of anything except getting through each day as it comes."

"That's probably a good thing to do right now. I'm glad we had a few minutes to talk. We may not get a chance again for a while. I can hear Beth and Daisy on the porch. I'll go find out what's going on then come back and help you in the kitchen."

Anna didn't have a chance to respond. Lance called her from the other room. "Anna, can you come here, please?"

"Sure Lance, what do you need?"

"My prisoner needs food. Can you find something he can eat with his hands?"

"Sure, I have some venison roast left over from last night. I'll slice that. Do you think the venison and a couple slices of bread with butter will be enough?"

"That'll do. Put it on a cloth, no utensils, and a tin cup of water. That should do him just fine." Marshal Chambers wasn't taking any chances with the prisoner. He had Jessie untie Dean's left hand so he could feed himself, then tie the right hand to the ropes on his feet. His gag was removed and Dean ate his food then asked for a cup of coffee.

"I like it black and *hot*," he demanded.

Lance shook his head. "Coffee you can have, but not hot."

This made Dean mad and the filth that came out of his mouth made Lance mad. "If you don't stop that filthy talk, I'm going to stuff that sock back in your mouth and gag you again. Is that what you want?"

"What I want is the whole lot of you *dead*. How long are you going to keep me tied up like this? I'm tired of sitting here on this hard floor."

"You'll stay tied up until the other marshal gets back and we figure out what to do with you. You might as well lay down and take a nap."

"What makes you think your other marshal is going to come back? If it's Fred that got away, that marshal won't even know who or what killed him. He'll never see it coming. Fred is the most cunning killer I ever ran into. That's one reason he hides out here, he's wanted all over the country. He's *mean* and just pure evil. No, that other marshal ain't coming back."

Josie was in the kitchen with Anna and heard the exchange between the two men. She stepped out the back door and took a deep breath. Anna followed her out. "Are you worried about Rand?"

"Sure, I'm worried about him and dad. It was a lot harder to watch them leave this morning than I thought it would be. I'm not one to sit back and wait. Part of me knows they can take care of themselves, but there's another part of me that can't help but fret. I suppose that's part of being a woman."

"I know you're right but I've always worried when I knew it was time for Dean to come back home."

"Anna, is Fred as mean as Dean says he is?"

"I've never seen any of it, but Dean always threatened me when he was leaving saying if I didn't do what he told me, Fred would tell him and I would pay dearly for it. He always held it over my head that Beth Ann would pay too. The stories of Fred were more than horrible, but guess it could have just been talk."

"That must have been an awful way to live."

"It still is. Having Dean in the house terrifies me. If he got loose he would do everything he said he would and take great joy in hurting me and Beth. As long as he's alive, I'll never feel safe."

"I'm sorry, Anna. It'll all work out, you'll see." For a few moments the two women were quiet then Josie broke the silence. "I think I'll go to my wagon and take my wig off. Rand would probably like to see me as myself when he comes back. That will keep me busy for a while. I'll come back to the house and help with the evening meal before too long. Maybe my men will be back by then." *Please, God, protect them and bring them safely back to me.*

"That's the entrance to the canyon down there, George, I mean, Mitch. Calling you Mitch is going to take some getting used to."

"Don't worry about it. I'll answer to both names."

"Rand spoke quietly, "I didn't go down there when I followed him before. I went up the trail over to the left and found myself on the edge of the canyon. Let's go that way and see if he's there. Might save us some trouble."

"Lead the way; I'll be right behind you."

The two men soon found a place behind some brush and looked down into the canyon. "We're in luck, he's down there. There are five horses in front of that old shack," Mitch whispered.

"Yeah, one looks like his mount and one is a heavily loaded pack horse. The other three are the mares that were with the black stallion."

"I don't see the black stallion, do you?" Mitch sounded worried.

"Not . . . yet . . . *there* he is."

"Where? Point him out to me."

"Close to that stand of trees on the right side of the cabin."

"All right, I see him now. Is he tied up there?"

"I can't tell for sure but it does look . . . Uh, oh, he's got wind of us. That horse is looking right up here. He'll give us away sure enough when Fred comes out."

"What do you think we should do, Rand?"

Suddenly, the door to the cabin opened then banged shut. Fred came out shrugging on his coat. He checked the horses one at a time then walked the short distance toward the black stallion, who was eyeing the man suspiciously. As Fred stopped and checked his rifle, Mitch realized what he was going to do. "He's going to shoot the black, Rand! We've got to stop him!"

Rand shouldered his rifle and took aim. "He may be out of range but maybe we can scare him back into the cabin." The two men fired several shots, and sure enough Fred dashed back to the cabin.

Mitch was angry. "Why would he shoot such a valuable horse?"

"If that's your friend's stallion down there, he's well known. Fred probably intends to destroy the black and when the mares have their foals he'll make some good money selling them, or raising them himself for race horses."

Mitch started to move away. "I've got to get down there and make sure he doesn't kill that stallion."

"Wait a minute, Mitch. You stay here and keep him in the cabin. Whenever you see him at the door or window, fire a shot down there. Keep his attention up here and maybe I can surprise him by crawling through the brush and tall grass."

"That's quite a ways to crawl, Rand."

"Yeah, but I don't see any other way, do you?"

"I guess not. Be careful. Josie will never forgive me if you get shot."

"The same goes for you. He may have us located us now so watch yourself."

Getting through the opening of the canyon was fairly easy. Rand found a rigged gate of sorts to keep the horses in the canyon. He left his horse there, and found a position where he could not be seen, but had a good view of the canyon. Then he studied his options. *There's more cover going to the left, but Mitch is up there and Fred will be watching that direction. The right side is how I'll have to go. Sure hope I don't have to crawl through mud and water around that pond.*

A third of the way, Rand found enough cover to slip through the trees and brush without crawling. Soon he was on the ground again making his way through tall grass. Rand was not the only thing in the grass right then. He came to an abrupt halt when a water snake slithered across his hand. A low groan sounded in his throat. *Now why did that have to happen? The flies and mosquitoes are enough of a problem without snakes. Sorry, God, but you know how I feel about snakes. Please keep them away from me even if they are harmless.* More cautious where he put his hands and elbows, Rand moved on.

The black horse was only about twenty feet away when Rand came to the end of the grassy area. The horse's head was down, eyeing Rand suspiciously. "Hey, Midnight Thunder, don't give me away." The black lifted his head and his ears twitched. "That's a good boy. Is that your name, Midnight?"

The closest cover was in the trees where the horse was. Rand lifted himself out of the short grass and dashed to the only tree that was big enough to conceal him. The black horse side stepped and nickered. "Easy now, Midnight, keep quiet."

Curious, the horse lifted his head and sniffed the air, then took a couple of steps toward Rand. The rope he was tied to was not long enough for Rand to reach. "Sorry, Midnight, we'll have to get more acquainted later. Right now I've got business to tend to."

Rand watched the cabin and the rim of the canyon where Mitch was. There was nothing to give him a clue of what was transpiring. *Something is wrong. It's too quiet. There has only been one shot since I left Mitch, and I'm pretty sure that was from Mitch's rifle. What is Fred doing in that cabin, or is he in that cabin. Maybe there's a way out the back.*

Taking a chance, Rand dashed to the back of the cabin and sure enough there was a window. On the ground was a thin piece of deer skin that had obviously been covering the window. Rand investigated and found the cabin empty. Outside again he searched the ground for tracks or any kind of clue to tell him where Fred had gone. But Fred was good. He had left few signs of his passing except for a couple sprigs of smashed grass on a steep trail up the hill behind the house. In about twenty minutes of climbing, Rand stopped to catch his breath and listen. *Looks like I'm almost to the top of the canyon. Where are you going, Fred?* Only the sound of warm breezes rattling the leaves in the trees could be heard. So he continued on.

Suddenly, Fred's trail turned sharply to the left and Rand's heart thudded faster as he realized where Fred was going. *He's going for Mitch! That one shot from Mitch gave his location away . . . .* He had no time to go back for his horse, Rand kept moving. Well aware of the danger of being jumped himself, he left the trail and headed to where he had left Mitch. At the sound of voices he halted in his tracks, listening. Moving ever so slowly, he snuck close enough to see who the voices belonged to. Surprised, he found himself looking at Little Danny who was confronting Fred. And Fred was standing over Mitch, dangerously close to the edge of the canyon cliff. Mitch was lying on the ground, not moving.

"I don't want to hurt you mister," Dan was saying, "but you can't roll my friend off the cliff. I'm mad that you hit him on the head and I have a terrible temper, so don't make me hurt you. Put your rifle on the ground and we'll wait right here for the marshal."

Fred seemed to be frozen in place. Dan didn't have a weapon that Rand could see, but Fred was wearing a pistol and had a rifle in his hand. Having the giant of a man come out of the trees had shocked Fred for a moment. But that shock wore off and Fred's rifle came up. The sound of a gunshot echoed in the canyon.

Chapter 11

DAN'S KNEES BUCKLED AND he sat hard on the ground. "Hi, Marshal Trinity. Sure glad to see you. Thought for sure I was a goner."

"You all right, Dan?"

"A little shook up but I'm fine. When I saw what that man was going to do to Mitch, I didn't think about what I was doing. I just walked right up to him and told him he couldn't do it. Wasn't very smart, was it?"

"It was a brave thing to do." Rand knelt down beside Mitch and saw he was breathing and trying to open his eyes. "Why don't you carry a rifle or pistol, Dan?"

"Look at my hands. My fingers are too big to pull a trigger. I have a big knife but I don't like to use it unless I have to. Usually, I can pound a man into seeing things my way but I don't like to fight, either. Honestly, though, most men don't want to fight *me*."

Rand smiled at the gentle giant. "I can see why. You're a good man, Dan. Glad to call you a friend." Mitch moaned. "Looks like he's coming to. Would you get the canteen off the horse over there?" While Dan went for the canteen, Rand took a moment to look over the cliff and find Fred's body. Sure enough, he was on the rocks at the bottom.

Rand tended to Mitch as Dan took his turn to look over the edge of the cliff. "Not a very pretty sight down there. That was the strangest thing I ever did see. It was almost like he was flying off the cliff backwards. You shot him square between the eyes, you know. It just lifted him in the air and he went over with his arms out like wings. Do you want me to go get him, Marshal Trinity?"

"No, thank you, Dan. We'll all go down there when Mitch is ready."

Mitch sat up, rubbing his head. "What happened?"

"That man, Fred, conked you on the head with his rifle, *that's* what happened," Dan told Mitch. "You must have heard him cause you turned your head just in time and didn't take a direct hit. Looked like it just grazed the side of your head. Does it hurt much?"

"Hurts like thunder. What in the world are you doing here? You're supposed to be back at the house with the others."

"I was digging a hole with Jessie to bury the outlaws when I heard shots way off. I figured it was you and the marshal shooting it out with the man who got away. And if he was *here*, he wouldn't be around the house. Thought you might need help, so I came to see. Ran most of the way. You know I can run pretty fast with these long legs."

"Better be glad he got here when he did, Mitch," Rand told him. "If he hadn't, you would have been at the bottom of the canyon instead of Fred. Dan walked right up to him and told him he couldn't push you over the cliff."

Mitch looked up at Dan. "Did you kill the outlaw, Dan?"

"No, Marshal Trinity shot him right between the eyes and he flew off the cliff backwards. Strangest thing I ever did see. I guess the marshal saved both of us."

"Well, thanks to both of you. Now let me see if I can stand." Mitch got to his feet and brushed the dirt off his clothes. He decided he was fine except for the side of his head. "Burns like it's on fire."

"I'm sure it does," Rand told him. "Scraped the hide off the side of your head. We need to get you back so the women can tend it. But first we should get the horses out of the canyon. Dan, you seem to be good with horses. Do you think you can make friends with that big black stallion down there? He's tied to the tree down by the cabin. It will probably be best if you can go in first and see if he takes to you, then walk him back to the house. Put him in the barn and give him some grain. Mitch and I will follow with the other horses."

"Sure, I'll give it a try. It will be a pleasure to make friends with such a fine animal. Is that Midnight Thunder, Mitch?"

"I won't know until I check for the one identifying mark on him. At the top of his neck at the base of his throat is a small diamond-shaped white spot. It's the only white on him. Look for that and we'll know for sure."

"Are you all right with Dan taking the black back to the ranch house, Mitch?"

"Sure! I'd trust Dan with any horse, or my life for that matter."

Dan was eager to meet the black stallion. "I'm going now, Marshal."

"Sure, go on ahead. And, Dan, if we're going to be friends I want you to call me Rand."

Dan had a huge smile on his face as he turned and loped off down the hill. Rand and Mitch watched until he disappeared from sight. "Do you think we might ride double down to the entrance to the canyon, Mitch?"

"I don't see why not. It's not very far so let's get going. Breakfast was a long time ago and I'm getting hungry!"

"Oh my, don't you look nice!" Anna commented when Josie came into the kitchen. I can see why Rand is attracted to you. That black wig was nice but I think you definitely look better as a blond. You're a very pretty woman, Josie."

"Thank you, Anna. After wearing a wig most of the day I had to wash my hair to get it looking decent. That's what took me so long. It's still damp so I'll leave it loose for a while. Now, what can I do?"

"Help *me* decide what to do. Everything is ready to eat. Should we go ahead and feed the ones that are here, or should we wait for everyone else?"

"I don't see any reason to wait. We don't know when Dad and Rand will be back, so let's go . . . ."

Josie didn't get to finish her sentence because Beth Ann burst through the back door.

Ma! Little Danny is coming off the mountain with a black horse. He's almost here!"

"Is he by himself, Beth?" Josie asked.

"I didn't see any one else," Beth answered.

"Maybe Dan will know something about Dad and Rand. Let's go find out where he found the horse and see if he knows anything."

The three women hurried through the front room and told Lance where they were going. They joined Daisy who was in the yard, watching Dan. "Where is Jessie?" Josie asked.

"He's working on the hole that Danny started."

"What hole?"

"Dan and Jessie said we needed a hole to bury those outlaws, so they picked out a spot on the other side of the bunkhouse and started digging. Dan thought he heard shots way off and decided to walk that way. By the look on his face he has a story to tell." Daisy giggled. "You know how he loves to tell a story, Josie. I bet this will be a good one."

"Hello, ladies," Dan greeted. "What do you think of this fine looking horse?"

"He's magnificent," Josie told him. "Is it Midnight Thunder?"

"I'm happy to tell you *yes*. He is the one you and your dad have been looking for."

"Have you seen them, Dan?" Josie asked, trying not to look worried.

"Yes, again! They'll be along pretty soon. When I get this horse taken care of I'll tell you all about it. Watch yourselves now and don't get too close. He's a bit nervous right now with all the new people. Rand told me to put him in the barn and take good care of him."

"Is Dad and Rand all right?"

"They are just fine, Miss Josie. Your dad has a scrape on his head, but he's all right. That Marshal Rand is taking good care of him."

"How did he hurt his head?"

"You'll just have to wait till I tell you about it," Dan said, as he disappeared into the barn.

The women laughed at Josie as she put her hands on her hips and huffed, "Men! They just don't understand us women. Doesn't he know we've been waiting all day long, and I don't like to wait?"

Daisy took Josie's hand. "Let's go see how Jessie is doing with that hole and then go wait on the porch for Dan to tell his story."

The small group was waiting for Dan to finish pampering Midnight Thunder when a commotion from the side of the mountain drew their attention. "It's Dad and Rand!" Josie jumped up from the porch steps. "Hurry, Beth, let's go open the gate to the pasture, they have several horses with them."

Beth and Josie dashed for the gate. After the three mares were safe in the pasture, the rest of the group, chattering like magpies, surrounded Rand and Mitch as they led their horses toward the barn. Mitch asked, "Have you seen Dan?"

"Yes, Dad, he's in the barn taking care of Midnight Thunder. We've been waiting for him to come tell us what happened."

"There will be time later to tell what happened. Right now I want to ask you women if there's any food around. I am a starving man and would appreciate whatever you can find to fill my stomach."

"There's plenty of food ready, Dad, but you need to come to our wagon while the women put the food on the table. There will be nothing for you to eat until I doctor and bandage your head."

"Well, then, let's go, I'm a hungry man!"

The women set up a table outside on a patch of grass so everyone could eat together while the men took care of horses and washed up. Then they all headed for the food. Later that evening after the outlaws were buried and all the chores done, the company of people sat around a fire in the ranch yard. Rand and Lance talked quietly together while Mitch and Dan told their stories.

"What are you going to do with him?" Rand nodded toward Dean. He was tied up on the porch so Lance could keep an eye on him.

"When the ladies moved the table outside, it caused Anna to remember there is a trap door under the table that leads to a hole under the house. She says there's nothing down there but a very small room with dirt walls and floor. She has never used it, so it's empty as far as she knows. There are no windows and the only way out is up through the trap door. I need you to check it out and make sure there's no way to escape. One of us can make our bed on top of that trap door for the night."

"That sounds as good as anything I can think of." Rand was quiet for a few moments. "I'm going to leave first thing in the morning, Lance."

"I thought we would all leave first thing in the morning. Maybe you better tell me what you have on your mind."

"I'm going on ahead with the prisoner. If I travel light and ride steady for most of the day, I can reach Winchester where there's a sheriff and a jail to put him. The sheriff can help me find someone to go with me the rest of the way to Lexington, then I can turn him over to the local authorities."

"I can ride with you, Rand."

"I know, but you would slow me down, Lance. And what if you have a spell with your heart again? I think you should stay with the wagons and make sure the stolen money and goods get back to Lexington. That judge friend of yours will want to talk to Anna and I figure you'll want to be in on that. Besides, driving one of the wagons would be easier on you than riding a horse. The wagons have hiding places in them that were used during the war to help runaway slaves get into Ohio. Would be a good place to stash the loot. First though we need to talk with Mitch and his bunch to make sure they're all right with taking the risk, but I think they'll help. Mitch will want to take responsibility for Midnight Thunder, but besides the stallion we have about twelve to fifteen horses, a milk cow, and some chickens to take care of. We need to get the prisoner behind bars and I don't want him around any of these people. I won't take that chance."

"It galls me to admit it, but you're right. I'm starting to feel like an old horse put out to pasture. These are good people, Rand, and that girl of yours is a dandy. She tried to hide it, but I could tell she was like a caged animal all day, waiting for you to get back."

Rand grinned at his marshal friend. "You don't know the half of it. Sometime I'll have to tell you about when we first met." Rand made eye contact with Josie across the fire. She was watching him and he could see a slight smile on her face.

Lance chuckled and clapped Rand on the back. "I think she would like to spend some time with you, so go talk to these people and let's make our final plans. We still have some work to do tonight."

Standing in front of the group, Rand called for everyone's attention. While he told them of his plan for getting all of them to Lexington, Anna quietly made her way over to Lance.

"Lance, I need to ask you something," she said softly.

"Sure, Anna, just ask."

"I know I need to talk to Rand before we leave here tomorrow, but I'm really nervous about it. It's tearing me up inside to think how he might hate me, that he might not accept Beth Ann as a sister. Would . . . would you be with me when I talk to him?"

"If that's what you want, I'll be glad to be with you. It's time you talked to him and the right thing to do."

"I sure hope so."

"You need to know that Rand is leaving first thing in the morning with the prisoner. If you're going to talk to him it should be tonight. I'm sure Rand will want to spend some time with Josie, so when he comes in we can catch him in the kitchen and you can have your talk."

"All right, thank you, Lance. I can't tell you how special it's been for you to help me and just be with me the last few days."

"You've been good for me too, Anna. We'll talk more after we see the judge but I want you to know I care a great deal about what happens to you and Beth Ann." He reached over and gently squeezed Anna's hand, then turned his attention to the conversation around the fire.

The first thing to be done after they all agreed to Rand's plan was to secure the prisoner in the cellar. Rand took a lantern and checked out the dirt room. He cleared out cobwebs then asked for some blankets and laid out a place for Dean to sleep. "This is the perfect place for him," he told Lance when he climbed out. "There's no way he can get out of there."

A fierce battle of wills ignited when Rand held a gun on Dean and told him to climb down the ladder and get some sleep. "What are you talking about?! I'm *not* going down in that hole!" Dean raged and cursed them all.

Rand felt his impatience getting the best of him. "If you don't get down that ladder *right now*, I'll throw you down head first. Now move!"

"Untie my hands then," Dean ordered.

"No, you can make it down if you're careful. Maybe you can free your hands when you get down there. It'll give you something to do until you fall asleep."

Dean glared brimstone at Rand. "I won't sleep tonight. What I'll do is enjoy making plans to kill all of you." His eyes strayed to Anna who was standing in the doorway with Josie. "Especially *you*. I'm going to kill you if it's the last thing I do!" He was partway down the ladder when he stopped and glared at Rand. "What's your name, little boy marshal? I want to remember your name so I can kill you, after I kill *her*."

"My name is Rand Trinity, U. S. Marshal, and you're not going to live long enough to kill anyone."

Dean stared at Rand. "Did you say Rand *Trinity*?"

"Yep, that's what I said. Will you get a move on?"

Dean's mouth twisted into a hideous sneer and a short burst of evil laughter filled the room. He looked at Anna in the doorway with vile hatred. "Does he know who you are, Anna? Well, now, isn't this interesting. I can tell by the look on your face that he doesn't even recognize his own mama. Meet your mama, little marshal boy. Meet Mrs. Annabelle *Trinity*."

Muffled laughter was the only thing that could be heard as the trap door slammed shut. Beth, standing behind Josie, had heard everything. "What did he mean, Ma? Is Rand the little boy you left a long time ago?"

Anna's face had drained of all color. She dropped her head. "Yes, Beth, I'm so ashamed of myself that it's hard to say, but Rand is the boy I abandoned so many years ago." She looked up and found Rand staring at her. "There's no excuse for me, Rand. I don't blame you if you hate me. I just hope someday you'll find it in your heart to forgive me."

Like the flames of a campfire that flickered and danced, so was the emotion in the eyes of Rand Trinity. He searched the faces of the people in front of him. *They all knew.* Confusion and doubt clouded his mind as he stared hard at the woman who said she was his mother. He remembered her face when she had first seen him in the lantern light in the attic. *Of course, I look like my father. Uncle Scott told me that many times.* Acceptance of the truth came as the memories of a six year old little boy confirmed what he was being told. *It is her. Why didn't I see it sooner?* Pain and anger crowded his heart so tightly he felt on the verge of smothering. Without a word, Rand turned and slammed his way out the back door.

Chapter 12

ALONE IN THE WOODS behind the house, Rand sat on the first log he came to. Hard as it was for him, in his heart he *knew* it was true. He had come face to face with his mother. *I never thought I would see my mother again. Never! Maybe I just wanted her to be dead. It's like I blotted her out of my head and never thought of her again. God, what now? I don't know what to do, what to think or how to feel.*

"I really wish you'd shot that man dead."

Startled, Rand looked up. "Honestly, Josie, you've got to quit sneaking up on me. It's a wonder I didn't shoot *you* dead just now."

"Don't you know I'll always find you when you need me? Besides, I think I need you more than you need me right now. It was one of the hardest things I've ever had to do when I watched you and Dad ride out after Fred this morning. And, even harder to see you walk out of that kitchen just now. So much happened after you and Dad got back that we haven't had time to even talk to each other. But, I'll understand if you want me to go away."

"No, I don't want you to go away. I was going to find you when things settled down. Come on over here and sit with me."

For long moments, Rand held Josie in his arms. Words weren't needed, just being together was all that mattered right then. Rand's stomach was tied in knots when he'd left the house, but peace finally settled over him. "Why didn't you tell me, Josie? How did you find out?"

"I figured it out after Beth Ann and I met in the meadow the first time. She was in such emotional pain and needed a friend to tell her troubles to, she blurted out the story. I almost told you that night but changed my mind. You had a dangerous job to do the next day and I didn't want you to be distracted. I told Anna that if she didn't tell you, I would."

"My feelings may change, but right now, I don't feel any hate for her. I've hardly thought of her at all over the years. My life was good with my father and after his death, with my uncle and cousin. Now I have *you* and nothing else is important."

"I'm glad you don't hate her, Rand. Hate can change a person, make them bitter and destroy their life. I want you just like you are."

Rand squeezed Josie tighter. "Josie, when do you want to get married?"

"Yesterday."

"I'm serious. Today when we were coming back to the ranch, I couldn't get you off my mind. I don't want to wait a long time for a wedding. There will be stretches of time my job will keep me away and I want to take advantage of every moment we have to be together."

"I'm serious too," Josie said. "I would marry you right now if there was a minister anywhere around here. That's about the only thing I want, to be married by a minister. And of course, have *you* for the groom."

"How about when we get to Lexington, we find a minister and get married then?"

"That would be wonderful, Rand! My family could be there." She paused. "I guess there is *one more* thing I want before we marry."

"And what would *that* be, my sweet Josie?"

"A perfect day! If you could make peace with your mother, then *your* family could be there too."

Rand groaned. "Oh, Josie, that might take some time."

"You'll have time. About four or five days. That should be plenty of time."

Rand stood and pulled Josie to her feet, taking her into his arms again. He kissed her and whispered in her ear. "I'll do everything I can to make your day perfect."

"*Our* day, Rand, it will be *our* day."

"Judge Cramer, there is a man to see you."

"Tell him to come back," Samuel. "I don't have time for anyone else today."

"I think you'll *want* to see *this* man, Judge."

Judge Lowell Cramer looked up from his writing. "Who is it that you think I'll *want* to see, Samuel?"

"It's that young red-headed U.S. Marshal that was here a while back."

That got the Judge's attention. "You're right. I *do* want to see him! Send him in."

Rand stepped into the judge's chambers, walked right up to the front of his desk, and stood respectfully waiting to be acknowledged. The judge scowled then sat back in his chair. "Sit down, Mr. Trinity. I see you came back empty handed. I should have known better, but I suppose you did the best you could."

"Yes, sir, I did the best I could."

The judge shook his head. "No sign of Lance, huh?"

"Oh, yeah, I found Lance Chambers."

Rand tried not to grin but the look Judge Cramer gave him made it impossible. "I can see you're enjoying yourself, Trinity. Out with it, then. Start from the beginning and tell me the whole story. Don't leave anything out."

For the next couple of hours, with coffee and pastries, Rand told Judge Cramer all that transpired since he had left Lexington on this assignment.

"Well, bless my soul that *is* good news! How much do you trust this bunch that is bringing in the stolen money and valuables?"

"I'd trust them with my life and if I had anything of value, I would trust that with them too. They're good people, Judge Cramer. It would have been a very different story if they hadn't helped me and Lance."

"Lance, that son-of-a-gun! I can't wait to see him. How far behind were they?"

"Well, it's hard to say for sure. They had a number of horses, a cow and some chickens they brought with them. I figure a couple more days. Anna was going to give the cow and the chickens away to the first farm they came to. They should be able to move faster after they get rid of that milk cow. Mitch and Josie are going to see that Lance sees a doctor in Winchester. His leg may need some attention."

"Anna, now she's the one that was with that Dean guy?"

"Yes, she and her daughter were kept like prisoners up in the mountains. From what Lance told me they've been treated quite badly for years."

"What do you think of her situation, Rand?"

"That's something I'd like for you to ask Lance."

"Why do you say that?"

"He knows her better than I do. She splinted his leg and took care of him for several days while he was in hiding."

"As a judge for many years, I've learned to read people pretty good and I think you're not telling me everything."

"That's why I want you to talk to Lance about her. It's guess work on my part, but I think he's attracted to her. From what I saw it seems to be mutual. Lance and I never talked about it, so let Lance tell you about her."

"All right, I'll do that. I need to get home anyway, should have been home an hour ago. What are your plans now?"

"A good meal and a comfortable bed for the night are all I need right now. I'm going to ride out to Philip Dawson's place in the morning and tell him about his stallion, Midnight Thunder. I figure on going back to find my friends and thought he might like to ride with me."

"Sounds like a good idea. I saw that horse race this last May. Almost made me wish I was a betting man. Fast, man that horse is fast!"

"Oh, yes, another thing," Rand said. "Where's a good place to buy a ring?"

"Ring? What kind of ring?"

"A . . . well . . . a wedding ring."

"Now, did you forget to tell me something?"

"Not really. Mitch Morgan and his daughter, Josie are people I knew from the Cheyenne assignment. Josie and I are going to get married before we leave Lexington."

"You don't say! Well, congratulations, young man. I can tell you exactly where to get a ring. You tell the owner I sent you and he'll give you a good price."

"Don't you look deep in thought," Josie remarked. "What's going on in that pretty little head of yours?" Josie and Beth were riding together behind the wagons, and were in charge of the horses.

Beth sighed. "I was just thinking about Make Believe Meadow and wishing I could go back there and never leave."

"Goodness," Josie said. "Why would you want to do that?"

"It was fun and . . . ."

"And *what*?"

"Safe."

"Oh, I see. Are you getting nervous about what might happen in Lexington?"

"Yeah, I guess. There are so many things to think about, like what's going to happen to my ma. Lance told her she would have to talk to the judge. What's going to happen to my pa? I still can't believe I have a brother, what does he think about me and ma? That's just a few of the things on my mind."

"Of course you're right, but Make Believe Meadow isn't the answer, Beth. I have a secret to tell you."

"What secret?"

"Well, it's not really a secret, I just haven't told anyone yet. You are the first one I'm going to tell. Rand and I are going to get married when we get to Lexington." Josie was pleased with Beth Ann's reaction.

"Really? Wow! Are you going to have a *real* wedding and everything? I've never been to a wedding."

"Yes, but not big or fancy. Just a wedding in a church with a minister. My family and friends will be there and I want you to be there too. Would you please be my bridesmaid, Beth?"

Beth shrugged her slim shoulders. "I don't know *how*."

"Nothing to it. You just be with me that day. We'll go shopping and get us a nice dress to wear. I'm so excited I'm about to bust. You know, when I marry Rand, you'll be my sister."

Beth smiled for the first time that day. "I would like that a lot! Can I tell Ma?"

"Sure, go ahead. And, Beth, don't look back at the past. Let's look forward to the future. We'll make our own memories and sneak in a Make Believe Meadow once in a while, just for the fun of it."

Josie was deep in thought when she spotted a rider coming towards them. *Rand!*

"Hey there, pretty lady. Can I ride with you?"

"Oh, Rand, it's so nice you came back. Hey, I like that nice scarf you have around your neck."

"Thanks. A sweet, little old gray-headed lady knitted it for me."

"Nice, really nice. The color goes real good with your red hair."

"Thanks. You know, I never did get to thank her."

"Oh, I think she knows." Josie noticed some extra men ahead of the wagons. "I see someone talking with Dad. Did they come with you?"

"Yes, Mr. Dawson and three of his hands came with me. They're going to take Midnight Thunder and the three mares back to his ranch. We've all been invited to stay there when we get to Lexington. I was really impressed with that ranch of his."

"That was nice of Mr. Dawson to invite us."

"I couldn't wait to see you, so I left him with your dad."

"You look good, Rand. How was your trip with Dean? Did he give you any trouble?"

"Oh, yeah! But not any more than I expected. He was a pretty desperate man and it was good to get him into the jail that first night. The sheriff in Winchester got in touch with a retired sheriff who lives there and he rode into Lexington with me."

"I'm glad you had someone with you. I was worried."

"How have things gone with your bunch?"

"Remarkably well. After we got rid of the milk cow we made good time. Lance saw a doctor in Winchester and he put on a different, more comfortable splint on his leg. He thought it would be fine and Lance might not have a limp if he takes good care of it."

"How are they doing?" Rand nodded toward Anna and Beth.

"They've both been quiet most of the time, especially Anna. Their life has been turned upside down and they don't know what their future holds. I feel sorry for both of them. I just told Beth Ann that we are getting married before we leave Lexington. I asked her to be my bridesmaid. I hope you don't mind."

"No, I don't mind if that's what you want." Rand reached over and took Josie's hand, gently kissing the back of it. "You can invite whoever you want as long as I am there and you say, 'I do.'" Rand dropped her hand. "Here come the Dawson ranch hands. Let's get the three mares for them."

Two hours later the tired group started looking for a place to camp for the night. As they neared Lexington, more and more homes and ranches appeared along the road. Rand was riding by the first wagon, talking to Lance. "Rand, over on the left there's a big dairy farm. Why don't you go flash that badge of yours and tell them a group of people need a place to spend the night. If it will help, tell them you have a wounded U.S. Marshal that needs to rest. Oh, yeah, tell them you'll pay them for their trouble."

"Hmm, I guess that's not a lie," Rand responded.

"I promise the part about the wounded marshal needing rest is *not* a lie. Most people are eager to help when they know who you are."

Rand was back in about twenty minutes. "He was agreeable, Lance. Go on down the lane and take the wagons east of the big barn. There's a fire pit and plenty of room for the wagons."

"Sounds good, let's go make camp."

The farmer came out and met everyone as they were arranging their wagons for the night. Rand noticed he was particularly taken with Little Danny and his horses. "These are fine, beautiful horses," the farmer raved.

"Thank you, Mr. Gustow. They are shire draft horses. That's how I make my living."

"I could use a couple of horses, but I don't have a need for draft horses."

"You should talk to the marshal. Maybe he would make a deal with you and give you a couple of our extra horses for letting us stay here. I can't say for sure, but it won't hurt to ask." Dan reached down and picked up an orange stripped cat that was rubbing against his ankles. He started petting it.

"I've got four of her kittens in the barn that are ready to give away. I noticed the young girl over there fussing over Snuggles. In the morning, why don't you and the girl go pick out the one you want, and you can have them."

"Thank you. I might do that. I'll talk to Beth Ann and see if she can take one."

"I'm going to go find that marshal and see if we can deal for a couple of your horses. Nice talking to you."

That evening while they were eating, Rand and Josie told everyone they were getting married before leaving Lexington. For a while there was a lot of happy wedding talk. As the women were doing clean up after their meal, Beth Ann asked, "Do any of you know what's wrong with Danny? He's so quiet tonight and he's way over there sitting by himself."

Josie took a deep breath and exhaled slowly. "I'm afraid it's the conversation about a wedding. Dan has prayed for years that God would help him find a suitable wife. Most women are afraid of Dan. He doesn't think there is a woman who will have him and he is destined to live his life alone."

The ladies' eyebrows shot up when Beth declared, "We should pray *right now* that God will find him a wife. I don't like him feeling so sad."

"You are right, Beth, let's pray right now." Josie didn't wait but bowed her head and said a simple prayer. "I'm glad you thought to pray, Beth. Now let's go sit by the fire for a while."

The next morning found Rand and his group getting ready to pull out of the farm yard. Beth remembered the kittens. Anna and Josie were standing together when Beth approached them. "Ma, have you decided if I can have a kitten or not?"

"I guess it will be all right. Josie said if it became a problem she will take it for you."

Beth hugged Josie, then her mother. "Thank you! I'll go pick one out." As she hurried past Dan, she told him where she was going.

"You go ahead; I'll be there in a few minutes."

Beth entered the barn and stood still, waiting for her eyes to adjust to the dim interior. Slowly, she made her way to the middle of the barn and was surprised to see someone else there. A woman's voice spoke, "What are you doing in the barn, little one?"

"The owner of the farm said I could pick out a kitten to take with me."

"Did he, now?"

"Yes."

"And what is your name?"

"Beth Ann. What is your name?"

"Yolanda."

Beth Ann moved closer to the woman, hesitated only a second, then held her hand out to the lady. "Pleased to meet you, Yolanda. Do you know where the kittens are?"

"I do. Let's get them and take them out to the sunshine so you can pick the one you want." As they gathered up the kittens, Yolanda commented, "You're not afraid of me. Most young people are afraid of me, because I'm so big."

"No, I'm not afraid of you, and you're not *so* big. Little Danny is bigger than you."

"Do you know how silly that sounds? A little boy, this Little Danny, is bigger than me."

"He's not a little boy, he's a *man*. A most wonderful, nice man."

"And where is this wonderful, nice man?"

"I'm right here," a masculine voice said from just inside the door.

"Bless you, Beth Ann, you are not a liar," Yolanda whispered to herself.

"Do you need help with the kittens?" the masculine voice asked.

"No," answered Yolanda. "We are going to take them out into the sunshine so we can see you better . . . I mean, see the *kittens* better."

"Good idea. Bring the kittens out so we can *all* see things better." The voice had a touch of playfulness in it.

Yolanda placed the kittens on the ground and Beth Ann was so delighted, she didn't notice that Dan was no longer interested in the kittens.

"I've never seen a woman as tall as you," Little Danny said.

"I've never seen a man as big as you. How tall are you?"

"I'm eight feet three inches. I doubt you'll ever see a man bigger than me."

"You're probably right. I can see you would like to ask, but are too polite, so I'll just tell you, I'm seven feet two inches, without my shoes on."

Dan took in all seven feet two inches. She was tall and big boned but had pretty womanly features. Her blond hair fell down her back in one thick braid. "Forgive me for being so bold, but you are the most beautiful seven feet two inches I've ever seen. Do you live here?"

"This is my home. My father owns this dairy farm."

"You milk cows, then?"

"Not if I can help it. I like horses better than cows."

"What do you do all day, then?"

"I'm a seamstress. I had to learn at an early age to sew my own clothes. A lot of the women in Lexington come here for me to make their fine gowns. What do you do?"

"I raise shire draft horses. I have a place down south along the Cumberland River."

Beth interrupted, "Dan, I'm going to take this one. Can you tell me if it's a boy or girl? Josie said for me to pick out a girl."

Dan looked utterly lost and flustered. Yolanda took the kitten. "Let me have it, maybe I can tell. She lifted the kitten and examined it. "I'm pretty sure it's a girl, Beth Ann. Why don't you show your mother and ask if it's all right to take this one with you. You picked the prettiest one."

Beth headed off to the wagons that had pulled around the barn and were waiting for Dan. Teasingly, Yolanda said, "Since we're out in the sunshine, Little Danny, do you like what you see?"

"Very much, Miss Yolanda. Do you like what you see?"

"I'm delighted with what I see, but it's what's on the inside that matters most. Why don't you go tell your friends you are going to stay here for a few days. Tell them I'm going to make you some winter shirts and trousers. You'll have to stay here so I can take your measurements and fit you once in a while. That is . . . if you would like for me to sew you some winter clothes."

Dan grinned as big as his face would allow as he crossed the yard to where Josie and Rand were sitting their horses. "I'm going to be staying here for a few days. Miss Yolanda is going to sew me some winter clothes. Will you please forgive me if I don't make it to your wedding?"

Josie smiled at Dan and looked over at the waiting Yolanda. "She is very pretty, Dan. You stay here, and if you see happiness coming your way . . . grab it, and *don't let go!*"

"I will. Thank you for understanding."

Rand leaned over and quietly told Dan, "We'll be back this way in a few days, but if you need to escape, find the Dawson Ranch on the other side of Lexington."

Dan leaned toward Rand. Very seriously, he said, "I'll see you in a few days."

Epilogue

AT THE DAWSON RANCH, Rand and Josie finally found a few minutes to themselves. "Are you happy, Josie?"

"More than I could ever express. Mrs. Dawson and the pastor's wife did a wonderful job decorating the church sanctuary. The ceremony was almost perfect."

"What do you mean, *almost* perfect?"

"Well, it's nothing to fuss about, but I thought the minister was a little stuffy. Maybe the right word is *stern*. I know marriage is a serious thing but it should be happiness and joy also. He wouldn't even bring his wife to the party the Dawson's are giving us. I think his wife really wanted to attend."

"Look at it this way; we wouldn't be having as much fun now if that stuffy preacher had come."

"You're right. I didn't think of it that way. Everyone seems to be having a good time. Poor Beth can't get away from the Dawson's twin sons. She's just glowing today, all dressed up in her new outfit."

"If you ask me, she's too pretty, and those boys are being a little too friendly."

"Why, Rand Trinity, you're acting like an older brother."

"I don't know about that, but I can tell we're going to have to keep an eye on her when she comes to visit this summer."

"We will. I was so happy for Anna when the judge released her into Lance's custody. She told me Lance has a house on some property next to his daughter and son-in-law. His daughter has a new baby. Anna and Beth are going to live with her for a while to help with the house and baby."

"I hope Lance knows what he's doing."

"Don't worry. He's a grown man. And a Godly man at that. He'll know what's right. I saw you talking to your mother last night. What did you say to her?"

"Not a lot. I just told her how I felt."

"How do you feel?"

"Like I told her, it may take me a while to adjust to having a mother again. I told her I didn't hate her and wanted her to be happy."

"And . . . what else?"

"That I couldn't call her *mother*. I'll just call her Anna."

"And . . . that's it?"

"Mostly. Except I told her she looked real nice and I am glad she was coming to the wedding."

"And . . .?"

"You sure are persistent. I told her if anything happened to her that we would take care of Beth Ann."

"I'm so proud of you, Rand. Are you happy?"

Rand's hazel eyes met Josephine's dazzling blue ones. "*Happy* isn't the word for what I feel right now. I love you more than I ever thought possible. You're beautiful, smart, fun, talented, make a marvelous chocolate pie and can throw a wicked knife. The only thing that would make me happier, is to take you away from here and kiss you senseless."

"Where are you going to take me? You haven't told me yet."

"I guess I can tell you now. Judge Cramer told me about a fancy new hotel in Lexington. I've made reservations there, for tonight. I didn't know whether to take the room for another night or not."

"One night will be fine. I would feel selfish staying longer. My family is ready to go home, we've been gone for quite a while now."

Rand stood to his feet, pulling Josie up to hers. "Are you ready to leave, Mrs. Trinity?"

"Yes, Mr. Trinity. I can't wait to experience being *kissed senseless*."

IF YOU ENJOYED THIS ADVENTURE OF THE LAWMAN WITH
RAND AND JOSIE BE SURE TO LET CONNIE KNOW. THERE
JUST MIGHT BE ANOTHER ADVENTURE ON THE WAY.
CJAUTHOR@CUSTERTEL.NET

IF YOU ENJOYED THE LAWMAN AND HAVE NOT READ THE
HIGH MEADOWS TRILOGY BY CONNIE AND HER SISTER, SANDY,
YOU WOULD PROBABLY ENJOY THESE BOOKS TOO.

BOOK ONE – THE HOPE OF WIND RIVER
EBOOK IS WIND RIVER

BOOK TWO – LITTLE MOSES

BOOK THREE – FRONTIER SOLDIER

Printed in the United States
By Bookmasters